BY NICOLA DINAN

Disappoint Me
Bellies

DISAPPOINT ME

DISAPPOINT ME

A Novel

NICOLA DINAN

THE DIAL PRESS
NEW YORK

The Dial Press
An imprint of Random House
A division of Penguin Random House LLC
1745 Broadway, New York, NY 10019
randomhousebooks.com
penguinrandomhouse.com

Originally published in the United Kingdom by Doubleday, an imprint of Transworld Publishers,
a part of Penguin Random House UK.

LIBRARY OF CONGRESS CATALOGING-IN-PUBLICATION DATA
Names: Dinan, Nicola, author.
TITLE: Disappoint me: a novel / Nicola Dinan.
DESCRIPTION: First edition. | New York, NY: The Dial Press, 2025.
IDENTIFIERS: LCCN 2024052166 (print) | LCCN 2024052167 (ebook) |
ISBN 9780593977873 (hardcover; acid-free paper) | ISBN 9780593977897 (ebook)
SUBJECTS: LCSH: Transgender women—Fiction. | LCGFT: Transgender fiction. |
Romance fiction. | Novels.
Classification: LCC PR6104.I53 D57 2025 (print) |
LCC PR6104.I53 (ebook) | DDC 823/.92—dc23/eng/20241118
LC record available at https://lccn.loc.gov/2024052166
LC ebook record available at https://lccn.loc.gov/2024052167

Printed in the United States of America on acid-free paper

9 8 7 6 5 4 3 2 1

First U.S. Edition

Book design by Sara Bereta

BOOK TEAM:
Managing editor: Rebecca Berlant • Production manager: Maggie Hart •
Proofreaders: Pam Rehm, Vicki Fischer, Cameron Schoette, Ruth Anne Phillips

The authorized representative in the EU for product safety and compliance is
Penguin Random House Ireland,
Morrison Chambers, 32 Nassau Street, Dublin D02 YH68, Ireland,
https://eu-contact.penguin.ie.

No person is fewer
than two things
Two people
And if such two people are at least two people
then how many people are we?

DISAPPOINT ME

Max, 2023

I

It's four a.m. and the house party hasn't thinned. New Year's! Everyone wants to go to a party, but nobody wants to host a party, and so a party's a party and people will stay. At a certain stage of life, people leave house shares for smaller flats, because they can afford to live alone, or because they're in a couple, or because their parents give them some money for a modest two-bed, though they'll assure you they pay the mortgage themselves. In all cases, houses become less like places you live and more like homes, less like places you're willing to trash. House parties are rare. Caspar, who lives here, is a friend from university. We were also in a writing workshop with my ex-boyfriend, Arthur, though I've obviously since left. Now I barely see Caspar outside of these parties, which he continues to invite me to despite our estrangement.

I'm flirting with sobriety, which means I've only had two drinks and the small bump of ket that Caspar just offered me. The decision to restrict is not because I'm an alcoholic or addict. I've always been able to pull back, to eventually say no, to go home early. I'm restricting because drugs and alcohol make me feel bad. After Arthur broke up with me, I'd wake up with a gravitational compression that anchored me in bed. I'd be much worse the day or two after a bottle or two shared between friends. It shouldn't have been a revelation that alcohol is a depressant, but my baseline finally dropped low enough for me to notice it. Since stopping, I've been more emotionally robust, and also more superior, as if I'm the first person in history to wake up to the dangers of hedonism.

I'm dancing with my eyes shut, because I'm dancing with Caspar and his eye contact is severe. He's brilliant. I don't particularly like him, and so I'm saying this in an objective sense. A genuinely brilliant mind. He did a PhD in PrEPenomics, and then went on to write a book of essays on pre-millennium London club culture, which he was not present for, published by an independent press stocked only in Hackney bookshops. It sold a lot more than anyone anticipated, thanks to a well-known actor-singer-cross-stitch-artist who posted a nude selfie with Caspar's book covering his crotch. It sold a lot more than my book of poems, obviously, because who in the world buys poetry anymore? After the crotch selfie, Caspar got a U.S. deal. And a German one. Even a Japanese one. He is glamorous in a way that will wear off for me. Time is kinder to men, even gay men. I won't always be beautiful. I think about that a lot, now that I'm in my thirties. Now that I'm thirty. My marionette lines are a giveaway; even though I insist to myself that it's the structure of my face, that I've always had them, I know they're getting deeper. How long have my eyes been shut?

I open them. Caspar's gone. I survey the crowd and regret it immediately. Some people should really stop taking drugs. I scratch the ketamine off the hem of my nostril and look up. Lights! A light machine shoots lasers across the room, creating an illuminated sheet overhead. Simone and Eva are next to me. Simone never sweats. She's in a boxy blazer with matching shorts, like a child in their dad's suit, but sexy and poised. She is my favorite person in the world. Eva, her girlfriend, is not. It's not because I'm possessive, I just think Eva's a little boring. She's a fashion videographer for cool brands with asymmetrical knitwear and expensive shoes that look like Transformers. People who do jobs like that are only ever interesting on paper. Except Simone. Simone often defends Eva's right to be boring to me, in neat aphorisms that are conflicting but even in the strength of their presentation. *Listen, Max, everyone becomes boring when you've spent enough time with them.* Am I boring, Simone? *No, but she talks about things that we never talk about.* She does talk about Crocs a lot, though.

Eva places her hand on my back. I feel my own sweat against the curve of my spine.

"I love your bag," she says.

It's a vintage, black leather baguette. I don't think she actually likes it; she just wants to endear herself to me, maybe because she knows that I know she's boring.

"Thank you," I say. "I love your Crocs."

I feel hot, and only in the unpleasant sense of the word. I wish I wasn't wearing a silk slip. My awareness of my moist armpits is acute. I shut my eyes again. Maybe I should actually be grateful for Eva. I've lost many friends to heteronormativity in the last couple of years. Even queer ones. Engagements. Cardigans. Looking out at the sea while rubbing the outside of their arms.

Eyes open again, and I look toward Simone. She gurns so much. Not judging, just observing. Her teeth chatter like she's naked in the Arctic. I've known that noise since we first took MD on a side street off Lan Kwai Fong sixteen years ago. Simone grabs my hand and brings her mouth to my ear, and I know what's coming. Rattle, rattle, rattle.

"It's like they're talking," she says.

"What are they saying?" I ask.

"Help."

We laugh. I lean away and search my handbag for gum. Eva's palm slides over my arm.

"I love your bag," Eva says, again.

"Thank you," I repeat. "I love your Crocs."

I know I've long been the perpetrator of many of these looping conversations, and my penance is to bear my own annoyance and smile. I take out the packet of gum from my bag, stacked pillows of xylitol, and pop out a couple for Simone and Eva, and then one for myself. Simone throws it into her mouth, nodding at me through droopy eyes.

Eva pulls me and Simone farther into the living-room-cum-dance-floor. I look at them, and suddenly they're bent backward. Who the fuck brought out a limbo stick? Am I doing limbo? I throw my spine back like it's a normal thing to do. It's not like they just found a stick outside. This is a stick of specific length, circumference, and texture. Who brought this?

As I'm upside down, my eyes go to Carla, a Spanish woman I know through Caspar, who Simone once said looks like Poundland Arca. Carla and I are friends, in the sense that we're both trans and therefore vaguely supportive of each other on social media. Her sequin dress is lovely. So slinky. When I swing back up, I'm thinking of microplastics. I try to keep dancing, but purse my lips, imagining those little beads slipping from those sequins and into the sea, and into the fish we eat, and into our bodies, clogging up hormone receptors and pulping our gametes. While I've already met a version of this apocalypse, it's not a fate I wish to befall everyone else. Is this what abstinence does to a person? When you can't turn the world to mush, make everything dissolve and stop making sense. When the mind can't crowd itself, where is it left to wander?

Carla comes off the decks. One of several bleached buzzcuts ascends to replace her.

"You were so, so good," I say.

"Thank you, baby," she says. "You look amazing."

"I love your dress."

"Same," she says. "You look amazing. Let's go upstairs."

She grabs my hand with a violent tug, pulling me out of the room and toward the staircase. Our skin contact is feigned closeness through shared experience. We met a few years ago. All I remember from that evening is that she gave me a cigarette and told me there was a man who paid her top dollar to smoke vapes from her butt, and that she could introduce me if I wanted. I think she still sees him, even though her paintings are selling okay. The next week we went for a drink at a bar in Dalston. I was mortified by how rude she was. Some trans women serve cunt, in that they're quite rude, because when the world shits on you it's easy to be a little mean, but she sent a negroni back for having too thin an orange slice on the rim. No amount of pain excuses that.

We sit on a beanbag upstairs. Three men in mesh tops are on the couch to Carla's left. One of them looks forty-five, another looks thirty, and the twink closest to Carla looks too young to be here. The forty-five-year-old squirts G from a dropper into a glass of orange Fanta.

"This is my friend Max," Carla says. "She's a lawyer."

"That's amazing," says the twink. "You must be so smart."

"Sometimes," Carla answers for me.

It's unclear to me what Carla means, even if sometimes is probably appropriate. I'm not that smart. Most lawyers aren't. Law's a career built on privilege and rote learning. I work four days a week as legal counsel for a tech company. They claim to have AI that can review contracts, except it can't and it's actually me reviewing them. I am the robot, signing off my emails to clients with its name, Owl. I spend any downtime at work labeling contracts, teaching the incompetent AI how to read them so that one day it might replace me. Even at four days a week, I am grossly overpaid. The fifth day is supposed to be for poetry, though I've stopped writing.

"I like your shoes," the thirty-year-old says to me.

"Thank you."

I bought them to celebrate getting the deal for my book of poetry. There was no advance, but it made sense to buy shoes. They're all scuffed up now, because they're platform brogues and the rubber soles knock against the leather when I walk. It breaks my heart.

"Do you want some?" the forty-five-year-old asks me, holding up the vial of G.

"No," I say. "I'm okay."

The twink racks up lines of coke for himself using a slotted spatula. My mind wanders to Arthur. Part of me thought he would be here. We exist on separate rocks in the same ecosystem. It's what made the decision to come here mostly sober even easier, because drugs and alcohol soften my tongue and limbs and memory into gelatine, coaxing me to cradle the monster swaddled in vintage Carhartt. *I only asked about jawline surgery to be supportive of your transition, Max.*

I don't know if it'd hurt more to see him with a cis woman or another trans woman. Either would make me feel like I wasn't enough, maybe because the brain searches for the reasons it wants, caught in a strange loop of self-reinforcement. I wonder why I'm here. At thirty, I still experience the pressure of seeming like I'm having fun, of doing a lot, or at least doing interesting things. It's why having my book published was so satisfying for a while. A cold pearl of disappointment weighs on my stomach. Why am I here? The question presses itself hard onto my all-too-conscious shoulders. The party has to end, people. We can't do this forever. And why not? I have no answer, other than my own feelings of emptiness. Maybe I'm projecting. I look across the room. There's a thin white woman wearing a low-rise miniskirt and a bra made of chains, dancing completely out of time to the music on the speakers. It's probably rude to stare. I think of how nobody, not a soul in the world, would think a woman like that is trans. It's a far cry from what I might hope for, that people would believe you if you told them that I was or wasn't.

"Hold this for a second," Carla says.

She passes me a fifty-pound note.

"Why do you have a fifty-pound note?" I ask.

I roll it into a tube for her.

"A man in a fedora tipped me with it at my pub job, baby," she says. "He slipped it into my panties when I brought him a sausage roll. I should've kicked him out, but I wanted to keep the money."

Carla racks up two lines with an unstamped coffee shop loyalty card. They're fat lines. Slugs. My eyes drift again to the dancing woman, and Carla gently takes the note out of my hand. I hear the wind through her nostril. She scratches her nose with a bejeweled acrylic nail, and we both look over at the dancing girl.

"She's trans, you know," Carla says. "I think she's twenty-five. She's a model. She transitioned when she was thirteen."

Fuck. I grab the note, and for a moment I think of snorting the slug, but hand the note back to Carla. I don't feel better. Not even righteous.

"Maxy wrote a book," Carla says to the three boys, putting her arm around me.

They nod, because nobody really cares. Nobody reads anymore. Writers will soon be redundant, AI will replace us, and my decided departure from poetry will look less like failure and more like expedience.

The twink and the thirty-year-old start kissing.

"Are you going to Dionysus?" the forty-five-year-old asks.

I shake my head.

"I don't go to that anymore, baby," Carla says. "It's not queer. It's gay."

She's right. Every queer night I used to go to has been colonized by muscle gays. It's simply not for me anymore. Is tonight? I look toward decepto-trans again and start to feel creeped out. It seems impossible to dance this out of rhythm for this amount of time. It's inhuman.

Carla and I leave the beanbag holding hands and walk out to the hall-way. I notice her notice me looking at the dancing girl back in the room.

"Don't you just get jealous?" Carla asks.

"Of what?" I ask.

"Of her."

"No."

"You're lying." She pushes my shoulder, but gently. "You're jealous. You're beautiful, but you're not that beautiful. Every doll is jealous of her."

"I'm not jealous."

"Just admit it, baby."

"Did you see her dancing?" I ask, trying to tame Carla's aggression, because I feel too sober, like my walls are too high to just admit that yes, I feel a bit jealous.

"You're fucking jealous," Carla repeats.

"I'm not fucking jealous."

"You're fucking jealous," she says. "This is literally your problem, Max."

"What is literally my problem?"

She doesn't know me well enough to know what my problems are.

"Just admit you're jealous," she says. "And you'll be free."

She grabs my wrist with cokey force.

"I'm not jealous," I say, raising my voice enough to reveal that I am indeed jealous.

The three men on the couch are looking at us open-mouthed through the gap in the door. Victory registers across Carla's face.

"By the way," Carla says, "maybe this is a bad time to tell you, but I slept with Arthur. He is not a good man."

I want to numb my despair. I want Simone. I'd even take Eva. It's a terrible feeling. I want to hold it together. I turn away from Carla, holding the banister to swing myself around. As I launch down the stairs I miss a step and lose my balance. I start to tumble. I hit my head. Simone screams my name.

I WAKE UP IN A hospital room. How did I get one to myself? It's quiet and eerie. I hear only the clicking of doors and soft steps from outside. I can't see anyone in the hallway through the open door. Every hinge of my body aches.

An Oedipal tension swallows me. Not because I want to fuck my parents—I don't—but in the prophetic sense, because I went into the night sober, trying my best to do no harm, to be dignified. I barely drank, I declined lines, only to fall down the stairs and end up in the hospital anyway, remembering little of how I got here other than fragmented memories of a taxi and a flashlight in my eye. Then a young doctor saying to keep me in until a consultant arrives in the morning so I can have a CT scan, but that he was pretty sure I was fine. I'm fine.

I want to be responsible. I want to feel responsible. I want an Eva. Or another Arthur. Can finding a boyfriend be my New Year's resolution? Can that be something that a person resolves to do? Is feminism dead? I feel very alone. Maybe the most alone I've allowed myself to feel since Arthur broke up with me. This is like a vision of my future. In twenty, thirty, fifty years' time, when my parents and my brother, Jamie, are dead and I'm single with no children and my friends are too ill or too far to visit. I could be in a hospital one day, alone, with nobody to see me. What kind of future is that?

There's an IV drip in my right hand, which feels melodramatic and wasteful. As I dislodge the needle from my vein, spots of blood spill into the canyons between the bones on my hand, which I wipe on the bedsheet. I read the Post-it atop a pile of fresh clothes, all mine.

Gone home. Will stop by yours to pick up more stuff. You don't have a concussion, but they're keeping you for a scan. Phone charging next to wall. Back soon. Simone.

I climb into them, my joints so creaky they might pop. Flared jeans, a T-shirt, a cropped jumper, and a light jacket. My spare keys are in a nylon cross-body bag I bought to cheer myself up after the *Guardian* shat on my book. These clothes don't feel like enough, but when I check my phone, the weather app informs me that it's sixteen degrees Celsius. On New Year's Day. The world is ending. I fold and put the Post-it in my back pocket, because maybe one day I'll find it funny. Maybe one day this will feel funnier than it is. I'm not a myopic person.

I limp into the dreary halls of Homerton Hospital, feeling all chafe and lesion. It feels trite to describe a hospital as sickly, but this hospital feels sick, like the off-white wallpaper might peel off to reveal clusters of black mold. It's as if each person who enters these hallways leaves a bit of their illness behind, and it's collecting in the speckled linoleum and the smell of antiseptic blasting out of the vents. Nobody seems to notice me leaving through the glass-fronted doorway.

I walk for a while until I reach a bench that faces a church. It's an enormous, eighteenth-century building, yet fails to be imposing. It's built with what seems like modest house brick, and the tower that spears from its center is faded, simple in its edges. There's no intricacy. It's plain but beautiful. Not for a moment do I contemplate finding God. Even at my lowest—please may this be my lowest—I am not tempted by religion. God won't find me a boyfriend. I can't imagine the men at Christian coffee mornings will take me.

I take a deep breath and drop my head into my hands. Jealousy and weak joints got me here, although I know that none of how I'm feeling is really to do with the fall. The fall, if anything, is the mere sum of my failures. Life feels harder than it used to. I'm jealous of Caspar, of that girl who danced weirdly, and on some level of Carla, too. I was jealous of Arthur, awful Arthur, of seeing his books in shops, of seeing him speak at talks, even though, like Caspar, he's brilliant—

objectively—and deserved it all. All of it makes me feel ashamed. Disappointed.

I walk by the palm trees at Hackney Town Hall. Sometimes when I see people gathered outside, taking pictures for their stripped-down city weddings, the extreme diminution of ceremony makes all of it feel appealing. I can see the town hall from the window of my place, an ex-council flat on the top floor of a mansion block. I rent, because although my parents offered me a deposit, I declined. I didn't want to be like the people I grew up with in Hong Kong, who live unblemished lives and are out of touch. There was some pride in this, except I now realize that declining a deposit is even more out of touch, and that I can only afford my rent because my salary from my AI job is too much for what it is.

I know that my Thatcher Flat is part of the problem, the way I've colonized this part of Hackney. Being a bit Chinese doesn't absolve me of this. I come from a long line of colonialists. My grandfather, who worked for the British government, raised my mum in colonial Hong Kong. My parents raised me in neo-colonial Hong Kong. This is neo-colonial Hackney. Self-awareness doesn't make it better. It probably makes it worse.

When I open my front door, Eva and Simone are standing in the living room, looking at me. Simone in her expensive jeans and white shirt, with her black leather jacket with flames cut out of brown leather. Eva's in a floor-length kilt. Their hair is so glossy, even though they probably barely slept.

"Maxy," Simone says, hugging me. "I thought you were missing. The hospital just called. You're supposed to have a scan—"

"I left," I say.

"I know," she says.

"Should we go back?" Eva asks.

Both of us ignore Eva. I can hear tears in Simone's voice.

"I'm sorry you woke up without us," Simone says. "We slept and came back to pick up some of your stuff. I didn't like the clothes we picked out for you. We were about to head back."

"It's fine," I say, suddenly feeling self-conscious of my appearance. "The clothes are fine."

Simone shouldn't feel bad about sleeping. I should feel bad, guilty. I'm terrible. I begin to cry. Simone hugs me harder. Eva comes in and fills the gaps, so that I'm encased in a zorb-ball of flesh.

"I'm sorry for ruining your New Year's."

"You fell down the stairs, Max," Simone says. "That could literally happen to anyone."

"Literally anyone," Eva adds.

"Can we just stay here for a bit?" I ask. "I don't want to go back right now. They said I'm probably fine."

Simone purses her lips.

"Okay," she says.

I walk over to the couch I bought from a second-hand store. My eyes roll over the rest of the furniture, a lot of which I bought on eBay with Arthur's help. He had a car, so he drove us around London to pick stuff up. His stain is everywhere. His book is still on the shelf. Simone and Eva sit down at the round dining table, fitted with four chairs. They look at me with soft stares.

"Are you hungry?" Simone asks. "Do you want breakfast?"

The word summons it. My stomach grumbles in response.

"I think I have stuff for a carbonara."

Simone's ready to say that's not breakfast food, but she doesn't.

"Don't move," she says.

For the next half-hour I drift in and out of consciousness, my body aching for sleep. Big nights are always on borrowed time, even if you're sober, or trying to be. There is always a debt to pay. Robbed hours, installments of naps in the days after, pennies of energy scraped from a groggy brain and eyes, all to satisfy the serotonin-hungry bailiff.

The sounds of knocking ceramic and sizzles are split by Eva and Simone's quiet bickering. I miss it. I miss it all. Even the bickering. It's easy. It's simple.

They drag on for longer than it takes to make a carbonara. As Simone carries a pot of pasta into the living room, I can smell the rendered fat of lardons, twisting up from the browned bits I know are at the bottom of the pan. The sharp, full smell of Parmesan. The steam billows out of the knock-off Le Creuset and lures me to the dining table. Simone places a nest of pasta into my bowl, together with some asparagus. The carbonara is delicious. Salty, rich. They did well.

We eat in silence. They are walking on eggshells, and I resent that. I'm made of harder stuff. Soft feet are not welcome. No tiptoes.

"New Year's resolutions?" Eva asks.

"That feels pointed," I say.

All of us laugh. I try to think of things other than how alone I felt this morning. My mind comes up blank.

"What about writing more?" Eva asks.

"I guess writing made me feel less alone, but maybe I'd rather just not be alone anymore."

"Did you feel less alone with Arthur?" Eva asks.

"I guess," I say. "But I also felt very jealous, and wasn't very happy with him, which also makes a person feel very alone."

"Maybe you could try again," Eva says. "Have you thought about it? I mean, have you been dating?"

"Not really," I say, scraping melted clumps of Parmesan off my plate with my fork. "Maybe I should."

"New Year's resolution," Eva says.

"Yeah," I say. "What's yours?"

"I don't know," she says. "Maybe build a shed or something."

Lovely, boring Eva.

*　*　*

I INSIST THEY GO HOME after breakfast, promising I'll go to the hospital as soon as I wake up from my nap. My dress from last night is draped over my desk chair. As I change out of my clothes, I feel lonely. Lonely when the house is empty, lonely when the house is full. I'll go back for the scan tomorrow.

II

I NEVER WENT BACK FOR THE SCAN. I STARE AT THE VINYL CUT-OUT PLAS-tered on the WeWork bathroom wall. It's a Beyoncé lyric, and every time I look at it, I wonder what she'd think about her songs encouraging the professional-managerial class to shit like a boss bitch, or if she even knows what WeWork is. It feels impossible to imagine Beyoncé knowing about WeWork, but it also seems impossible for her to be completely oblivious that it exists. Can someone comprehend the scale of their omnipotence?

I let the thought take me away, because I'm sitting on a closed lid, no intention of excretion. In my sudden desire to run toward responsibility, I have decided to commit more to work. Offer my hands more frequently. Move from quitter to contributor. The product range of legal services our AI, Owl, can provide has—allegedly—expanded to include finance documents, such as those for simple derivative transactions. Owl cannot actually do this—the dawn of generative AI has not touched my workplace—and so I've been training junior lawyers in this exciting new frontier of fraud.

Work isn't working for me. I'm not like Simone, who throws herself so deep into her job that only she can let herself down. She believes in the big picture of what she does—she loves fashion, she loves scouting for new faces, starting the careers of impressionable young women. Unlike for her, there's no higher purpose for me. It was supposed to be poetry, but what's the point in that? Einstein worked as a patent clerk while he developed his theory of relativity. His menial job helped to change the world. My poems help no one, except sad women and gay men who intend to stay that way.

I flush the toilet I haven't used and wash my hands. Life isn't simple for anyone. Simone broke up with Eva a week into January, only a couple of weeks ago. *Look, Max, she's a woman without substance, and there's not enough of me to fill her up.* I was a little surprised by Simone, but that's unsurprising. Maybe I was being melodramatic on New Year's Day, but I still feel deflated. Falling down the stairs will do that to a person.

At the sink, I check my phone and see a message from Vincent, a man I matched with on a dating app, confirming the time for our dinner. In the time since I last used them, dating apps have only declined in terms of functionality, quality, and inclusivity.

Every man's profile confesses that he is both overly competitive and would like to travel to Japan. To protect my soul, I refuse to scroll through profiles, waiting for men to like me first so that I can wield the axe. The experience is otherwise too degrading. My profile already says that I'm trans.

Eager as I was to start the year dating, the validation from strangers finding me attractive was quickly replaced by the disgust from strangers finding me attractive. Vincent, however, is handsome, and while he's my height, if he and I were melted down he'd occupy more volume, which is all that's important to me. I have no reason to expect it will be bad, but little reason to expect it will be good; dates often feel like something one should do, like replacing a Brita filter or using black mold remover for the corners of your bathroom, rather than something meaningful. While I'd like to draw a distinction between dating and those chores, which keep a house and body safe, we live in a world that pathologizes singledom, where being single means being alone. With every headline of an octogenarian dying two weeks after their spouse, we believe it more.

When I return to my desk, it's nearly the end of the day. Maeve, blond-bunned legal counsel, hunches in her chair, chin pushed forward, running her finger along a line of text on the screen, glare trapped in her enormous glasses. She approaches her job with much more enthusiasm than me, even if she produces largely the same output in five days that I do in four. What is the big picture for her? The singularity?

"Plans for tonight?" she asks.

I purse my lips. Why do people only ask questions to be asked them in return? I wish everyone would pack it in and just talk to themselves.

"Just seeing friends," I say. "You?"

"I have a date."

"Ah," I say. "Good luck."

She responds with a knowing look.

"It's not a first date," she says.

"Exciting!" I beam with a frozen, toothy smile.

I could ask more questions, but why?

OUR TABLE IS IN A corner by the window, and I sit on the benched side. There's a solo diner sitting along the same bench with her back against the window. An empty table of two separates us, thankfully. There is a special kind of embarrassment that comes with other people hearing your conversation on a first date.

My phone lights up with a text from Vincent, saying he was held up, that he'll be fifteen minutes late, and encouraging me to choose a bottle of wine. I am still courting sobriety, though I've decided to make a marked exception for dates. The stakes feel higher, and I don't trust enough in my skills as a conversationalist.

I open up the dating app on which I found Vincent and scroll through a few faces, trying to find a man-shaped safety net. Too many minutes pass before I catch myself and call Simone.

"He's late," I say. "I'm literally here swiping through men on my phone."

"While waiting for your date?"

"Yes."

"That sounds really unstable," she says. "Do you have other dates lined up?"

"No," I say.

"That's insane."

"I work two jobs, Simone."

"Who do you think you are?"

I laugh.

"Are you sticking to Veganuary?" she asks.

Falling down the stairs called for another layer of asceticism. I've decided it won't continue past January, because it's brought me no real happiness, only flatulence.

"I'm going to try—"

"I just think you're six years too late to—"

"Bye."

I hang up as Vincent walks in. He smiles and kisses me on the cheek, all with a billowing smoothness. My expression lifts. It's not about looking better in person than in pictures, but a static frame cloaks posture and luster, dulls the kindness in a person's eyes.

It is said—in the Bible, I'm sure—that men know within seconds of meeting you whether they'd like to sleep with you. What an incredible burden. How much sweat, chemical exfoliant, and ripped activewear is laid at the altar to shift those odds. And so preoccupied with our supplication, we barely consider our attraction to them, if at all. Release me from my chains, I beg. Would I have sex with Vincent? I guess. If he's nice.

As he strips off his coat and pulls up his jumper, I look beneath his armpits to see if there are any yellow deodorant stains. I wouldn't mind either way, but I think it says something about a man. There aren't. Thankfully. He gets into the chair. The bench I'm sitting on is raised in comparison, and so I feel like I'm towering over him, which I hate. The light on his face is gentle, rounding his sharp cheekbones, enhancing the glow on his tanned and poreless skin. He has lovely, dark eyebrows. My mum would be happy. Not just because he's Chinese, but because she's obsessed with skin. According to my mum, you can't judge a book by its cover, but you can judge a person by theirs.

"How was your day?" I ask.

He sighs, shrugging his shoulders with a soft smile.

"This deal keeps dragging on," he says. "And the partner on it's a dick. You know how it is."

"Kind of."

The hours working in-house, where I am, are less punishing than private practice. I left that life when I lost my appetite for a work environment that rewarded undiagnosed personality disorders. It also felt modern and well to have a day a week to invest in my hobbies, to potentially turn that hobby into a career. That didn't work out, so whenever someone tells me they work at a law firm, like now, I experience a stubborn flash of greener pastures across my frontal lobe, a quick flush of unquelled regret and abandoned prospects. I pour him a glass of wine from the bottle.

"What's the partner like?" I ask.

Vincent laughs.

"He's one of those young dads with toddlers who—"

"How young?" I ask.

It's a reflex—my first question whenever I find out anyone has, or is having, children. Being a childless person who doesn't know how I feel about children or when I might possibly have children, and hearing about children, begets the existential: am I falling behind?

"Young," he says, "like, mid-thirties."

This kindles some relief. Not just the stranger's age, but that Vincent thinks having children in your early thirties makes you a young dad, too.

"Anyway," he continues. "His only outlet is work, so he always gets fucked up at office parties. Like, offering associates lines and getting mad when they go home early."

"Has he gotten in trouble?"

"He offers selectively."

"What's the criteria?"

Vincent lifts a fist with three fingers outstretched.

"Single, male, only a little less senior."

"What!" I say. "Give the girls their lines."

"Yeah," he laughs. "The last frontier of workplace sexism."

A waitress comes to take our orders. I turn to Vincent.

"I'm doing Veganuary, by the way," I say.

"I didn't realize that was still a thing."

"It's not, really."

"Why didn't you say anything?" he asks.

"I'm happy for you to eat fish," I say. "And I checked if there were vegan dishes. I'll even share."

"How sweet of you."

I order some inari sushi and miso aubergine, and he excitedly adds a couple of other things he thinks I'd enjoy, like agedashi tofu and pumpkin tempura, as if I've never had them. He orders a modest platter of nigiri and sashimi.

"When did the partner get made up?" I ask.

"A couple of years ago."

"How many years qualified was he?"

Vincent smirks a little, and I wince at myself for asking these questions.

"Nine," he says, pausing to take a sip of wine, and then looks at my eyes more closely. Too close. Slow down, Vincent, we just met. My body's down here. I want to lean back. "You're part Asian, right? I feel like you are, but your surname came up as Murphy when you messaged so I couldn't be sure."

"I'm only a quarter," I say.

"Really? You look more."

"Thank you. People say that a lot," I say. "I think it's because I have dark features."

"Chinese?" he asks.

"Yeah."

"Me too," he says.

"I know."

"How?"

"Your name comes up as Vincent Chan when you text," I say. "And you look Chinese."

He takes a sip of his wine, then unbuttons the cuffs of his shirt and rolls them up a little. I notice a red stain along the stitching of one. His watch is nice. Annual-bonus watch.

"Are you Irish?" he asks.

"I think it'd be quite annoying if I said I was," I say. "Like those Americans with shamrock keychains."

He laughs.

"I grew up in Hong Kong," I say.

He lights up.

"My parents are from there," he says.

"My mum grew up there, too," I say.

"Where did you live?"

"Lamma Island."

23

"That's so random."

"My dad really wanted to live there," I say. "Have you been back much?"

"Not really," he says. "I did a secondment out there a few years ago for a year. They asked me to stay on, but I ended up coming back."

"Why?"

"My girlfriend at the time was still in London. It sort of made sense." He puts his glass down. "It would've been nice to stay, though."

It's nice that he came back for her. There are questions about exes we all want to ask, most of them not appropriate for a first, second, or even third date. But patterns matter. What tore you apart? Unresolved generational trauma? Maybe it's for the best—a world with all cards on the table is one where people are forbidden to change. But can't I at least toe the line?

"Were you together for long?"

"Six years," he says. "We broke up two years ago. She lives in Australia now."

"Whoa," I say. Good riddance. "And since then?"

"Nothing, really," he says, and, as if to remind himself: "Six years is a long time."

"Mm."

Six years is a long time. It is also reassuring.

"How about you?" he asks.

"We were together for two years," I say. "We broke up last year."

"Three weeks ago last year?" he asks.

I laugh.

"No," I say. "A while before that."

The agedashi tofu comes on a small plate. Four cubes coated in a light battered skin, soggy where the stock has seeped in. When I pick one up, its skin falls off like a silk robe from a nude body, and the tofu drops back into the bowl, a lithe wobbly box. Vincent laughs. I'm unsure if at it or at me, at the weak constitution of the batter, or at the way that I hold chopsticks, which I blame on being left-handed. I laugh, too, anyway. I place the skin down on my plate and nudge the naked soy onto my spoon.

"Would you ever move back?" he asks.

"No," I say. "I like what the UK has to offer."

"Like what?"

More accessible gender recognition, which is saying something.

"Mayonnaise and single-use plastic."

He smiles. His uni nigiri arrives, soft tongues of urchin draped over ovals of rice. He picks one up, eats it, and nods to himself with a smile. The rest of the food follows. I wish I wasn't doing Veganuary.

"Why did you decide to do Veganuary?" he asks.

I almost tell Vincent that I fell down the stairs. Part of me knows that he'll find it funny. But then I remember how I once went on a date with a man who told me he'd slept over at a colleague's after work drinks, whereupon he wet the bed. I laughed at the time, but also decided not to see him again.

"Water," I say instead.

"Water?" he asks.

"It takes seventeen thousand liters of water to make a kilogram of beef."

"I think I've heard that."

"Yeah," I say. "It's wild."

I pulled this fact from a presentation by a clean water charity when I was at school. That number stayed with me. Seventeen thousand.

"Do you like your job?" I ask, taking a piece of the craggy pumpkin tempura on the plate between us, and worrying for a moment that I seem obsessed with work.

He places his elbows on the table and hums, looking at the wall to his right, as if I've asked an interesting question.

"I do," he says. "Now that I've moved firms the hours aren't so bad, and once you're senior enough the job becomes pretty relaxed because it's like muscle memory. Like I said, you know how it is."

"Sort of," I say. "Do you want to be a partner?"

My voice is impassive. I don't want him to think I'm asking because I care about money. I don't. At least, not a lot.

"I think so. It's definitely on the cards." He pauses, picking up a piece of sashimi, arching its back over his chopsticks before dipping its toes in the soy sauce. "It's one of those things that's hard to admit, though."

"What do you mean?" I ask.

He fights to swallow his food.

"Saying you never wanted it is like a safety net, right? Easier to back down from."

What he says tickles an embarrassment in me. It's familiar. I don't think I'd be as embarrassed by the poetry if I hadn't secretly hoped it would work out much better than it did, that it could grow into more than something I did alongside my day job, that some critic of renown would declare me a genius. Miss Byron. I insist that Vincent eats some of the tofu, and he settles on half of one cube, which he separates by holding one chopstick in each hand. I try to badger him into eating more, but he says that I should eat it.

"Do you like your job?" he asks, dabbing his mouth with a napkin.

"No."

"Why not?"

I explain to him that I'm an adult woman impersonating legal AI, which feels illegal, and that it reduces my degrees and qualifications to a means of gatekeeping a job that most people, with enough on-the-job training, could do. I also share how I suspect that in a few years, maybe less, this ship will combust, and that I should probably move before it does. He laughs. I laugh. For a moment I wonder if we're laughing too much. After all, this is my career.

"What would you rather do, then?"

I wonder if I should mention my poetry collection. It makes me cringe, but I also want Vincent to think I sparkle, that I'm interesting, and maybe a book is a good way in.

"I sort of write poetry."

"Really?" he says, surprised. "What kind of poems?"

"What do you mean?"

"I don't know, really." He takes a moment. "What are they about?"

"People, I guess."

"People?"

"Yeah," I say. "Relationships. My body."

"Must be lovely poems."

I don't like the euphemism. *Look at the poems on her.*

"Sorry," he says. "Bad joke."

"Fucking perv."

He laughs. He knows I'm joking, which is nice, but is it? Would he know if I wasn't?

"I had a book of poetry published a year ago," I say. "Just over a year."

His jaw drops. I blush a little and look down at my plate. Vincent's not acting. Maybe he is a little. But it's a nice feeling.

"What's the book called?"

"Small and Humble."

"Why?"

"It's a Shakira reference."

"Is it?"

"It's from 'Whenever, Wherever,'" I say. "She's talking about her boobs."

His eyes flash down to my chest and back up again. I'm not sure he even realizes. I take a sip of wine, but he doesn't take his eyes off me. Mine dart in and out of his gaze. There's something in me that can't handle it, being observed, and I start to panic about what he's seeing, as if the review from that queer periodical is tattooed to my forehead: "when the most superficial layer is lifted, there's not much there." I don't see myself as a particularly ashamed person. Only a healthy amount. But that's what this is, isn't it? Shame.

"That's really amazing," he says. "I don't read much poetry, but I'd love to read yours."

I smile—maybe I'll show him. It'd be a relief to share them with someone who doesn't interrogate form. He picks up one of the pieces of vegetable tempura. I watch him take a bite. He has lovely, wide, full lips. There's a fleck of tempura batter holding on to the corner of his mouth.

"Oh shit," he says. "Do you mind?"

"What?"

"I just ate your tempura," he says.

"What?" I ask. "Everything's to share."

I reach for his second piece of uni nigiri with my chopsticks. He looks at me open-mouthed as I eat it, then laughs through his nose.

"Veganuary?" he asks.

I wave my hand to dismiss him. The uni is delicious. Not in any miraculous sort of way. I've only been vegan for two weeks.

"Actually," he says, "is tempura even vegan?"

"What?"

We look it up on his phone. It isn't. A notification from a dating app appears at the top of the screen, which he hurriedly swipes away with his thumb. How many dates does he have lined up? Am I playing it wrong?

"All the better I had the uni," I say, pretending that I saw nothing besides eggs in batter. "Anyway, what would you do?" I ask. "If you could do anything."

He plants his elbows on the table, then looks up in thought.

"I think I might still be a lawyer," he says. Dear Lord. "That's really dull, isn't it?"

"It is a bit," I laugh. "Seriously?"

"Yeah," he says. "I think I'm painfully pragmatic. It ticks the boxes. And I think I do like it. It's not perfect, but I do enjoy it."

I tell myself that I can't fancy people for their jobs, that artists and writers are often quite annoying. They will make ugly art about you. Donate their belongings to charity and a story about a vengeful ex will appear in *Granta*. *It's not you, Max.* It was.

"Which parts do you enjoy?" I ask.

"I like it when a new deal comes in, and you read about the companies, the business case for the transaction." He's bobbing his head from side to side as he talks. "Which tells you how the client sees the world, and it's just interesting seeing all these different perspectives."

He catches himself, as if embarrassed by his own enthusiasm. We smile. I understand then that he must really like his job, because no M&A lawyer does that kind of background reading on clients unless they care about the bigger picture. Otherwise, they just mark stuff up using precedents, not engaging with the soul of the documents, if documents can be said to have a soul. He enjoys his job. The simplicity is refreshing. And yet he's not boring. Not like Eva. Why am I thinking about Eva? Let the girl rest.

Vincent finishes the remaining nigiri and offers me the last bit of chicken yakitori, which I decline. I feel a bit bad about fucking Veganuary up, but can't resist when he suggests matcha ice cream and red bean. As I inhale the creamy green, I worry about leftover smears around my mouth. I dab my lips an inordinate number of times. A waitress clears our plates and we ask for the bill.

"I'd like to get this one," he says.

"Let's at least split it," I protest.

"I was late." He waves a hand. "Let me. You can get the next one."

I feel a warmth in my chest. I let him pay. It's not that deep.

After fifteen minutes of walking side by side, we reach the junction where I go right for home, and he goes left toward his flat in Highbury. Dinner could've been bad, or just okay, but it was good, and within that good is a kernel of possibility, of progression beyond Arthur—the first time I've thought about Arthur this evening. Or was it the second?

"Would you be up for another drink?" he asks.

"We could go to mine?" I offer, maybe too quickly.

"Sure."

He smiles. We go right, and he reaches for my hand, a perhaps too intimate gesture, but which nobody does enough. A woman wearing a baby-pink beanie walks between us, and we synchronize letting go to allow her through, rejoining seamlessly. I notice that his face is red, and I point it out callously before realizing that it's probably Asian flush, and that doing so might be insensitive, and then he hides his face behind his hands and laughs until I look away. It's sweet to see a grown man hiding behind himself.

"Is it your mum or dad that's Asian?" he asks, just as we reach an intersection at Kingsland Road.

"My mum," I say. "She, like, really plays it up, though."

"How so?"

"I think she's in denial about growing up around white people in a big house on The Peak," I say. "She speaks in Cantonese idioms that I'm pretty sure she just googles." Vincent laughs. "She only started taking lessons when we moved back to Hong Kong, because she didn't speak any Cantonese growing up," I continue. "My grandmother didn't think it was useful to learn, which says a lot, and she died when my mum was young, anyway."

"What kind of idioms?" he asks.

"Fat dou jau fo," I say. "When she's mad."

"What?"

"I'm probably not saying it right," I say. "She probably doesn't either. It means something like, even Buddha gets angry."

"Oh!"

Vincent laughs, and then repeats the idiom, but with the correct tones.

"She'd love that," I say.

We walk a while longer, and then I lead Vincent toward my flat.

I take a couple of beers out from the fridge while he pokes around. We sit on the sofa.

"Have you dated any trans women before?" I ask.

He startles at my directness. I can't help myself.

"A couple of dates."

I think of Carla.

"Who?"

"What?" he asks.

I flush red.

"I might know them," I say, only half joking.

"I've never *dated* dated a trans woman," he says. "And I don't think you would, anyway."

"But you've slept with one?"

"Yeah," he says.

"Why is that?" I ask, and it's too late before I realize that an interrogation is not very sexy, but it's a compulsion, and I want to know. Nobody else would ask these questions for me. Except Simone.

"There aren't that many around. On the dating apps, I mean. I guess statistically. But I'm glad to have gotten the chance to. I feel lucky. To have met you, I mean, not—"

I laugh.

"It's true, though," he says. "You're very pretty."

I think I like Vincent, not just because he said I'm pretty, but because of the way he said it, his face turned away from me at a slight angle, bashful, like it was something he wanted to confess but was scared to. My blushing doesn't feel like my own; a tender infection spread from his cheeks to mine. Vincent looks at the bookshelf behind him.

"Is your book up there?" he asks.

"No."

"Why not?"

"I just don't see the need."

"Oh," he says, eyes static on the spines. I feel glad that I recently binned Arthur's book. "I still think it's amazing, though. To have done that."

I give him the same placid smile I give anyone who uses that line. I kick off my shoes. He does the same, pushing at the heel of one loafer with the heel of the other. I see a stitch at his big toe. The only thing more impressive than a sock with no holes is a mended sock. I bring my feet up to the sofa. He twiddles his fingers, pretending to pick dirt out of an already clean nail.

"I've had a really good evening," he says.

"Me too."

He gives me the look. That weird, dumb glare that men give you before they kiss you, a moment of vacancy before leaning in, a twisting of the head as if it were a star-shaped block to push into a baby's shape sorter. He kisses me. On the lips. Full, just wet enough. A few not-quite-closed-mouth kisses, and then a brief assembly of tongues. His body on top of mine. He rubs his hand along my ribs, along my butt, across my pants, but gently. My hands should probably do something, so I run them across his solid chest, and then briefly over his hard-on. He kneels upright to unbutton his shirt, then helps me pull off my top. When his chest descends back onto me, he undoes the buckles and Velcro of my kilt, and a finger slips beneath my underwear.

I smile and laugh a little and he smiles and laughs a little. I realize then that he hadn't asked the question he may have wanted to, but instead was fine to wait and see. Maybe he doesn't care. Regardless, it's nice that he didn't ask. Sometimes it's just nice to meet someone and have sex and enjoy yourself like every other person in the world, without a pre-coital interrogation, a kindness I didn't extend to him.

Once naked, we move into my bedroom, our clothes draped over the couch and across the floor, like a waterfall of inside-out fabric. He asks me the right things, and with healthy eye contact. *Does that feel okay? How about that?* I can't help but compare his body and its motion to Arthur's. It's involuntary. There are things I notice yet can't fully explain; how Vincent moves with more patience, and yet also with more timidity, how his lips linger for a semibreve rather than a crotchet, how he's not rushing for release. There are things Arthur did that Vincent does not—bites on my thigh, pressing forehead to forehead—buttons Arthur knew to press. But maybe those buttons vanish and resurface like blisters. It's easy to forget they're a function of time, of learning, of growing into another's curves.

After he cums, he tends to my body until I do, too. We move into the bathroom for a shower, and he lets me go first. He watches me through the glass panes, his eyes on soapy boobs and thighs.

"What?" I ask.

"You're so beautiful," he says.

Sometimes compliments feel like something I could subsist on entirely. When I'm done with the shower, he hops in. I brush my teeth, then offer him my toothbrush as he wraps himself in a towel.

"Are you sure?" he asks.

"I think we're beyond that."

Vincent laughs. He thinks I'm funny. And pretty. I think the same of him. I do. I sit on the curve of the bathtub as he brushes his teeth. Vincent seems tidy. He seems organized. He mends his socks. Maybe it was a mistake to offer him my toothbrush—he might think it's gross—but he might also just like me. There doesn't seem to be a question of whether he'll stay over. In my room, he inspects the photo of me and Simone on my desk.

"Who's this?" he asks.

"Simone," I say. "We went to school together in Hong Kong. And university here."

"She's very pretty," he says.

"She's half Filipino," I say, as if that explains it. "She's gay," I also add, for reasons I don't want to think too hard about. "I'm sure you'll meet her."

What an odd thing to say. Why would I say that? I'm coy and careful. But Vincent smiles and doesn't seem to mind. What would Simone think of him? *Wow, Max, a Chinese lawyer, your mum really got to you. If anyone says he's gay for dating a trans woman, show them that picture of him in a shacket at the pub, holding someone else's sausage dog.* Vincent gets into bed and rests his head on my chest.

"What are your friends like?" I ask.

"A lot of them are married," he says. "Or engaged. Or getting there."

"I'm sorry," I say.

He laughs.

"Yeah, it's sort of that time, isn't it?"

"Not really for mine."

"No?"

"Well, a few," I say. "I'm just in denial. I have a friend from school who's getting married. Emily. Me and Simone are bridesmaids."

"You don't sound too excited."

"I think I just find it all strange."

"Hmm."

He lifts his head to kiss my nipple, then places it back down.

"I think I've changed my mind," he says.

"About what?"

"I wouldn't be a lawyer if money was no object."

"What would you want to do?"

"Play the clarinet."

"The clarinet?"

"Yeah. I used to be really good at it."

He looks up at me.

"When did you start?" I ask.

"I was eight," he says. "My dad started learning piano at the same time."

"Really?"

"Yeah," he says. "He'd always wanted to learn. We used to duet. He still plays."

"Were you in an orchestra?"

"I joined a jazz band in school and at uni." He pauses, shifting his body a little to draw himself even closer to me. "I always think those concerts are some of my happiest memories. I'm not sure I've felt as much like I was part of something. I'd never be, like, world class or anything, or even properly professional, but if money didn't matter then maybe I wouldn't have to be. I could just play in a jazz band with a few friends and have a good time with them. Maybe I'd feel like a loser, though."

"A loser?"

"If people asked me what I did, I might feel like a bit of a loser saying that I play in a really average jazz band."

I pause.

"Does that matter if you're happy?" I ask, with genuine curiosity.

"I think feeling like a loser could make me unhappy," he says. "And there's a lot of pressure on me."

"Where from?"

"My parents," he says without hesitation. "They're proud of me. I think that's worth a lot."

"I can see that."

VINCENT WAKES UP AT SIX thirty to go home and get changed for work. He leaves me a note by my bedside, written on the back of a grocery receipt that I'd left in the kitchen. He could've sent me a text, but he wrote a note, and ink has a permanence that pixels do not. I fold the receipt and keep it in the bottom drawer of my bedside table.

VINCENT, 2012

III

I'M AT SUVARNABHUMI AIRPORT, BANGKOK, WAITING FOR MY BACKPACK at the conveyor belt. There's been so much buildup to this. Part of it still feels like a miracle. Gap years, especially before university, are the whitest of white people bullshit. I had to present a detailed twelve-month costed budget for my dad to even consider it. *Hah! You think you don't need to make money? Chi sin.*

This is my first time in Asia, outside of visiting my grandparents in their tiny flat on the edge of the New Territories. My backpack was a present from my parents for my nineteenth birthday. A tall one, designed so that some of the weight sits at my coccyx. It was really nice of them, considering how much hair they pulled out over the trip. I think it was them finally accepting that I was going traveling. Who knows—it's a Chinese thing. Everything's in code. It's all fucking cipher. Hieroglyphics. Body language. Interpretive dance. Alan Turing couldn't crack it.

I'm alone here. Fred's not joining for another few days. He's decided to extend his stay in India, even though he's already been traveling there for months. He messaged me about a week ago, explaining that . . . *um . . . I just think I need a bit of a time out . . . my head's a bit, like, I don't know, man, fucked up right now. I was talking to someone and they said this meditation stuff helps . . . a place opened up and I just took it. I'm sorry, man, but I'll see you in ten days . . . in Thailand, I'll fly into wherever you are . . . I haven't booked my flights yet.*

Have you booked your flights, Fred? *Yeah, man.* Are you sure? *Yeah, man, chill.* I want to be angry. I am angry, but he's quiet about this stuff, and I know he doesn't talk about it to other people. There's trust between us. But still, would he have screwed over anyone else? Anyone who didn't already know he's a bit fucked in the head?

Now I'm thinking about all the stuff Fred has done over the years. He used to call me Foot-long Wong. My surname isn't even Wong. It's Chan. He'd seen my dick. It wasn't any smaller than his, but the implication of the joke—the issue with Foot-long Wong—was that my dick is small, because I'm Asian, and that's why the joke was supposed to be funny. He did stop everyone else from calling me it, though, but only when he finally decided it was offensive.

There's a girl my age standing close to me. She's wearing a leavers hoodie. 2011. Same year as me. Her hair is in a messy bun on top of her head. She's alone. About five meters away. Could I say hi? Hey— are you getting a cab? Do you want to share one into the city? Whereabouts in the UK are you from? Oh, I only know because of your leaver's hoodie. Feels like a British thing. And I guess this plane flew in from Heathrow.

I don't know why my heart's beating like this. I don't really understand why this is so hard. Just fucking talk to her. You're not a virgin. You can talk to girls. You're okay at this. Not great, but okay. Some of your best friends—well, friends—are girls. Okay, I'm going to do it. I take a deep breath. What's that Japanese word for feeling 80 percent full? I don't know, but it feels like that except with my lungs and air. As I start to walk toward her, she takes her bag from the belt and walks away. She looks back at me before she goes through Customs, but she doesn't smile. I've missed the window.

I wilt. My shoulders drain toward my stomach. Fuck Fred, man. I don't want to be alone here. The months leading up to this trip have been torture. Even after agreeing to let me go, with the exception of buying me the backpack, my parents committed themselves to making travel as unappealing as possible. Mum had just gotten an iPhone, and so looking shit up became a billion times easier. She'd sit next to me on the brown leather couch in the living room, slowly typing things with her red-nailed index finger.

"So terrifying," she'd say.

"What?"

She'd hold the phone toward me, always with an article about a young Brit abroad who died in a zip-lining accident, or who vanished into the sea after taking too many drugs at the Full Moon Party, or who ended up with a monster hospital bill after a motorcycle crash that insurance wouldn't cover.

"Can bankrupt us. Just stay alert."

When Fred said he wasn't going to meet me in Bangkok, I knew that I couldn't tell them. They would've lost it. Not let me go. All my friends said that they couldn't actually stop me. They're all white—they don't understand that I'll be asking for permission for the rest of my life. And maybe my parents would be right to stop me. White people can be a safety net. You get treated differently, even by Asians. At least that's what I've experienced at home, and I felt that I'd probably be treated like a white-person-by-proxy rather than an Asian, even in Asia, if I was with Fred. But I wasn't going to let it ruin the trip. I'd saved for six months for all this. Pushing cans of tuna and celery and wine along a checkout counter at Sainsbury's. Asking for IDs from teens and older ladies who looked like they needed a boost.

My bag arrives, tag wrapped around the strap at the top. I head toward Customs. I'm nervous about being stopped. It's that article my mum showed me about a foreigner being convicted of drug trafficking, after which she bought me a lock for every pocket of the bag, even the internal ones.

"Could be you," she said. "Be careful."

I carry my bag into the hostel lobby, which looks cheap but grandiose. Terra-cotta tiles line the steps up to the entrance. A middle-aged woman in a white collared shirt greets me harshly. She sits behind a counter made of laminate disguised as wood. She is tiny—her shoulders barely go much wider than her head—but she's sitting on a very high stool, bringing her up to eye level with me. She wiggles the mouse of the desktop computer, first soft, then hard, before banging the space key with her index finger.

"Name?" she asks.

"Vincent Chan."

"Passport?"

I swing my backpack off my back, undoing the lock on the front zip and taking the red booklet out of the pouch. She types details into the computer with only two fingers. I sign something.

"Go up two stairs," she says. "Room five, bed four. Lower bunk, okay?"

"Thank you."

"You Thai?" she asks, even though she's seen my passport.

"No," I say. "British."

"British?"

"British-Chinese."

"Ah, okay. Chinese."

She hands me a key.

"Got locker under bed," she says.

"Okay."

I go into the room of four bunkbeds and throw my bag onto my lower bunk. A shirtless man lies on the bed across from me.

"You all right, mate?" I boom.

I don't think I've ever said that in my life, I just want to signal that I'm British. And I know that's shit, that I'm caving in to racism, kind of, but I've seen how people react when they realize that my parents' accents match their faces. I don't want people to treat me that way. The guy lifts his head from his phone.

"Hey, man." He's British. He looks back down at the screen for a moment. "Joe."

"Vincent."

His skin is golden, but blemished with red patches, like scars from a hot whip; on the top of his cheeks, the ridge of his nose, what I can see of his shoulders.

"Did you just get in?" he asks.

"Yeah," I say. "How about you?"

"Ah, I've been here for a week. I'm heading to Phuket after this."

"Are you traveling alone?"

"I came here alone, yeah. But you pick up mates pretty easily. We're heading out to get some food tonight. You should join."

OTHERS FROM THE HOSTEL ARE with us, including a brunette, Bex, who told me within minutes of meeting her that she's going to Cambridge. We head to a bar on Khao San Road after dinner.

Red lanterns hang from the ceiling. Are they flammable? What if something catches fire? There's a long bar on one side of the room. Pictures of white tourists with the owner are plastered across the mirrored back, colonizing the space around the nozzle-topped bottles of alcohol. 'Starships' by Nicki Minaj blasts from a speaker. There's a level of buzz excessive for ten P.M. White people tumble around, screaming at one another to go to the beach. Joe's ordering shots at the bar.

"Four." He holds out four fingers. "Shots." He mimics the action of taking a shot. "Tequila," he says slowly.

I cringe. The woman behind the bar nods, expressionless, probably strapping TNT to him in her brain. For a moment we make eye contact, and I feel embarrassed, so I look back at the pictures of tourists. The shots come. It's cheap shit. Even I can tell that. My flush intensifies. It's only this bad when I'm dehydrated. We bob along at the edge of the dance floor.

Constellations of Thai girls are dotted around the Caucasian crowd, pearls in the sea of sweaty tank tops and brown shorts. More pristine. Makeup, maybe quite heavy, but artfully slapped on. Thick-drawn brows, candy-pink lips, in form-fitting dresses in bold colors that loop around nice tits and thin necks. One of them is tall. Joe's breath is in my ear.

"Like the ladyboys, Vinny?"

I realize what he means, but I don't even know if she really is at all. How does he know for sure? I blush again. The curious look on my face melts into a hard expression.

"Fuck off," I say.

I shouldn't have reacted so strongly. It's such a giveaway. Have I been caught? Shut up, Vincent! You were just looking. You're allowed to look. And who said he can call me Vinny? Why do people always call me Vinny?

"Gotta be careful," Joe says.

He cackles in a way that forces my shoulders toward my ears.

"What is it?" Bex asks.

"Vinny's found a ladyboy," he says.

Bex takes aggrandized offense.

"They're not ladyboys," she says. "They're transsexuals."

I'm not sure if transsexuals is right, but maybe that's just because it's a word I see a lot in porn. Transsexual. TS. Porn words don't feel right for the real world. I'd never call a Black person ebony. I look into the crowd and see another white boy from the hostel, hunching over one of the Thai girls. Not one of the ladyboys, or at least I don't think so. He looks so dirty in comparison to her. It feels a bit gross. I wonder if they'll fuck. Where they'll fuck. Back at hers? Is he allowed to take her back to the hostel?

Bex turns to us, and we dance. She pulls my head toward her, her sour breath in my ear.

"Just so you know," she says, "I have a boyfriend."

I lean away from her and nod. There is not a speck of sexual energy between us, and I almost take offense, but any protest would simply confirm to her that I do, in fact, want us to do it. My eyes drift back to the tall lady. The tall maybe-though-maybe-not transsexual. I'm not gay. I've never found someone who wanted to be a man attractive, unless any of the girls I've fancied wanted to be men. I look away again, this time for good.

Jᴇᴛ ʟᴀɢ. I ᴄᴀɴ'ᴛ ɢᴇᴛ to bed, even after pumping myself full of beer and spirits. I'm dehydrated. My head is scrambled. The small backpack, detachable from the big backpack, is next to me on the bed. I fiddle around for the zips until I find my pack of cheap cigarettes and a lighter.

I go up to the hostel rooftop. There's a girl sitting by a table—the girl from the airport. I start to walk toward her, wanting to say that I recognize her. I know she saw me, too, so it would be an ordinary thing to say, right?

"Do you want a cigarette?" I try.

She looks at me and smiles.

"I'm actually heading back to bed." She clears her throat. "Night."

She walks away and I'm alone again.

I sit down and light a cigarette. They're bad quality, the cheapest of the cheap. It feels like I'm putting my mouth over the pipe of a rusty car, breathing in exhaust fumes.

I hear shuffling behind me, flip-flops on dusty tile. I turn around. A different girl. She's tall, wearing a top with thin straps and loose trousers. Blond hair wavy and just past her shoulders. Hot, I guess. She sits next to me. I offer her a cigarette.

"No, thanks," she says.

"Can't sleep?" I ask.

"Jet lag," she says. "I only got in a couple of days ago."

"I got here today," I say. "Are you going to be traveling around?"

"Kind of."

"Kind of?"

She yawns.

"I have an operation in a few weeks," she says, and I'm taken aback by her abruptness, the plain way that she says operation.

"What kind?" I ask.

Who asks that? None of your business, Vincent. She turns away from the landscape and looks at me.

"The lifesaving kind," she says.

"Oh, shit. I'm sorry."

There's a small curl in her lip.

"Don't be."

Maybe she's got a wooden foot. She needs a prosthetic. Is Thailand good for prostheses? Can foot surgery be lifesaving? I don't know. I need to move the conversation along.

"Are you here alone?" I ask.

"Yeah," she says.

"Did you want to be?" I know I should stop asking questions, but I can't help myself. "Like, did you not want people around for surgery?"

"I wanted to do it alone," she says. "Maybe I'll regret it. I don't know. My mum really wanted to be here. I felt bad saying no, but I felt like . . ." She pauses. "I don't know. I'm twenty-one, you know?"

I nod my head, even though I don't know. She pulls up the thin fabric of one of her trouser legs and scratches. The sound of her nails against her skin is gentle. Her long fingers draw red streaks across her leg, the flesh becoming distended, deformed, wobbly.

"Fucking bites," she says.

"They don't really seem to go for me."

"Bad blood, then."

I laugh. She curls her lip again, and a hot pang of nerves flares up in my chest.

"Yeah, maybe," I say. "What's your name?"

"Alex."

"Short for Alexandra?" I ask.

"Just Alex."

"That's modern."

What a weird thing to say. That's modern. What is wrong with me?

"Yeah, I guess so," she laughs, rearranging her hands. "Where did you grow up?"

"Near Cambridge," I say. "Ely. How about you?"

"Hackney."

"That's in London, right?"

"Yeah. East London."

London, and instantly I know Alex is much cooler than I am. I can feel it. She can feel it.

"Did you like it?" I ask.

"Kind of," she says, recrossing her legs. "It's changed a lot. Did you like Ely?"

"It was all right," I say, though I feel the conversation beginning to slow under rusty pleasantries. "It was actually quite shit," I add, and she looks a little more interested. "There was nothing to do. And I went to school in the center of Cambridge and lots of people were just bell-ends." I think of Fred. "People were also quite racist."

"That doesn't surprise me," she says.

44

I think about telling her about Foot-long Wong, but it feels weird putting the foot-long in her mind.

"People called me Vincent Ching Chong all the way through primary school," I say, and Alex's jaw drops a little. "You kind of wish that if people were going to be racist then they'd be a little more creative."

"I was bullied a lot in school," she says.

"Really?"

"Yeah."

"They were probably just jealous," I say, cringing immediately, because even though I aimed for teasing, it ended up at groveling, and I feel like I might as well have tipped my hat toward her and called her m'lady.

"Did people call you Vincent Ching Chong because they were jealous?"

"Yeah," I say. "I had a really sick bowl cut."

She smiles. Maybe I've won her over.

"What are you doing tomorrow?" I ask.

"I wanted to go to this gallery. And this floating market. They're a bit out of town." She looks at me. "Do you want to come with?"

"I'd love to," I say.

She smiles, like she was worried I'd say no.

"Let's meet for breakfast at ten? Is that too early?"

"That's perfect," I say.

"Cool."

We sit in silence for a little while. I yawn, then put my cigarette out. I feel tired again, and so I stand up and stretch my arms above me. My T-shirt rises a little, and I hope that she's looking at my abs. That's really stupid, I know, but she might like them. It's not like I'm stacked, but I have a nice body. I draw my shoulders back and squeeze my biceps, then relax back to normal. She's looking off into the distance.

"I think I'm going to head back to bed," she says. "I'll see you tomorrow, yeah?"

I nod. Maybe too eagerly. When I head back down and crawl into my bunk, onto my narrow mattress, thoughts of Alex cloud the dark, muffle the sounds of bodies around me, and I feel warm. It's a crush, and it's silly, and maybe it's not anything and maybe she wasn't even flirting, but I feel a bit less alone.

MAX

IV

VINCENT AND I ARE AT THE TATE MODERN TO SEE A JAMES TURRELL installation, enough dates along that I've stopped counting. At Simone's insistence, there were also dates with other men. A man who was cast as the dull husband in *Hedda Gabler,* and for good reason; another "musician" who read my poems while making me listen to his EP— the kind of experimental techno that sounds like two pieces of scrap metal fucking.

I mentioned that I'd struggled to get tickets, and a few weeks later Vincent bought some without asking. It's a kindness I'm not used to in dating. I went to the internet to ask if I was being love-bombed, but apparently he may just be nice. One eye open, though. Always.

We walk down the concrete slope of the vast Turbine Hall.

"Giles Gilbert Scott designed the power station," I say. Power stations make me homesick. They remind me of the one on Lamma Island, close to the beach by our house, where I could swim in the salt water and bury my brother, Jamie, in the sand. Vincent smiles at me. He likes facts. He holds my hand. "An early-twentieth-century architect," I say. "He designed Battersea Power Station as well."

"What do you think he'd make of the spin classes there?"

"Imagine trying to explain that to him."

"So dystopian."

When we reach the bottom of the Turbine Hall, we leave our coats in the cloakroom and move into the adjacent Blavatnik Building, arranged around the irregular corners of the structure's quadrilateral husk. I think of another fact.

"Blavatnik's an oligarch. He gave hundreds of millions of pounds to build this."

"I don't think he's an oligarch," he says, and I'm caught off guard by being fact-checked. "I don't think he's even Russian, and he's cut business ties with Russia, anyway."

"Has he got you on retainer?"

Vincent laughs.

"I'm not saying he's a saint," he says. "Nobody makes money like that without a little bit of exploitation."

It's a low bar, but it's nice that despite his career, working on acquisitions for oil and gas, fast fashion, and tobacco companies, he has mostly favorable politics, even though he excuses himself as being a mere facilitator of the bad. He's clever. When I first met Vincent, I thought I was smarter than him, in the same way I think I'm smarter than most people when I first meet them, a sure-fire sign that I am probably, in fact, quite stupid.

"Thank you for buying the tickets," I say.

He smiles. It's hard to communicate without overdoing it that I really am quite touched. I was behind thousands of people in the online queue, so I'd shut my browser off and convinced myself that I didn't actually like James Turrell that much. There are skylights in every British home with an extension. Who needs to see another? Vincent must've signed up for notifications for when a new batch was being released. There's a hopefulness in that, which I find endearing.

"It was really sweet of you," I add.

"You can get the next one."

We wait in a short queue, and then all of us are let in one by one by a Tilda Swinton–looking waif.

"Hi," Vincent greets her with striking warmth. "We've got two tickets?"

We walk into the exhibition space. There's a dark wall, and illuminated on it is an orange rectangle. There is a set of black stairs beneath the orange. Part of me is a little disappointed, especially when I compare it to the last time I saw a James Turrell installation.

It was at a festival held in the grounds of an enormous estate north of Cambridge. The festival was incredibly crusty. No adjustment to the vibe for time of day; pounding techno through morning and night. I would wake up so desperate for lyrics that by day three I began to hallucinate them. I went with Simone. A small carve-out from the chaos was the tour of the sculpture park. Our tour guide was a local teenager who did bumps of ket throughout. He told us how he'd kept tabs of acid in his pocket, and when it had rained two days before they'd bled into his thigh, and he'd spent ten hours thinking he was in Tetris. He led us to the wooden structure housing the Turrell, and we sat on the benches, staring at the small, square skylight cut out of the top. It was blue. Just a clean square of blue. I was so taken by it, how the monochrome sky, cut up so neatly, was so simple yet beautiful.

This indoor gallery space feels less impressive. This is just a wall with an orange rectangle on it.

Tilda Swinton tells us to take our shoes off, and to put on slippers before going up the stairs. I briefly worry about hygiene but decide to relax. As we walk up, I can see that what I thought was an orange rectangle simply projected is actually an opening, an entryway into another room, illuminated plainly in that orange, and much wider and taller than the entryway, extending deep into the building. I can't work out the mechanics, how all of this fits within the exhibition space, and I feel moved, being consumed by this static color. I hold Vincent's hand and I don't want to let go.

A woman too old to be wearing a beanie with animal ears holds her hands up and spins, her bearded partner taking a photo of her. She is the type of person whose quirks consist of kitsch clothing and an unwavering belief that her love for the most successful media ventures of my lifetime—*Friends* and Harry Potter—somehow makes her unique. Is there a special place in hell for me? Vincent and I recently had a conversation about our self-perceived flaws.

"I'm quite judgmental," I'd said.

"Really? I don't see that."

If he could look inside my head, he would run.

Vincent looks back at the woman and smiles at me with a quick lift of his eyebrows. He then stands in front of me, placing his hands on my shoulders. I can see the entrance through which we walked, and everyone else.

"What are you doing?" I ask.

"It's just nice to see you like this. It's like a painting."

He holds my shoulders there for a little while longer. Do I like him? Do I really, really like him? I am aware that there was a shift—sometime after Arthur—when I stopped caring about flutters and cared more for caring, for feeling like a priority. When I stopped questioning if I found people hot and thought more about whether they were nice. When things stopped being about what someone was, who their friends were, what they did for work, and more about how they were.

I've been thinking about the hospital, and when I do I watch myself falling down the stairs in third person. The source of my personal crisis was not the fall; it was merely the point of inflection. I don't want to overegg the omelet, but still, I can't help but go back to it.

Kristen Johnston once had an unforgettable one-episode stint on

Sex and the City, snorting coke at a party where the average age was fifty-five, lighting a cigarette by an open window, screaming that New York used to be the most exciting city in the world, and then falling out of said window to her death. That scene was what made me go ankle-deep into sobriety. I'd seen that episode once when I was a teenager, illegally streaming already old episodes on my laptop on Lamma. Again when I'd finished my law conversion and was nursing a post-celebratory comedown. And eleven more times nine months ago, after Arthur broke up with me, when I rewatched the entire series start-to-finish and that scene became something else. I once heard that Putin often watches that video of Gaddafi being dragged out of his car and murdered by a mob. That scene was my Gaddafi video. It was a crippling fear of being left behind, of being unable to see when my life needed a change in direction. When I spend time with Vincent, there's a sense of safe harbor, holding me back from falling down the stairs or out of the window, from waking up in a hospital alone. We step out of the room and down the stairs. I stuff my feet into my trainers while he ties his laces carefully. A flick of hair has separated from the pack and dangles between his eyes.

"Your hair looks really nice like that," I whisper.

"I thought I'd try something new."

"It looks nice."

He places his arm around my waist and grabs a little. A small wiggle of his fingers, just to let me know he's close. We leave the exhibition space for the cafe. I ask him to find a table near the window while I get two glasses of wine.

"My mind's kind of blown from that," he says. "It was just light."

"Was that your first Turrell?" I ask, taking a sip of wine.

"First Turrell?"

"I know," I say. "I'm a cunt."

He laughs, dropping his head over his forearms on the table.

"So it wasn't your first?" he asks. "You didn't say anything."

I smile. There wasn't really room to. *I got tickets to that exhibition—three thirty next Saturday.* Sure, that sounds lovely. *Done.*

"Where did you see it?" he asks.

"There's this sculpture park outside of London on the grounds of Houghton Hall, and they have one of his installations there."

"Why were you there?"

"A festival."

I consider telling Vincent about the tour guide, about the acid that dissolved into his thigh, how it looked like his face was melting as he took us around the sculpture park. I know he and his best friend took shrooms on his gap year in Thailand, and that some of his friends do coke on the weekend, but I decide not to say anything, buckling under the pressure to upgrade my palatability.

Vincent reaches into his backpack and takes out a Tupperware, looking around him like he's handling contraband. He lifts the lid to reveal two slices of cake and I clap. Layers of white sponge, separated and coated in a faintly purple icing. He unfurls two forks wrapped in kitchen towel.

"Lemon and lavender," he announces. I take a bite. "Is it good?"

I nod. It's delicious. Tangy but light, airy but satisfying.

"Yeah." I swallow. "Really yummy." My fork plunges down for more. "I kind of want to learn."

"I could teach you."

"Have you taught much before?"

"No," he says. "I mean, I kind of taught Fred, I guess. We baked together a lot when I was a teenager."

My eyebrows shoot up. Vincent's best friend. Who I've yet to meet.

"He was kind of depressed back then," he says. "I thought it'd help."

"Did it?"

"Sort of. I don't know." He shrugs. "My mum would get really mad when we did it at mine." He clears his throat. "Vincent Chan! Too much cake. Too much butter. Can get fat and die of heart attack."

I laugh.

"It's so funny," he says. "We used to keep it a secret from all our friends as well."

"Very homoerotic."

"Right?"

"It's sad you had to hide it, though."

"It's the world we grew up in," he says. "Pretty much still are in."

I look out toward St. Paul's, taking another bite of cake.

"Would she like me?"

I feel pathetic right as the words leave my mouth.

"My mum?" I can't bear to nod. "Ah, Maxine, Maxine." Another impersonation of his mum. "So pretty. Ngaan hou tai. Lawyer. Still Chinese. Very good."

If anyone should be allowed to do an impression of Vincent's mum, it's probably Vincent, but there's something about it that will always feel a bit off. I laugh, anyway, even if it's hard to imagine that's all she'd think.

I'M WATCHING VINCENT'S BACK MOVE around the kitchen as he cooks a one-pot chicken rice, stirring aromatics into the chicken fat he's rendered out of the thighs.

You should marry a nice Chinese man, Maxine. My mother said that to me when I fled to my parents' after Arthur broke up with me. We were sitting at the rosewood dining table in the family room, across from each other, our plates filled with Indian takeaway. She said it, then laughed and covered her face with her hands together, fingers elongated, blood-shellacked nails pointing toward the ceiling. Weird. It was, in my mind, one of her desperate attempts to seem more Asian, not realizing her behavior would only make me too embarrassed to ever introduce her to a Chinese man. She was tipsy, which she never really is except on special occasions because of Dad's sobriety, but he was away, so we shared a bottle of wine. I took the bait.

"Why?" I asked.

"Dependable. Hard-working."

"That's racist."

When she released her hands, her face was stern.

"It's not racist," she said. "It's culture. I'm Chinese."

I didn't have the energy to explain to her that, in liberal society, much discrimination comes from people who think they're on the inside. I also didn't have the energy to explain that some Chinese people are actually quite racist.

"Not all Chinese people are raised the same," I said.

"It's culture," she said. "It just is, Maxine."

"Do you want me to order a husband from Guangdong?" I asked. "Do you want to tell him I'm trans, or shall I?"

Mum scoffed.

"There are plenty of Chinese boys in England, Max." She said this so earnestly, as if I genuinely didn't know.

"Chinese boys who've grown up in Britain are British, Mum. They can be just as shit."

"I know that, Maxy," she said. "But the culture's still there. Like it is with me."

"Is it?"

Mum sighed, exasperated.

"It's just my advice. You can take it or leave it, okay?"

I said nothing.

"It's just my advice," she repeated.

The high stool in Vincent's kitchen is hard on my bum. I'm trying to drink the chilled white slowly. It's a Hungarian semi-sweet, which I only know because Vincent told me. His friend Fred brought it back from a business trip for him. Fred, again, who I have yet to meet, but whose mark is everywhere. The wine is quite nice, even if we're not supposed to like sweeter wines. People always want dry.

The perspiring glass drips onto a cork coaster. I asked if I could do some chopping—spring onions, garlic, ginger—but he said no because he's hosting, though I've never extended the same generosity to him, and so I'm sitting here doing nothing. The exhaust fan is no match for the smell of sizzling lard, which I know will seep deep into my clothes. I wouldn't mind. I'd wear this as perfume. It's delicious.

"Where's the recipe from?" I ask.

"Well, it's kind of a play on Hainan chicken rice," he says. "But I saw a video of someone making it online. A South Asian woman. British, though."

"I think I've seen the same video."

"It's weird, isn't it?" he asks with his back to me.

"What is?"

"When people who seem outside of your culture present you things from inside it. I don't know. Part of me gets defensive. It's stuff I should've learned from my parents. Sometimes when I cook for them I get a little annoyed that they're too impressed."

"You feel like they should've taught you more?" I ask.

"Exactly," he says. "Or do more."

It's getting warmer. Vincent's thrown the rice and stock into the pot. The steam begins to cloud, beads of condensation forming on the glass of the shut sash window by the side of Vincent's kitchen. I get up to open it, and, for the first time, see two Fuchsia Dunlop cookbooks in the very narrow bookshelf by the window. *Every Grain of Rice. Land of Fish and Rice.*

"Do you like Fuchsia Dunlop?"

"I hate her," he says, and I laugh. "She's more Chinese than I am."

He covers the pot and turns back to me, examining me in the way that he does. I'm finding myself more able to endure his lasting stares. I always lamented Arthur not seeing me, often quite literally not meeting my gaze, and here I am, shying away from Vincent's.

What my mother says rings in my head again. Vincent is dependable. Vincent is hard-working. I'm walking a fine line. Maybe it's because Vincent is Chinese. Maybe we, my mum and I, can say that because we are Chinese. Can we? Can I? Am I, even? But Vincent is those things, regardless of the reasons why. Vincent speaks to safety. I take a sip of wine as he turns back to the stove.

I wonder if what I think I know about this man is accurate, or whether ruminating, tracing the outline of him again and again, has thickened my belief in a person that simply isn't there. It's difficult to know if the qualities I see are ones that will stay, what is show and what is character. Kindness can be a veneer, stripped as soon as it's safe for cruelty and apathy to crawl out of the hatch. But there are few shortcuts to knowing someone, and so what's a girl to do? Either tread with suspicion, or trust the sales pitch and the white-toothed smile.

I look at the records on the shelf to my left. Six are displayed so that you can see their covers. One by Frank Ocean, another by Laura Marling, things that remind me that a person is not a shell. Vincent shuts the pot and leaves everything to boil. He places his forearms on the countertop, sitting across from me.

"Thank you for coming over," he says.

"Thank you for having me."

"You're very beautiful, Max."

"Thank you."

He always says this. I never know whether to say it back, because a mirrored compliment can be a platitude. It serves nobody but the giver, fills a gap that guilt may otherwise fill. I've learned just to say thank you. Sometimes I get anxious because I worry that he values beauty too much, because then I, counterintuitively, begin to worry that I'm not, that he'll find someone prettier, or realize that I haven't always been as pretty and recognize that's something that matters. Could I even blame him? I'm the vainest bitch I know. I hate this feeling. I'm thirty. It's so embarrassing.

"It's kind of hard to believe you're trans sometimes."

"You can't say that, Vincent."

Contrition grips his face. I suppose gaffes like this are inevitable. I'm still disappointed.

"Fuck, yeah," he says. "I'm sorry."

"It's fine."

"That was stupid."

"It's fine."

I smile, limply. At least he knows it was stupid. He turns back to check on the rice and gives it a little stir. Worry is matched by flattery, because there's part of my brain that still hears the statement as too much of a compliment, which makes taking genuine offense hard. When we were younger, Simone used to say thank you when people said she didn't look Asian. It's not a compliment, Simone! *Well, it's not a crime to look Venezuelan.* Simone hasn't done that since we were teenagers. Now she wants more than anything to be seen as Filipina, uploading photos of her many attempts at adobo or jars of papaya pickle. I can understand that when it came to race, part of how well you were doing was how well you hid it, at least back then. I hate that it still feels the same with being trans. For me. I can't ignore that the hiddenness, the cloaked transness, might be why Vincent thinks this will work.

Vincent serves up two plates, and we sit next to each other at the kitchen counter. The grains of rice are swollen with lard, each a bullet of salty, greasy umami.

"This is absolutely delicious," I say. "I love family recipes."

"Yeah," he laughs. "Generations back."

He moves in his chair so that our knees touch. I feel warm. These aren't sparks, but I'm glad that they aren't. I'm not sure I believe in the virtue of sparks. For many years it's been hard to separate love from anxiety, from push and pull. The manic rush is more a desire to be loved than love itself, a desire that explodes at any sign that love may recede, that it is in short supply. My worries about Arthur gave me diarrhea, forcing me into a six-week course of hypnotherapy to settle the distress signals from my brain. Evacuate, evacuate.

"Have you ever slept with a man?" I ask.

I don't know why I've asked the question, but I also don't know why I haven't yet asked it. He has a mouth full of chicken rice. He gestures softly to his undulating jaw, and I watch as it quickens. He attempts to swallow, then coughs, and as he reaches for the water I rub my hand along his back, patting with the pads of my palm.

"Kind of," he says, shoveling rice around his plate with his fork and spoon, hunched over his forearms again, like he's digging for words around the seared and braised meat. For a moment, I feel relief. "Hand job. Once. But I really wasn't into it. I think I'm attracted to femininity, but I think I'm also just attracted to women. I like boobs."

"Have you heard of the phrase gynosexual?"

I've never said that word out loud in my life.

"Yeah," he says, exchanging his fork for his glass of wine. "I don't feel like that works for me. I'd just say that I'm straight. It feels simpler."

"You don't have to call yourself anything you don't want to," I say.

It feels like an empty thing to say, even if it's true.

"Have you ever slept with a woman?" he asks.

"I've thought about it, but no."

He looks at me, really looks at me, and then wipes something from the corner of my lip with his thumb. I feel shy and dab my mouth with my napkin, which is actually just a bit of kitchen roll. There's another question that I want to ask. It's hard to know why. Am I being vulnerable, or am I just seeking reassurance?

"Do your parents know?" I ask.

"What do you mean?"

"That you're dating a trans person," I say. "That you would date a trans person."

His face tilts back toward his plate.

"No."

"Why?"

"My parents take me talking about dating someone quite seriously," he says. "I don't always tell them about that stuff."

"But do they know you would?"

His jaw slides sideways; he hunches over a little more.

"It hasn't come up," he says, placing a hand on my knee. "When does stuff like that really come up? But I would tell them. I mean, I'll have to tell them, right?"

I chew on this. His parents would probably think I'm well educated. He knows, through our conversations, that my parents are, by most standards, well off, even though they'd never say it. *We're comfortable!* That I'm also a lawyer. It would help, I imagine, that it's hard to believe I'm trans sometimes. Maybe he hasn't thought too much about the trans question because there is little to navigate in the annals of heteronormativity. Isn't that the appeal?

"I want to be clear that I've never really had hang-ups about this stuff," he says. "It just hasn't come up with my parents. You don't need to worry, okay?"

There is a bluntness in the way that men often say this, betraying the fact that they do indeed have hang-ups. *But you're a woman, so there's nothing to work through. Who even cares?* Arthur wasn't like this. He once admitted to hang-ups, and that was much less challenging because it was honest. It's hard to know if the shoes are on the wrong feet if you refuse to look down. For all his faults, Arthur could at least look at himself. And yet I want to believe Vincent. I almost believe Vincent. I'm not sure I want to know much more.

"Okay," I say. "I was mostly just curious."

Vincent doesn't let me wash up. When he's done, we hold hands. The soap's roughened his skin, dissolved the natural barrier that should coat them. And then we move to his room and have sex, and I remind myself of all the things I like about Vincent. About having sex with Vincent. The way he doesn't look away from me when he licks my nipple. The way he bites his lips at the simplest thing, so much that sometimes it feels like it must be an act. The way he likes to hold my hand while he's fucking me.

V

"SHOULD WE GO FIND HIM?" VINCENT ASKS.

"Drinks first."

We move to the bar. The hairstyles in the crowd are a mixture of she/they mullets and he/they yellow. We're at Caspar's book launch, at a rooftop venue in Spitalfields. It's a Thursday. Books always come out on Thursdays. The chairs and lamps—all mid-century, all vibrant pastel—are set on an electric-blue carpet. The sofas hug the squiggling internal walls, separated by bushels of tropical plants. It's all very Caspar. So is the book. Essays about gay dating called *Grind Out*. The cover of the hardback is an ass—just an ass. Vincent and I are holding our newly bought copies in one hand, although he holds his back to front, and our negronis in the other as we move into the crowd. I haven't seen Caspar in months, not since I fell down the stairs at his party, and as he approaches, I feel nothing but dread. He's wearing a black bodysuit with cut-outs, and over it a leather harness, tucked into a long skirt sewn from clashing tartans. None of it works together—it's a sartorial war zone for young designers.

"Max!"

"Caspar! Congratulations."

He kisses me once on each cheek, then holds my arms with his sweat-slicked palms, looking me right in the eye.

"How is your body?" he asks. "Are you healing?"

"Yeah," I say, looking toward Vincent. "This is my boyfriend."

Caspar looks at him, hands still locked on to my upper arm fat.

"So nice to meet you," Vincent says.

Caspar releases me to kiss Vincent's cheeks.

"Did you come from work?" he asks Vincent, eyes on his suit.

"Yeah," Vincent says.

"Are you a banker?"

"I'm a lawyer."

"Oh." Caspar turns to me. "Are you still working at that law firm?"

"It's a tech company," I say. "Are you still working for that property developer?"

"They're architects. And I'm quitting."

Half of queer culture is fronting as an artist while working in an office. It's the new, more grueling system of artistic patronage.

"You're going to write full-time?" I ask.

"I know," he says. My face smiles, my body groans. "Anyway, I'll see you both in a bit, okay?"

Vincent and I find a quiet corner on one of the benches on the outside terrace. Spring has come early. As Vincent puts his arm around me, his elbow dips into the water feature behind us.

"Fuck," he says.

I helplessly dab some of the excess from his suit jacket with my cardigan. He takes it off, and I use it to draw some of the fluid from the damp elbow of his button-down. Water aside, Vincent looks suave, freshly ejected from the bowels of the city.

"Do you guys actually like each other?" Vincent asks.

"I literally don't even know at this point."

"Why was he asking you about your body?"

The time has come. I keep dabbing at his shirt, avoiding looking Vincent in the eye.

"I fell down the stairs at his party on New Year's."

"Were you drunk?"

"No, actually."

"Were you hurt?"

"Yeah, but not badly. Just, like, bruising. Simone took me to the hospital."

"Shit."

"It honestly was not that big a deal." I pause. "I was supposed to have a CT scan but left."

Vincent retracts his elbow. There's shock across his face. He looks so confused. Yes, I too can be irresponsible. Sometimes I find it hard to do the right thing.

"You didn't go back?"

"No."

"Will you?"

"If something were to have happened, it would've."

I wave at Simone as she appears on the balcony, wearing expensive loafers and leather trousers. Her white shirt collar is pointy and ironed. There's a spicy margarita with a bird's eye chili garnish in her hand. She and Vincent hug, a tight embrace. Simone likes Vincent.

"You look handsome," she says to him, hand on his chest.

"How are you?" I ask.

"Very good." She takes a big gulp of her margarita. "That girl I scouted, Xenia, booked a big job."

"The one with no eyebrows?" I ask.

"Yeah."

"Can I see?" Vincent asks.

Simone takes out her phone, showing it to Vincent. In the picture— one of Simone's Polaroids—Xenia's wearing low-rise jeans and a crop top.

"Wow," he says.

He doesn't get it.

"It feels like having proof of concept," Simone says. "But I think we can do it. I feel excited."

When we saw her in London Fields, Simone was unsure of Xenia's body, which surprised me because I'd thought that things had moved along.

"You can be bigger now," she said. "But you can't really exist in between bigger and smaller, or maybe in between, like, big, medium, and small."

"Why?"

"You have to fit the samples how they're made," she said. "You can't just be any size and expect it to work."

"Can't we?"

"I know. It's fucked."

Vincent gets up to use the loo. Simone turns to me with a grave look.

"Arthur's inside," she says.

My ribs tighten around my heart. There was a good chance he'd be here—better than good. Arthur got Caspar in the divorce, and our writing group, which previously included me, Caspar, Arthur, and a burlesque performer called Calypso who wrote obsessively about body hair. I voted against her joining.

I can't deny this is partly why I asked Vincent to come with me. People shouldn't be worn as clothes, and especially not as armor, but isn't this what we're supposed to do? Bring people into our lives, allow ourselves to be brought into theirs.

"He's doing a poetry reading," she continues.

"How do you know that?"

"We said hi."

"He doesn't even write poetry."

It stings. Caspar and I workshopped my poems together. *You have a crisp, salient voice.* Did that mean nothing? I might have said no, but why wouldn't he ask? I put my drink down to check the acknowledgments of Caspar's book. I'm not there. Arthur is. Even Calypso. I roll my spine back into the seat. The ice in my negroni is melting, mellowing its syrupy taste.

"Eva's also here," Simone says.

"Why?"

"She filmed some pride campaign that Caspar was in. They're friends now."

"Pride? But it's only April."

"I know," she says, rolling her eyes. "It's like buying Christmas decorations in September."

She finishes her margarita in another big gulp.

"Did you say hi?" I ask.

"Yes," she says, looking down at her empty glass.

"And?"

"It was cordial, but I spent some of it gushing about how great the last few months have been, which made me question if they've been particularly great."

"You've done a lot," I say, because she has. "How was she?"

Simone cocks her head toward me.

"Fine."

Vincent comes back, smiling.

"I think your friend's about to do a speech."

As we get up, I pick up Vincent's book, forgotten on the bench.

"Here," I say. "My ex is doing a reading, by the way. Sorry."

Vincent smiles.

"I think I'll be okay, Max."

Caspar is standing on a chair. Clusters of people gather at his feet. While Caspar's team fix a technical issue with his microphone, Vincent grabs my bum, then kisses me on the cheek. It's not appropriate, but it's okay. I like it.

"I want to thank my agent, my publisher, my queer, chosen family." The crowd whoops. "And, of course, my parents." He points to two people in their sixties near the front, clutching each other in a tight embrace. Then he talks about the improbability of him being here, of the times he felt so lost and alone that living past thirty wasn't something he could comprehend, and I look toward his mother, and she has tears in her eyes, and I realize that I wasn't aware that Caspar had gone through anything like that, even though Simone and I have known him since university. I suppose I've seen a lot of his writing, but writing can be so distant, especially something like a book of essays. I suppose intellectualizing our experiences is just another way to depersonalize them, strip them of pain we would otherwise feel and replace it with pain we can merely think about.

"I wish I could show this book to the twenty-two-year-old who gave himself a kidney infection from holding in his pee. Or the twenty-three-year-old who didn't leave his house for months, because he felt himself sinking deeper and deeper into shame."

Simone mouths the word fuck to me. The honesty is startling. I wonder if it is necessary, and then question if I'm the problem. Caspar tells us how writing a book about queer love feels like a testament to the distance he's traversed.

Although it feels like Caspar came out at birth, it was only a couple of years after we graduated. And then I remember Becca, his university girlfriend—a posh white woman who now has a kid and once told Simone that she looked like Pocahontas.

Simone and I exchange looks. The wash of guilt across her face is also on mine. While I forever float in my own life story, I rarely wade into other people's. Is that a bad thing? The crowd claps for Caspar. Simone leans into me.

"God," she says. "It's so easy to forget all of that stuff. How different people become."

"Yeah."

"It's kind of like how I knew you before you transitioned, but when I imagine us as kids I just see you as how you are now."

I can't help but feel a twinge in my chest. I struggle to accept that reality, that Simone and I weren't—or at least weren't seen as—two girls together at school. It feels so wrong to overlay those facts across the present. I'm not sure how to respond.

"I can't really imagine you with long hair," I say.

If it's hard for Simone, then it's probably hard for anyone who knows me to really picture me as a boy, including Vincent. To experience someone else's past with the richness of the present feels impossible. Vincent hasn't spoken to me much about trans things. He's asked the basics—when I knew, how long I've been on hormones, the horrors of accessing trans healthcare on the NHS—but not the detail, about how it all was for me.

There's some misdirection at most celebrations of overcoming adversity. *It's all behind me! I'm fine! Would an ashamed gay wear an eight-hundred-pound kilt? I think not.* But we carry our shame and scars with us. At least, I do. There's no doubt about that. I'm not sure if Caspar's even happy. He makes a big thing about being alcohol-free, but I'm pretty sure half of that is just because he really loves GHB.

Are the worlds of Caspar and Vincent troublingly far apart? By troubling, I mean for me. Vincent is watching with his mouth ajar. He's clearly moved, but I want to dive into him, inspect the firing neurons to measure the breadth of the gap, see the extent of his empathy.

"We have a few readings tonight," Caspar says. "Not my own work, because you should all just buy a fucking copy"—he chucks the book at one of his friends at the front. The crowd laughs—"but I thought it'd be nice to have some poetry. I asked my friend Arthur to do a reading."

Vincent shoots me a look. I return it, scrunching my lips and my eyebrows. I don't want him to think there is any joy in this—there isn't. Arthur stands in front of the crowd, and I feel deeply embarrassed by him, his slouch, his unkempt hair, his oversized T-shirt and thick corduroy trousers. I cling on to Vincent. I can't believe the motherfucker's writing poetry.

"Hi everyone," he says, meekly, unfolding the poem from his back trouser pocket. He clears his throat, rubs his nose, and then clears his throat again, as if the world has nothing but time for him. "Winds hurtle." He takes a breath. "Across the surface." He drags his hand in a straight line in front of him. "Of mellow water." He pauses, longer than necessary. "Each body a pond, pillaged and abandoned by conquest." He looks at the audience. "Bodies without a name, moved if not by wave then plane."

Vincent looks at me with a smirk. Simone isn't next to me anymore, but at the bar, and another girl has moved into her place. There's a glint in her eye as she watches Arthur, and immediately I know that they're fucking. I almost want to laugh. I hold on to Vincent's arm a little harder, rubbing my thumb along the smooth weave of his jacket sleeve, refusing to listen to the final verse of Arthur's poem.

"The scroll unfurls." Another long pause. "Sins smudge the ink."

Everyone claps. Arthur catches my eye and smiles. I return it, but the flutter inside me vanishes as quickly as it appears, the final wiggles of a severed tentacle. It's dead. There's no brain there. I exchange a smile with the girl who's sleeping with Arthur, which unfortunately invites her to lean into me.

"Wasn't that beautiful?" she asks. "I spoke to him about it. It's about the refugee crisis."

"Which one?"

"Oh, I think, just, like, generally."

"Oh," I say. "Cool."

My chest starts pulsing with church giggles, and I bury my face in Vincent's neck. He rubs my back, slowly, as if he thinks I'm crying, but then he starts laughing, too.

We retreat to a curved sofa in the corner of the room.

"It was like a really bad version of your poems," he says. "It just wasn't very good."

I recently gave Vincent my poetry collection. He liked it. It meant a lot.

"I could see how he tried to play with imagery in a similar way," he continues. "I'm sure you were an influence, but he fell a bit short."

"It might be poor form of me to talk shit about an ex."

"Not even a little? Not even tempted to call him a white savior?"

I laugh.

"All four of his mothers are therapists," I say. "And I think it shows."

I watch Vincent's brain crash as he tries to compute. Simone appears with three cocktails.

"That poem was terrible. I hope you feel good, Maxy."

"Mm."

I shouldn't, but I do.

"He's coming," she says, waving limply.

Arthur approaches us with a strong gait. Simone sits closer to me, linking our arms. I do not want this.

"Just wanted to say hi," Arthur says.

I introduce Vincent as my boyfriend, and he gets up to shake his hand. Arthur gives me a kind look, as if to say, good for you, which makes me want to tell him to go fuck himself.

"Cool poem," Simone says.

"Thanks." He looks at me. "Did you like it?"

"Sure," I say. "Well done."

"You should come back to the workshop."

I'd rather die.

"Oh, yeah, maybe," I say. "How are you?"

"Yeah, I'm good. You seem well."

"Yeah!"

Awkward silence hangs in the air.

"Anyway," he says. "It was nice to see you guys."

We all say goodbye. I can breathe.

"Workshop?" Vincent asks.

"I left it when we broke up."

"Why?"

"Because he said he was fine for us to both be in it, and I wasn't, and I didn't want to see him because he broke up with me."

"That's so unfair."

"Right?" Simone scoffs. "It's always be chill, be fucking chill. I'll put his fucking body on ice."

"Whoa," Vincent says.

I laugh. She holds the anger for me. I'm grateful for that, mostly because rage is unbecoming. It was quite literally my downfall.

"Do you think I should go to therapy?" Vincent asks.

"What?"

It is the weekend after Caspar's launch, and we are on the Overground to Fred's birthday. Vincent holds a cake tin in his lap. Its contents are magnificent—three tiers with delicate piping.

"It's weird," he says. "People always say that everyone should go, but Caspar's speech really made me think how everyone has stuff to unpack."

"Like what?"

"I don't know. Don't we all have stuff?"

It's easy, perhaps too easy, to respond to someone's problems by telling them to go to therapy. Childhood trauma? Therapy. Divorce? Therapy. Poverty? Therapy. It's the safeword of the emotionally illiterate, a convenient yet enlightened way to throw the discomfort of care into someone else's lap, as if each kind of care is interchangeable. But my own cynicism aside, our minds are cluttered houses, boxes piled up to the mold on the ceiling. And the funny thing about minds is that we're trapped inside with no way to open the door. Vincent's right. We all have stuff that needs unpacking, and therapy helps us find the box cutters, the bin bags, the shelves. But you can never force people into it. That's how you get Arthurs.

"You could go," I say. "I would never force you. But it can be helpful."

"I'll think about it," he says.

We leave Hackney Wick station and walk toward the Olympic Park. Vincent said it would be a picnic. It is not a picnic. As we approach, I see large tables, white tablecloths and people in white aprons preparing food. Caterers. No picnic has caterers. It's not far from what Simone and I grew up with—moneyed heteronormativity—and to have spent years away from it doesn't mean I've forgotten how to swim. As we get closer, I see a man that I recognize from pictures talking to a park ranger, pointing at a printout. It's Fred.

"What's he doing?"

"Those are the park regulations," Vincent says. "He asked me to find and send them to him."

People slowly turn to wave at us. There's a conversation among the men on one side of me, and a conversation among the women on the other. I make a note to join the women after introductions. What would they possibly do if there were a couple of gay men here? Would the bottom join us? I can't take my eyes off the baby in the pram, rocked back and forth by a blond woman. I don't have friends with children. I don't go to parties with children. I look toward the food table again. There are sweaty jugs of Aperol spritz, skewers of meat and veggies arranged in pyramids, crudités and halloumi slices in circles, a graveyard of sticky chicken wings, two entire salmon filleted upon beds of roasted tomatoes. Beneath each woman's light jacket is a summery wrap dress, and I feel relieved, because I predicted this and therefore wore a summery wrap dress. One woman is wearing green leopard print. Aisha, I presume, because she's the only one who isn't white.

"Vincent!" Aisha marches toward us, posture upright, fringe un-moving. She kisses Vincent once on each cheek and turns to me to do the same. "I'm Aisha. Fred's partner."

"Max," I say.

She's half a foot shorter than I am. Her features are sharp, her cheekbones cutting through the planes of her face. Hair in a neat ponytail, not much makeup. Vincent has told me we have lots in com-mon. *You're both creatives doing non-creative jobs. She makes rugs. No, I know it's not the same as poetry.* Vincent also said she's from Singapore, which is something, I guess. I say hello to the rest of them; they re-ceive me with warmth.

Most of the men are Vincent's and Fred's friends from school, and they resume their conversations soon after kissing me hello, their en-thusiasm popping and receding like fireworks. I feel like an append-age until I meet Fred, who has appeased the park ranger, shaking his hand and sending him off. Fred has waves in his golden hair, pushed out of his face by some God-given force, and large muscles, all of which make me distrust him. His trousers, T-shirt, and overshirt are all loose enough, and his trainers cost three hundred and fifty pounds. I've seen them online.

"Max," he says. "Ah! I can't describe how nice it is to finally meet you. I've heard so much."

He gives me an almost imperceptible up-down, and then smiles at Vincent.

"I've heard a lot about you, too," I say.

I have. Luminous ringleader Fred. Left a boutique consultancy to become the COO of a start-up. Literally always working. Very clever. He doesn't earn as much money now, though still a lot, and has ample share options. Best friend. Oldest friend. Did a lot of traveling with Vincent. Lived in Hong Kong, just like me, but for work. It's hard to track the depressed teenager who needed Vincent to bake with him to the man I see now. Was it therapy? What is he carrying?

"Vincent was telling me about your poetry," he says. My heart drops a little, but then I remember what Vincent said at Caspar's launch, about my poetry being better than Arthur's, and this buoys it. "I looked you up and found one you wrote in that journal? About MSG? I thought it was moving."

"You found a poem about MSG moving?" I ask.

"It has a bad rap," he laughs. "I'm an ally to the cause."

I do like that poem—it was pre-book and published in a well-known literary magazine. I remember when the email came through saying that it'd been accepted. I felt like a success, even though I was paid nothing for it.

"Thank you," I say.

"I haven't read that one," Vincent says.

"I'll send it to you," Fred says before I can. It'd be more appropriate for me to send it to Vincent, but Fred has spoken with such confidence that I almost believe it makes sense for him to send it instead.

One of the catering staff pours champagne into flutes, and another hands them out on a tray. Fred asks us to sit down, and so I circle the table to find my name. Surprisingly, there's no seating plan. Aisha slips into the seat next to me before Vincent can, and so he's relegated to a few seats down, and the woman with a baby sits across from me, the little creature writhing in her lap until it latches on to her breast.

"I'm Annabel," she says.

"I'm also Annabel," says the ginger woman next to her.

Will they reveal over lunch that I, too, am Annabel? I feel at sea.

"I heard you used to live in Hong Kong," Aisha says. "It's where Fred and I met."

"I think Vincent mentioned," I say. "I grew up there."

"How long have you been with Vincent?"

Doesn't she know?

"A few months," I say. "And you're married to Fred?"

"I am," she replies. "When did you move here?"

"When I was eighteen. For university. And you?"

"Two years ago. I couldn't wait to leave Hong Kong, though."

"Hong Kong sounds so nice," Blond Annabel says, heavy on the so. "I actually love Asia. We were in Phuket for Christmas. We were really worried about the flight but it ended up being all right with the bassinet." She looks down at her baby. "We were fine, weren't we!"

Jesus Christ. I give Blond Annabel what she wants and steer the conversation firmly toward her baby. I ask how old she is, and then ask questions about what the baby can do—whether she's said any words, can crawl or roll over—and after a while it feels like I am asking someone about their car or Swiss Army knife.

"That's so nice," I say.

"It is! You'll know one day"—and then Blond Annabel gasps, and she puts her hand over her mouth—"I'm so sorry. That's so insensitive."

"No," I say. "Don't be silly, it's fine. Seriously."

My head quickly swings from side to side, and I see that nobody is really paying attention, other than Aisha and the Annabels. I feel a prickly heat across my cheeks, a slapping reminder that I'm the other, that people are thinking about medicines and genitals and internal organs and other things that are none of their fucking business. What if I don't want kids? Why does everyone assume that this is a tragedy? I take a breath. Each second of silence makes floor space for awkwardness. I know how I'm reacting has nothing to do with my thoughts on parenthood, other than an angry feeling that people are thinking about it for me.

"Please come up for food!" the caterer shouts.

I am relieved.

Aisha and I stand in line hip-by-hip. She pinches my arm softly, then whispers in my ear.

"That was really fucking weird," she says.

"Thank you," I say, feeling too small to say much more.

"I have PCOS," she says. "The assumptions hurt."

We pass Fred on our way back to the table, and he stops to kiss Aisha on the cheek.

"Enjoy the food, girls."

She gives me an apologetic smile. Back in my seat, I poke and bite at a piece of halloumi. It was left out to sit for too long, and tastes like a tire dug out of the sea. Next, a bite of the baked salmon. It's soft. Garlicky, soy-saucy, umami-y.

"I've heard about your poetry," Aisha says.

"I've heard about your rugs."

"They're quite painstaking."

"My poems are quite bad."

"Are they?" she asks. "Weren't they published?"

"One of the quotes on the front cover was, fans of the grotesque and imaginative could like this," I say, at which Aisha cackles. "A reviewer suggested I crowdfund for breast implants."

"Why?"

"To do the world a favor and stop writing poems about having small tits," I say. "I think the worst part was that my ex suggested it was a good idea."

Aisha laughs even louder this time. I'm taken by how little I feel at what I've said, how something once anguishing and hurtful has smoothed into a pebble, a small anecdote to skip into the lake of conversation. She hasn't reacted how Simone did when I told her. *Is he fucked in the head? Jail!* It's not like Simone can't take a joke—it's the shift in my delivery. It's not that deep anymore. I can't help but feel happy for it. I bite into the chicken wing, feeling comfortable enough with Aisha to chew the bones clean.

"So why did you leave Hong Kong?" I ask, licking the marinade off my fingers.

"To escape the white people."

I look around at the crowd of girlfriends and boyfriends, Vincent and Aisha palm trees on a white beach.

"How's that going for you?" I ask.

We laugh.

"Who's that?" Aisha asks.

Blond Annabel turns behind her, and we all look at the woman waving. It's Carla—Poundland Arca—wearing a microskirt and folded silk scarf tied behind her back as a top, immune to the slight chill. I haven't seen her since New Year's. This entire week has been a violent collision with my violent collision. I'd almost forgotten about her sleeping with Arthur, but for the most part have forgiven it. We are, at the very least in my mind, unified against him.

By the time I stand up, she's almost behind me. I don't know why I feel like I've been caught doing something dirty. Cheating on queerness. Fell down the stairs and woke up a trad wife. I fight the urge to cover the flowers on my dress with my arms. We kiss once on each cheek.

"Hi, gorgeous," she says.

"So nice to see you."

She surveys the outdoor lunch.

"So Nicky Hilton."

I'm not sure Nicky Hilton has ever been to the Olympic Park in Stratford.

"It's Fred's birthday." I gesture toward him. "He's my boyfriend's—Vincent's—friend."

They wave to Carla in turn. Vincent gets up to join us.

"Wow," she says, sizing Vincent up. "New boyfriend! So you've recover—"

"You weren't at Caspar's book launch?" I interject.

"No, baby." She shakes her head, hip cocked. "I don't like book people."

"Why not?" Vincent asks.

"They take a lot of words to say simple things," she says, rolling her hands in front of her.

"Fair enough." Vincent laughs. "How do you guys know each other?"

Carla and I look at each other.

"From, like, around," I say.

Carla nods.

"Anyway, baby, I've got to go see Michael."

"Who's Michael?" I ask.

"The vape guy."

The man she sucks nicotine into her ass for. Carla starts laughing at my recognition, and I can't help but laugh with her while Vincent stands on politely. Carla and I air-kiss twice goodbye, with plenty of space separating lip and cheek.

WE WAIT FOR THE NEXT Overground train on a sun-drenched bench.

"Do you think Fred had a good time?" I ask.

"I hope so. He's been feeling quite down recently."

"Anything in particular? Or just run-of-the-mill existential pain."

"Think his work's been stressful because of the downturn. And he's prone to sadness, anyway."

"He seems to really love Aisha."

"I guess it helps to love someone when you're feeling low."

"That's the first party I've been to with a baby."

"It's weird, isn't it?" Vincent puts his hand on my thigh. It sends a soft shiver up my spine.

I decide to tell him about Blond Annabel's gaffe, and as I do, his jaw drops, and then his forehead falls into his hands, shaking in the gap between his thumb and forefinger.

"Fucking hell," he says. "I'm so sorry."

"It just made me feel out of place," I say.

"Fucking yeah."

We wait in silence until the train arrives. Sat down in the near-empty carriage, he rests his head on the glass window behind us.

"Do you want them?" he asks.

I look away, toward the handrails, the doors, the red emergency lever that stops the train.

"I think life often works in reverse when you're queer," I say. "Children aren't a given. It's an opt-in, not an opt-out. As Annabel pointed out."

I smile at him. He returns it.

"But do you want them?" he asks.

I purse my lips. It's hard to explain how little I understand myself when it comes to this. I often say I don't, because we live in a world where kids cost a lot, and I live in a city that costs a lot, and that means making sacrifices I'm not sure I can make. And there's the fact that I'm sans womb, and that means exploring other options, all of which cost money. And none of these methods—private adoption, surrogacy—are without ethical questions. But all of these points escape the essential question, which is, do you want kids? Without barriers, would you want them? To answer yes makes the blockades more painful, and I'm not sure I want to invite that in. Is contemplating children just another hook on to which I can hang my feelings of inadequacy?

"I don't know," I say. "It just feels complicated."

"Yeah, they are."

"I guess they're an insurance policy against loneliness," I say. "But is that a good reason to have them?"

"It's sort of selfish," Vincent says, holding my hand.

"Yeah," I reply. "I also don't know if I'd be a very good parent. I worry I'd be like my dad."

"What do you mean?"

I haven't told Vincent much about Lamma. It doesn't feel like there's much to tell. We could talk about the fire, but whenever I recite the story in my head, it always feels lacking. I imagine his response. *Do you really think that's why you're not close? Everyone was fine, right?*

"He was kind of detached, I guess," I say. "And my mum wasn't home much. She spent a lot of nights in Central because the ferries to Lamma stopped before midnight, but Dad didn't want to live anywhere else."

"Funny that you and Jamie became lawyers like her."

"Jamie would remind you he's a barrister, not a solicitor," I say. Vincent laughs. "But I feel like we're often doomed to repeat the failings of our parents."

"And hate them for it."

I probably shouldn't be so dramatic. Vincent's told me *I love you* never leaves his parents' lips, and of the burden of their expectations on him as their only son, even though his sister is an investment banker. I have it pretty good—my parents don't really expect much of me at all.

"I think you'd make a good mum," he says.

I squeeze his knuckles.

"Do you want them?" I ask.

He pauses.

"I've never looked into the future and not seen children," he says, "but I don't think that means I want them."

"That's what I mean."

"But it doesn't sound like we're far apart, does it?"

"It's a mirror image," I say. "Like your left hand and right hand."

"What?"

"The same thing, but not perfectly superimposable. The same but in reverse."

I place my hand over his. He rests his head on my shoulder, slouching into his seat, spreading his legs long and wide.

"Carla seemed funny," he says. "What does she do?"

"She paints, but also does other stuff."

"Is she trans?"

"Yeah."

"All your friends are so interesting."

Are my friends really that interesting? Is interesting a euphemism? I'm not sure I want to know for what.

"They're fair-weather friends," I say.

"Not Simone."

"We'll be buried in the same grave."

"What will the tombstone say?"

"No boys allowed."

Vincent laughs.

"Who's the vape guy?" he asks.

"A man pays her to smoke vapes out of her butt."

Vincent sits up from surprise.

"Whoa," he says. "Is that even possible?"

"I guess."

"Is she okay?"

"I think so."

Is she okay? Or does life on the margins mean one becomes inured to experiences others would describe as traumatic, too readily collapsing them into funny anecdotes or chapters in self-development?

"A man once paid me to stand on his dick," I say. "I wore trainers. I didn't have to take my clothes off."

"What? When?"

"When me and Simone were at uni. She waited outside for safety."

Vincent sits back; I wait for him to formulate a question. Maybe I've said too much. It's not as if I owe him this information. It doesn't even feel like it was me. Not anymore.

"What did it pay?" he asks.

"Fifty pounds for half an hour."

"Is that the going rate?"

"I don't know. It felt like a lot at the time. I didn't do it again. I felt really sad after."

"I'm sorry."

"For what?"

"That you felt sad."

He holds my hand again. The train stops. We watch passengers board and alight.

"Do you really see yourself as queer?" he asks.

"I suppose," I say. "Why?"

"I don't know. You look the way you do, and you only date men. It doesn't feel so queer to me."

This disarms me far more than I want. I could take offense, but he's also right. Identities don't mean much to me outside of their relationship with the material, and if I'm not performing queerness, if what I'm perceived to be is just a woman, and one who isn't trans or gay, then where does identity really take me? What cause does it serve? I squeeze Vincent's hand.

"Hey, I was thinking, you know that medication you take to reduce your testosterone?" he asks, voice hushed.

"Yeah?"

"What's it called again?"

"Cyproterone acetate," I say. "Why?"

"When I first told Josh about you he asked if your medication had side effects."

I feel a hot prickle of annoyance. Blond Annabel's husband. Of course.

"Why?"

"He's a doctor."

"Then surely he can find out by himself?"

"I know, I'm sorry," he says. "I realized that I don't actually know, though. About the side effects."

I sigh.

"Weight gain," I say. "Brain tumors."

"Really?"

"Yeah, it's a very small risk, but they say it can happen."

"Fuck," he says. "I'm sorry."

"It's okay," I say. "It's not something I really think about."

"He also asked if you froze your sperm."

"Vincent," I plead. "That's so weird and invasive."

"I know, sorry," he says. "I think he was just throwing the kitchen sink in."

"I would rather smoke vapes out of my ass forever than have a room of people discuss my body."

I slap my forehead to my palm. Vincent separates them and holds my hand.

"I'm sorry," he says. "I just felt bad. For not knowing how all this stuff works."

Maybe I should've told him, but he hadn't asked.

"I froze my sperm," I say. "Not that I'd ever use it."

"Oh," he says. "Why not?"

The train stops at Dalston Kingsland and fills. Vincent moves the cake tin onto his lap.

"I thought I'd use it if I ended up with a woman," I whisper. "Some people experience a shift in their sexuality when they go on hormones."

Vincent raises his eyebrows.

"But I didn't. So I especially can't imagine using mine," I say. "And even if I did, I'd still feel weird about it."

Vincent nods, slowly. I don't say that whenever I've imagined having these conversations, my body has always felt, in one way or another, like a concession, that in some way I'd owe some enormous debt to any man who'd jump through the many extra hoops to have a child with me. Letting him use his sperm seems like the least I could do.

"There are plenty of ways to make a family," he says. "I think there's latitude to rewrite the book a bit."

He recently started reading *Detransition, Baby.* I wonder if that's where this has come from.

WHEN WE GET BACK TO his, he takes a seat on the balcony. I sit on his lap. He inspects the fabric of my dress with his fingers and kisses my shoulder. I keep my head fixed forward, as if the touch of his puckered lips on my bare skin does not make me melt, because I'm scared of my weakness for tenderness, and how I can rise with the simple fact of a man's—of Vincent's—touch. He kisses my neck. The tickle makes me laugh, and my head falls back and we begin to kiss again, and from behind me he plays with my breast.

We go inside. He lies on the bed, playing with himself through his trousers. I stand before him and slip the straps off my shoulders. He smiles at my half-naked body. I hook my thumbs at the waist and pull the dress down. He's smiling, a smile of desire, of deep want and wonder, one which reminds me that, to him, my body is not a concession.

THE NEXT MORNING, VINCENT GETS a call. His father has had a heart attack. He mumbles as he packs a bag, then runs out of the flat without saying goodbye.

VINCENT

VI

ALEX SITS ALONE AT A TABLE FOR TWO IN DENIM SHORTS AND A T-SHIRT. She looks up from her book, folds the corner of the page and smiles at me. The beginnings of a good day stir in my belly.

"Have you eaten?" I ask.

"I have. But I'll wait for you."

I go up to the breakfast counter. The toaster is a conveyor belt that crispens the bread as it sails through, dropping out the other end. Kind of like a car wash. The opposite of a car wash.

I sit across from Alex. Does she have to watch me eat? Am I eating okay? There was a time when I had trouble keeping my mouth shut when I chewed. It was when I started school. Kids made fun of me and said it was gross, but all I was doing was what Mum and Dad did. My sister was like me. We became self-conscious, and on the few occasions we went to restaurants, we'd beg them to chew with their mouths closed. We even invented a code word so we could say it without saying it. Magical Chicken. Code for: close your fucking mouth. They'd roll their eyes and scold us. *No respect!* They don't chew with their mouths open as much anymore. I guess over time that shame bled

83

from us to them. I wipe some crumbs from the corner of my mouth as I swallow.

"What are you reading?" I ask.

"*Half of a Yellow Sun*," she says. She nods her head toward the case of books at the side of the room. "All the other books are the same. Take nothing but photos, leave nothing but your copy of *Shantaram* on the communal bookshelf."

I don't know what *Shantaram* is. I laugh, anyway. She smiles.

"How's it been for you here?" she asks.

"What do you mean?"

"It must be kind of weird," she says. "You could pass for Thai, but you're still a foreigner traveling around with white tourists."

"Yeah." I feel some relief at the question, that someone could know without me explaining. "I'm probably not treated as well. By the locals, I mean. Or by white people. It's kind of, like, the worst of both. I've only been here a day, though."

"I can see that," she says. "Hopefully it gets better."

"Have you made friends in the hostel?" I ask, taking a bite of toast.

"You."

I smile.

"Besides me," I say.

"I hung out with this one girl. Her name is Bex."

"I met her last night."

"Everyone's a little basic," Alex says, shrugging.

I think of the set of T-shirts I brought with me. How they were packaged at Uniqlo as a three-pack of basic T-shirts. He wears basic. He is basic. How long until Alex is bored of me?

"I also feel a bit on the outside of it," she says. "I've got my own room."

"Fancy."

"I killed a cockroach in the bathroom this morning."

* * *

ALEX HANDS ME ONE OF the earbuds plugged into her iPod. I stare out the window of the air-conditioned carriage. We're listening to Frank Ocean, who I know some of my friends like but who I've never really listened to properly. I ask her what the song is. It's Forrest Gump, and when we get to the end, I ask if she can play it again. We talk over the sound. She's in her final year of philosophy at UCL. She's never liked it. She's taken some time out. For medical leave.

"Do you have any hobbies?" she asks me.

The clarinet. I'm no prodigy, but I'm quite good at it. I've been playing since I was eight, after a couple of years of not taking to violin or piano. Playing a melody on it always feels like I'm sailing, just gliding through the notes with the force of my breath and small movements of my fingers. It feels like magic. But people think the clarinet is gay, and boys will always tell girls at parties that I play it to shit on me, or laugh when I bring my case into school, calling it my handbag. Sometimes I wish I played something sexier, like the saxophone or even the trumpet, but at the end of the day, I do just like the clarinet.

"I play instruments," I say, hoping she'll leave it at that.

"Which?"

I purse my lips.

"The clarinet."

"That's cool. Like, in an orchestra?"

"Jazz band."

"I'm so jealous," she says, turning down the music a little. "I've always wanted to do that. Are you doing music at uni?"

"No. Law."

"Why?"

I think about all that stuff I grew up with, about being a provider, about being a good son, and how studying something like music or psychology or English or art was never even a consideration. I can't imagine that conversation. But Mum, I love music. *Love? Love?! Love don't pay the bills!* Alex feels clued in, but there's only so much she can understand, and I did choose law on my own, it's just there isn't a clear border between my choices and theirs. I want security, but I also want to make them happy. Isn't that just as important? Is that kind of want not equally important? Want is a complicated word.

"I want to be a lawyer," I say.

ALEX TAKES CAREFUL PICTURES OF the boats at the floating market, of butcher's knives and cut-up fruit. She buys a packet of jackfruit, undoing the plastic wrap as we sit down on a bench. I refuse her hand sanitizer before picking up a piece.

I offer to take a few pictures of her on her camera. It isn't digital. I haven't really seen someone use one of these since I was a kid. I expect her to laugh when I ask how to use it, but she places her hands over mine, showing me where the shutter is, how to focus. I take one of her on an over-water walkway in between two boats. She doesn't smile. I hope it's a nice photo, even if it has nothing to do with me. She asks to take one of me, and I let her, and I wonder if I'll ever see the finished thing. She said to me on the train that she doesn't have Facebook. It was just another way for cunt bullies to fuck with her, and she doesn't feel the need anymore. There are questions I have, like, how do you check who's going to a party? How do you stay in contact with randoms like me? But I don't ask, because the answers seem obvious.

And then I feel a rumble in my lower belly. I try to ignore it. It comes again. I know that I need the bathroom. Quickly. I'm literally going to shit myself. The rumbles turn into sweats, and I feel like my body's about to plunge out of my asshole.

"I need a toilet," I say.

She reaches into her bag and gives me a packet of tissues, plump and unopened with sprigs of lavender over the front. She knows. I remember seeing a toilet sign in a complex near the front of the floating market and start running that way.

"I'll wait for you here," Alex shouts after me.

The men's smells like the walls are lined with fecal matter. I cannonball into a cubicle, undo my shorts and squat over the toilet. Everything explodes out of me. For a few seconds it feels like I'm dying, great flood upon great flood, but then everything settles, and I use the entire packet of Alex's tissues cleaning up. When I walk out she's waiting there for me, not in the market like she'd said, smiling.

I've never been so embarrassed. And I feel like a bit of a loser, but it seems like she doesn't care. It'd be a bit shit if she cared about a little shit. A lot of shit. She doesn't know how much shit there was. I think I fancy her, really fancy her, even though it's only been a day. Half a day. Maybe this is just a cute part of our origin story. We'll look at this in the future and laugh about how I nearly shat myself in Thailand.

"You okay?" Her smile breaks into a laugh.

"Yes" shoots out of my mouth, an offensive defensive, and she laughs again, and I feel like even more of a dick. "It was probably the jackfruit."

"I don't think it was," she says. "I don't feel anything." She starts rummaging through her bag. "And I don't know if food poisoning works that quickly. You should've cleaned your hands, anyway."

Alex pulls out some hand sanitizer and squeezes a small slug onto her palm, and then onto mine. The synthetic smell of watermelon rises up from my hands. She holds out the tray of jackfruit. Please. Let it go.

"No, thanks."

She laughs and eats another piece. A trail of saccharine saliva-tinged juice runs down her finger.

The next day, Alex leads us through a shop in Chatuchak Market exhibiting local artists, and she talks to the shopkeeper about them, who they are, where they studied. She doesn't buy anything, but everyone looks happy to talk to her anyway. I imagine introducing her to my parents. I haven't introduced a girl to them before. I guess I keep my parents hidden. It's not that I'm embarrassed by them, even if they can be embarrassing. Fred gets it, and I feel like Alex would, too. She's charming. It's white girl charm, but she doesn't talk down to people. I picture her on the sofa, watching Cantonese dramas with my mum, engrossed in the swinging swords and impossible leaps, sucking on sour plum candy. *A-lix! Eat more.* I shrug myself out of the thoughts, even if they're pleasant. Always going into the future. Getting too deep too early. Alex shakes the man's hand and says goodbye.

"You know which questions to ask," I say, walking through a narrow corridor of hanging T-shirts and ornaments.

"They're basic questions," she says, then pauses. "The questions come if you really want to know something. Should we go to the gallery?"

We walk to the train station, and in the carriage my sweat cools on my skin. We sit in silence for some of it, but it doesn't feel bad. That's good, isn't it? We get off at the stop for MOCA, walking toward the entrance, past a huge sculpture atop the water feature that looks like a lotus flower made of large white bubbles. I offer to pay for the tickets, and Alex confidently leads us through the exhibits, like she's been here a thousand times before. I read all the labels because I want to show her that I can take information in, that I'm not an idiot, but I retain none of it, because I'm an idiot. I want to say something about them, ask some questions. *The questions come if you really want to know something.* Maybe I don't want to know. I guess I just want to talk to her.

As we sit in front of three enormous paintings, each as tall as a house, but narrow, one each for heaven, middle-earth, and hell, all I can think about is how she's heading to Koh Samui tomorrow because she wants to be near the beach.

* * *

BACK AT THE HOSTEL, WE bump into some of the others, including Bex, though we don't do much beyond saying hi. Bex is smirking. It's crazy how you can be miserable with sunburned Brits who smell of Sudocrem one night, and then be happy with someone you actually like the next. We head out to a restaurant together, and on the way Alex picks up fishcakes served in a banana-leaf tray, and then a banana crêpe.

"Leave space for dinner," I say.

"I'm just trying. We might as well."

She offers me a couple of small bites but eats the lion's share. She's so thin. Where does it all go? Does she take dinosaur shits? She suggests somewhere a bit nicer for dinner, and we find a complex of restaurants a twenty-minute walk from our hostel and sit down on a bench with a beer. We get a few curries, one with flaky pork shank and another with steaky monkfish, each in rich warm sauces—orange and red splotches, like the sun. It feels fancy, the first time a meal's making a dent in my budget, but it's worth it with Alex. We spoon the curries onto our plates with some rice. I want to ask her about the surgery. What it is. But I don't. It's none of my business—I don't want to say the wrong thing.

"Has your friend been in touch?" she asks, licking some sauce off her thumb.

"I'll check when we're back at the hostel," I say. "He got out of his meditation thing today. He'll fly wherever I tell him to meet me."

"From India?"

"Yeah."

"So last-minute?"

"He doesn't really care about money."

"Where's it going to be?" she asks. "As in, where are you going?"

"I'm not sure," I say. "I'm going with the flow."

"What's the flow, though?"

"As in, I'm seeing where things go."

"I know, but what are things?"

"I don't know."

Silence grows. I feel sad. It'd be so simple to say, I want to spend more time with you. *Sure, come with me.* But within those words is a destitute soul, a neediness I'd rather hide. I feel sad.

"Do you want more of this?" I ask, hand on the serving spoon, already halfway to her plate.

She nods. I ladle some of the meat and soupy broth next to her dome of rice. I spoon some food into my mouth, my jaw lethargic.

"Why don't you come with me to Koh Samui?" she asks. I feel the light return to my face, and I almost squirm at my transparency. "Your friend could meet us there. It's a long journey, but it's supposed to be really beautiful."

I think about Fred. He'd like to be in Koh Samui, but he'd also like to party.

"Do you think you'll go to the Full Moon Party? It's nearby, right?"

Alex lets out a gentle scoff.

"It's not on when I'm there," she says. "There's the Half Moon one. I can't really see myself going, but I guess I'm not against it. Like, morally."

I nod, eating a bit of fried fish. I offer her some, scraping off a small bone with the spoon. I couldn't see her there, either. She seems too clean, too assembled. Alex sort of just floats around, swift but smooth. I don't think I've seen a drop of sweat on her. I'm a beast in comparison, sweating for the both of us, huge dark rings in the armpits of my basic T-shirts.

"I think Fred would probably want to go," I say. "I'd probably have to go with him."

She plays around with her food.

"We could look into it," she says. "I guess it'd be interesting to see. So do you want to come with?"

"To Koh Samui?"

"Yeah."

"How are we getting there?"

"Overnight train to Surat Thani, then there's a ferry," she says. "The tickets are, like, twenty quid. We can get the train tickets back at the hostel, and we can just get the ferry tickets when we get there." She pauses. "I get nervous traveling alone, to be honest. It'd be nice to have company."

I smile. A plan's there, even if it feels like she could take it back at any moment. Still, I imagine people at the hostel asking me where I'm heading next. Overnight train to Surat Thani. With Alex! We're meeting my friend over there. A few days ago, the trip I'd saved up for felt like it'd come to nothing, but now it feels real.

"I'll message Fred tonight," I say. "To let him know."

She smiles, and I feel reassured.

"What's Fred's deal, anyway?" she asks.

"He's a good guy," I say. "A bit all over the place."

"How so?"

"He was supposed to be in Bangkok with me," I say. "But he only told me a week or so before I flew over that he'd canceled his flights to do this silent meditation thing."

Alex scrunches her eyebrows. I don't want her to think I'm the type of person who puts up with that, or the type of person who people would do that to, even if I am. And it's complicated with Fred. He's a good guy, and if he said he was in a bad way, he was in a bad way.

"That's kind of fucked up," she says.

"No," I say, shaking my head, spooning up the last bits of rice from my bowl. "It's fine. I'm pretty good on my own. And I think he really needed it."

"You're a good friend."

"You'll like him," I say. "Honestly."

I imagine Alex and Fred together for the first time, and it occurs to me that she could really like him. I really hope she doesn't like him, at least not in that way. It's a coupling that would work, in that Aryan could-be-siblings could-be-dating kind of way. Shit. I slurp some of the dregs of curry.

I LIGHT A CIGARETTE ON the way home, and after I put my lighter back in my pocket, Alex reaches for my hand. Thoughts about Fred vanish. My heart jolts. I squeeze a little, not resisting a smile, catching her eye. She's smiling, too. I feel a warm rush. This stuff is so difficult. So much time wondering if someone likes you, if signs are signs or delusions.

"Do you want to stay in my room tonight?" she asks as we approach the hostel. "I kind of get freaked out sleeping there alone."

My face, already red from heat and dehydration and flush, gets redder.

"Yeah, why not?" I say, as if she's offered me a fucking Oreo. "I'd like to, I mean."

For some reason, I think about that tall woman from a couple of nights ago, and an unpleasant feeling takes hold of the neat image of me and Alex holding hands. It's not like Alex knows that I found that woman attractive, but I imagine her finding out, and it feels like there's a rat inside me, and all I want is to scrub my insides with steel wool, remove the dirty footmarks and droppings. I take a few deep breaths, focusing on the soft warmth of her palm until that rat loses power, softens into a plush toy, until it seems odd and ridiculous and far away.

I get ready for bed in my dorm, write to Fred to tell him the plan, then walk up to hers, taking the steps two at a time.

Alex lets me into her room. She changes in her bathroom with the door shut and comes out in a tank top, which you can kind of see her boobs through, as well as some cotton shorts. I'm sitting upright in the bed, back against the headboard, like I'm waiting for something, kind of because I am. It's awkward, as if I don't really know why I'm here, like we need an excuse for my presence. She fiddles with the air-conditioning, standing with her side to me, her hair behind her ears, the gentle waves falling onto her back, still but dancing.

When she sits next to me on the bed, it's clear something needs to happen. Someone needs to do something. We look at each other, and she leans in and kisses me. Her lips are soft. She slides down on her back. I've got one knee on either side of her. I place a hand on her tit, and she places three fingers on my chin. I back off. Why does it always feel like I've done something wrong? Should I have asked?

"I'm okay with just kissing for now, I think," she says.

She sits up to lean in for another kiss, but it's like someone's pulled the plug on me, and that zap between us has fizzled. She pulls away again, and then I'm lying next to her.

"Maybe we could just cuddle?" she asks.

She turns her back to me, and I lay my arm over her waist, and we inch closer and closer until her body is enveloped in mine.

IT'S THAT MIDDLE-OF-THE-NIGHT-HANGOVER feeling, like someone's put a vacuum cleaner to my ear and sucked all the moisture from my brain. I get one of the big bottles of water at the end of the room and glug it down, but when I get back into bed my tiredness doesn't mellow into sleep.

I take a piss in Alex's bathroom and check my phone. Four A.M. Fred's messaged to say he's booked a ticket to Koh Samui. He'll get there before us. I need fresh air, to clear my head because my thoughts are racing.

Nobody's upstairs, except Bex.

"Hey," she says.

"Hey." I pull up the seat next to her. She seems drunk. Too drunk to be on a roof alone. "Did you go out?"

"Yeah." She lets out a bellowing yawn. "What did you do?"

"I went for dinner and drinks with Alex."

"Oh, yeah." She yawns again, and this time I catch it, mimicking it, a quiet echo. "You've been hanging out a lot."

"Yeah, we have."

There's some silence between us. I'm about to stand up, because maybe my head's cleared enough and I'd rather lie in bed awake than sit next to Bex, but then she starts to speak again.

"You know she was born a man, right?"

My body goes stone cold, all except my face, which feels like it's on fire. I'm not sure what I've heard, if I've heard right, or if I'm on edge in a way that's tweaked the hairs in my ears, picking up words that aren't there. At the same time, I don't think I've heard wrong. My brain hasn't substituted letters. Worn a fan. Torn a ban. Bex said Alex was born a man. What else could Bex have said? I don't respond.

"She's a tranny," Bex slurs. "A transsexual, I mean. She used to be a man."

She's assessing my face for a reaction.

"You didn't know?" she asks.

The blood in my chest rinses down toward my legs, weighing them down to the floor. I'm not sure how I'm supposed to act.

"Are you joking?"

"I'm not fucking with you," she says. "You really didn't know?"

It sounds accusatory, even if a little stupid. There's a spitefulness in the way she's dropped the bomb. I don't know how to play this; too much going on in my head. Is it more embarrassing to show outrage? All I can think is, of course—of course Alex is a man, because of course that's the way the world would play me. Some sick irony. Well fucking done. Bex has taken the pen. She's already writing. Everyone is writing. People think I'm gay. It sucks being disrespected, but even more for something that I'm not. I don't know what to do. Do I play mature?

"No, I didn't," I say.

"That's why she's here. For the surgery."

"You shouldn't be spreading people's personal business like that."

"Aren't you guys fucking?" she asks, her voice peppered with a little anger. "Wouldn't you want to know if you're fucking?"

"Wouldn't I have known if we were fucking?" I ask, and I'm angry. She must be really fucking drunk. "We're not fucking."

"Okay." She holds up her hands. "Sure. Just letting you know, though. In case you wanted to go there."

"Right." I pause. "Thanks. I'm gonna head back down."

I walk back, but to my own dorm. I lie in bed, feeling concussed. Do I care that Alex is a tranny? Yes. But also, I don't know. Should she have told me? I don't fucking know. I'm panicking. She's fucking taunting me. I like normal girls. Fuck. I can't back out of Koh Samui. Fred's already going. I have to go with Alex. I thought I liked Alex, but why? I'm not gay. I feel like I'm naked in public, but I'm not gay, so I'm not actually naked. I'm making no fucking sense. I'm not gay. Alex looks like a girl. I'm just a boy who found a girl hot. There's nothing wrong with that. Fuck. We're not fucking. Nobody thinks we're fucking.

MAX

VII

VINCENT AND I ARE SITTING ON THE TRAIN TO EDINBURGH, NEAR WHERE my parents live. I always struggle to say why they live there. We have no extended family in Scotland. They had no friends in Edinburgh before they moved, let alone the village where they live. It's like they shut their eyes and stuck a pin into a map, promising themselves to question it no further.

It's far from me and Jamie, and Jamie thinks that is exactly why they live there. *Would you expect anything else from Mum and Dad?* They've always moved as a unit. I can't imagine liking a place and one person enough that those two things combined would be all I need. It makes the world seem so small, so perverse.

This whole trip feels perverse, given what Vincent's going through. He's been with his family since the call. His dad is alive, though not well. He's recovering from surgery to put a defibrillator in. I thought we would cancel the trip, or that he might drop out, but Vincent said he wanted to be around a family that wasn't his. Simone slept through her alarm and is coming later—she's the kind of person who'd rather buy a new ticket than run for a train.

The last time I saw Vincent was a couple of weeks ago, in Ely, when I brought his work laptop from London. I had to get spare keys from Fred. I insisted on doing it—I didn't want him to have to come to London, to take that time away from his family. We had a quick coffee before my journey back, and I didn't expect nor want much more—he looked depleted.

I haven't been sure how else to help him. Before his dad's heart attack, Vincent brought over a bag of nice clothes he no longer wore so I could help him sell them online. Since he left for Ely, I've thrown myself into vivid descriptions and well-lit phone photography to make myself useful. A lot of them have sold—not that I've told him, because I don't think my ongoing negotiations to extract more and more cash from teenage boys would be particularly uplifting. I also bought him a framed poster of *Chungking Express*, which I've now hung up at mine because I'm scared of smothering him.

It'd be easier to help if, in some sense, his family and I were part of the same world. From where I'm standing, I don't know the ins and outs. He will often scratch the surface of the bog, then retreat with a truism and a sigh. *I just imagined my dad dying on loop, Max, and I felt like a toddler left in a supermarket, that fear of losing someone forever. Oh well, everyone gets sick, I guess!* I don't know what to do, other than hug him, remind him that I'm here, because there's a clear unease, a tightness in his shoulders, a division of mind. He's not okay, but I don't really know how to make him okay.

Fred has been much more helpful. He returned with a suitcase full of traditional Chinese medicine after a business trip to Hong Kong, sending it to Vincent's house in Ely in a taxi. *No, Vinny, not a cent, man, not a cent. It's the least I can do.* Fred even checked up on me. What's the least I can do? He wants a weekend away from family, with my family. It feels paltry that all I'm offering are trite words and a plan we already had in the diary.

There's an open Tupperware between us, dark-chocolate miso

brownies inside. He said they were quick to make, that this is his go-to recipe in times of crisis. I pick at crumbs, flattening them, pressing the grease onto my fingers.

"Are you nervous?" I ask.

"I'm nervous," he says.

"I understand that."

I hold his hand. We're both looking out of the window. My eyes dance between the blurred trees lining the tracks and his translucent reflection in the glass.

"Look at this," he says.

Vincent holds out his phone. His father is by the piano in the living room I've only seen photos of. Vincent's standing next to him, clarinet in hand, sheet music on a stand. They play a duet, slowly, Vincent looking over at his dad's fingers, adjusting his pace. It's very sweet.

"When was this?" I ask.

"A couple of days ago."

"Why didn't you send it earlier?"

"I was kind of embarrassed."

"It's really special."

I squeeze his hand.

Not far from Edinburgh, he locks his phone, looks at me, and takes a deep breath.

"I told my mum about you," Vincent says, and my heart sinks. A quiver slaps my lip. I look out of the train window. I'm being fragile. A woman of weak constitution. He hasn't even said anything and already I want to cry. Not happy-cry. Not grateful-cry because he's told his mum, just cry because he told his mum and I feel bad, because his family is going through a lot, and because news of a trans girlfriend could only make things worse. It's a terrible feeling, being outside of a life you shouldn't have to justify your claim to.

"Max?" he asks.

I look at him, not knowing what to say, but temper my expression. I don't want Vincent to know that I'm upset. It doesn't feel like it's my place. Do I look upset? It'd be nice if we knew the ways in which our faces betrayed us.

"I told my mum," he repeats.

I only nod because I can feel the wobbliness in my throat.

"She'll be fine," he says.

Which means she's currently not fine, and this adds weight to my dismay. He's so sanguine, as if there was no other outcome but for her to be a little upset. I can't help but imagine the conversation. *Max is trans. Translator? Trans fats? Transgender.* Stunned silence.

"So she's not fine now?"

He takes a deep breath, and holds my hand. My fingers are limp in his grip.

"I don't think my parents really think about this kind of stuff. Trans stuff. And so the language wasn't all there. I did it with my sister there. She was helpful. We're going to wait to tell my dad, though."

I pause, then look at the window, at the electricity pylons and green fields and clusters of sheep.

"She kept asking if this means I'm gay."

"Because it'd be so wrong if you were gay?" I ask, plainly, but I can see from Vincent's face that he feels attacked. I'm not judging. Sure, the world expends too much energy convincing people that men aren't gay, and it's exhausting, but I just want to know the depth of his mother's homophobia.

"No, Max," he says. "That's not it. She's just a bit confused about what it all means. She asked if it meant I'd never have children."

I take a deep breath.

"How did it come up?" I ask.

"I think"—he pauses—"when someone's ill, people want to plan and to know that things go on. For my mum that means starting a family." Vincent sighs. He's looking out of the window as he speaks to me. I try to meet his gaze through the reflection, but his stare is fixed on the fields. "So she asked what the plan was, when I was going to get serious, so I told her I was seeing someone who I cared about, and that I wasn't sure if I even wanted children, anyway."

"Is that true?"

"I don't know."

"What'd she say?"

"You must have children," Vincent says, his voice a severe imitation of his mother. "Who will take care of you otherwise?" His expression relaxes back into his own. "And then I explained that it was complicated, and it seemed the right time to discuss the trans thing."

"What else did you say?" I ask.

"I said we haven't been dating that long, but that it was really just like dating a woman who's infertile."

"Like?"

I can't help myself. Vincent puts his hands on his face.

"That's not what I meant," he says.

Moments like this are peppered across life. Brief glimmers that present you with a difficult question: is this really how they see me, is this what I really am to them, or is it a mistake, merely quibbling over semantics? And that question is in fact a choice; the mask rises as quickly as it slips, leaving you to choose what to believe. I allow my tongue to recede, for the poison to retreat up the tubes in my teeth. I choose to believe him. It's just semantics.

I understand that Vincent's dad had a heart attack, how this conversation with his mum came to be, that I was a chip used to appease her, although perhaps unsuccessfully, because I don't have a womb. In my mind it might have been a year, maybe two, or even longer, until Vincent told his parents. It felt unsaid that their conservatism would silence him until he was truly sure about me, and I've felt fine about it, because at least it makes a little bit of sense. I only met two of Arthur's four mums, anyway, and only once and twice respectively, although it always felt like more of an Arthur problem than a Max problem.

Vincent squeezes my hand once, then twice, then lets go. Even though I know he's being reasonable, I can't help but want him to apologize to me for how I feel about myself. What is my face saying?

"Hey." He reaches into his bag, laughing. "She gave me these before I left." I take the pamphlets. Surrogacy pamphlets. I flick through them. UK surrogacy law. Options abroad. What we—Vincent and I, or any other couple suffering beneath the palm of a pushy Asian mother—can expect.

"Vincent," I say. "What the fuck."

I feel sick. It's clear from his face that he thought I'd find this funny. He reaches back for them, contrite.

"Sorry," he says. "I'm really sorry. I think I misread this. I just thought that maybe it was progress or something."

"As long as there's a biological grandchild."

"I'm sorry."

"We shouldn't even be talking about this," I say.

We shouldn't. His father is ill, but also, this relationship is new. I am speechless. I want to pull the emergency brake and launch myself into the moors.

"Have you told your parents I'm cis?" he asks.

I can't even pretend to smile. His face falls. We sit in silence for the rest of the journey. Tendrils of guilt sprout from my stomach, but still, I can't quite force myself to say that I appreciate that he took this step, because I want to wish it all away. If I admit this to him now, the sadness will show on my face, and I don't want to be upset when I see my parents. I want to show them that I'm in love, and it's hard to perform love through reddened eyes.

When we're off the train, I reach for his hand. That's all I can muster for the moment. We let go when we reach the turnstiles, beeping through to my parents, who are waiting for us on the other side. It's kind. They wouldn't do this for Jamie. In part because Jamie is driving up in the Audi he bought in February, even though it adds several hours to the journey, but also because, in their eyes, he doesn't need taking care of.

"Hi, Mum." She takes me into her arms as Vincent and my dad shake hands. Her dark bob smells like lavender. When she releases me, she inspects a lock of my hair between two fingers. "What is it?"

"Nothing!" she says. "You look pretty. Clean and healthy. Shiny."

"When is my hair ever not—"

"Hello!" She turns to Vincent, enveloping him. "It's so nice to meet you."

"Hi, darling," my dad says to me.

His hugs are always light. He seems unsure of his own embrace, like he doesn't know how to hold another body. It's not because I'm trans—we're a little beyond that. Jamie would say it's because he's not drunk. Maybe that's true, though sometimes it's hard to know if that's the reason. He hasn't had a drink since we lived on Lamma.

We put our bags into the boot and get in.

"This is a gorgeous car," Vincent says, addressing my father, rather than my mum. Maybe it's because he's the one driving, but I know it might just be because he's a man, even if Vincent knows my mum earned every penny that paid for it. I wince.

"Thank you," my parents say in unison.

We drive out of the city. My mum asks after Vincent's father, and he puts on a brave face while recounting the last couple of weeks to them. She probes for details with a polite indifference, but I know what she's doing. It's the same thing everyone does when anyone dies or falls ill. People are desperate to hold one report card against another, to ask: could that be me? The city deconstructs into countryside, and it strikes me how this must all feel more familiar to Vincent than it ever has to me. British countryside. Suburbia. To me it still feels like the weirdest place on earth, these weekends when we come together as a family in a village none of us has ties to.

We arrive at the gate of the house and the car snakes up the driveway. I watch Vincent take it in. The sandstone cube, a set of wide windows on each side of the front door, the gravel around his feet. I wonder what my parents' house says about me, what he feels. Is it surprise? Or an of course?

"Beautiful," he says, addressing my mum as we walk in.

The tallest and scantest bouquet of flowers I've ever seen is on the table at the bottom of the stairs. An artful bunch of imported twigs.

"That bouquet is hideous," I say.

"This is not your house," Mum says in mangled Mandarin, winking at Vincent.

I glare at her. Vincent hardly speaks Mandarin. She speaks even less. I, after many failed years of lessons at school and university, speak only a little. I'm relieved Vincent can finally see the way my mum cosplays as a Chinese person.

Vincent and I carry our stuff upstairs, into my room that's not quite my room. It once had things like graduation photos, matriculation photos, school-age photos. When I transitioned, I asked Mum to clear them out. I don't know where they are. In storage. In the bin. I still haven't shown Vincent old photos of me, mostly because he hasn't asked. I'm not sure if it's because he doesn't want to see them—if he wants to deny history—or if he's being polite, or if he simply hasn't thought about it. He scans the bare walls. It doesn't really look like it's my room. There's so much Foucault on the top shelf, and I couldn't tell you anything about him, except that on the scale of male philosophers, he is among the more fuckable. Vincent puts his bag at the end of my bed and stands by the window. As he turns around with his hands on his hips, I wonder if now is the time for me to apologize, but I don't.

"It's really nice here," he says.

I sit next to him on the window seat. He puts his hand on my thigh. Now is the time.

"Thank you for telling your mum," I say.

I want to tell him that sometimes I feel less than, how the feeling that I am bad news to break has made those feelings worse. I also want to tell him about how that day with his friends—that thing with Blond Annabel—has stuck with me. About that awful sticky sensation that I've struggled to completely parse, which today feels alive and tentacled, and which reminds me how terrible it is to be the other, outside, for my body to feel like a burden. And for that I feel guilty, because I've tried so hard to be proud.

Vincent looks out of the window.

"She'll be fine," he says again.

I squeeze his thigh. We stand up, and as we turn away the faint sound of an engine grows louder. We look back out. Jamie's car rolls up, grinding the gravel on the driveway.

"Nice car," Vincent says.

Jamie waves at us from below. He's dressed just like my dad. Fisherman-knit jumper, lovely chinos.

"You guys look alike," Vincent says. "Same coloring."

By the time we walk downstairs, Jamie's in the hallway. I hug him. He holds me tight, unlike the way Dad does, and then he shakes Vincent's hand, and when Jamie says, "Hey, man, great to meet you," his voice drops an octave, and Vincent responds in a similarly deep boom. He hugs Mum, and when he hugs Dad I have to look away. It's like getting two action figures to embrace. So awkward. Are they doing this for Vincent? I guess there's always face to save.

We migrate into the sitting room, though Jamie doesn't even sit down before his phone rings.

"Work call," he says.

"Already?" Mum asks.

He vanishes upstairs. My parents are in the green armchairs, across from me and Vincent on the pink silk sofa. There's a bowl of White Rabbit sweets on the coffee table.

"I haven't had these in so long," Vincent says.

My mum beams. He starts to peel the rice paper off.

"You can eat the paper," I say.

"Oh, yeah," he says. "I forgot."

Mum regales us with stories of growing up in Hong Kong. I can see Vincent's jaw struggling with a White Rabbit as he listens. They're extremely chewy. I'm chewing one, too, just so I can dissociate. My teeth knead it like dough, and it sticks and imprints onto my molars, releasing dribbles of milky sweetness that climb up my enamel, gums, and tongue. Nobody wants to hear about her childhood home on The Peak. So out of touch. He leans in gently toward her. Body language that shows he wants to listen. Vincent's extended family lives in small apartments in the New Territories. Does he not find this cringeworthy? Maybe we make excuses for people we're trying to impress. Maybe I'm too hard on her, but she's also very annoying.

"Even as a child, you really got the sense that something was going on," she says.

"I can imagine."

"I suppose when you're there you still get the feeling that things are happening," she says. "Just scarier things." And then my mum's face curls into an aggressive expression, like Vincent's just thrown a vase at the wall. Vincent hasn't done anything wrong, she's just about to speak Cantonese. She says something I don't understand.

"I do," he says. "I was only ever there to visit family when I was young, and then I moved back out for work for a year. But I do miss it a bit. I should go back." He pauses. "I should warn you that my Cantonese isn't very good."

Well, neither is hers. Mum gasps, anyway, and says something in Cantonese again. Her tone is sharp and vicious. She looks like a white person doing a racist imitation of a Chinese person. Vincent smiles and nods. He probably didn't understand what she was saying. I finally manage to swallow the White Rabbit.

"Am I cooking tonight, Mum?"

"If you'd like to."

Mum usually fills the fridge before I arrive, expecting me to cook. I like cooking for people, I just don't like what it brings out in me. It's a bit pathetic, the way I watch someone as they bite into the food, seeking reassurance, calling out my own mistakes before someone else does. The basil went in too early. The noodles are sticking because I didn't rinse them enough. It's a neediness I've suppressed in most other areas of life.

"I'll have a peek in the fridge," I say.

"Can I help?" Vincent asks.

"Not really, but you can come with me if you want."

I stand up and walk through to the foyer, half expecting Vincent to follow, but he stays with my mum. Is that a bit crap of him? Chatting while I'm working. I suppose he should get to know her, but the optics are off, even if it's unlike him. He should know that.

The kitchen fridge is full. There's no reason or organization to the items on the shelves. Aubergines. Kai lan. Spinach. Broccoli. Carrots. Greek yogurt. Pecorino. Parsley. Coriander. Gochujang. Unopened harissa that doesn't need to be in the fridge. I check the cabinets on the other side of the kitchen island. Bread flour. Pasta. White jasmine rice. When I turn around, I see my dad standing in the doorway and scream. The man takes serial-killer steps. Tiptoes around life in fur slippers. He's so boyish—his face never quite sure what's going on, his hair still a little mousy brown.

"Sorry," he says.

"It's fine."

"Everything okay?"

"I'm just looking for some stuff to cook."

"Ah," he says. "What do you think you'll make?"

"I've seen this woman cook a creamy pasta, but with gochujang," I say. "Or I could make these stuffed flatbreads. And some roasted veg with chickpeas and harissa. What would you prefer?"

"The flatbreads sound delicious."

"Sure."

We stand, looking at utensils around us, as if a bottle opener or whisk might inspire some conversation. I turn around and fill a pot with hot water. I'm going to cook the pasta. The flatbreads wouldn't take much time; I just don't want to make them. I turn the heat on full.

"How are you doing?" he asks.

What would a world where I told my dad about my and Vincent's conversation on the train look like?

"I'm okay."

"How's the job?" he asks. "At the tech company. Still good?"

"Oh, it's fine."

"Challenging?"

"I pretend to be a robot, Dad."

"That could be challenging."

"I sign my emails off as Owl."

The doorbell rings.

"That must be Simone," he says, leaving me to get the door.

"Hi, Uncle Peter!"

Simone's warm voice flies through the house. My family loves Simone. Sometimes I wonder if they love her too much. *Simone's job sounds so interesting. Mother Agent. What a wonderful job title. She should write a book about it! That and her love life!* If Simone pissed on the flower beds, they'd thank her. My parents always lamented my International School accent, are frequently pleased that it's become more British, but they seem to love it in Simone, whose accent, if anything, has just calcified. American, but not grating, the upward lilts of her intonation dulled.

"Aunty Melinda!"

When the pot reaches a rolling boil, I chuck the rigatoni in and join the congregation in the hallway. They cluster around Simone like she's a celebrity, like she's handing out gold bars from the pockets of her pinstriped trousers.

"What have you guys been up to?" she asks as we hug.

"I'm just cooking," I say. "Vincent and Mum have been talking Hong Kong."

"What are you making?" she asks. "Do you need any help?"

"Pasta." I turn back to my dad, who looks at me with a small gap in his mouth, wide enough to slot a pair of chopsticks in without touching his lips. "I'll do the flatbreads tomorrow. I think people want an early dinner," I add, not knowing if it's true.

Part of me worries about the data he collects from moments like these. I always have. *Maxine doesn't like me. She's uncomfortable around me.* Though, to be honest, I do the same with him. It's hard to shake, and I know it all started after the fire on Lamma, after which I became something else. I look at my dad, who is fiddling with the sleeves of his jumper. Even at his age, he is like a man in someone else's clothes. It's the complete lack of confidence, so worn down. Worn down by what? My mother, who worked when he didn't. Child-rearing. The shame that keeps his alcoholism in check. Maybe I should've cooked the flatbreads.

"You can come watch," I say to Simone, then turn my attention to everyone else. "Be ready to eat soon."

Simone follows me, and I stand over the pot until the pasta is soft with bite, reserving some cloudy pasta water and draining the swollen rigatoni from the pot, piling it into the colander.

"I forgot to put on deodorant before I left," Simone says. "I spent so much of the journey trying to decide if I smell."

She holds out her armpits for me. I move from the sink to give them a quick sniff.

"It just smells like skin," I say.

I drip ingredients for the sauce into the pan. The gochujang begins to marble in the cream, until the sauce emulsifies into a rich orange, thick like a melted oil pastel. I hear the sound of the fridge opening.

"Can we drink?" she asks.

"Yeah, the wine's for us," I say. "Mum still drinks with guests. Same as usual."

"Just checking." There's a glug and a clink before Simone hands me a glass of white wine. "Emily wants to call, by the way. I finally looked at the wedding website. Have you seen it?"

"Only to click attending."

"So we're definitely going."

"We're bridesmaids, Simone."

An unspoken con of my transition was that people became more likely to ask me to be part of their weddings. Emily picked sentimentality over reality. Us over people she actually sees on a weekly basis. Apparently, it's so, so nice to have friends who took you to the hospital to get your stomach pumped when you were fourteen by your side at the altar.

I'm not sure what's left of my friendship with Emily. Whenever Simone and I see her, we hear the regular platitudes of how amazing it is that with certain friends, you don't have to see one another for years and it all feels like normal, as if to suggest the distance that's grown between us is artificial, societally imposed, a figment of time and space, all dissolving on reunion.

"Could you start grating some Parmesan, please?" I ask.

"There's a picture-annotated timeline of their relationship," Simone says. "It feels really unhinged to manufacture joy like that." I hear the block of Parmesan knocking against the bowl. "Nobody who's happy works that hard to prove it. A couple of years. No more."

"Maybe three years," I say.

"Should we get the call over with?" Simone asks.

I look at the pasta. The steam in the colander will ripen it beyond al dente, but I also want to get it over with. I take the sauce off the heat.

Emily picks up on the second ring. It's a video call.

"Hi-igh!" she says.

Simone and I mimic her, involuntarily. Her hair looks incredible. And her skin. She gets a blow-dry twice a week. Is she using a ring light?

"You guys look so cozy," she says. "How are your parents, Max?"

"They're fine," I say. "How are you?"

"I've had the craziest day. I picked up the dress!" She claps her hands. Simone and I do jazz hands, involuntarily. "Picked out wedding bands." A large rat—allegedly her dog—springboards onto her lap. We aww. "Took him out for a long walk around the Burg."

"Wow," Simone says. "It's hardly past noon there."

"I know," Emily says, revering her own efficiency. "Can you guys send me your measurements? We need them for the fittings in London."

"I already sent them," I say.

"In case they've changed," she says, as if I'm stupid.

"Do I have to wear a dress?" Simone asks.

"I'll have to see, okay!" she says. "But you'll be comfortable either way." It's unclear if that's a demand or assurance. "Also, Max, me and Fraser have had a think about Vincent." I look around me, because God forbid he can hear this. "And we think we just have to stick to the one-year rule."

"That's fine," I say. "I mean, I didn't really even ask or expect it."

"I know!" she says. "But I know how much you like him."

I look around again. Simone nudges me under the table. I pinch her thigh.

"It's fine, honestly," I say.

"What if I got back with Eva?" Simone asks.

"Do you plan to?"

"No," she says. "Genuinely just curious."

"I think that resets the timer, honestly. Anyway." Emily claps again. "It's so amazing we can do this together. Like we've always dreamed." She puts a hand to her chest. "And you, Max," she adds almost tearfully. Of course, she's referring to my transition. I force a smile, concerned that inducting me into this ceremony is her attempt at allyship. If this is trans rights, I will do some trans wrongs.

Simone moves the conversation on. There's brief talk of work before we wave goodbye and hang up.

"Like we always dreamed," Simone says. "I don't want to wear a dress."

"What the fuck is the Burg?" I ask.

"Williamsburg."

Simone and I laugh. I think Emily feels as if we are as close as we were, because for her, she is the same person with a new backdrop. Simone and I have spent years carving difference—in what we wear, in how we look.

I heat the sauce back up and mix the pasta in.

"Help me plate," I say, and she sidles up next to me. "Have you actually been thinking about getting back together with Eva?"

Simone's shoulders tense. I slide a portion into a bowl from the ladle, but Simone is slow to garnish.

"I'm not going to break no-contact," she says. "So it doesn't matter." She pauses. "Obviously there's always an internal back-and-forth." She holds a hand up above her shoulder. "Did I do the right thing?" And then the other. "Could I be aromantic?"

"But you fall in love."

Simone strangles a bunch of parsley, dismembering it with a knife.

"I wish I could squeeze it out of me," she says. I imagine Simone holding her heart in her hands, forcing the feeling out of it like whey from a cheesecloth. "But Eva was really boring, right?"

"So boring."

"Even if we were friends—"

"Would you want to be friends?" I ask. "I mean, it's not uncommon to be friends with your ex. In our circles."

"Just because gay people do it doesn't make it right."

I finish filling the bowls. Simone sprinkles the parsley.

"What if I can't handle boring?" she asks. "Isn't life boring?"

"Eva wasn't safe-boring, she was just quite boring to talk to."

"She did talk about Crocs a lot."

"I feel like we talk a lot about Eva talking about Crocs a lot."

Simone sighs.

"But I fell in love for a while," she says. "There was good there. We had nice conversations—it's not like she was always dull."

"It's interesting," I say.

"What is?"

"That you're making excuses for falling out of love."

"Mm, yeah."

Simone rinses her hands, and we carry the bowls into the other room.

"Dinner's here!" Simone says.

"Maxine," Mum says, Vincent next to her on the sofa. "You could've given Simone a little bit of a break."

"I wasn't working for long," Simone says. "Emily called."

"How is she?" Mum asks. "Still letting men treat her terribly?"

She scoffs, cruelly.

The table is set with the nice silverware that we keep in the living room. It was probably Dad. It's quite sweet of him, and I feel a little bad, because maybe he wanted to be useful but didn't feel like he could stay with me and Simone. Mum calls for Jamie, but when he arrives he stands above us at the table, looking at us intently. Simone and I exchange a look. He's going to announce something.

"I have something to announce," Jamie says, taking a deep breath. "Me and Maria are pregnant."

My jaw drops, and without a further word I know the facts. Accidental pregnancy. Discovered post breakup. Maria will keep the baby and Jamie will be a father. Today doesn't need more baby talk. I groan. An unspeakably scrunching migraine seizes the left side of my brain. Bile climbs up the back of my throat. The room is silent for enough time for me to gather my attention. Dad purses his lips. None of us have met Maria, though they were together for over a year.

"Maria?" Mum asks.

"Yes," he says.

"You broke up two months ago," Mum says. "Are you back together?"

Jamie looks confused, like he expected champagne and confetti cannons.

"No," he says. "But she's pregnant. She got pregnant while we were still together."

"Were you trying?" Simone asks.

"No," he says. "But we were using natural cycles."

Simone cocks her head toward me with a microscopic lift in her eyebrow. *Uh huh.* At once, everyone has the information they need. Everyone is caught up. We're quiet again. Jamie holds one fist in the other.

"Are you getting back together?" Mum asks.

Jamie looks annoyed. I look at everyone's bowls of pasta. They're getting cold.

"No," he says. "We're not."

"That's great," Dad says, with a gormless smile.

"But Jamie," Mum continues. "How—"

"It's called co-parenting, Mum."

Mum's skepticism has charmed the venom from his fangs. The tension is strange and unbearable.

"More and more people opt for non-traditional arrangements now," Simone says.

"Yeah, definitely," Vincent adds. "Have you read *Detransition, Ba*—"

I start clapping, because I think it's what Jamie needs and I'm suddenly overcome with emotion, not because I'm jealous, but because Jamie's announcement has split the ceiling separating me and the weight of today, of Vincent telling his family, of how I'm just like a woman who's infertile. A baby in the family. Am I smiling oddly? There's a tear falling down my cheek. Everyone is clapping. I stand up to hug Jamie, and then I feel another tear, and I look at my mum and she's crying, too. It's not clear if she's happy or sad or stressed. Simone has the fingers of one hand in the other palm, like at the end of the clap, the shape of a tulip. There's not a tear on her face, but why should there be? I look at Vincent, who's looking at me with a wide smile and wider eyes.

"Do we have champagne or something?" I ask.

Mum scuttles out of the room and returns with a bottle. She pops it open and starts pouring a glass for everyone but my father. Is the food going to get too cold? We should really start eating. Mum runs back into the kitchen to get a bottle of kombucha for my dad. We're all standing, bringing our glasses together, and I can't help but look at Dad. The kombucha somehow seems punishing, gut microbiome aside. Sometimes he seems lonely, and that loneliness reads not in what he says, but in tiny movements. A limp wrist as he brings his tumbler toward the maelstrom of clinking glasses, the roundedness of his spine as he walks, the slowness as he rises from and descends into his chair.

We finally eat a lukewarm dinner. I'm not sure if people want to talk about the baby, but it feels inappropriate to move on from such enormous news. Simone helps to fill blank space and smooth tensions. *What do you envision with respect to co-parenting? Can I see a picture of Maria? The baby's going to have a striking face.*

It sinks in that it really is that easy for some people—you just cum in someone and call it a day, and then these torturing questions about family vanish, because you're having a kid, and there's no interrogation needed. There's no planning, no agonizing or mental gymnastics to convince yourself that life-limiting biology is taking you where you're supposed to be. Let's say that I stay with Vincent, and we decide not to have children, then what if he decides one day that he wants children and abandons me for the easy route? Where does that leave me? I pierce another piece of rigatoni with my fork. Too soft. Tastes perfect.

"Will you cut back on work?" I ask Jamie.

The room goes quiet.

"No?" Jamie answers, with the defensiveness of someone who has trauma-bonded with the Civil Procedure Rules. "People work and have children."

"Okay."

"Yeah," Jamie says, and then, with his head in his bowl, "you guys might know one day."

I open my mouth to say something, but then I don't. I'm not sure what I was going to say. He said it so casually, as if equally to me, Vincent, and Simone. Part of it is laughable, because he has no real experience of being a parent, only news of a pregnant ex. Yet under his posturing wisdom, beneath a simple might, is a fair assessment that the barriers I perceive may be hurdles, rather than walls. Yes, we all might know one day.

Simone reinstates herself as the center of my family's interest, made easier by the fact that everyone needs time to process Jamie's news. They ask about her models. She tells us about a girl—Xenia, the one with no eyebrows—who's blown up, shows us her social media, her thick black ringlets falling onto Issey Miyake pleats or frilly Ganni collars. Mum, never one to moderate her obsession with beauty, or being told what is beautiful, gobbles up her grid, flicking down and down as she chews on the pasta, which I notice nobody has commented on. As if reading my mind, Vincent squeezes the top of my arm.

"This is really yummy," he says. "As always."

Vincent and I offer to wash up when everyone's done. I can see Simone and Dad smoking from the window. She knows what questions to ask him. It's easy between them.

"My head really hurts," I say, the tension in my skull transmuting to nausea in my throat.

"What is it?" Vincent asks.

"Migraine."

He rubs a soft thumb on my head before nudging me away from the sink. I take a seat by the counter. Maybe it's fine that he didn't help me cook. He rinses dishes before putting them in the dishwasher.

"I'll take over," Dad says, appearing at the doorway, Simone nowhere to be found.

"We can do it," I say.

"Please," he says to Vincent. "You're the guest."

"Oh no," Vincent says. "It's fine. I'd like to."

"I insist."

Dad's voice is kind but firm, and Vincent steps back a little.

"How does it feel knowing you're going to be a grandfather?" Vincent asks.

Grandfather. My shoulders knot from the question.

"Hm," my dad says as I start to scrub the pan. "It's surprising."

Very surprising.

"But it feels good," Dad says. "Doesn't it, Maxy?"

"It feels good," I say. "A nice surprise. Just surprising."

"Yes. It'll be nice, spending time with a grandchild. A fresh start."

Fresh start. The knots tighten. It's really all he has to say—I fucked up the first time. It's unclear how much he, and therefore we, will actually see the baby. The parameters of the co-parenting arrangement remain vague. I haven't shared much of our family lore with Vincent, other than the fact that Dad and Jamie don't get along, but at the same time I don't really know what there is to say. This has been going on for years. There was an altercation from which they never recovered. None of that speaks sufficiently to the space between Dad and Jamie or even to Dad and me, the long erosion from which a fissure becomes a canyon.

"Babies feel like that," Vincent says. "A fresh start."

My dad smiles downward and nods. When the dishwasher is on, we return to the family room single-file. Sitting between Vincent and Simone, I exchange smiles with Jamie. A baby is literally going to fly out of Maria, a woman who several months ago I wasn't even sure was real. There are other questions I have for Jamie. Why didn't you tell me before Mum and Dad? Is this really going to work? Now doesn't feel like the time.

"Aunty Max," Simone says.

The room is still, and everyone else is listening, as if Simone's asked me a question.

"A traunty," I say.

"What?" Mum asks.

"Trans aunty," I say. "Like guncle, but for trans women."

Simone laughs, which permits my mum to laugh, and Dad laughs into his glass of water. I look at Vincent, who shifts a little and wears an awkward smile.

"But how does it feel?" Jamie asks.

"What?" I ask.

"To know you're going to be an aunty."

He genuinely wants to know. I don't like his tone. It's a little interrogative, as if it is a bona fide mystery as to whether it would be a positive for me. Did my family really think that outside the privacy of my own brain I would make this about myself?

"It feels special," I say. "I'm happy for you, but also just excited to spend time with your baby."

Jamie gets up from his seat and hugs me. He holds me longer than he needs to. Did he doubt I'd feel good about it? A family forum seems an awfully inappropriate place to ask about it, even if he actually believed that I might think his baby would be really terrible for me. I sit down. Vincent places his hand on my knee, and when I place my head on Simone's shoulder, she plays with my hair. I feel as if I'm the focus again. Is everyone thinking about my lack? How big is this elephant? I want to receive these small tokens of affection, but sometimes they feel no different to when I see someone with a rainbow lanyard smile at me. Fuck off.

"Would anyone like more wine?" Mum asks.

Everyone declines, and disappointment sprints across and vanishes from her face. She doesn't get to drink often. I stand up and start collecting glasses. Vincent helps without me asking. In the kitchen, he hugs me tight from behind.

LATER, IN MY BEDROOM, VINCENT unpacks his suitcase while I lie in bed. My eyes trace the unsteady ridges of a thin crack on the ceiling, emanating from the light fixture and tailing off halfway toward the wall.

"How are you feeling?" he asks, his back still toward me, moving things between his suitcase and the wardrobe.

"I don't really know how it'd work," I say. "Jamie's so dysfunctional."

"Is he?"

"He doesn't have time to be a dad. He didn't even have time for a relationship."

Vincent sits on the window seat.

"Why did he and Maria break up?" he asks.

"He said Maria wanted too much from him," I say. "And that he didn't have enough to give between her and work."

"And he thinks a kid is—"

"I know," I say. "Every day I'm grateful that he's my brother and not my boyfriend."

"That's gross, Max."

We laugh. He changes into a T-shirt.

"I sort of meant to ask how you're feeling, though," he says.

"What do you mean?" I ask, even though I know what he means.

"About the baby."

I don't think I should have to spell it out for him, or say anything at all, because I really think if he were to examine the evidence, the day we've just had, he would know exactly how I feel. But maybe that's a tall order, and maybe sometimes life demands spelling things out for people, and that's nobody's fault.

"It's just a bit overwhelming," I say. It is. As is the presumption that things are hard for me, so much so that it's sometimes hard to admit it when they are. "I thought I'd reached a place where I barely thought about being trans, where it just wasn't part of my every day, but now—"

"What's changed?" he asks.

"It's just this year. Being in a new relationship." I sigh. "And that age. Feeling like people are graduating into these things that don't feel made for me. I want life to feel simple. And when you tell me that your mum will be fine—"

My voice cracks. He's standing now. His arms are flat against his sides. Why is he standing like that? Like a pencil.

"But it just happens, right?" he asks. "If your mum wasn't, like, this Sinophile—"

I snort-laugh and wipe some tears from my eyes.

"Yeah, but if she wasn't, if she was just some posh white woman, and you brought home an Asian guy, and they were a little weird about it at first?" He puts his hands by his hips. "You know, I'm just saying it happens to a lot of people."

"It's not the same."

"But it kind of is," he says. "I'm not saying that to dismiss things, I'm just trying to make you feel less alone. Like, sometimes we feel on the outside of things, and it's okay to feel shit."

I breathe a long, loud breath out of my nose. It feels like too much has been shared between us and I'm scared. What I want to say is that it'd be much simpler for him without me, especially in a time of crisis, when his family needs him. But I can't say it. I don't want him to realize it's true. I tell myself to stop making everything about me. Stop dropping myself into the broken pumps of his father's heart.

"You're right," I say. "I'm sorry."

"It's okay," he says, voice small.

We pause, looking at each other. It seems for a moment that neither of us will move, that neither of us will ever move, but then he makes the slightest lean and I lift up the duvet for him to come in. And I hold him, snaking my arms around his body, because I want to say sorry without saying sorry again, because I don't want him to be so far away. Our breathing evens out, syncs up, and I exhale the hurt from the leaflets and the train.

After a while, he shifts, back still to me, his body curled further.

"I need to talk to you about something."

The brief calm recedes. My heart rate rises.

"What?"

"I want to pull out of that flat. I offered in a rush and it doesn't feel right. Just with everything that's going on." He pauses.

"Do you—"

"Do you think I could maybe stay with you when my lease ends?" he asks. "Just until things with my dad get better?"

I take a deep breath, grateful it wasn't something worse. That we're okay.

"Yeah," I say. "Yeah, sure."

By the time his lease ends, we'll have been together for five months.

So soon. So risky. But his dad is ill. His work is always busy. It's nice that he asked, that he wants to. It's not as if I haven't thought about it, that I haven't ruminated over his expiring lease, but I was worried about extending myself too far toward him.

"Let's sort it out when you're back," I say.

We swap positions and he holds me, then starts to kiss my neck. My T-shirt doesn't come off when we have sex, but he still feels beneath. When we finish, he spoons me, with only the bedside light beside me on.

"I see what you mean about your dad and Jamie."

"Yeah," I say. "It's been like that since Lamma."

"You always say it so ominously."

"Lamma," I repeat, hoarsely.

He laughs.

"Lamma," he says. "What happened?"

"My dad set a carpet on fire."

"A carpet?"

"He was drunk and fell asleep with a cigarette in his hand. I was coming downstairs for some water and saw it."

"And then?"

"I ran and put it out with a cushion."

"Oh my God," he says. I can feel him raise his torso. "How big was the fire?"

"I don't know." I massage my forehead with my hand. "It happened really fast. It was sort of crazy."

"What if you were asleep?"

"I wasn't, though."

I shut my eyes.

"Where was your mum?"

"Work, obviously. It was the weekend."

"And he woke up?"

"Yeah," I say. "I was crying and screaming. Even after it was out and he was awake, I couldn't stop shaking him. I'm not sure why. He just looked at me dead with the emptiest stare ever."

"What did he do?"

"He replaced the carpet with the one we had in storage and told Mum he thought it looked better." I sigh. Vincent's holding my arm, tight. I don't know if he realizes. "For some reason she agreed. She didn't even notice the missing cushion."

"Okay," he says. "I sort of meant whether he freaked out."

"I think we were just in shock."

"Were you okay?"

"I was fifteen."

"But were you okay?"

"It was fine."

"And so Jamie—"

"I kept it a secret until Jamie was back from uni. I shouldn't have told him. He lost it, couldn't get over how Dad had put me in danger, kept catastrophizing."

"But that was true?"

"I woke up, though." I sigh. "Anyway, after that Jamie kind of blew up at my dad."

"And then?"

I shift a little out of Vincent's embrace, and with a gentle palm he encourages me to twist my body so that I'm facing him.

"My mum got really mad at Jamie for breaking my trust, which didn't make sense to me at the time, but she was obviously just deflecting, and then my parents went into their room to talk."

"What did she say to him?"

"Like I'd ever know."

"But it worked, no?"

He starts to draw a finger along my cheek.

"I don't know," I say. "Look. Jamie is not a healthy person. He's always been so full of panic. His outbursts were a nightmare for all of us. He always hated my dad. Like, swearing around the house at the empty bottles piling up when my mum was gone. But he's also very protective of me, so when he felt like my dad put me in danger, it gave him a reason to never forgive him."

"And you?"

"What?"

"Did you forgive him?"

I look down toward his chest. He kisses my forehead.

"I guess it's not really about forgiveness. I feel really bad for saying it, but I kind of liked my dad drunk."

"Hm?"

"When he got sober it was like he couldn't even be near me. I stopped feeling like we could talk, like somehow I'd become this puzzle to him."

"Wasn't he more present?"

"I mean, I guess. But not really there." I take a deep breath. "Before he stopped drinking, we would get under a blanket on the couch and watch movies, and he was really affectionate, in the way a lot of dads should be but aren't."

"Yeah," he says. "Mine wasn't."

"God, I'm so sorry," I say, wiping a tear from my eye that I didn't realize was there. "I keep talking about my own shit—"

"I kind of don't want to talk about my shit right now."

I turn around and nestle my back into him.

"I mean, he definitely became more functional. A million times over. And he went to therapy. And AA. And instead of isolating at home he'd meet my mum at the IFC roof in Central for lunch. He's always cooked and cleaned for us, also, and sorted everything while Mum worked . . ."

"But."

"I feel like I lost him."

"Really?" Vincent asks.

"I just know he holds it against me—that I told Jamie. The whole thing."

"Are you sure?" he asks. "You were a child."

"Sometimes you just feel it. It's not like he'd admit it. But sometimes you just know."

Vincent gives my arm a squeeze.

VIII

"YOU LOOK BEAUTIFUL, MAX!" EMILY SCREAMS.

I'm standing on a small podium in a fitting room, confronted with at least a dozen too many mirrors. Emily—a brunette white woman with a voluminous blowout—and Michelle—a Hong Kong Chinese woman with a purple Chanel flap bag—look like slightly diverse Barbies with champagne flutes. Simone sits between them on the satin sofa, slouched onto Michelle's shoulder. It's like an anxious hallucination. I look at my reflection, at the thin straps, the sweetheart neckline, tight bodice, skirt hanging loose off my hips. So much dusty pink. Why are bridesmaids' dresses always this color? Or that horrible sage green. Made to look like flowers or stems, to remind the world that we are delicate things, ready to be yanked from the soil by rough, manly hands.

"Do I have a tummy?" I ask.

"Everyone has a tummy," Simone says.

"But do I have a tummy?"

"You actually look small enough," Michelle says.

Simone laughs quietly.

"Thank you, Michelle."

Michelle has flown in from Hong Kong, en route to Emily's hen in Vegas. She is rich—Hong Kong rich. Maybe by virtue of her upbringing, or her wealth, Michelle is at least a decade behind in socially liberal politics. When I came out as gay, she told me we could go shopping together. When I came out as trans, she also told me we could go shopping together. She understands that casual racism is not okay, but will still also openly say, as a Chinese woman, that she is not attracted to Asian men. Neither Simone nor I have seen her for a couple of years.

I don't know the last time the four of us were together. These are the women who, as a gay kid with survival instincts, I latched on to at school. With everyone but Simone, there has always been some distance, some hiding, and even though I hid from Simone, too, we at least had it in common.

Emily steps onto the podium and stuffs her finger into the back of my dress, tugging at it. The dress shop tailor joins her.

"It's perfect, no?" Emily asks the woman.

"Yes," she says. "Very nice."

"Well, let's just hope nothing changes."

By nothing, she means me. The dress isn't going to shrink in protest at heterosexual union, camp as it is. I take a seat, and the woman brings out Simone's dress. Simone gets up and holds the hanger, and I can see the dread on her face. My heart sinks for her.

"It's going to look great," Emily says.

Simone disappears into the changing room.

"Are your parents still in Scotland?" Michelle asks me.

"Yeah, they're fine. Still in Edinburgh."

"Where are Simone's now?"

"Phuket."

"So sad that everyone's left Hong Kong," Michelle says.

"How's Aunty Yvonne?" I ask.

Michelle's mum was terrifying. A stern woman, sitting all day by a dining table eating lychees and drinking expensive wine. It was hard to imagine cancer striking her, that somehow she wouldn't just scare the aberrant cells into submission.

"She just had her annual scan," she says. "All clear."

"I'm so glad."

"How's Uncle Peter?" Emily asks me, sitting down with us.

My friends have always liked my dad, a much softer version of their own fathers. There's a collective pity for him. They know about the alcoholism, though I'm not sure they ever noticed it.

"He's okay," I say. "My mum as well."

"My mum stopped drinking recently," Emily says.

"Did she?"

"It got quite bad after the separation," she says. "God, did I tell you she's wearing a wedding dress to the wedding?"

"What?"

"It's insane," Michelle says. "Show her the picture."

Emily shows me a picture of her mother, Julie, in what is definitely a wedding dress.

"She says it's not a wedding dress because it's cream," Emily says. "Look at the lace!"

"Can't you just say no?"

"She's giving us money for the wedding."

Simone comes out from behind the curtain. Michelle and Emily cheer. I can't. I know she must hate it. The long, floor-length satin, her bare back dramatic against the high neck. She looks so unsure of herself, turning around slowly, like a broken ballerina in a music box. Emily and the woman stand behind her.

"We should take it in a bit," Emily says.

The woman pulls, folds, and pins, and I can see Simone wince as the fabric clings even tighter to her bust and waist.

"You like it, right?" Emily asks. "I just thought it had a bit more of a masculine vibe compared to Michelle's."

"Because it has a high neck?"

Emily, affirmed, beams.

"Yes! Exactly."

Does she think gay women are self-conscious about their sternums?

I think of Simone at our graduation prom, with her long red dress, in the arms of the captain of the rugby team. I also remember the jealousy I felt, wanting to be as beautiful as her, for a man like that to like me, maybe even love me. It's funny that for some of us, being a beautiful woman in a beautiful dress that beautiful men want to fuck is a dream, and for others it's hell on earth, and sometimes it's both at once.

"Do you feel good?" Emily asks.

"I just haven't worn a dress like this in a while," she says, running her hands along the bow of her hips.

"Do you remember what you used to wear out to Dragon-I?" Michelle laughs, looking at me for confirmation. I pretend not to notice.

"I was a teenager."

"Do you not like it?" Emily cocks her head.

"No," Simone says. "It's fine. I just thought it would've been—"

"Is it a huge deal?" Emily asks. "If it's a really big deal we can look into something else, I honestly just thought—"

"No, no," Simone says. "It's fine. It's nice."

"Are you sure?"

"Yes," she says. "It doesn't have to be a thing. It's just unusual for me. I can't remember the last time I wore a dress. It's nice."

Simone looks shrunken, a little shriveled. A sad, gay raisin. Emily turns to me and Michelle.

"Can you guys stand together?"

All of us stand shoulder to shoulder. Emily takes a few pictures, then hands her phone to the tailor, who takes a few more. I squeeze Simone tight, and then again as we let go of one another.

* * *

WE CELEBRATE—THOUGH MUTEDLY, AHEAD OF Emily and Michelle's early morning flight—at a Chinese restaurant in St. James's. The staff do not allow us to order wine without the sommelier. I know this dinner will be outrageously expensive, and so I try to soothe myself. Emily has paid for the dresses. Michelle and Emily live abroad. You're not going to the hen. You can pay for the three-figure Peking duck. A man in a tall chef's hat slices through the crisp brown husk of the bird. I feel the onset of a headache. It must be the day drinking. We wrap the small ears of flesh in thin pancakes.

"Mm!" Emily says. "I completely forgot to ask about your brother."

"Jamie's fine," I say. "I think he's having a baby?"

"What?!"

Michelle and Emily glow with maternal longing.

"It's a messy situation," I say.

Simone swallows a large bite of duck.

"He got his ex-girlfriend pregnant and she's keeping it," she says. "Jamie's involvement TBC."

"Do you think he'll be a good dad?" Emily asks.

"Um." I genuinely haven't considered the question, at least in those terms. "Not to shit on my brother or anything, but I really don't know."

"Oh." Emily looks disappointed.

"God," Michelle says, "do you remember Jamie beating up Tom Stacey for bullying you?"

"I obviously remember Jamie beating up Tom Stacey for bullying me."

Honestly, how could I forget? It became a whole thing. Parents got involved. No harm came to Jamie because he'd finished his exams and was going to university. Nobody ever touched me again. Jamie was protective, but I think he also just wanted someone to punch. There was a lot of bad energy swirling around back then. Dad still drank. We suffered through Jamie's constant panic about failure, all while everyone beyond the four walls of our home thought he was okay. It's always been that way with him, his insecurities a tool to bludgeon others.

"Tom Stacey was so hot," Emily says, eating a clove of fried garlic whole. "He's, like, really not anymore."

"I've seen, actually," Simone says. "So sad."

Emily sighs with hefty remorse.

"Early thirties hits men hard."

Plain, but true. Beauty, much like hairlines, recedes.

"I went to Lamma recently and thought of you," Michelle says to me.

"Remember how we used to go to the beach!" Emily says. "With the power station. Do you think that was safe?"

"I kind of don't really want to know," Simone says.

"And that fried chicken stall," Emily beams.

"It's still there, you know," Michelle says as she puts more vegetables onto my plate.

That was the first place my family and I ate, while we rolled our suitcases from the ferry to our new home. I was eleven. It's funny to hear them talk about it with nostalgia. Emily, who lived in Deep Water Bay, on Hong Kong Island with a nice beach of its own, always complained about having to come to Lamma. They all complained about coming to Lamma. They made it sound like a pilgrimage. Simone would maintain that she had to stay over, as if that was the only way to justify the journey. It was only a twenty-minute ferry from the pier in Central.

"Maxy, with how your dad is doing right now, do you think I could put him in touch with my mum? For sober stuff?"

"Yeah, sure," I say. "I'm sure he'd be fine with that."

I don't know if he'd be fine with that.

"When did he stop again?" Michelle asks.

"After the fire," Emily and Simone say.

I look at Simone like she's betrayed me, because maybe she has. She stuffs a tofu puff into her mouth while Michelle's face surges with the jolt of a resurfaced memory.

"Oh my God, of course," she says. "He set your house on fire."

"He didn't set our house on fire . . . It was just the carpet."

"But it was really scary for you," Emily says.

I'm pretty sure, when I first told them, Emily said I was being over-dramatic.

"It was fine."

"No, it wasn't," Emily says. "You were so stressed about it. It was a big thing. And then when Jamie—"

"Oh my God, yeah, sorry, I remember. Sorry," Michelle says. "He went ballistic at your dad, and then he got sober, but was still so off with you about it?" Michelle turns to Simone, as if I'm an unreliable source. "Right?"

I look at Simone, hoping for support.

"I mean, it was scary," she says. "You were a teenager."

"Simone."

"Max," Emily says with an unsure smile. "It's fine. He's still sober."

"Yeah, exactly." My voice is sharp. "It's fine."

"Oh my God, I remember." Michelle exhales. "And then after that you guys never talked about it. That's honestly so crazy looking back—"

"Guys," Simone interjects.

I want to scream. Simone massages her eyebrows with her fingers. Emily bites her lip.

"I just . . ." I say. "I just really hate—"

"Did you ever talk about it?" Emily asks. "As in, your family?"

"Not really."

"What do you mean?" Michelle shakes her head. "I always forget how white you are."

"Guys," I say. "Come on."

My cheeks go hot. I remember it all. Keeping everything a secret until Jamie pressured me into telling him what was wrong. Crying at school. The girls surrounding me. Me begging them not to tell their parents, which, to their credit, I don't think they did. The table falls quiet. I'm flushing with old scraps of embarrassment and shame. At having an alcoholic dad, and at myself, for inviting that chaos in, for letting it rot.

"Think of the good that came out of it, though," Emily says. "Him going sober. I think my mum will be happier. She already is."

"I think that's just the wedding dress," Michelle says.

The girls laugh. I manage a chuckle. I slouch in my chair. Simone reaches for my hand beneath the table and gives it a squeeze, and then another. The table goes quiet with tacit understanding. Nobody says sorry. There's nothing to apologize for.

"I can't believe you guys aren't coming to the bachelorette," Michelle sighs.

It's unclear if she's expressing sadness or disappointment. Emily gives me and Simone an expectant look.

"It was literally so expensive," I say. "I couldn't justify going for a weekend."

"No. Me neither," Simone adds.

"Also, I don't think I would've felt comfortable flying to Nevada as a trans person."

That seems to close this line of conversation. I am grateful for the nuclear option, even though I have no idea whether or not it's safe to fly to Nevada as a trans person.

Emily's mum messaged me and Simone separately to let us know how much she wished we could be there for the hen. Neither of us responded. It's not just Michelle joining, anyway. There's a whole bunch of Emily's friends, who she is probably much closer to.

"Your boyfriend looks handsome," Michelle says. "I can't wait to meet him."

"He's not coming to the wedding," I say, taking a sip of wine, avoiding Emily's gaze.

"How long have you been together?"

"Maybe five months?" I keep my eyes on my wineglass. "Not long."

"It feels quite serious, though."

"His dad had a heart attack," I say.

"Oh my God." Emily gasps.

"So stressful." Michelle puts her hand to her chest. "That people just die?"

I put my chopsticks down.

"He's alive. I think that's forced us a bit closer. Made it more serious, I guess. He's also met my family and stuff."

"They're living together," Simone adds.

"What?" Michelle and Emily say.

"Temporarily."

"Do you like him?" Michelle turns to Simone.

"Yes." She leans back into her seat. "Much better than the last one."

"Such a dick." Emily shakes her head.

The rest of us share a solemn nod. I don't think Michelle even met Arthur, but I suppose people tell stories, and that's enough. I reach for another pancake.

"Is his family nice?" Michelle asks.

I feel my face go hot.

"I've only met his sister," I say, not making eye contact. "Because of everything with his dad. She was perfectly nice, though. She helped him move in." I take a breath then look at her. "Do you think you'll get engaged soon?"

"Austen's going to propose next March."

"Oh, how do you know?"

"I asked him."

"So you proposed?"

"No?" Michelle looks confused. "I set a date for him to propose to me."

*　*　*

SIMONE INSISTS ON ORDERING THE taxi to Camden Road. Carla has a show at a gallery there. It's an achievement. A series of portraits painted of trans women, a lot of them nudes. Michelle and Emily decided not to join. Vegas, baby. We're by the side of the road, the evening unusually chilly for early summer.

"Five minutes," Simone says. "I fucking hated that dress."

"Yeah," I say. "It wasn't you."

"Am I being difficult?"

"What? No."

"It's not like I'm trans," Simone says. "Like, I almost feel if I was trans I could justify not wearing that dress."

"I do get what you mean. I think they just don't get how uncomfortable it made you. Maybe you could tell her?"

"I'll probably be fine," Simone says. "Ugh. I'm such a fucking coward. You know how some people will always make you feel small? And it's not even them, it's just me, feeling trapped. Or stunted. Something."

"Oh my God, Max," I say. "It's, like, so, so nice you're a girl now because we definitely couldn't have included you in the wedding if you were a boy."

"Oh my God, Simone," she says. "You used to be such a dick-guzzling slut, can't you wear the fucking dress and shut the fuck up?"

We laugh. I feel the wine.

"I think Eva's seeing someone new," Simone says.

"Is she?"

"Yeah, which is fair. After this long. It always stings, though, doesn't it?"

"It will never not sting."

I think about the girl from the book launch, the one standing next to me when Arthur read out his poem, and how a couple of days after, when Vincent wasn't in close physical proximity, I felt less than. It took all of me to avoid research, learning about her, seeing if she was better, finding ways to prove that she wasn't. All an exercise in proving I'm unworthy.

"I'm sorry," I say. "That's a horrible feeling."

"Don't you sometimes feel like you're going to be left behind? Like a single washed-up party girl?"

"Simone." I put my arm around her. "Literally all the time. But we hardly even go out anymore."

"Isn't that worse?"

"You're so interesting, though," I say. "And high-achieving."

"That's true, at least I have that." She hugs me. "I'm sorry about the fire stuff."

I take a deep breath.

"It felt like an interrogation."

"PC Michelle," Simone says.

I laugh.

"It's so weird," I say. "I told Vincent about it recently. When we were up at my parents." It sort of just feels like this awkward thing hanging over me. Like it's never really over."

"Some things are never really over."

"Mm."

THE CAB ARRIVES. IT SWERVES through traffic before dropping us in front of the gallery. We take a glass of white wine each as we enter and stand in front of the first painting.

It's a nude mounted on the wall, a trans woman painted in blue with her legs splayed, genitalia on show. She looks familiar. I could probably find her in the small gallery crowd. Simone moves on to the next painting, but I can't help but stay near the entrance, next to the wide window by the door, looking at onlookers on the street. The gallery's next to a bus stop. I watch a couple walk past, the woman oblivious, the man's face wrought with sudden alarm. He nudges the woman and they take a few steps back, staring wide-eyed at the body. When I see a couple of teenage boys catch their first glimpse, I turn. I don't want to see their reaction.

"Max!" Carla shouts, coming up the stairs from the bathroom, wearing a tight black dress flaring out at a dropped waistline. "You came!"

We kiss each other on the cheek. Twice, of course.

"Thanks so much for inviting me. I brought Simone. We were at a bridesmaids' dress fitting."

Carla cackles.

"You're so crazy," she says. "Always doing funny things."

I guess it is a funny thing.

"Congratulations," I say. "The paintings are beautiful."

"Thank you, baby," she says. "So much last-minute stress. They wanted to move that one by the door farther in. Swap it with one of the butt paintings."

"I like that one," I say. "It's brave."

"Brave?" She raises her eyebrows. "It's not brave. It's a body."

"I—"

"Hi!" Simone says.

"Hi, baby."

"Congratulations. The paintings are beautiful."

"Thank you, baby."

Carla leaves us. We move through the gallery, through a room full of people admiring naked bodies painted in mournful blue and green hues. Squatting, bending, looking in the mirror and examining. What a world of difference between outside and in. A lot of the people here were also at Caspar's, although I can't see Caspar himself. Maybe there was some beef with Carla. It's hard to keep up.

The final painting is the smallest. A detailed portrait of a woman curled up on her bed in the corner of the room. She is maybe the size of an apple, or a satsuma. We bend our knees and lean into the little room within a room.

"What do you think she's doing?" I ask.

"Journaling, sleeping." Simone sighs. "Waiting for the sweet embrace of death."

We lean out.

"I think I should start writing again," I say.

"Mm?"

"As in, properly. I've only written a couple of poems this year."

It's not because I want to be productive. This isn't about wasting time. It's just that life has been collecting at my feet—a lot of happiness, but also some shame. I'm not sure if the way out of pain is to swim through it, but I'm not sure there are many other ways for me to make sense of it.

"Why now?" Simone asks.

"I don't know."

We move to stand at the edge of the concourse, holding out our empty glasses for a refill.

"I like it, don't I?"

"You used to," she says. "Maybe focus on doing it for yourself."

"That can be hard."

"It isn't."

"Isn't it?"

"I do everything for myself," she says.

VINCENT

IX

THERE'S NO REASON WHY WE CAN'T GO ON AS NORMAL. ALEX AND I JUST kissed a bit. No lines were crossed. She doesn't have to know that I know. I'll just try to find her gross. Remind myself that there's no point wanting someone if I'm never going to act on it.

I'm pissed, though, because out of all the girls I could have met at a hostel while traveling, why did the one I like have to be trans? Alex felt special, but how would it even work? It'd be a life of explaining shit to other people. What would my parents think? Mum would combust. Dad would pretend he hadn't heard. I imagine telling him at a supermarket, tapping watermelons to find the right timbre for ripeness. Dad? Did you hear me? *Overripe.*

I stay in bed until the woman at the front desk comes to the room. She screams at me to leave because I haven't paid for late check-out.

Our train to Surat Thani isn't for a few hours. I find Alex down-stairs with her bags, and I don't even have to try to not want her. There's a white-hot barrier around my body.

"Hey," I say.

"Where did you go last night?" she asks, her face investigative.

"To the roof and back to mine."

"Oh," she says, as if I could've gone anywhere else. "I went to another one of the floating markets this morning. It wasn't as good as the one we went to."

I give her a flat smile and a small nod, like I don't care.

"I sorted out your ticket, by the way," she says.

"Oh, cool." I pause for a moment. "Thanks."

I should ask her how much I owe, but I don't. I'm looking through my phone, at nothing in particular. I don't know how I feel. I know that I'm being cold, that I'm punishing her for something. For not telling me. For being. I'm mad and I feel self-conscious. What if other people in the hostel know and are looking? It's stupid how quickly these things change, how I was a dog humping her leg yesterday, and today she's humping mine and I just want to chuck her into the sea. She sits next to me and so I get up and take *Shantaram* from the communal bookshelf.

"*Shantaram*?" she asks.

"Yeah?"

We sit in silence, and she's playing with her nails. I wonder what she's thinking. Does she think I'm being weird?

"We should probably leave in, like, forty-five minutes," she says.

I don't look up from *Shantaram*, which I'm only pretending to read.

"Cool," I say.

"Is everything okay?"

"What?"

"Is everything okay?" she repeats.

"Everything's fine."

I find myself trying to spot male inflections in her voice, trying to see if she looks at all like a man, staring at her throat, her jaw. I think about how when she laughs, it's kind of low. All that history, the before, makes me want to squirm. How could I want that? I don't want

139

it. We sit in silence, passing time. She asks me if she can leave her bags with me so that she can go for a walk. I think about my parents again.

We leave when she comes back, taking the Blue Line to Hua Lamphong rail station, bags on our shoulders. She stops trying to make conversation, except for asking me for the ticket money with her arms folded. Occasionally, we catch each other's eyes, but it's like we're drifting from each other in real time, if we were even in any way together. More like pulling two things apart before the glue's dried, hapless white strings falling between two pieces of paper.

Crowds of people wait in the central foyer of the rail station with the curved roof. Alex takes our printed tickets out of her bum bag and passes mine to me without a word. We check the electronic display boards, then find the steel-sided train on a platform.

We have two seats facing each other and a window to our left. They're gray-green and leather, and soft, and the whole carriage is clean and modern even though the tickets were cheap. There's a big berth overhead, which I guess is one of the beds. I don't know where our other bed is going to be, but they can't make us share, right? I look at the menus in front of us, with Thai food, all costing just under two hundred baht. Alex is staring at me.

"Are you going to tell me what's going on with you?" she asks.

My face is slapped with heat.

"What do you mean?" I ask.

Alex rolls her eyes.

"You've been funny with me the entire day," she says. "You left my bed in the middle of the night and didn't come back and now you're being fucking weird."

"I'm not being weird," I say. "I just wanted to read and I didn't feel well. And I couldn't sleep in your room."

"Did something happen?"

"No," I say, sounding as surprised as I can. "Why would anything have happened?"

"I'm just trying to figure it out."

"There's nothing to figure out," I say.

She puts her elbows on the table and puffs through her lips, looking out onto the station platform from the window next to us. I'm taken by her directness, not letting things simmer for longer. It's so plain and simple. What's up with that? I'm being stupid. We're not in the hostel. There's no reason for me to be paranoid. There are no eyes on me and Alex, assessing what we are, what I am. Just be friendly. Keep distant, but friendly. Rational.

"Maybe getting with each other was a mistake," she says, her eyes on me, a tentativeness in the lift of her eyebrows. I don't say anything for a little while. "I'm sorry I invited you into my room. It's my fault."

"It's okay," I say. "I mean, you don't have to apologize. I guess just because we're seeing Fred, you know. Maybe it makes sense not to hook up."

"Yeah," she says, placidly, eyes back out of the window. "You're right."

"Yeah."

My stomach plummets a little, and I'm swallowed by regret, which surprises me because she's giving me what I want. This is how it's supposed to be, so why do I want to hold her hand? I take a deep breath. These feelings will go away.

Our train leaves the station, and after a while, things between us start to feel back to normal, if normal is a step behind where we were yesterday, firmly in chat and laughter. We talk and talk. *What?! You've never seen* The O.C.? *I would've died to be Marissa Cooper when I was younger. When I was mad at my mum, I would scream that I wished I was born in California.* Sometimes I think good conversations are like those little robots that hoover the floor for you. Roombas. Knocking into things and going in a spontaneous new direction, with no end in sight.

"What kind of lawyer do you want to be?" she asks.

"I don't know," I say. "I always thought it'd be cool to work on patents and stuff."

This invites a long lecture about capitalism from Alex. She tells me about how she sat outside the London Stock Exchange with some friends for Occupy London.

"Someone had a sign there that said Rosa Parks Died For This."

I burst into laughter, feeling relieved I know who Rosa Parks is.

"Why'd you go to the protest?" I ask.

Her jaw drops, but she's playing.

"Because I care, Vincent."

I've never been to a protest. Sometimes I wonder if I even have opinions, let alone good ones. If pressed on stuff, then I can come to a view, but I don't spend my day thinking about the world. It'd be nice to be someone who did, to be a bit more like Alex. Fred thinks about the world. He reads a lot, dropping quotes into conversation when you least expect it, sometimes in a way that makes me feel stupid. *Large parties are so intimate, there's no privacy at small parties. What, you haven't read Gatsby?*

We order dinner, and as we eat I tell her about some of the food we used to eat when we went to Hong Kong. She gasps at pig intestines.

"It's just offal," I say, even though I wanted to shock her. "I thought you were a good eater."

"I am!" she says. "I just can't deal with certain parts. Like tongue." She fake-retches.

"Tongue's good!"

"It's like making out with a dead cow," she says. "It's bestiality and necrophilia in one."

The feelings will go away. It's just nice to talk to her again. When the food is cleared, attendants fill the carriage, folding and flattening the seats to form a bottom bunk. The carriage melts into quiet, and I watch the bottom of Alex's bed. It's a strange kind of intimacy, lying beneath someone like this. I can't help but draw the outline of her back and hips and legs from under the berth, using my memory of the night before. They don't turn the lights off in the train, so I curl up in the shadow cast by Alex's bunk. I slow my breathing, imagining that we're syncing up, though how would I ever know? I want to ask her if she's okay up there, if she can sleep with the light on, but I don't. I fall asleep, hugging my backpack, thinking of Alex.

In the morning, Alex's pale legs climb down the ladder, the zips of her bum bag clicking against the steel. She sits at the other end of my bed as we wait to alight from the train, and I keep checking my bag to make sure I haven't lost my passport, wallet, and phone. We drift in and out of sleep on the minibus, and then on the three-tiered ferry, Alex resting on my shoulder, my cheek on the top of her head.

I rub my eyes as we approach Koh Samui. The sea is impossibly blue and crystalline, full brightness and saturation and contrast. Alex yawns and looks out of the window, too. It feels like we're sharing this together. Is that stupid?

The shore muddies the clarity of the water close to the pier. We step off, and the morning heat beats onto us. Sweat beads across my back, wetting and conjoining the humid layers of skin, shirt, and nylon bag. We're soon in a taxi, on the forest-lined road toward the hostel. My eyes follow the rise and dips of the power lines above the road, stacked and crowded, a barrage of rubber eels flying above the tarmac.

"How long's the journey?" I ask.

"Am I your mum?"

I laugh.

"Fred must already be there," I say.

"Do you think he'll like me?"

"Yeah," I say. "I do."

I don't really know what Fred wouldn't like about her. Sure, she's trans, but it's not like Fred is going to find out, and who's to say he'd even care. I guess Fred still throws the word fag around sometimes, but not super recently, and definitely less since it stopped being okay. I also don't think he'd ever call an actual gay person a fag.

Alex cracks open a window. The taxi driver looks back. The air-conditioning's on. Alex smiles, and he smiles back. White girl shit. The roads get busier, and we slow down as we approach a strip with shops and bars and restaurants. I'm peering out, looking at unlit neon signs, dull and dusty in the daylight.

We arrive at the hostel at Chaweng Beach. It's ridiculously nice for a hostel. Big white reception, with open glass doors and brown fans swinging above. Alex is paying for a private room. Fred and I are sharing—it didn't cost much more than two beds in a room of eight. I also thought Fred might like some privacy—he's been holed up in an ashram for more than a week, surviving on boiled vegetables and five hours' sleep a night. I'm still not sure whether he's doing well.

We hand in our passports to check in, waiting at the counter.

"Vinny!"

Fred appears from the side. His hair is blonder, with thin, sun-bleached streaks. He's wearing shorts that end just above his knees and a billowy shirt, mostly open, bronzed chest, little bleached strands of hair poking out. He's golden. Not even that reddish tan most white people get. We do that thing where you grip hands then bring your bodies close then pat each other on the back.

"It's so good to see you," he says. "I really mean it."

"You too, man."

I mean it.

When we separate, I look toward Alex, turn back to Fred, and see him look at her for the first time. I feel an immediate dread. Sometimes you can tell that someone's into someone else. It's a hungry smirk, a lift of the eyebrow, a deep breath. They hug hello. What's Alex thinking? *He's so handsome. And charming.* And Fred? *Wow, nice boobs.* My stomach scrunches. I try to reassure myself. Nothing is going to happen. It can't, because then he'd find out, and he wouldn't be into that.

OUR ROOM DOESN'T LOOK LIKE a hostel room. We've got doors that open to the pool and there's vinyl of coral behind the bed. Fred's claimed the side of the bed near the windows, but his stuff is spread all around, in the way I'd expect it to be. We lie on our backs.

"How's it all been, man?" he asks.

"It's been good," I say. "To be honest, Bangkok was pretty shit at the start. I don't think I'm good at traveling alone."

"I'm really sorry."

He looks genuinely remorseful. I'm not going to milk it.

"I don't think I've ever felt that terrible," he says. "I felt like I was in a black hole. Ruining the best time of my life."

"For the whole time you were in India?" I ask, unable to imagine feeling that way for months. "Did you make friends at hostels or anything?"

"Yeah," he says. "And I got with a few girls and stuff, but I got so in my own head about it all being meaningless. Traveling. Going out. Seeing shit. Life, even. I didn't know what to say to myself."

We're looking at each other now.

"Sorry, Fred," I say. "Do you think you're better now? After it?"

"Yeah," he says. "I'm feeling a bit more excited. I feel like I've got some tools."

"What do you mean?"

"We spent the first days sitting down and focusing on our breathing," he says. "That's all you have to do, focus on your breath, until you stop sinking."

I purse my lips. It's hard to be mad at him. It's not like I've had

to go through it to know it sounds bad. I don't even have to understand it.

"I'm really sorry, again, Vinny."

"It's fine," I say, rubbing my eyes. "It's been fine, honestly. I've just
been hanging with Alex."

He raises an eyebrow.

"Alex," he says. "She's fit. Have you guys?"

"We're just friends."

I feel a nip in my gut. Is it because I'm not telling the whole truth,
or because I see the gears turning in Fred's head? I get up to chug
down one of the free bottles of water, then sit on the edge of his bed.
He's wearing a wicked smile.

"You like her, though."

"No."

"You do."

"I don't."

"You're blushing," he says.

I try to wipe it off my cheeks with the back of my hand.

"You like her."

I push his knee away. He softly kicks the back of my shoulder, and
then again. I grab his ankle, and he pulls me back by my shoulders
and soon we become a human pretzel, wrestling off the bed. I land on
my hip with a thud, shouting ow, then pin Fred to the floor. We're
laughing. I'm laughing so much it's hard to stay on top. Our bodies
flip and he punches me in my side.

"Fred," I say. "That hurt."

He whines my words back to me. He laughs, standing up and wiping sweat from his forehead. I catch my breath on my back, reminding
myself that we were just having fun, that he didn't mean to hurt me.

"Want me to kiss it better?" he asks, tousling his hair.

"Fuck off."

I peel myself off the floor.

"Should we find Alex and get some lunch?" he asks.

We walk up two floors to her bedroom. She opens the door with wet hair, thin straps of her bikini tied behind her neck, an inches-long pair of board shorts sitting low on her hip bones and held up by a crinkled white waist band. Fred's behind me, leaning on the banister. He's looking at her—I know it. I imagine him falling back over the railing and enjoy the thought.

We walk in a three. Alex asks Fred questions that triangulate us, reporting things I said about him, allowing Fred opportunity for elaboration. *Vincent said you went to school together. Vincent said you're going to Durham. Vincent said you were in India. Vincent said you did that meditation stuff.* Fred asks Alex questions. Things about UCL, about her mum, growing up in London, all of which makes me feel invisible, even though Fred's just catching up.

I know you can't own someone, that you can't stop them from getting to know other people, but I think I do want to do that. Keep Alex in a box. I try to shake the thoughts out of my head. Alex and Fred won't become a thing because Alex is trans. Fred wouldn't have sex with her if he knew.

I'm walking a couple of feet behind them because the pavement is narrow on the way to Chaweng center. A woman calls us into a restaurant that's by the roadside, with open walls and high ceilings and swinging fans, plastic chairs and tables, and we inspect the menu, which is the same as in every other tourist restaurant in Thailand. We sit down, and Alex asks the waitress whether the salads can be less spicy.

"I can't tell you how good it feels to be speaking to friends," Fred says.

I don't know what he's talking about. Alex is hardly his friend.

"I can't believe you didn't speak for ten days," Alex says, and she genuinely looks amazed, impressed. "I would've gone crazy."

"My brain started feeling like mush. It was honestly like I ran out of things to even think about," he says. "They wouldn't let you read anything. You couldn't even wank."

"Not in front of Alex, Fred."

Alex laughs.

"They couldn't actually stop you, though?" she asks.

"I wanted to follow the rules!" Fred says. "By the end of it I genuinely saw a tree with a curvy trunk and thought, wow, quite fit."

Alex cackles. I'm giggling into my palms.

"You know when the wind hits the branches in just the right way."

"Stop it, Fred," I say.

We're all laughing now.

"Why'd you want to do it, anyway?" Alex asks.

"Just thought it'd be a good challenge." Fred smiles. This isn't the Fred from our room, talking about black holes and despair. It's outside Fred, lively, confident. Part of me feels angry, or wants to get mad at him, catch him out in a lie, but then again, we're all lying. All I've done for the last day is lie. But if only she knew. If only he knew. "Anyway," he says. "I was talking to someone at the hostel about this Half Moon thing."

"Do you really want to go?" Alex asks.

"Yeah." Fred's surprised. "Don't you guys?"

"I'm not sure," Alex says.

Fred looks toward me.

"Isn't it a bit overdone?" I ask, though I don't think I've ever cared about something being overdone.

"Overdone?" He furrows his eyebrows. I blush. "We're already here. It's one night. We should just do it." His voice is pleading. "We'd have a really good time."

"Yeah," Alex says. "Maybe you're right."

She gives in much faster than I thought she would, and it makes me see her differently—as more malleable—and I'm annoyed at her for it. She must really like Fred.

※　※　※

ALEX MEETS US BY THE hostel pool. There are signs saying that we can't drink in the water, but the two other clusters of people are holding Smirnoff Ices above the waterline, dribbles of the milky-white falling into the chlorinated soup. Fred buys a few and returns, bottle caps off. As I sip the cloying liquid, Fred starts splashing Alex at the pool edge, giggling. She pushes herself off the ledge, the water climbing up her ribs.

"Why do you wear those?" Fred asks.

"Wear what?"

"Those shorts," he says. "Instead of a normal bikini."

This is so awkward. I look off toward the beach, at the low, undulating waves, pretending I'm not here. I don't want to cringe. Nobody thinks I have a reason to cringe.

"I just like the look of it, to be honest," she says.

"I think bikinis look a bit nicer."

"Do you wear all of your clothes for other people?" she asks.

I smile and look back. Fred's smiling, too.

"Isn't that the point of it?" he asks. "You wear clothes because of how you want to be seen by others. If there was an apocalypse and you were the only person on earth, do you really think you'd be wearing clothes?"

"It can still be about self-expression," Alex says. "Even if I want to be seen."

"Sure, but self-expression to whom?" he asks.

"Think about language. Like, talking. It's not just about being heard."

"We wouldn't speak if there weren't people there to hear us."

"But I probably would," she says, facing Fred. "This conversation, for example," Alex continues, "isn't just about trying to impress us, it's about trying to impress yourself. Your self-image."

"Hah," Fred says, sounding pleased, like a proud parent, like her words are his indirect doing. He smiles, then floats on his back. Alex paddles away.

I sink into the water, blowing bubbles out of my nose. There's a feeling I sometimes get around Fred and my friends, like I'm an observer rather than a participant, where I recede inches into myself, from human to husk. Maybe it's not too far from what Fred described. A black hole. There are so many things I could blame it on, but when it happens it feels like there are gaps in the circuit board, absent connections in my brain. Did I skip a chapter of child development? Am I just really fucking weird? It's never like this when it's one-on-one; I just get swallowed up in groups a bit. Swallowed up by people like Fred. I come up for air.

"Fred," Alex squeals.

Fred laughs. She's looking at him with her mouth agape.

"What's up?" I ask.

"He pulled my shorts down!" Alex's voice feigns outrage, which makes me feel a little gross, because she seems to not really mind. I see another girl roll her eyes. I imagine she's jealous. Of the way Alex looks. Of the attention Fred pays her.

I give a disappointed smile, a raise of my eyebrows, all toward Fred, who doesn't look my way. They're hanging on to the edge of the pool and I feel out of place. It'd be a nice picture, them with their elbows on the infinity pool like that, but I'm not here to take photos of them. I push myself out, grab one of the towels we brought and leave, deciding I'm not going to look back. Neither of them calls after me.

IT'S EARLY EVENING AT THE hostel bar, and a guy in a Tiger Beer wifebeater, burned red like a boiled lobster, leans forward, telling us and two other people a story about a ladyboy at a bar in Bangkok.

"You could tell right away, but he spoke in that way"—he begins to speak in a helium-y, grating, lifted falsetto—"hey, boys." He scrunches up his face, pushes his lips into a duck pout and waves. "And Johnny's like"—he points to his friend next to us, in a Tiger Beer snapback and a Red Bull wifebeater—"can we see your mangina?"

People gasp, including Fred. Not in an offense-taking way, but in a no, you didn't way. I look at Alex, who seems disturbed. I don't want to give it all away by being too serious, so I glance back at lobster-boy and give a faint chuckle.

"Did it show you?" the third boy asks, wearing a brandless wife-beater and army shorts, no snapback.

"Don't call someone it," Alex says, but it's a gentle reprimand, and I feel a little sad because underneath all this she must be hurt. The boys look at her. "That's not okay. You can't call someone an it."

"Yeah, guys," Fred adds. "Come on."

Fred says it halfheartedly. He's playing both sides. I'm embarrassed for Alex. Would I even have said something if I was her? I remember that photo from my fourteenth birthday, when all my friends pulled their eyes back and shouted my name. *Say Vincent!* I didn't say a word. I don't even have small eyes.

"Was he-she okay?" the third boy asks.

"Just call her she," Alex snaps.

I go on alert. Is she giving it away? Everyone ignores her.

"We saw the mangina," Johnny says.

Lobster-boy takes out his phone to show everyone a picture, and everyone, except Alex, but including Fred, leans in to look at it. They all scream. Lobster-boy turns the phone to show Alex, but she cringes away from the screen, saying she doesn't want to see it. It seems like any moment a bomb could detonate. The third boy asks if any of us have seen a Ping-Pong show. He tells us that he saw a woman squat over a cup, and how a terrapin fell out. Fred has his hand over his mouth, laughing.

The conversation moves on, but I can't help but think of how terrible Alex must feel, and so I sit next to her and bring my mouth to her ear.

"He's such a tool," I say.

She laughs.

We drink on, get drunk, then move on to the strip and into a club. I'm sweating loads, but so is everyone around me. We jump from bar to bar, and I see Fred and Alex talking intensely, and part of me worries that they're going to hook up, so all I can do is keep drinking more. Syrup and spirit in buckets splash onto sweat-damp clothes. A girl dances close, her butt slowly approaching my groin like a Toyota into a parking spot. For a moment I think I'm going to pull, but then I feel something come up my throat. I stumble into the club toilet and throw up and throw up and throw up, so much, until I start to see the tail ends of what I ate for dinner. Full chunks of chicken. I'm a real fucking wreck right now, but I don't want any help, so I stagger the however many meters or kilometers back to the hostel without saying goodbye to Fred and Alex. I know they're just doing what we're supposed to do, but I can't take it. I don't want anything to do with them. Maybe Fred was right. I get where he was coming from. What's the point of this? What's the point in any of this?

MAX

X

IT'S LIKE AN ANGRY TWINK HAS POURED POPPERS INTO MY SKULL. I PRESS my head into the forest-green tiles of the bathroom wall. Another migraine. I knead my temples with my fingers before returning to the restaurant. Fred booked it, one of a cluster of new-ish upscale places doing tasting menus in Hackney. There are nine courses. I mourn the death of large plates. Where did they go? Can they take me with them?

My leather maxi has been too tight since the first course. Every dish is Asian-inspired, but in a way so light it's hard to detect. I wonder if I could be described in the same way: Asian-inspired white woman. I return to our table outside, each of us lying to ourselves that it is warm enough to eat al fresco, wrapped up in our light jackets.

"Are you okay?" Vincent asks as I sit.

"Migraine," I say, shaking my head.

"Oh no," Aisha says.

"Do you get them often?" Fred asks.

"Recently," I say. "It's fine."

I bite into stout-and-treacle loaf served with Japanese pickles. I've been getting migraines more and more, to the extent that, without me asking, Vincent brings packets of paracetamol out with us. He's bought me supplements he's researched. Magnesium. Folate. The migraines aren't completely debilitating, but they're a problem, and so I've booked a GP appointment. I haven't told Vincent—not after everything with his dad. I press my eyebrows together, hoping to release the tension in my head. A waiter collects our plates, and soon after they're replaced with a seaweed cacio e pepe. Just because you can, doesn't mean you should.

Vincent and Fred are in quiet conversation. I know it's about family. Fred's face is awash with sweet concern.

"What are you guys doing in September?" Aisha asks me.

She's sitting next to me, wearing a broderie anglaise dress with puffy sleeves. She looks fully covered above the knee, but you can see through the gaps in the embroidery. It's subtly sexy. Very mature.

"I'm not sure yet," I say. "I have a school friend's wedding. I'm a bridesmaid."

"From Hong Kong?"

"Yeah," I say. "My friend Simone's a bridesmaid, too. Neither of us speak to her much."

"One of those," Aisha says, setting down her fork, playing with her wedding band.

"Yeah."

"Can you trust the friends you make when you're half a person?" she asks. Both of us eye Vincent and Fred at the same time and laugh. They flash us a quick look, before turning back to each other. Fred puts his arm over Aisha's chair while she leans forward. "I mean, you can, but there's so much room to grow apart." Aisha pulls out her phone. "Anyway, one of my friends from Harvard has a holiday home in Provence that she never uses. She's letting me use it for a week. You and Vincent should come. It'd only be us."

"The wedding's actually in Bordeaux," I say.

"No way!"

"Are they close?" I ask.

"It's all the south of France, isn't it? It can't be that far."

We compare dates. I could go.

"I'd need to talk to Simone," I say. "I think our plan was to go together."

"Simone could always join," Aisha says. "There's room in the house."

It feels very generous of Aisha to let someone she hasn't met come along. Even more generous of Aisha's friend.

A waiter arrives with an ox-heart bao, garnished with rhubarb. I count how many courses in we are. Five. I get this same feeling whenever I see a play. No matter how good it is, I always seem to count down the moments until it ends, until I can get out of my seat and leave. I've never been a fan of theater. Culture that talks at me. The heart presents a surprising amount of resistance to the fluffy bao. Each chew releases the tangy marinade locked into the dense fibers of the meat. Only four more.

"When's the last time you were back in Singapore?" I ask.

"So long," Aisha says. "I don't really like going back. Can't be bothered with my parents."

"That bad?"

"No baby. White husband." She extends a finger for each felony. "Who's not Muslim. And works at a start-up."

Fred and Vincent look over. Is Aisha having an aneurysm? Who does this? Each finger is a bullet in his heart, or at least it would be in mine.

"Is Aisha listing my shortcomings?" Fred asks, with a careful, neutralizing smile.

He releases his hand from her thigh. I feel bad for him. It seems like he does a lot for people. Enjoys doing things for people. I'm sure he's a good husband, although who even knows. Your friend will break up with her perfect boyfriend, only to tell you he tortured animals and was breastfed until he was eleven.

Aisha isn't done.

"I left a stable job at McKinsey to work better hours." Her pinkie goes up and she lifts her other hand to continue counting. "Moved to London to be farther away from my family and closer to Fred's. Make rugs in my spare time."

"What's wrong with the rugs?" I ask.

"It's time that could be spent rearing children and caring for the husband they don't approve of." She looks at Fred. "Sorry. My mother always says the rugs won't keep me warm at night."

"But they literally would keep you warm at night," I say.

"I know."

Aisha's rugs are beautiful, delicately needled in the style of Mughal miniature paintings. Her talent is unbearable. She's not even queer. It's not fair. I thought she'd be making rugs with large, geometric shapes and block colors.

"Anyway," she continues, "I'm a disappointment."

"Weren't you a Kennedy scholar?" I ask.

"Yup."

Aisha takes another bite of her bao. I hear the sound of knives scraping plates, tines on ceramic. Aisha is one of the most accomplished people I've met. It's all over the internet. She was short-listed for the Fitzcarraldo Essay Prize with an essay exploring the line between submission and assimilation of Tamil Muslims in Singapore. She doesn't even want to be an essayist. She wrote it over a bank holiday weekend. What astounds me is that there must be a part of Aisha that believes it—that she is, in fact, a failure. One of life's great ironies is that many people are successful precisely because they'll never feel like it. And I wonder how she reconciles that with the people she surrounds herself with. Does she think we are shallow and incompetent? Part of her must resent herself, which means that part of her must resent us. Where does that resentment go?

"Moving back isn't off the cards," Fred says to me.

"It's much easier to have kids in Singapore," Aisha says. "You can have maids—"

"Helpers," Fred says.

Aisha rolls her eyes. Yuck. Vincent and I exchange a quick look.

"It's the same thing," Aisha says.

"Words matter, don't they?" Fred says.

Maid feels nearly as Victorian as servant, a reduction of a person to a simple noun. Is helper that much better, though? By avoiding maid, what we're really saying is that we're not the kinds of people who'd hire a maid. Yet, if you're still exploiting foreign labor at low prices, does politeness do anything but assuage your guilt? I don't say any of this. When we were still at school in Hong Kong, Emily once told Simone that she looked like a maid. Simone threw a pillow at her. *You're a fucking racist bitch, Emily.*

A waiter comes and replaces our baos with smoked brisket and chanterelles.

"Vincent told me you're going to be an aunt," Fred says, lifting a glass. "A traunty."

I laugh. Aisha claps. I still don't think I've fully processed the news that Jamie is going to have a baby. When I last went over, he was surrounded by books about neonatal development, including three copies of *The Book You Wish Your Parents Had Read*, which I assume he plans to give to our parents. *There's so much to learn, Max. That's the problem with Mum and Dad, they just thought they could walk in unprepared and smash it.* A baby isn't an exam, and if it was, he'd be failing. He missed her twelve-week scan for a meeting. *Look, if I don't have a job, there's no money, and if there's no money, the baby dies.* Maria is a management consultant.

We all clink our glasses.

"It's a bit of a weird situation. I don't know if Vincent said." I pause. "I don't know if my brother's ready to be a dad." The mood falls. Was that a cruel thing to say? "I mean, having kids isn't always a good thing."

"People surprise you," Fred says. "No one knows how to be a parent before they become one."

Three dessert courses follow in quick succession, with wine pairings that become progressively sweeter. A forgettable pastry followed by an orange roly-poly with black sesame sauce, the fluffy sponge grounded by the slick, fatty paste. A delicious oil-spill. Finally, a tea-flavored jelly to finish.

When the bill comes, we split it in two. Fred pays for Aisha, and so for optics' sake I pick up the bill for Vincent. For feminism. He'll bank-transfer me his share right after. We go to a pub round the corner, one I don't like because everyone looks and dresses like me—oversized leather jackets and ribbons in their hair. Fashion is dead in a ditch and it's wearing cowboy boots.

Fred buys a round, bringing all four drinks back by himself, plopping frozen margaritas from a slushie machine in front of me and Aisha, kissing her on the cheek as he does. Aisha remains inert.

My phone vibrates in my bag with a call from Simone. I go outside to answer it.

"Max," she says.

There is nothing I like less than people calling me and saying my name. It is panic-inducing. It feels cruel. Even if there is bad news to deliver, this doesn't feel like the way to do it.

"Is everything okay?" I ask.

"I think." She takes a deep breath. "I think something bad is happening."

Her voice is quivering, unseated. It's alarming.

"What?" I ask, the panic solidifying into something true. "What's happening?"

"One of the models posted my emails," she says. "They're calling me toxic."

The panic settles. They're just emails.

"What do the emails say?"

"Check your messages."

In the emails, a model—the one with no eyebrows, Xenia—tells Simone that she's signing with a well-known agency and will terminate her contract with Simone. Simone's entire business model is scouting new talent, developing them a little and helping them get signed to bigger agencies. Simone then takes a cut of the new agency's fees in perpetuity. The model has effectively cut Simone out. Simone's responses, now public, are an uncanny lapse in professionalism.

Burn bridges like this and you'll drown.

Metaphor or death threat?

You are totally disgusting. Inside and out. I've done so much to support you, and you've done fuck all to appreciate it.

Is this how people in fashion speak to one another? The closest I've got to a fuck you in any job has been a Rgds. The model shares her struggles with body image against one of Simone's emails.

I'm sorry you couldn't handle the clear and empathetic advice regarding your measurements.

These are horrible messages. I'm surprised, but even more surprised at how disappointed I am, that I could be this disappointed in Simone. Threatening to drown young girls. Who does that?

"What do you think this means?" I ask, not sure what I mean by the question.

"I have people messaging me calling me a cunt, Max," she says. "It's completely misogynistic."

"What is, sorry?" I ask.

"The messages I'm getting."

I purse my lips. Don't say anything. She'll see the light eventually.

"And for what?" she says. "Stating a fact of the industry?"

I think about Aisha earlier, airing what her parents think of Fred in front of me. Facts can come in humiliating packaging. There's whispering and there's shouting. There's hand-holding and there's punching.

"I'm freaking out. What if this is the end?"

"The end?"

"Of everything," she says.

"Everything?"

"Max," she says. "My career. People get ruined for this stuff. Even people who I know would've said worse are liking it. It's so unprofessional!"

"What is?" I ask.

"The comments!"

Simone unleashes a guttural scream, muffling it halfway through with a pillow.

"Look, I'm really close by with Vincent at a pub," I say. "Should I come over? We can work it out."

"You don't have to."

"We're not far," I say. "I'll come."

I go back into the pub, explain in jumbled sentences what's happened, handing my phone over to show them the pictures, as if that will ease things along. Fred stoically looks at the emails. Aisha sucks air through clenched teeth.

"Shit," she says.

It's unclear whether this is out of empathy or cringe, though one could argue all cringe demands empathy. In any case, I could perfectly imagine Aisha being in Simone's shoes, even more than I can imagine Simone being in Simone's shoes.

"It'll blow over," Fred says, before looking at Aisha. "Right?"

"No?" she says. "I don't think it's helpful to pretend."

"Is it not?" Fred asks.

"These are crazy messages, Fred."

For a moment, there's an electric tension suspended between them. It's weird, and obviously reaches beyond Simone. Fred turns to me.

"Scandals often feel new and complex, but their lifespans are short. Like an octopus."

"An octopus?" I ask.

"They die fast," he says.

"Oh."

I don't know why they're trying to reassure me. I'm not at the center of this. Vincent insists on coming with me. We walk for twenty minutes to Simone's flat on the south side of the canal and buzz in.

"Do you mind just waiting here first?" I ask Vincent, who nods.

As I climb the stairs to her flat, I'm nervous. When she opens the door she's crying, in a way I haven't seen since we were young. If I shut my eyes, she could have long hair, eyeliner the whole way round her eyes and a dip-dye. It's hard to digest these uncomfortable collisions with the past, to not take them as evidence that we haven't changed much at all, that all those extra layers are just onion skin. Translucent, immaterial. My unease dissolves to pity.

Simone has already poured me a glass of wine. I sit in an armchair, and she slumps into the soft groove of her Togo sofa.

"So," I say.

She looks at me. I realize she won't start.

"Those emails were quite scary, Simone."

"Max!"

"What's going on?" I ask. "Sorry. But that can't be normal, can it? That can't be how you normally speak to people?"

It occurs to me that I genuinely don't really know what anyone I'm close to is like to work with.

"Obviously not!" She buries her face in her hands. "I was just." She pauses. "So angry. I knew when I was typing how crazy I sounded, that she'd probably tell people that I'm fucking crazy, but I honestly didn't care. I just thought—this is my life. She's fucking with my life." She slouches even deeper. "I woke up and checked my phone and there were these emails sent at one A.M. from that stupid girl telling me she was leaving. Who the fuck sends an email like that at one? I just lost it."

"But this has happened before, right? Like, surely you've been cut out—"

"She wasn't the same," Simone says. "I landed on a fucking gold mine."

I don't like that she's referring to young women as gold mines.

"Why didn't you just call me?" I ask. "Or something."

"Max," she says. "I don't know. I just felt really angry. Am I not allowed to feel angry?"

"Yeah, you are."

She groans.

I reach out and place my hand on her shin, squeezing it.

"People are so fucking dumb." She sniffs. "Is Vincent still at the pub?"

"I left him downstairs."

"What?" She scrunches her eyebrows. "You left him outside? Why would you do that?"

Simone makes me go get him, and as I do I feel sheepish. I was just trying to be a good friend. There's another glass of wine waiting for him when he enters. Vincent sits next to her on the couch. His presence seems to calm her. She might be trying to save face, but I don't think that's a bad thing. People closer to you put up with your worst, even if it's bad for you—spiraling is easy when it's done against a frictionless surface.

"How are you doing?" he asks.

"Terribly," she says.

"The storm always passes," he says. "It's time, though. It just needs to pass. You're going to feel better about this tomorrow."

"That's not true," she says. "We don't know what the fallout's going to be."

She's right, though Vincent leans forward, elbows on his knees, glass of wine between his hands, as if he's really thinking the problem through. Maybe it's genuine, or maybe he's just trying to show that he cares. Simone clears her throat.

"Do you think it helps that . . ."

"What?" I ask.

"That I'm"—Simone pauses—"a queer woman of color."

Vincent entertains the idea with a lift of the eyebrows. Aisha using the word maid refreshes in my brain. Solidarity, when convenient, seems to be the ailing motto of wealthy minorities. We all lean back.

"To be honest," I say. "No."

Simone nods.

"It's not like I haven't struggled with food," she says.

I think that might make it worse. I shift my bum a little.

"Right or wrong, people do just forget about things." I take a sip of wine. "If you think about it, the people who still get punished for something they said years ago are the ones who won't shut up about how they were punished."

"Or make a career out of it," Vincent adds.

"Yeah," I say. "And you're an agent. Models are desperate for agents. Agencies will always want you to scout. Just remember, the life cycle of a scandal is short."

"Like an octopus," Vincent says.

"What?" she asks.

"They die fast," I say.

Simone still looks despondent. Though I'm trying to sound reasoned and empathetic, I worry I've been too blunt, that my words sound too rehearsed, too lawyerly. I think back to when I've felt like shit. On New Year's Day, after I fell down the stairs, when instead of trying to talk me out of my feelings, Simone just stayed with me. It's obvious that we can't always reason with emotion—that sometimes we just need to wait.

There was one summer, when we were both back in Hong Kong, and after I'd figured out I was trans, when I couldn't stop crying because I wouldn't be able to change my gender marker on my Hong Kong ID card until I'd had gender reassignment surgery, which at the time felt like so long away and too much change to bear in one gulp. Simone migrated to Lamma for a few days, and we sat on the couch and binged episode upon episode of *The Real Housewives,* watching grown women lob prosthetic legs across rooms and accuse each other of having Munchausen's. I move next to her and let her rest her head on my lap.

Vincent clears his throat.

"I get why you want to think it all through," he says. "When life's in a tailspin all you want is control. It's been like that with my dad." The mention of his dad draws Simone out of her fugue. Her head lifts; she's attentive. Vincent keeps talking, though he doesn't make eye contact with either of us. "People just want to feel like the future is still intact. My mum's been crazy. It's even been hard for Max." I could cry. His dad had a heart attack, and he's telling Simone it's been hard for me. "And it sounds so dumb, but it is just a day-by-day thing."

I smile at Vincent.

"We could sleep on the couch tonight?" he adds.

Simone's shoulders rise.

"Yeah," I say. "Why don't we just stay over?"

"Are you sure?"

"Yeah," we say. "Of course."

SIMONE GOES TO BED. VINCENT and I stand in the bathroom. I wait until we've spat our toothpaste out to whisper.

"I feel really sad she'd do that."

"Yeah."

"Should I feel guilty?" I ask.

"For what?"

"She didn't call me."

"I don't think that's your fault," he says. "She knows how to call."

"But maybe I've been less—"

"It's not your fault."

He hugs me before we retreat to the sofa bed, facing each other, wearing Simone's old Lao Gan Ma T-shirts.

"I think it's so special how close you and Simone are," he says. "How close you've always been."

"I guess it's the same with you and Fred."

Vincent purses his lips.

"Is it not?" I ask.

"I mean, yeah," Vincent says. "But we didn't go to uni together like you guys. And after our gap year we stopped speaking for a while."

"Why?"

"Hm." Vincent takes a breath. "We drifted, then drifted back, I suppose."

"It's good you guys found each other again."

"Yeah."

I nestle further into Vincent.

"I wrote a poem today."

"What about?" he asks, tucking some hair behind my ear.

"Some old memories."

"How did it feel?"

"It felt okay," I say, and then I think about what Vincent said about his dad, how beautiful I thought it was, and I know that I need to shuck the oyster, release the milky flesh. "But I've been feeling like a bit of a failure. When I write and don't think it's good, but also because of other stuff going on. I feel so bad saying it. It's so selfish. But those surrogacy pamphlets made me feel like a failure." I pause. "I'm not saying it's the same for me as women who learn they can't have kids, who have all the right parts but learn not everything's working in the way it needs to for children. I'm not saying it's the same—"

"But I imagine it might feel similar," he says.

"We'll never really know that—" I stop myself. Who am I appeasing? What am I trying to prove? "But it's just the standard you compare yourself to. I feel like I've less to offer."

"Max—"

"I know."

He hugs me.

"At least you're writing more," he says.

I sigh.

"Sometimes writing makes me feel like a loser, because I just remember those feelings of failure." Vincent's face melts into a sympathetic smile. I draw my finger along his sternum. "I really wanted to be a success, to be invited places to talk and read, and none of it really came to be. It feels like I'm picking the wound. I don't know, it all feels like an echo."

"Of what?"

"I don't know," I say. "Of how sad I get."

"I think I've been a bit anxious lately," he says.

"About your dad?"

"I don't know how to say it so it comes out right." He pauses. "I think moving in for a bit has made things feel very real. I'm just worried."

My stomach falls.

"About what?"

"I don't know. Sometimes I spiral over all the things I'd miss if we broke up. The echoes."

"I don't want to think about that, Vincent." I pull the blanket over my face, wrapping myself up.

I feel Vincent's arm around me, and his cheek on my rib.

"I'm not saying we're going to break up," he says. "Or that I want to. The opposite. I just wonder what would stick." He pauses. "You probably wouldn't like this, but I think if anyone mentioned poems or poetry I'd always think of you." He burrows his head into my armpit, such that his deep voice fills the cavern between sheet and skin. "I'd probably have to fight the urge to say my ex is a poet. And if someone mentioned Hong Kong I'd probably think of you, too, which is ridiculous because that's where my parents are from." He loosens his grip a little. "Or if I saw a White Rabbit I'd think of that weekend with you at your parents' and you trying to eat them." He imitates dramatic chomping, like a cow chewing cud. I laugh into him. We settle. "And I see you as so much more than this, but seeing news about trans people would probably make me think of you. I can imagine seeing a shitty headline and just thinking, I hope Max is feeling okay, and then feeling shit."

There's a moment of silence. I decide to play ball.

"I don't know if I could go back to the Korean place we go to," I say. "I'd probably avoid where your office is, and I'd think of you whenever I meet a corporate lawyer, which is too often. Also, I think I'd stop buying that high-protein yogurt. I'd just think about how much you like eating it and it'd make me sad."

"Could you go up a percentage?" He lifts himself from me. "Or do you think you'd just avoid the brand entirely?"

"Avoid it entirely."

I release my body from its cocoon. Cool air splashes across my face.

"I think I'm just feeling really porous at the moment," I say.

"What do you mean?"

"Like, I really feel like I absorb things. I feel more sensitive."

"Yeah," he says. "Same."

We stay still.

"This thing with my parents, Max."

I harden.

"Yeah?"

"It has nothing to do with you."

"I know," I say, though impassively, like the thought has sailed from brain to mouth, away from heart. "Sometimes it just feels like it."

"It shouldn't, though," he says. "You're at the center of things. For me, I mean."

"Okay," I say. "Okay."

Our breaths sync up on the mattress, and I wonder if I'm sold on being at the center of things. When you're the sun, you don't get much say as to what's sucked into your orbit. I don't want to be something through which other people plan. All I want is to be a speck, and Vincent a speck, too, floating in space together, almost as a unit, until something, if ever, forces our courses to split. The sentiment is sweet, nonetheless. I'm not sure I've ever been told I'm at the center of things. And then I remember the feeling of being in someone else's orbit, the determined tug of gravity around my waist, and how that was much worse.

XI

DR. PANDYA IS SHOWING ME A SCAN OF MY BRAIN ON A COMPUTER SCREEN. I have a brain tumor. The headaches got more intense, becoming the worst migraines I've ever had. I dismissed them, because—according to the internet—headaches rarely mean a brain tumor. I went to a GP, who referred me to Dr. Pandya, a neurologist, who, with the power of my job's private health insurance, ordered me a few scans. I booked our follow-up for a workday late morning, and now I'm here, in Dr. Pandya's consultation room, looking at her perfect skin while she tells me about my brain tumor. I wonder how long she's been on tretinoin. Can I ask her? Is that a medical question?

It's hard to imagine a world where Dr. Pandya's family isn't proud of her. How much training does it take to be a neurologist? I don't know, but she is a consultant, and she also looks my age. My parents would be proud of me if I was her. Not to say my parents aren't proud of me, but when they tell their friends that Maxine is working as a lawyer for a tech company, they don't tell them I sign off client emails with the robot's name rather than my own, or that I sometimes feed the AI misinformation so that I don't put myself out of a job. Dr. Pandya isn't even wearing foundation.

"Maxine?"

I look up, and Dr. Pandya tells me more. Research shows that the risk is cumulative when you take cyproterone acetate, my anti-androgen of choice. The longer you take it, the more it builds up in your body, and the more likely you are to develop the tumors. While the risk of tumors like these is very low—extremely low—they do happen, and they have happened to me. I already know about these kinds of tumors, because I was told about them when I started CPA.

I don't share with her that I'm familiar with the research, which is a little scant, and on the basis of that research I calculated that if I continued my HRT regimen for thirty-nine years, I would be at a 129 in 100,000 risk of developing one. Thirty-nine years, because I always thought I'd be kind of happy to make it just a little bit into my sixties. It'd be convenient. I barely contribute to my pension.

A hundred and twenty-nine in a hundred thousand is just over one in a thousand. I've long cycled through anti-androgens. It was spironolactone first. Mistake. My throat always felt dry, and my head was achy, and I pissed out all the water I drank, which was five liters a day. Then bicalutamide, which made sex and masturbation painful in a way it hadn't been before. Then CPA, which, aside from an initial two weeks of low mood and extreme lethargy, was almost perfect. A side effect, a very small side effect, especially at my dose of 12.5 mg every two days, was brain tumors. Meningiomas. What Dr. Pandya is telling me I have.

It occurs to me that we might've found it had I done the scan on New Year's Day. For the love of God, free me from the shackles of Caspar's staircase. I want to ask Dr. Pandya how badly I've messed up. It seems a waste not to—it's rare that a post-mortem of our mistakes can present such clear yes or no answers; usually the counterfactual is buried in other uncertainties. But I don't now want to draw attention to my idiocy, and Dr. Pandya can't undo the damage she's here to fix.

She shows me the scan and points to where the tumor has bubbled up in my brain.

"It's a sphenoid wing meningioma, which means above the ear and behind your eye. It's not encroaching on the optic nerve, yet. Fortunately." She points to the area that the tumor's in. "The tumor is the white mass."

"Right."

The white mass. White-on-white crime. The tumor is huge, and for the first time today my breath escapes me. I knew I was in for a tumor, but did it have to be so big?

"Most meningiomas are benign, meaning they don't spread, and your MRI gives indications that this is the case, so if it's removed then it's unlikely to recur." She takes a breath. "But we can't be certain until we have a sample that a pathologist can review in a lab."

"And you get the sample through—"

"Surgery."

I ask the only question that seems relevant or important. The one I've seen on television.

"What are my options?"

"Well, surgery," she says. "We'll arrange a consultation. Another option is monitoring, but I'm conscious the tumor is already quite large, and close enough to the optic nerve."

I feel ill. I am a white mass, growing whiter, about to eject a green mass onto the beautiful neurologist. She shifts on her stool. I appreciate the way she's sitting. Leaning forward, her elbows resting on her thighs. It's a posture that implies togetherness, as if it's me and her fighting this thing together. We are at the helm of the *Titanic.* I'm flying, Dr. Pandya! I meet her stare, and I know that I look like I'm caught in the headlights.

"Are you okay?" she asks.

"It's just a lot?"

"I'm sorry," she says.

Both of us look at the scan again. There it is, the tumor.

"I understand," she continues. "It sounds like a lot."

"Could surgery kill me?"

"The surgical consultant will go over all of this." She purses her lips. "But there are always some risks with surgery."

"Okay."

I have more questions. If I'm unlucky enough to have a tumor from CPA, am I more likely to get another since I'll always take CPA? Should I stop CPA? What do I tell my boyfriend? His dad had a heart attack recently. It feels like these may be questions for a different day. Dr. Pandya lets me go. We book in a date for a surgical consultation.

I've always thought that depressed or anxious people, or at least those who've flirted with depression or anxiety, may fare better in a crisis, because the worst has always been in their field of vision—looming in the corners of an already gray landscape. I have no evidence for this, except that I've been depressed and anxious—and sometimes think I might still be—and I have always been calm in a crisis.

I'm late for lunch with Aisha. I don't want to cancel, even if it almost feels inappropriate to go—a completely unserious course of action. At the same time, there are two options before me—believe that I'll be okay, or believe that I'll die—and in either case saying some hellos and goodbyes makes sense.

THE CAFE IS FULL, AND SO we're sitting on two stools facing out onto the junction between two busy streets. Our flat whites come. I take a sip, pulling at the milky heart on the surface.

"I went to the doctor today," I say.

"You did?"

The waiter is back to take our orders. Aisha orders the mackerel and potato salad with the in-house mayonnaise. I've had it before. It's not good, but my head is too scrambled to order anything different.

We swivel to face each other, our elbows on the green wooden table. A tumor. The drama. It's rare to have news that demands this kind of attention. It's not Munchausen's—I literally have a tumor.

"So, you went to the doctor?" she asks.

"I've got a tumor."

Aisha's face drops. She reaches out and holds my hand, remaining silent. I guess I'm supposed to continue.

"I'm going to be fine. It's at the front of my brain. Around there." I gesture around my skull with my hand. "It's kind of crazy, looking at an MRI of your brain, having a doctor point to a mass that shouldn't be there but is."

"You have brain cancer?"

"I don't think it's cancer," I say. "They think it's unlikely to be malignant."

"So it's okay?"

"No, they won't know for sure until they see it up close," I say, unable to stop myself from imagining the surgery, what it'll take to remove the thing in my head—the cutting, the peeling, the drilling. Cut. Peel. Drill. "But there are some risks." I roll the words around my mouth like a marble. "Like a small risk of death."

"How small?"

I feel like I can see a wobble in her lip. She looks genuinely scared. Why aren't I? All I feel is cold.

"I think quite small," I say. "I haven't had a surgical consultation. But, like, it is brain surgery, so I feel like there's always going to be some risk. I mean, they haven't actually told me."

This must be a coping mechanism. I'm shutting down, talking about a low risk of death as if it's a plantar wart. Panic starts to creep up on the edges like frost. I could die. I really don't want to die.

"It's going to be fine," I say.

Aisha takes her hand from mine and puts it to her chest.

"Okay," she says. "Okay. How did Vincent react?"

"I haven't told him yet." I take another sip of coffee. "I came straight here. He didn't even know about the appointment. I didn't want to freak him out, with everything with his dad."

Aisha looks alarmed.

"So you've told me before Vincent?"

"Only because I've seen you first," I say. "Don't tell Fred until I've had a chance to speak to Vincent. Please. I need to do it in person."

I think of Jamie. I should tell him, too, right? Our mackerel arrives, draped over the mounds of diced potato, a reclining pale lady in an oil painting. Aisha picks up her knife and fork. I hunch over my plate. The mackerel flakes apart. I look at her, and then I think of Jamie again. And then my parents.

"Are you okay, Max?" Aisha asks.

"I'm just thinking about my brother."

"And the tumor?"

"Yes. And the tumor."

"How do you think he'll react?" she asks.

"I don't know how he's going to react," I say. "I'm not sure I'm going to tell him."

"Max—"

"Family's hard, isn't it? There's already the whole thing with the baby, right?"

"What whole thing?"

"I mean, nothing new," I say, taking a bite of potato. It has a lot of kick. Not that easy with potato salad. "I just mean everyone has a lot on their plate right now."

It's true. Vincent's dad had a heart attack, my brother is having a baby, and Simone's had her own drama. There was fallout for Simone. Consequences. A large agency cutting ties. A few more models poached. After a certain age, if people don't become their families or partners then they become their jobs. Simone is no exception, and so her career almost imploding has been a trauma akin to a near-death experience.

Aisha holds her knife and fork in the polite way, combining everything to take a large mouthful. I realize how unkempt I must look next to her, bent over my plate. I'm trying to carve an igloo out of the potato salad. It collapses. I should've known better than to trust simple starches. There's nowhere to hide.

"Maybe just start with Vincent," she says. "Then work from there."

"Yeah," I say. "It'll be fine, though. We honestly don't have to talk about it."

Aisha nods, as if understanding that we don't have to means I don't want to. I deconstruct the mound of potato with my fork. We eat in silence.

"I think I might be cheating on Fred," she says.

I cough.

"No fucking way," I say. Aisha nods, wide-eyed. "Who is he? Or she? Or they?"

"He's my neighbor. As in, kind of, but across the road." She puts her cutlery down neatly on either side of her plate. "He's not even a world apart from Fred, except he has this, like, round, dumpling face," she says. I nod, imagining her making out with a giant char siew bao. "Sometimes you can see him masturbating in the window, one foot on the ledge. Me and Fred once saw him together, but one day I was working from home alone and I joined him."

"What?" I ask. "By the window?"

"Yeah."

"Can he definitely see you?"

"We've been doing it at the same time every week for a month." Aisha pauses. "And he gave me his number when we bumped into each other."

I'm surprised at Aisha. Would I have been surprised at Fred? I just don't think he'd wag his dick at his N1 neighbors. Does this make Aisha queer-adjacent? Whacking off in the window almost feels like a canonically gay experience. There's a lesson here, between this and the rug. Perhaps this is what they mean when they say people contain multitudes? Aisha groans.

"He's not even a world apart from Fred," she says again.

She and I aren't that close. We're new friends, so how does she know that I won't tell Vincent? Maybe we know each other at a convenient distance. I'm a bartender, a hairdresser, a nail tech. I don't know her well enough to call her out, to even know where her cheating falls in the broader constellation of her life.

I could just be something into which Aisha can blindly decant her words, but I also told her about the tumor, and before my boyfriend, and there's at least some relief in knowing her life is a mess, too. Perhaps it's a kindness from Aisha—call it schadenfreude, call it gratitude.

"What does he do?" I ask.

"He's an architect," she says. "He has, like, a skill."

"That's quite hot. He's probably really good at DIY."

"I don't know," she says, and then, as if to remind herself: "I still love Fred."

I don't move my face, but her expression sours, like my placidity has made a pointed accusation.

"I do," she asserts.

"I believe you."

I take another bite of my food.

"Can you be in love with two people at once?" she asks.

"Are you in love with window-man?"

"No," she says. "But what if it gets there? It doesn't mean that I don't love Fred, right?"

"I think you can be," I say. "In love with two people."

"How do you know?"

I clear my throat and sit up a little. Her elbow is on the table, her forearm holding up her head, looking at me.

"I don't know," I say.

Aisha lets out a low, steady, disappointed hum.

"I'm too young to be having an affair."

"Is it an affair?"

"Isn't it against the rules?"

"I feel like we get into relationships without knowing what the rules are."

"But it feels like a betrayal."

"Then I guess it's worth examining," I say. "People of all ages cheat."

"But to be married and cheat, to wank in front of someone else." She picks up her empty flat white and sips. There's no slurping; nothing drips from the cup. "It's an affair."

"Relationships sometimes allow for what a lot of people consider cheating," I say.

"Ours doesn't," she says. "We're not like that."

Lots of gay couples would actually find this very exciting, but I don't think telling her will help. Sometimes I forget that Aisha's my age. There's a togetherness in Aisha that betrays thirty-one. How old do I seem?

"And being divorced. It's, like, something I thought could happen when I was, like, fifty, but now I could literally be divorced. I mean, what the fuck, Max?"

Poor Fred, whose happiness seems semi-contingent on marriage. Still, divorced at thirty-one doesn't sound too bad. I think it'd be quite on brand for me. Simone would think it was chic, my parents would be amazed I had gotten married in the first place, and Jamie would probably say he knew it would happen. It's never too late to start over, and thirty-one doesn't feel late at all. Lots of people, like me, are at the beginning. I don't want to die.

"You don't have to get divorced," I say. "I think there's a set way people expect you to react to these things, but life's more complicated."

"Mm."

We sit in silence for a few moments.

"I kind of always imagined I'd get a brain tumor," I say. "And now I have one."

Her head drops into her hands.

"Shit, Max, I'm so sorry, what am I saying?" she says. "You have a brain tumor."

"I'm not saying it to minimize anything, Aish." I've never called her Aish before. "I'm just saying you can't really plan for tumors or falling in love." I pause to clear my throat. "Divorce can be a freeing thing."

"Can a brain tumor be?" she asks.

"Probably not."

I wonder if they'd be better off without each other. Part of me thinks so, but I really don't know—I'm sure not even Fred and Aisha know. My phone, face-up on the table, lights up. It's Jamie. Aisha and I stare at it. I reach to answer, expecting him to somehow know about the tumor, to scold me for telling Aisha first.

"Max," he says. "Can you come over for dinner?"

He sounds distressed, the same staccato rhythm of flustered speech he'd call me with the night before his university exams, early in the morning in Hong Kong, telling me he was going to fail. The way he still occasionally does with cases. But he usually launches into the root of his stress, never an invitation.

"Are you okay?" I ask.

"Can you just come over for dinner?" he asks, hurriedly.

"Why don't I come round now?"

"I'm working," he says. "I'll be done at six."

Ah. Shit. I'm at work, too. I forgot. This is my work break.

"Jamie," I say. "Are you okay?"

"I'll see you later," he says, hanging up.

I picture him in his work clothes—an ironed shirt and trousers even at home—pulling his hair out, dark rings around his eyes. My heart fills with worry.

"Is he okay?" Aisha asks.

"I don't know."

I stare at my phone, screen locked to onyx, and for a moment I feel relieved, to worry about someone who isn't myself.

* * *

I DON'T USE THE BRAIN tumor to escape the office. In fact, I go back, because if I'm home alone all I'll think about is the tumor. Is this why people are so burned out? Answering emails on their deathbeds. I take my seat next to my colleague, Maeve.

"You were gone for a while!" she says.

"My doctor's appointment ran over."

Even with her enthusiastic, purely observational sincerity, I still feel defensive.

"Everything okay?" she asks.

"All good. Were you out for lunch?"

"I went to that new sushi place with a friend," she says. "The one round the corner."

"Was it good?"

"It was too spicy."

"What?"

"They put wasabi between the fish and rice."

I'm so hollowed out that I can't even laugh at her. I stay at my desk for a little while longer, going through contracts that some juniors have marked up. I start writing notes on how they can follow my already detailed instructions better. I'm not going to die, but if I was going to die, would this be how I'd want to spend my final days? I think about Queen Latifah in *Last Holiday*, in which she finds out she has a brain tumor and liquidates her assets to go on a luxury ski holiday in the Czech Republic. It turns out she's misdiagnosed, but she has a new circle of wealthy friends and starts a successful restaurant. My life is not a movie. You can't live like you're dying unless you're definitely dying. It's irresponsible. The nerves, or fear, find their way to my hands as I type.

I have to get up. I go to the bathroom and cry, staring at the cursive vinyl on the wall. You get what you wish for, except wish is crossed out and replaced with work. What the fuck did I do to get a tumor? I don't want to die. I really don't want to die.

* * *

JAMIE LETS ME IN WITH a quick wave, phone to his ear on a work call. I'm ten minutes early, and I see a flash of annoyance cross his face. I start taking the groceries out of my bag while he finishes his call upstairs. Jamie lives on the top two floors of a Georgian terrace in De Beauvoir. He bought it move-in ready. It's a few cuts above a flipped home—herringbone floors with solid wood, stone countertops, long pendant light fixtures—but it's plain. Jamie wouldn't think to decorate. He's too busy. He wants convenience. He wants things to be nice, not charming.

He trundles down the stairs when he's done. Without a word, he falls onto his large, green velvet sofa, and screams into a matching pillow with beige trimming. The screaming stops only for a moment before it starts again. I clutch the bag of pappardelle so hard that it cracks. I put it down, then wander over to Jamie, perch by his outstretched body and place a hand on his knotted shoulder. When he finally stops, he turns his head. His eyes are red. This is too wordless, too guttural. I feel both scared and incapable. In the pit of my stomach, I know that something terrible has happened either with work or the baby. I'm not sure which one would be worse for him.

"Are you okay?"

He looks up at me like I'm stupid.

"No, Max." His arm contorts so that he can wipe his eyes with the back of his hand. He looks like a mangled corpse. "Maria called me this morning. She's having an abortion."

"Fuck," I say. "What did you say?"

"What could I say, Max?" His voice is angry, and I want to tell him not to take that tone with me, but I tell myself he's just lost a baby, even if I'm not sure it was really his baby to lose. "She said I wasn't going to change and that she knew the baby wouldn't be a priority for me, and that she didn't want to do it alone. I tipped her over the fence."

"Could you still—"

"It's already gone," he shouts, shaking his hands.

My eyes go to the stacks of books on parenting. I wonder if he'd made real headway with them, but it'd be cruel to ask. I rub my hand along his back, reminding myself that words might be of little use. And what words would there be to say? There may never be a good time to tell Jamie that Maria might've been right, that maybe he simply wasn't ready. It's hard to be sure if you're ready for anything, but I think you have to create space for things. Little grows in dark, cluttered rooms.

"I'm so sorry, Jamie."

We stay put for a long while, until he gets up and walks upstairs. For some reason, I follow him to the bedroom door, which he slams behind him. I usually feel resilient to his moods, but the weight of the day has caught up with me. Maria has aborted a fetus. I have a tumor, possibly an operation to excise it that could kill me. A tear trickles down my cheek. It doesn't make sense to do much else other than cook.

I put a pot on to boil, then begin to slice the tomatoes along their equator. When I was a teenager I heard Nigella refer to the midsection of a cherry tomato as its equator and I've been saying it ever since. Glugs of expensive olive oil drip into the Le Creuset pot. The edges of the garlic slices shrink and crispen. I put the harissa in, and then the tomatoes, salty pasta water, and then some capers and lemon zest. My eyes feel crinkly from dried-out tears.

Jamie comes back down when the food is nearly ready. People have had babies for years, and if microplastics don't sterilize us to extinction, people will go on having babies for years after. It's not a revelation that having a baby and being a parent are different things, that it takes more than the former to be the latter; it isn't a revelation, it's just a reminder that life is rarely ideal for anyone. There is probably a world in which Maria would've been happy to have the baby, and so she, too, is probably disappointed. It's not schadenfreude, but it's perspective. Jamie sets the table.

"Thank you," he says.

"Of course," I say, taking a bite. "I'm sorry again, Jamie. It's just—"

"It's what?" he asks, accusatorily, mouth full of pasta.

"Nothing," I say. "I was just going to say that it might be confusing now, but it might make sense later. You just need to take it day by day—"

"Fucking hell, Max," he groans, face in his hands. "Please don't patronize me with that day-by-day shit. This is the worst thing that's ever happened to me. Can we just sit with that?"

We sit with it. I'm slapped silent. Jamie's a dick, but he's in pain. I tear up again. He could try harder to be nice, but he's managing in the way he knows how to. I want to tell him about my tumor, to make him know he's being terrible, that he's not the only person in the world with problems. He looks at me as if there's something wrong with me, and then as if there's something wrong.

"I have something to tell you," I say.

Jamie's eyes swing up and his eyebrows rise. The deep, static grooves always on his forehead deepen and widen.

"What?"

"I have a brain tumor."

Jamie's jaw drops. He puts his fork down and puts his face back into his hands.

"It's likely benign. It's just there, like, this thing inside my head."

Jamie's face is still in his hands. I feel better.

"I'll probably have to have surgery to remove it."

"Is that dangerous?"

"I guess," I say. "They're cutting into my brain, Jamie. But it's not too close to the optic nerve yet," I add with confidence, as if I really know what that means.

Jamie's forearms move square on the table. He arches over his pasta.

"Okay. Not near the optic nerve," he says, resetting, as if he also knows what any of this means. "So we might be okay." He twirls his fork in one hand, and holds my hand with the other, giving it a quick squeeze. I watch as the pasta runs around the tines. I love that Jamie says we, but then I remember he also once said that both he and Maria were pregnant. We do not have a tumor.

"There's a chance of recurrence," I say. "And death."

He looks back up at me. I feel bad for trying to manipulate him, even though I'm not lying.

"It's small," I say. "I think."

He purses his lips. I can't help but feel he's processed it too quickly, which makes me think that he hasn't processed it at all. Why isn't he asking more questions?

"I feel like you're not registering this," I say.

"What?"

"You're not asking any questions."

"Give it a fucking second, Max," he says. "It's a lot to take in. Sorry." He sighs, gets up to refill his water at the sink, his back to me. "What comes next?"

"A surgical consultation," I say. "In a few days. I feel like the doctor didn't talk me enough through the risks."

"She should've told you."

"She's not a surgeon, though."

"But she can't leave you in limbo." He puts his glass of water hard on the table. "Have you told Vincent?"

"No."

"Why not?"

"I only found out today. It's something you'd do in person, right?" He nods.

"I'll tell him tonight," I say.

"Mum and Dad?" he asks.

"Tomorrow."

Worst for last. I imagine Mum's practical panic. *When's the surgery date? Are you taking supplements? C? D? B12? My friend from Hong Kong had a tumor last year. She died. This is serious, Max.* Dad's response would be just as unsatisfying. *Oh. Oh, dear. Well, we'll just have to hope for the best.* I can't be bothered with them.

"You're going to be fine," Jamie says, quick to resume his fragile rationality. "That's what matters. You're going to be fine."

"We don't know that."

"I'm just trying to be positive."

His reality at whose expense, I wonder. Regardless, I don't know what I want from him, or why. It's like asking a fish to bark.

"Yeah," I say.

I've barely touched my food. I dive in, one large bite at a time, probably swallowing capers and olives whole.

"You know what's stupid?" he asks.

"What?"

"I even booked a spa weekend for us last-minute," Jamie says, face back toward his plate. "For me and Maria. Next week."

"Really?"

"I was gonna surprise her."

"What if Maria had plans?"

"Maybe you and Vincent can go instead," Jamie says, ignoring my question.

"Why don't we go instead?" I ask.

"I don't know."

He doesn't lift his head from his plate.

"Okay," I say. "Let's decide later."

I'M STILL AWAKE WHEN VINCENT gets in, but I pretend not to be. There's a delicacy to his movements, a softness to the unfastening of his belt, to the removal of his trousers, his opening of doors. He comes to bed, and I turn over and place my head on his shoulder. He holds my forearm, draped across his body.

I could tell him now, but the scene is too gentle, too perfect for a tumor. He's moved in, and quickly and unexpectedly this flat has become a safehouse from the ills of work and family trauma. I ask myself, why corrupt the comfort? Why ruin a nice thing? No real answers come to me, other than the virtue of truth. But the truth will stick around until tomorrow. It can wait.

Come the morning, I hear things cooking. I smell soy sauce and ginger and oil.

When I go to the kitchen, Vincent, who's stirring a large pot of congee in a bathrobe, turns to face me. There's a mound of Spam cut into matchsticks next to a pile of pork floss on the counter.

"I woke up in a good mood," he says. "Thought I'd make a special breakfast."

A special breakfast. It's funny that in many parts of the world, ones with which Vincent and I are familiar, congee is painfully ordinary, and yet here it feels so special.

"Is that youtiao?" I ask, looking at the long fingers of fried dough on paper towels.

"Yup."

"You must've been up so early."

"I've been wanting to make it for ages."

We used to eat youtiao for breakfast in Hong Kong, though we never made it at home. When I was fourteen and read *The Grapes of Wrath* I would go to bed with a rumbling stomach. My only memory of that long, depressing-ass book is the mother frying dough because they were too poor to eat anything else. I was probably supposed to find it sad, but all I could think about was how much I love fried dough.

He ladles the gloopy porridge into a bowl for me, then drips some Kikkoman soy sauce over the top—ink over a wet canvas—scallions, Spam, and a little bit of pork floss, and then the youtiao across the top of the bowl. We eat across from each other at the round table in my living room. I look down at my spoon, at the unsure borders of rice, a gummy pool of burst cells. I feel a tingle in my head, and then I think about the tumor.

"I have to tell you something," I say.

He looks at me, congee dripping from his lips, like a rice paddy came in his mouth. I can't help but worry that it might all be too much, that all the stress with his father, together, may be more than he can handle. He's not going to chuck his father. I'm far more disposable.

"I'm going to be fine," I say, careful not to elicit panic. "But I went to a neurologist recently, and I have to have a surgical consultation soon." His mouth opens. I'm telling this all back to front, but I'm just trying to assess how to cause the least harm, how to make my tumor less of an imposition, an affront. On arranging words by impact, tumor ranks higher than surgery, even with likely benign as a prefix. "I have a brain tumor. It's likely benign."

Vincent drops his spoon; it disappears into a grave of bloated grain. "What?"

Tears form in his eyes already. He wipes his mouth and starts pacing around.

"I'm sorry," I say.

I go on to explain what might lie ahead, and with each word Vincent crumbles. I feel steady as I do it, as if he feels what I should feel, or can't, and it's a relief. As I calm him down, I start to believe the things I say.

He turns to me, eyes wet, hands on his hips. The contrast between his and Jamie's reactions is stark. No cold shutting down, but a little catastrophizing, and even though it could help Vincent to shut down a little, his reaction makes me feel cared for. It's a reaction raised in love and not neglect. It makes me feel loved, and guilty, for basking in his alarm.

"Do you think the scan from New Year's—"

"I don't know," I say, my eyes too heavy with shame to meet his. "I couldn't ask."

"Okay," he says. "Okay. It doesn't matter."

"It's probably benign," I repeat. "We don't need to worry."

He shushes me.

"Should I take time off work?" he asks.

"You don't have to."

"I'm going to."

He holds my hand and I start crying, too, because I see again the fear in his eyes, like he's worried I might really die. He's genuinely scared about something bad happening to me. It'd be fucked up if I'd made this up—completely—but if I'd known he would look at me like this, then it would almost have been worth it.

VINCENT

XII

THE STRETCH OF SEA CONNECTING KOH SAMUI AND KOH PHANGAN IS choppy, and the pointed nose of the boat thumps along the waves. Each time it drops, the vinyl edges of the orange life jacket scratch into my shoulders.

We're near the front of the boat, Alex and Fred behind me. Spritzes of seawater fly into my eyes, and as I'm about to rub them I remember the neon dots that Alex painted on my face. A line that starts above one eyebrow and ends beneath the other eye. I allow the itch to rise and fall unattended.

"Why's your hair up?" Fred asks.

"So it's not in your face," she says.

"I wouldn't mind that."

I sigh. Please stop.

"Do unto others," Alex says.

"Categorical Imperative," Fred replies.

Can this get any worse?

"What?" she asks.

"What you said," he says. "It comes from Kant."

"Who you calling a cunt?" Alex asks.

"He's a phil—"

"I know who Kant is."

They laugh. Why is he doing this? Why does she like it? Alex and Fred haven't hooked up, but I have a bad feeling, like it's inevitable. I can't tell them not to do it. Seeing them has made it crystal clear to me that I like her, which makes the feeling that she's getting further and further away unbearable. Maybe I could've just said how I feel to Fred, but it's too late now, and I'm angry at him. For no good reason other than he's enjoying himself.

"How are you doing, Vinny?" Alex asks.

"I'm good."

I hate that she calls me Vinny now, how some of Fred is rubbing off on her. It doesn't sound right coming out of her mouth. It doesn't feel right coming out of anyone's mouth. There's no way to correct her without it sounding like I'm telling her off. Don't call me Vinny! I prefer Vincent. I know what response it'd elicit. From her. From Fred. *What's the big deal? Literally everyone calls you Vinny.* And then I'd explain that it's always bothered me, that I've never really liked it, and then the question becomes: why didn't you say something earlier? And that speaks to something else even more embarrassing. Spinelessness. But I'd rather be spineless than stop being spineless and have people think I'm spineless.

"Do you get seasick?" Alex asks.

"Nah," I say. "Do you?"

"A little, yeah," she says. "I thought you might because your eyes are shut."

"Shutting your eyes actually makes seasickness worse," I say. "Water's just getting in them."

"You're probably taking the hit for the rest of us."

She places her head on my shoulder. I keep looking forward. I hope I smell okay. I just want to stay close to her. I've missed the window. I try to remind myself that nothing can happen between them. She wouldn't let it. He wouldn't be down.

THE MUSIC'S STARTED. HYPNOTIC TRANCE. There are fire dancers on tall wooden podiums surrounding a dance floor, and stairs up to a bar area with more seats. It's just like an outdoor club. People clap as a fire dancer shoots wide, streaky flames from his mouth. To some people this would be hell, and I think it might be close to mine. We order a jug of watery margarita from the bar, pouring ourselves glasses while we sit at one of the tables by the dance floor. We're in that in-between place, not drunk enough to have a lot of fun, sober enough to start feeling tired. We commit, observing what's around us as we suck the sugary drink up our straws. I take some cash out of my backpack to buy another jug, and we motor through that, too.

"Should we get a shroom shake?" Fred asks. I look at Alex, who looks at me. "C'mon, man."

So I'm the problem. I nod.

Fred heads off and returns with one in hand. We take tentative sips, passing it among us before we start gulping it down and move to the dance floor. What would my parents think if I came home and told them about this? Mum would dig out articles about tourists who run into the jungle or the sea after taking psychedelics. *What if this was you!* Dad would wait until the table fell silent to chime in. *Say no to drugs.*

The three of us stay close to one another, and the sparks I saw between Alex and Fred seem to have fizzled a little. We're here together. It's one of those moments when your head's out of the woods and you can finally think rationally, and you realize that all the panic was silly and you had nothing to worry about. Why would something happen between Alex and Fred? I've been making up signs in my head. She wouldn't hook up with him. He wouldn't go for it if he knew, and if he went for it then he'd know.

I feel a little nauseous, but I have energy, and I'm not really sure I see anything, like visuals and shit, but when I look at some of the club lights above me, those dancing radar streams, it's like they're pulsing a little. Do lights always pulse? Is that just how lights are? All three of us are in a sweaty pit of dancers. I don't think we've left for a few hours. Not even a break. This is great! Maybe it's the alcohol, the shrooms, or the fire. Maybe all clubs should have fire dancers? It adds something. It really does. I don't know what. Fire, obviously. But something else, too. I really need the toilet.

I put my arms around Fred and Alex.

"I'm going to head to the loo, guys," I say.

I maneuver out of the crowd and join the queue upstairs for the toilets. As I lock the door, I realize I need to poo, finding reserves of toilet paper I took from the hostel in my pocket. Am I high? My tank top's a sweaty rag at this point. I flush and head to the balcony where you can see the dance floor below. I spot Fred and Alex, dancing close. All I had to do was leave, and they're back on each other. I stand there, watching them, blaming myself for taking a shit.

I need another drink. I just want them to pull away from each other, because for a moment on the dance floor I really believed that it was all over, that I was crazy, that I could finally chill out. It's hard, because I thought the shrooms would dull the glow between them, but they've probably just made them feel more intensely. I feel more intensely. I like Alex. Really like Alex. I've fucked it all up.

I order a beer, and when I go back downstairs, they pull away from each other. That's a good thing! A really good thing! I don't care if I'm cock-blocking. We're dancing together again, and I give Fred and Alex sips of my beer. Would I ever have a threesome? Fuck. Threesome with Fred. I would rather die a virgin. I'm not a virgin, though. For real. We dance a bit more. When I check my phone, it's three A.M.

"Could we take a break for a bit?" Alex asks.

We head back out of the crowd and sit at a table upstairs. We're all drunk and loopy. Fred's hand is on Alex's thigh. His greasy fucking hands. I look away from them, into the crowd, and my eyes are swallowed by the dancing bodies, ninety percent white people, clunking around to this stupid music. I start to feel a bit cold. All the sweat on my body is drying.

When I look back at Alex and Fred, they're kissing. What the fuck? At the table? This is too much—I don't want to be here. Why would anyone want to be here? It's terrible. And I realize fully that I can't really stop anything. Things are going to be the way they're going to be. It doesn't mean I have to see it.

"Guys," I say.

They laugh, faces still close, then separate.

"I'm going to head to the pier," I say. "I think I'd rather just chill there."

"Are you sure?" Fred asks.

"You can't go alone," Alex says.

"I can, honestly. I just need a time-out. We'll get an early spot in the queue. You can just cut. You should enjoy the rest of it."

Alex looks unsure, like she's reading the start of an article about a missing tourist.

"Only if you're sure," Fred says.

I can't tell if he's pleased I'm fucking off, but I don't care. I need space.

"Yeah, it's cool, man."

We hug goodbye, and then I hug Alex.

"Be safe, okay?" she says.

I buy some fried chicken from a stall outside the party. It's going to be a long fucking wait on the pier. That's what everyone we've spoken to said. *Get to the fucking pier!* I decline a CD with some of the music from the night—track upon track of shitty trance—and walk the long way back. I'm one of the first in the queue. I lie down with my legs over the edge and my back flat on the wood, wishing I'd taken a CD so that I could at least have something to read. I shut my eyes. She's just a girl. There'll be more Alexes. But will there? It feels so stupid to be so scared, to have allowed those feelings to swallow me whole. Time goes by, and my eyes grow heavy and I fall asleep.

"Vincent!" voices call.

I sit up and look toward the other end of the pier. It's Fred and Alex. Why can't they leave me alone? There are protests along the pier about jumping the queue, but Alex and Fred ignore them.

They can tell I don't want to talk, and so we sit in silence. The boat comes a few minutes later. About a third of the queue, including us, gets on.

"Pier wankers!" Fred shouts.

So fucking embarrassing. Alex laughs. Why is she laughing? The crowd looks at Fred in disbelief. I want to crawl further into myself. Fred puts his arm around my shoulders.

"Thanks so much for queuing, man," Fred says.

I can see Alex and Fred holding hands from the corner of my eye, and I pretend to go to sleep so that they don't think I'm in a mood. It's hard to put my feelings into words that aren't petty. I'm jealous and angry and I hate myself for doing this to myself, for letting it happen like this. I imagine a thousand scenarios at once, and in all of them I handle it better. Tell Fred I like her. Just go for it with Alex and swear her to secrecy about the trans thing. She wouldn't have wanted Fred to know, anyway. Any other outcome than this would've been better—I've pulled the short straw.

We travel through the bobbing water in silence, watching the clusters of islands pass by, fluffy green hernias protruding from the sea, far away. We reach the shore and get a tuk-tuk back to the hostel. Alex sits in the back with me. I don't want her company.

When we arrive, Alex and Fred drop behind me, and I don't turn back because I know what it means. They don't have to say anything, and I don't want them to say anything. I take a shower under the now-flickering bulb, and I lie in bed, but I can't go to sleep. I want something to take my mind off things. I'd take anything. I want to punch a wall, but I'm not the kind of guy who punches a fucking wall. I'm too dehydrated to sleep, which means my mind is going in circles, but I'm too tired to get up for some water.

After half an hour, Fred knocks on the door. I wait until the third round of knocking before opening it. Stupid grin on his face, like he's discovered penicillin or something.

"Where's your key?" I ask.

"I think I lost it." He yawns. "I'll pay for it, don't worry."

He showers as I lie in bed. Does he know? If they had sex then he must do. Please don't say they had sex. I hate Fred. And Alex. It was wrong of them to fuck with me. Fred comes out of the shower, naked except for his boxers, and dives into bed with his hair still wet. We make eye contact, and it's a mistake because as soon as we do, he smiles, rolls onto his back and starts talking.

"Such a fucking cocktease," he says.

"What?"

"Alex."

"What do you mean?"

"She sucked my dick, but she wouldn't do anything else." He pauses, laughing. "I came on her tits, though."

I feel like I could explode. I'm in a heavyweight match between rage and disgust, in a ring roped with resentment and desire. I want to punish him, and the only way I know how is to shame him, and for someone who's got so little shame, I know there's only one thing I can say. The words come out like vomit. I can't stop them.

"You know she's a man, right?"

Fred laughs.

"Shut up, Vincent," he says.

"I'm not fucking kidding," I say. "She used to be a boy. I'm not kidding."

He laughs again.

"I'm not kidding," I repeat.

He just smiles, but when he sees that my face hasn't moved, he begins to register that what I'm saying could be true, that I'm not kidding.

"What?" He sits up.

"She used to be a man. She's transgender."

There's disbelief in his soft posture, but there's anxiety in his skittish arms and legs.

"There's no way."

"I'm not lying, man," I say, my tone accusatory. Of what? I don't even know. "It's true. I didn't think you'd actually do anything."

"Are you fucking with me?"

I'm trying to seem calm. Serious. I want him to believe me.

"How do you fucking know?" he asks.

"Some girl told me in Bangkok," I say. "She's in Thailand to get surgery. I'm assuming it's to do with that."

"She has a dick?"

Fred tussles with the blanket as he stands up, and he starts pacing around the room. I've never seen him like this, a foul mix of confusion and anger and disgust. He picks up the shorts he's thrown onto the floor.

"What are you doing?" I ask.

I'm suddenly filled with panic, the kind of panic that slows the world around you. He charges out of the room. I'm standing at the open doorway, knowing I need to do something. He looked so angry, like he was going to fuck something up. And then I realize what he's going to do. Fuck her up. I start running up the stairs, then along the patio toward her room, and soon I can hear crying and then Fred's angry voice.

"Faggot," he shouts. "Fucking faggot."

I burst through Alex's door. Fred's standing there. I can see Alex holding her knees at the far end of the room, crying, her shorts at her ankles. Blood's running down her nose, onto her tank top, a smear on her shorts. She's blubbering, saying something that sounds like no.

I turn to Fred, whose face shows he knows he's done something very wrong. The anger in his expression is gone, like he'd been sleepwalking and someone's woken him up. He stares at his hands. It's as if he's been framed, like the adrenaline obliterated his memory, a comatose hurricane.

"She—he—he fucking lied to me, man," he says. "I'm not fucking gay. I'm not fucking gay."

It's a bloody mess, this, and it's my fault. If I hadn't said something to Fred, then Alex wouldn't be on the floor, scrunched up like a ball of paper, red all over. Fred's standing there, waiting for me to do something, like a bystander gawking at a car crash.

"Just go, man," I say.

"What?"

"Just go back to the room."

Fred looks at his splotchy fist once more, then leaves, closing the door behind him. I take a few steps toward Alex.

"How did he know?" she cries. "How did he fucking know?"

"I told him."

She looks at me through eyes congealed with tears and mucus and obscured by bits of wet hair. She looks too tired to piece together how I knew to begin with. I expect her to be mad, but she just keeps crying, and then I kneel and hold her hand, and then she puts her arm over my shoulder, and we stand up and limp together, a clunky three-legged race to the bathroom. The fold in her body, the hunch in her back, tells me Fred didn't just hit her nose, but that he got a few kicks in, too. When we get to the bathroom, I let her sit on the toilet and she holds her head up. I've never done anything like this before, but I follow my instincts. I take the white, thin, scratchy hand towel, wet it under the running tap, and then dab it around Alex's bloodied nose, catching what's still wet and reintroducing moisture into what's dry, pulling and drawing it onto the fibers of the towel. Somehow I know that bedside manner outrides medical expertise; cells repair and link and join and organize, but the soul is porcelain. It feels important that I'm careful, that I care. I can't believe I fucking did this.

"It doesn't look broken," I say. "Your nose, I mean."

"Why did you tell him?" she asks, still sniffling.

"I don't know," I say. "I'm sorry."

She nods, almost imperceptibly. When my cottoned fingers wander too close to the curve of her nostrils, where the sides sew into her face, she winces, and so I withdraw and reapproach more delicately. I'm focusing hard because I know that if I don't, all that's there for me is guilt. After her face is cleaned up, and we can see for sure that her nose isn't broken, I hold each of her limp arms and inspect for damage, stains, marks. I wipe some blood away from her fingers.

When she's clean, she puts an arm around my shoulders and we stand up again. She turns her head to look in the mirror, and then the weight of her arm on my shoulder lessens, like seeing all the blood wiped away relieves some of the pain. We walk slowly toward the bed, and I tuck her into the sheets.

I wonder what Fred's thinking. He shouldn't have hit her. He really shouldn't have hit her. Was she in the wrong? Why did she have to go and suck his dick? Come on, Alex. Maybe it's wrong to trap a guy like that. I'm in the wrong, though. I know that. I don't have much else to focus on now. Regret pours in. My phone's in my pocket. Fred hasn't messaged me. I text him, but he doesn't respond.

It's seven A.M. Is that how little time has passed? Maybe I could go back to the room, but I don't think I want to see him. I know she probably should've told him, but he shouldn't have beaten her up. She shuts her eyes and slides down the pillow a little.

"Can you stay here, please?" she asks.

"Yeah," I say. "Sure."

"I just feel . . ." She pauses. "I feel, like—"

"It's fine," I say. "You don't have to explain."

AT FOUR P.M. ALEX STIRS, and I know that I'll face whatever interrogation I escaped this morning. I leave the room to get us some food and buy some time. As I wait for the takeaway, I think of what I'll say when she asks the inevitable. I backdate a few principles, a few courses of action. It feels simpler.

When I come back, she's sitting upright in the bed, and I can see more clearly that her left eye is bruised, and then shame washes over me, like it was my fist instead of Fred's, because it might as well have been.

"I brought some food," I say.

Steam clouds out of the polystyrene boxes. Alex stabs the bedspread with the plastic-sheathed chopsticks. She pokes the pad Thai around a little and takes a small mouthful. I open my own box and try to eat, but my eyes just drift back to her. After she swallows her first bite, she sets the box down.

"How did you know?" she asks, looking at me plainly.

"Bex," I say. "From the other hostel."

"Fucking bitch."

She picks up the box and starts poking again.

"Why didn't you tell me?" I ask.

"I don't know, Vincent," she says. "I don't owe you that information. I don't really owe anyone that information."

"I know, but—"

"And why did you tell Fred?"

"What do you mean?" I ask, as if I can skirt around the question forever.

"That I'm trans," she says, eyes on the food, mouth full.

"I just thought it was the right thing to do," I lie.

Alex sighs and puts the box on the bedside table. I can't look at her, so I keep my head down. I bite into a bit of fibrous, parched chicken.

"But he didn't know," she says, almost pleadingly.

"But he might've not done it if he knew," I say. "That's the point, right?"

"But he was attracted to me."

"But what if he's not attracted to the parts?"

"He didn't see the parts." Her voice becomes irate. "I didn't let him." I know that. I stop eating. The food doesn't taste like anything.

"If you think I'm in the wrong, then why did you stay?" she asks.

I think of something else to ask, afraid of the question, of my answer.

"Why are you in Thailand, Alex?"

"For surgery."

"What surgery?"

"That surgery."

"Right," I say.

Bex wasn't lying. If I'd met Alex later, then nobody would've had to discover anything. I feel a little excavated, like I've scooped myself out of myself.

"Are you okay?" she asks.

"Yeah," I reply, sitting back up on the bed, separating myself from Alex. "I should check my phone."

There are a slew of messages from Fred.

Hey man, can we talk?

Where are you, Vinny?

Vincent I'm serious we seriously need to talk . . .

I'm heading out for some food . . . I'll be back in our room in a bit.

The last message was twenty minutes ago.

"I should go see Fred," I say, and her face falls a little. He's already in the room—the black and blue on her face, the slice in her lip. "He's been messaging me. I'll be back, though, okay? We probably need to sort stuff out with the room. We're supposed to be leaving tomorrow."

Alex whimpers. It's a funny sound, but she has every right to sulk.

"I don't think I can leave tomorrow," she says.

"I know," I say. "I know. Let me just sort this out, okay?"

Alex reaches for my hand, and for a second, I flinch, but then I take her hand in mine and squeeze, gently.

I go down the stairs and turn right to my and Fred's room. The door's ajar. Fred's sitting at the end of his bed with a takeaway box on his lap, and he looks up at me when I come in. His eyes are red. He looks unclean. There are sweat patches in the armpits of his gray T-shirt.

"Where have you been, man?" he asks.

"With Alex."

"I fucked up," he says, rambling into his palms. "I fucked up."

I feel angry, like he's groveling at my feet for forgiveness that I can't give. I imagine myself kicking his head back, blood spraying up from his nose and onto the ceiling. I don't know what to say. Our stares meet each other's, his becoming more and more vacant.

"She can barely walk," I say.

He waits for more. I don't want to make this easy for him.

"There was a lot of blood." I cross my arms. "We—" I pause. "You beat her really bad, Fred."

I look away from him.

"Vincent," he says.

"I don't want to look at you."

"Fuck," he says, crying into his hands. "Fuck."

He groans. I look back at him. He pushes his palms into his eyes. I have no idea what else to say. I get that guys can be aggressive, I know how mad I sometimes get, and I've seen him mad, but Fred's not a violent person. He's punched cracks in his self-image. I know that some men hit women, then say they're sorry for it, that they hate themselves, and do it all again, but I don't think that's who Fred is.

"That wasn't you, man," I say.

"I know." He whimpers. "I know. Is she okay?"

"No," I reply. "But she'll heal."

He wipes his eyes and nose with the back of his hand.

"It wasn't you, Fred."

I don't know why I keep saying that. It feels wrong. It's like we're trying to convince ourselves we're not terrible, masking our disappointment in ourselves and other people. Me comforting Fred. Alex forgiving me. Fred asking about Alex.

Fred cries some more. I stroke my hand across his back, because I allow myself to pity him and I think it's what he needs. I think about Alex alone in the room upstairs, and how I'd rather be there than here, because even if it's true that this wasn't like Fred, I still don't know if I should be rewarding him with my comfort, to show him that he can do shit like that and still deserve affection. His noises subside. I release my arm and he draws his back up a little, so that he's only slightly hunched over his knees.

"Is she going to call the police?" he asks.

I feel angry again. Fred only caring about himself. Worrying if he'll get in trouble back home. I get up from the bed and brush the staleness out from my mouth in the bathroom. I stare at my face in the mirror. Tired eyes. Lines across my forehead.

"Vincent," Fred calls. "Do you think she's going to call the police?"

Christ, Fred.

"She could probably say that it's a hate crime," I say, brushing my bottom molars.

"What?"

I spit out the toothpaste. Streaks of red slash through the white.

"Vincent?"

"I said she could probably say that it's a hate crime."

"Fuck."

I could keep playing this game, but what's the point? I walk back into the room and pat my hands dry on my shorts.

"I don't think she's going to the police, though."

Relief washes over Fred's face. He hinges his back toward the bed, covers his face with his hands and sighs, lets out something between a laugh and a cry. I really want to hit him. I sit on the end of my bed and lie back, too.

"What are you going to do?" I ask.

Fred releases his hands from his face and turns to me.

"What do you mean?"

"Where are you going to head after this?"

"What do you mean, you?" he asks.

"I'm going to stay here for a while, I think. With Alex. She's in a bad way. She has surgery in a couple of weeks. I feel bad leaving her."

"What should I do?"

"I don't think you should stay."

Fred leans up on his elbows.

"So you're ditching me?" he asks.

"No, Fred," I say. "Ditching is what you did when you left me alone in Bangkok. You beat a girl up. We're still friends. We're always going to be friends. I'm never going to tell anyone what you did, but you beat someone up and she needs someone to be with her."

"It was—"

"You beat her up, Fred."

Fred leans back down and breathes out his lips, flapping from the force of the air.

"Do we still call Alex her?" he asks.

It didn't occur to me to call her otherwise. Not even to respect her identity or whatever, I genuinely just didn't think of it.

"I have been, yeah."

"How long until her surgery?" he asks.

"A couple of weeks."

"We could link up after?"

"Yeah," I say. "We'll check in."

Fred and I sit in silence for a while before I leave to make arrangements with the front desk. Fred agrees to leave tomorrow, to go to Koh Tao without us, and I email the hostel there to change the booking. At the front desk I tell them Alex is my friend, that she's sick and asked me to extend her room, and that I'll pay for another two nights with my card right now.

When I get back to the room, I hug Fred goodbye. The embrace is cold and distant.

"See you, man."

"Bye," he says. "I'm sorry."

I head back up to Alex, backpack on my shoulders.

"All sorted," I say. She smiles. I sit back on the bed. I lay out a plan, saying that after the swelling goes down in a couple of days, we can make the trip over to where her surgery is and get her settled. She nods to all of this, placid, and I realize that I might be overstepping. For a moment it feels like I'm fixing things, like I'm a bit of a hero, but then I remember this is all my fault. And not in a self-deprecating way, like taking on too much responsibility—this really is all my fault. Shame creeps in, and it makes me sad how quickly Alex wants to forgive me. How she's letting me take care of her. That's fucked up, isn't it?

"I don't have to be there, though," I say. "I don't have to stay with you if you don't want me to."

"I'm alone here," she says. "I want you to stay. If you don't mind."

We sit side by side as she flicks through what's on the television.

"I love this movie," she says.

"What is it?"

"*Lost in Translation*," she says. "It came out, like, ten years ago. Scarlett Johansson was seventeen in it."

"What's she doing in Japan?"

"Just watch the movie," she says. "It's not far in."

We sit in silence, and then she puts her head on my shoulder, and

I put my arm around her. Is this wrong? Wanting to touch someone when they're all bruised up like this? When it was your fault? I can't imagine what's going on inside her head, for her to be okay with this. Scarlett Johansson looks lonely and rides elevators with this older dude I recognize. They don't understand what they mean to each other. They're obviously not lovers, but there's love there. They just care for each other at the right time. Not everything needs a label. Alex moves deeper into me. The old guy whispers something in Scarlett Johansson's ear and I can't hear it, but I don't need to, and I reach for the remote and turn the television off and I look at Alex and her busted lip. I lean in to kiss her, and she kisses me back. The kiss probably reveals my motives for telling Fred—jealousy—but I suspect Alex already knows. I'm gentle, worried about the cut. I imagine the softest touch could hurt, even the quietest lick of saliva, but she doesn't seem to mind.

Her lips feel so nice. I'm hard. I reach my hand beneath her T-shirt. She's not wearing a bra. I roll my fingers over her nipples. I want to tell her I think she's hot, but I think that could be a weird thing to say. Not right now. Not after *Lost in Translation*. We take our tops off and I move so that I'm hovering over her, her legs either side of me. We kiss some more, and I pull away and draw my fingers along the side of her ribs.

"Are you sure?" I ask.

She draws my hand to the round of her hips.

"It's not as painful here," she says.

My hand rests there. I lean down and I lick her nipple, looking up at her, and she has her head back. You never know for sure if it's an act, if people are just pretending that things feel good to make you feel good.

"Is that okay?" I ask.

She laughs, looks down at me, and nods. And then she watches me as I lick her, and I look at her, and it doesn't feel creepy or too intense to be staring at someone like this. It just feels nice. I undo my belt and play with myself, and I pull down her underwear and feel there are two layers, two separate pieces, one lighter and the other more rigid, and I understand that's where it is, the first layer to hide, the second to hide the hiding. And there it is. I'm staring at it, and I can feel her looking at me look at it.

I rub it a little, not really knowing if what I'm doing is right.

"Is that okay?" I ask.

"It's okay," she says. "I just don't like it."

I stop, feeling some relief, and kiss her again while she plays with me, and when things feel right, I ask her if I can fuck her, if that would be okay, and she says yes and that there are condoms and lube in her bag, and I wonder why she brought her own condoms and lube, like, for what, for whom, but I don't question it and I get them and I put it on and I'm gentle. I go slow, and stay slow, because it still feels weird to go hard with someone who's all bruised up like this. The slowness is nice. It feels right. She moans. We stay like that, her on her back until I cum, and then I fall away next to her and hold her hand. We don't say anything. It's a lot to process, all of this. It's hard to believe this is all the same day, that only this morning we got back from the boat and Fred beat her up.

Alex hobbles to the shower and I follow her. I throw away the condom and help her wash herself. Back in bed, she's in the fetal position. I sleep behind her with my arm on the back of her thigh, where I know it won't hurt, and I don't know where to put my other arm but it's okay. It's okay. She'll be okay.

MAX

XIII

JAMIE AND I ARRIVE LATE FOR OUR SPA WEEKEND, JUST BEFORE SUNSET. The hotel room is absurd. The bathroom is the size of the bedroom. There's a clawfoot tub dropped by a window, with views of the enormous Somerset estate, surrounded by blue armchairs, as if this is not a bathroom but a place to entertain. They had no rooms with two singles, so Jamie and I are sharing the rosewood super-king. There was a bottle of non-alcoholic champagne and fresh flowers on the bed when we arrived, which he'd tried to cancel. I worry we'll spend the weekend fighting against the presumption of incest, which I can already see is stressing Jamie out. *I did call ahead to say we wouldn't need them. Could you please just check to see that I called? Surely someone took a note? So nobody took a note.*

"This place is ridiculous," I say, staring out of the bathroom window toward the far end of the property, beyond the manicured gardens and vegetable patches, at what looks like a herd of buffalo.

"They grow most of the food in the restaurant here," he says. "Including the buffalo milk."

I nod. I wasn't aware you could milk a buffalo. Or grow milk.

"I might take a bath," I say. "Do you need anything from the bathroom?"

"Nah," he says. "I'm going for a walk."

Before he leaves, he passes me a flute of the non-alcoholic fizz through a small gap in the bathroom door. I descend into the bath. It's been decided that I'll have surgery, that I have a 5 to 10 percent chance of major complications, like stroke, hemorrhage, changes in vision, and a similar chance of straight-up dying. I go to France with Vincent, Simone, Fred, and Aisha next week, followed by Emily's wedding with Simone, and the surgery is shortly after that. It made sense to be distracted, because as the surgery date draws closer, the risk of dying looms larger and larger, because when you think about it, 5 to 10 percent really isn't small at all. Every day passed is one step closer to death—that's true for everyone—but it feels as if I'm sprinting.

I didn't expect that when I assured people again and again that the tumor's likely benign, and that the surgery is unlikely to kill me, they would actually feel assured. I have tried very hard to feel the same, which has been difficult living with Vincent, because I can taste his fear in all my favorite meals, in all the cake he bakes, now without refined sugars. I'm trying to regulate my aversion to this kind of all-suffusing love, because I'd much rather he cared than not, but it's hard to receive care without believing I'm in danger, in need of it.

Romantic getaway. If I was in Maria's shoes—which I assume are sensible loafers—I wouldn't have expected flowers or bubbles or a super-size king. I can't help but think this was going to be, on some level, a declaration of love by Jamie, which seems dangerously presumptuous, something that could have erupted in flames. It makes me feel even sadder for him, how wrong he's gotten it all. I sink farther into the tub.

WE SIT ACROSS FROM EACH other in a room of heavy oak paneling, with light fixtures that look like clusters of solid gold bubbles. Dinner is seventy-five pounds for three courses—the oysters, which we also order, cost extra. The waiter explains to us that the vegetables grown on site lead each dish. I'm doubtful. The meats appear first in the description of each item.

Each main has a recommended cider pairing. Jamie explains to the waiter what he knows about the cider made at the production site on the estate, as if the waiter, who obviously knows all of this, will be impressed. Jamie refuses the recommended cider because he thinks the Signature Blend will be too sweet against the beef. The waiter wears a thin, hospitality-trained smile. I ask about a dish with cauliflower in it.

"We actually use the stem to make a puree," he says. "We don't waste anything, and the food doesn't travel far. It's a self-sustaining system. We like to talk about food feet rather than food miles."

We nod. Jamie looks enamored. Our ciders arrive with the oysters, which I immediately slurp up. Delicious. I love them, though I can never explain why, especially because, when you think about it, the better an oyster is, the less you can taste it.

"Don't you find food-feet zero-waste stuff so odd?" I ask.

Jamie tilts the last dregs of seawater from the oyster shell into his mouth.

"What do you mean?"

"Like, at what point did a culture of excess become something we would pay more money to avoid?" I ask, sitting back in the silk armchair. "Think about it. The way we look down on fast fashion. Food that isn't locally sourced. It's all in reverse to what it used to be. It's like we'll indulge in any values as long as there's a big price tag."

Jamie sighs. "Isn't there some objective good in sustainability, though? Would you rather this food was imported?"

"No," I say. "It's good. Some trends are better than others, but that's what's scary—it's a trend."

"I think the climate emergency is making sure it's not a trend," he says, taking a sip of cider, then nodding. "Mm. So good. Anyway, be a little more climate-aware."

"You ordered beef."

"Devon beef," he says. "And you ordered pork."

"Tamworth pork."

Jamie smirks.

"Just enjoy the oysters, Maxy."

My beets and buffalo curds arrive. I wonder if my eyes have settled on the very buffalo whose teat was yanked for this dish.

"Are you sure I can't give you money for this weekend?" I ask.

"It's fine." He waves his hand, head toward his smoked eel. "It would've been wasted otherwise. And I want to, you know . . ."

Yes. Treat me before I die. I push the beets around my tiny plate. They're light but salty. I can taste caraway seeds.

"How are you feeling?" I ask.

Jamie doesn't look up.

"What do you mean?"

"About the abortion."

"It's fine," he says. "Things could be worse."

"You could have a brain tumor?"

"Yeah."

Our mains come. The pork is extremely juicy. What's in the water in Tamworth? There's a couple next to us, much older, who seem to find us endearing. They don't know we're siblings. Jamie sees them, and he grunts to himself, which they notice.

"This is really creeping me out," he says.

"Relax, Jamie."

"What am I supposed to do?" he asks. "Lean into it?"

I dab my mouth with my napkin and clear my throat with the cider pairing.

"I'm just saying that you can't blame them," I say. "Was this whole thing with Maria supposed to be romantic?"

He scrunches his eyebrows.

"It was just going to be a nice break for her," he says. "The mother of my . . . I just wanted to do something nice, okay?" The couple next to us detect the animus in his tone. He's quick to draw the poison back up his teeth. "I wanted to show her that I really cared about her and the baby, and to make up for missing the scan and not answering calls." He pauses. "Maybe if I'd just told her before she—"

"I don't think this would've been decisive," I say, and I can see he's taken aback, as if he really thought a weekend away could've mapped out the course of deadbeat fatherhood. "This is a small thing." I pause. "A lovely and generous small thing, but a small thing."

"Is it not at least a big gesture?"

"I think big gestures are small things, but that doesn't mean they're not nice!"

Jamie sulks. I've said the wrong thing. Dessert comes. I have cream and rhubarb and Jamie has cheese, ever concerned about sugar.

Back in our room, Jamie takes the bolster from the sofa and places it in the middle of the bed. While he showers, I tuck myself in and go through the messages from Vincent. He's sent me pictures of what he cooked at his parents' that day. *Will bring some leftovers for when you get back!* I call Vincent.

"How is it?" he asks.

"Everyone thinks we're a couple."

He laughs.

"Feeling relaxed?" he asks.

"Not really."

"Try to," he says. "You deserve it."

A WOMAN WHO INTRODUCES HERSELF as Theresa Katherine leads me and Jamie through the medieval herb garden. She has huge blond waves and a tight face she'll swear is just SPF. We're in bathrobes and slippers, which feel improper to walk around in. I wonder if people are watching us. It's a beautiful day, regardless.

"What makes the herb garden medieval?" I ask.

"This is how herb gardens were designed in the Middle Ages."

The medieval period lasted a millennium. I don't bother asking if this is a composite of several gardens across those thousand years, or modeled after one taken from around halfway through. Jamie leans down and sniffs some rosemary. We continue walking the winding paths until we reach a glass-fronted spa. Theresa Katherine separates me and Jamie for our massages. In my private, marble-lined room, a sturdy, older woman who is impossibly named Belinda Jane gestures toward a massage table with a stomach hole. I remove my robe and tell her I'd rather leave my underwear on. I lie face down, my stomach exposed to the room's lavender-scented air.

"How far along are you?" she asks.

"I'm thirty."

"No." She laughs. "I said, how far along are you?"

I realize then that the stomach hole is for pregnant bellies. I'm staring at Belinda Jane's impeccably white shoes through the face hole. Her feet are still, like they're waiting for me to answer.

"I'm not pregnant," I say.

"But you booked the Mother-To-Be Total Body Experience?"

"I didn't book that. I'm literally not pregnant."

I lift my body up to look at her. She's clutching an iPad, swiping furiously, as if showing me the booking will spontaneously generate inside me a uterus and embryo.

"One second," she says.

While she steps out, I wrap myself in a robe and sit on the edge of the table. I could've explained that the massage was meant for Maria, who was pregnant but is no longer pregnant. I could also explain that Jamie is my brother and not my boyfriend, nor the father of my non-existent baby. That I can't get pregnant, and that the closest I've got is this tumor, and because of it I may not ever have kids by any other means. Because I'll be dead.

There'll be a note somewhere. Jamie would've told them to change it, just as he told them to change the flowers and bed and non-alcoholic champagne. I feel tense. No amount of medieval herbs could relieve it. I pray the massage therapist isn't disturbing Jamie. I can't bear the fretting. *You've got minions to milk buffalos but no one to put a fucking note through the system?*

She returns, apologizing, wheeling in another massage table without a pregnancy hole.

"There was a mistake in the system," she says. "The note wasn't picked up on. I'm so sorry."

"It's honestly fine." I shake my head. "I'm sorry for the fuss. I'm sure the Mother-To-Be Total Body Experience is lovely. Is there a big price difference?"

"It's two hundred pounds, so we'll refund you eighty."

Is this a pregnancy tax in action? Jamie was going to spend two hundred pounds on a massage for Maria in the hopes it'd prove he'd make a good father. How desperate, how misguided.

I lie down, and Belinda Jane punches the tension out of my shoulders and arms. It feels as if this is a ripe opportunity to contemplate parenthood, to dive into and evaluate the feeling of someone thinking I was with child, to assess whether I felt whole or validated or partial and denied, but the moment she pulls my arms behind me, stretching my back, I decide it feels like nothing more than a glitch in the system. It feels meaningless, which I suppose in itself is meaningful.

In the face of surgery, my brain is shutting down any contemplation of a future, especially one out of reach. Maybe people think of legacy in the face of their mortality, but let's say I survive, and allow myself to want children. Really want them. What does that change? Nothing actually gets easier.

I can't help but feel like a child myself, the way I've been feeling about death. I was ten when Mum's dad died, when the realization that life does in fact come to an end crystallized in my plastic brain. I'd lie in bed, dread multiplying like an algal bloom. My parents have never been religious, and so they never comforted me with promises that something lay beyond the veil. As I've gotten older, my fear of death has become easier to live with, but since the diagnosis, I've been feeling it in moments when I fall too deep into my own mind, including now, hypnotized by a pair of white tennis shoes.

Jamie and I are in the shallow end of the heated indoor pool, which covers most of the floor space of the modernized barn. Out through the glass walls, the weather's turned gray, rain patting onto the glass and obscuring the greenbelt view. I wonder how many trans people have been guests here. I don't think it's any sort of victory that I am.

There's a couple treading in the deeper water, away from us.

"Do you think they're siblings?" I ask Jamie.

Even he can't hold in a laugh. I think of home, or the home that once was. The beach, the hours sat with Jamie on the sand, the ripples curling up our shorts before tugging us deeper into the water.

"This sort of feels like when we were teenagers," I say.

"How so?"

"Being on the beach on Lamma. Sitting in the water together."

"Yeah."

He turns his body, resting his chin on his forearms, stacked neatly on the edge of the pool.

"I think when the time comes, you'll make a really good dad," I say.

He lets out a chuckle.

"Better than Dad?"

"Sure."

"That doesn't say much."

"He tried," I say, and before I know why I'm asking it: "Do you think I'd be a good mum?"

He seems to really think about it. Why does he need this long?

"You're caring and show up," he says. "So yes, you would be."

"Better than Mum?"

"Sure," he says, "but she wasn't so bad."

"How Freudian of us."

"Please don't say that."

I laugh before descending into the warm water, pulling my head beneath the surface, crouching and blowing water out of my nose so that I can stay on the blue-tiled floor. What does better even mean? More present. Less drunk. Jamie's certainly the latter, but not the former. And even then, how can we really know what a child-to-be's needs will be? It seems impossible to feel sure that anyone will be better than anyone. When I come up for air, Jamie's turned around, elbows behind him on the ledge.

"I still feel angry," he says. "It always comes back to them for me." I sit on the edge of the pool, wringing some water from my hair. "When I'm feeling stressed. Don't you think life would be easier if they'd been better?"

"Probably," I say. "But they're just people at the end of the day."

I think I forgave my parents a long time ago, even if sometimes I still feel the pain of being alone, of my inebriated father drifting closer and my sober father pulling away, of not knowing who I was and not feeling close enough to anyone to say anything about it. Feeling the pain often appears to me to be entitled, as well as talking about it, because I was in no way disadvantaged or abused. I'd say most children go through something similar, and without the luck of financial comfort. I guess when so many share the thorn, it becomes less sinister—just another thing that people have—no longer something we care to prune, even if we should. Jamie has the thorn, but he hasn't extended forgiveness. I don't know if it helps to put so much on them.

"I think this whole thing with Maria," he says, lifting himself out of the water. "The baby." He pauses. I bring my knees up toward me. "I was really ready to show that I could do a better job."

"A child isn't a way for you to prove something," I say.

This wipes the softness from his face.

"That's a pretty bad-faith interpretation, Max," he scolds. The nearby couple are staring at us. Jamie notices, too, and some softness returns. "I wasn't saying that. What's wrong with wanting to be better than them?"

"What does better mean?"

"You know what it means," he says. "Make sure they feel okay. Support them when they don't."

"But what does that mean?" I ask. "Were you going to work less?"

"Yes, Max. A baby forces life into place."

"Does it? Mum still worked," I say. "And why couldn't things be moved for Maria's scan? How can you expect people to wait?"

He's angry again. He looks like he's been stabbed in the heart, and I almost regret what I've said. Almost, because I meant it. A baby might change him, but he can't rely on it. Babies are too small to carry such a big burden. Jamie wipes away what might've been a tear and storms off, forgetting his towel. He returns a moment later for it, his wet feet slapping on stone, his stiff, bowed arms alternating back and forth like an action figure, all while avoiding eye contact.

"Jamie," I say.

He ignores me.

I dry off, get changed into my clothes, and return to our bedroom. Jamie isn't there. I start drawing another bath, because I'm not sure if the pool water was chlorinated, and I didn't want to use the showers by the pool. Vincent's been messaging every hour, asking me how breakfast was, how the massage was, sending an article on how acupuncture can decrease post-surgical inflammation. *We could both get it done. No pressure, but could be fun?* I'm not sure I want to respond.

While he's being kind, and while our plans for post-surgical recovery at least assume that I will live and be fine, the volume of his communication is overwhelming.

My phone lights up with a video call from Mum. I'm not sure if I want to endure her, but ignoring it would cause her more worry than me comfort. A stitch in time. Water plops out of the side of the tub as I reach for twenty minutes of a tedious lecture. She's sitting on a bench in the garden, accidentally switching cameras between a view of the house and her face a couple of times.

"Max," she says, and then, as if I'm the one who rang her unannounced, "you're in the bath."

"Hi, Mum."

"Have you looked at the post-surgery TCM recipes I sent you?"

I don't want to hear anything more about traditional Chinese medicine.

"The ones Vincent showed you?" I ask.

"We've been sending them to each other," she says. "Now I'm going to send you a list—"

"I'm in the bath, Mum."

"You don't have to read them now," she says. "The West doesn't provide an exhaustive template for how the body works." Why is she talking about the West as if she isn't the West? As if there isn't also groundbreaking and advanced medicine in the East. "The systems we've developed in—"

"We?"

"The Chinese."

I sigh.

"Trust it, Max."

I tell myself that she's trying, that her intentions are good and that I don't have to find her so annoying; that, to an extent, I am choosing irritation.

"I do trust it," I say.

"You need to do everything you can."

"For fuck's sake."

"Max."

"Sorry, but do you actually think I don't care about this?"

I can't help but feel like my mum is in denial, that doing Whatever She Can is a mere attempt to draw agency from fate, to shift responsibility onto me—to blame me for dying on a surgical table.

"I'm just trying to help, Max."

"Right."

My arm aches from holding up my phone. I take a couple of deep breaths, hoping to reset.

"You look pretty," Mum says. "How's Jamie?"

"He's fine," I say, then, lowering my voice to a whisper: "A bit difficult."

"Mm," she says. "He's going through a tough time."

"He's also just quite difficult."

"Yes," she says. "That too."

"I'm going to wash my hair now."

We say goodbye. I lather and submerge, allowing the suds to float up into the bathwater. When I rise up, I hear Jamie fussing around the room. He knocks on the bathroom door.

"We've got dinner in an hour," he says, matter-of-fact. "Can I use the bathroom, please?"

"I'm in the bath," I reply.

"Can you hurry up?"

I find the plug chain with my toes and pull.

WE HAVE A TABLE BY the window, looking directly onto the vegetable patch. I can see a man in a kitchen uniform hurriedly plucking herbs, speed-walking back inside.

Jamie ironed a shirt. He smells nice. He is, despite all his flaws, very handsome. It is probably a weird thing to say about my brother, but if people did think we were a couple, it'd reflect well on me.

"I'm sorry about earlier," I say.

"It's fine," he replies. "There's probably some truth in there." Jamie cuts into a selection of resort-cultivated mushrooms, a swirling mass of hats and trombones, applying a bit of cured yolk to the surface like oil paint. He raises the fork toward his mouth, then stops. "It sort of felt like my one shot."

"How?"

He lifts a hand, barrier between me and his mouth.

"There's never any time to date."

"You can make time."

"It's easier said than done."

"You know, you don't have to work so hard," I say. "People aren't making you."

This is a conversation he's had a million times. With me. Our parents. His ex-girlfriends, including Maria, I'm sure. Just not with a therapist he's wanted to stick with. He nods his head, but with a side-to-side motion that tells me he's bored of me.

"Sorry. Anyway, you're a man," I say. "There's no rush."

"What?" he spits. "And have a kid at fifty with a twenty-five-year-old just to stub out regret? What kind of father would that make me?"

"To be honest, Jamie, I don't know. You might be a really good dad at fifty, but you probably have some work to do. That's what I meant when I said what I said earlier." He's listening. Intently. Jamie's brain often moves so fast, eyes darting behind when he's talking to you, as if he's looking for someone better to talk to, even though his mind is just in a thousand places at once. Even when he's with me, it rarely feels like it. Now is different. "When it's right for you, you'll be a really good dad."

He starts nodding again, but he doesn't stop, and I can see his face getting redder. For a moment I wonder if he's having an allergic reaction, but then I realize that he's crying. He puts his knuckles to his eyes and his back moves up and down. People are looking. I get out of my seat and move behind him, wrapping my arms around his. He squeezes my forearm with his hand.

"Cry as much as you need," I say. "People will just think I'm breaking up with you."

He lets out a loud laugh, and then we're smiling again. He wipes his eyes with his napkin. When I sit down, my bag starts vibrating. I sigh.

"Vincent?" Jamie asks.

"Yeah," I say.

"Aren't you going to pick up?"

"We're having dinner," I say, and Jamie's expression is disbelieving. "It's been a lot. With the tumor. He's helicoptering me."

"But you're going to be okay?" Jamie asks, though it seems like he's asking about me and Vincent rather than me.

"I feel like everyone believes I'll be okay, but I don't really know." I pause. "It's so funny, Jamie." My voice starts to wobble. I can't contain it. "Like, so funny, because I've spent so much of this year thinking about all the ways my body fails me, and now I might literally die. It's a fucking joke. And I think it would've been picked up by the scan after New Year's if I'd gone—"

"What? You never went for the scan?"

"Don't, Jamie."

I try to breathe through the tears.

"It's been a good run," I say, "but I don't want to die."

"I don't want you to die, either," Jamie says in a shaky tenor.

I try to steady my breath as Jamie holds my hand. I can't look at him.

"And with Vincent," I say, "he's helping, but it's a lot." Jamie seems to understand. Being loved is a good thing—it's just hard for people like us to fully believe that someone will be there. "But I'm lucky.

There are distractions. Here, then France with his friends and Simone. Emily's wedding. I'm trying to not think about it."

"How is Emily?" Jamie asks, rubbing his eyes.

"I think she's fine."

Jamie nods. I feel bad, but I don't often wonder how Emily is. It doesn't feel correct for me to be a bridesmaid, and then I feel a twinge of guilt for being an absentee friend, for being neglectful. It's hard to think of it in any more poignant terms than this is just what life does. We all want to do better, but what does better even mean?

VINCENT

XIV

Alex and I are on Bang Saen Beach in Chonburi, under an umbrella we've rented for two hours. Fred messaged me last night, after a week of silence.

Hey man . . . just thought I'd let you know I've been thinking about you a lot

I know you probably don't want to hear from me, but can you give me an update?

I've ended up in Chiang Mai

Where are you now?

I've ignored him. I don't know when or if I'll reply, because to be honest I don't really know what to say or how to say it. I can't help but picture him going in circles. *Is Vincent sure she won't tell anyone? Should I wait in Chiang Mai for him? Is Vincent going to tell anyone? Am I a bad person?* Whenever I think of Fred, the reason for all this time I've gotten to spend with Alex starts to hang over me. It's unsettling. It doesn't feel good.

Alex's copy of *The Old Man and the Sea* is open and resting pagedown on her sunlounger, some sand in the curved spine, shaded by the large umbrella above us.

"You've read that quickly," I say.

"Hemingway's so easy," she says. "I like his prose. It's really crisp."

"That's a nice way to describe writing."

She smiles.

I wouldn't know if she's right. I've never read him. I've been on the same page of *Wild Swans* for the last fifteen minutes. I can't read in this heat, with so much to distract me. I found the copy on the hostel bookshelf. People have always told me that I should read it. I never did, maybe because I thought they were just recommending it to me because I'm Chinese, and there's also something off-putting about a book the size of a brick. Still, I've liked what I've read so far.

"The beaches here aren't as nice as Koh Samui," she says.

She's said this every time we've come to the beach. I don't know how she can say Koh Samui without wincing—I can hardly talk about it. She's right, though. This is a city beach, so what can you do? She gets up from the chair.

"Do you mind staying with our stuff?" she asks.

I nod. She starts walking toward the water, in those stupid shorts.

The undulating waterline dances between her waist and thighs. It's only a couple of minutes before she comes back and lies on the lounger next to me. She's silent, but I watch her body and look at her face. Most of the bruising is gone; the little that's left she covers with makeup.

I imagine telling my mum about all this. It's not like she'd ever find out, but I can't help but play it out in my head. *She's a man? You're a gay? How can she be a man and you're not gay? Vincent Chan, explain yourself.* I wouldn't know what to say other than I like girls.

Alex takes a deep breath as I settle back into my chair.

"Can you believe it's in a few days?" she asks, eyes shut, not looking anywhere.

"I can, actually," I say. "Not that I've been counting down the days or anything."

She opens her eyes to look at me and glares. I didn't mean it like that.

"As in, you've probably been waiting for this since you were two or something," I say. "I've only known for a couple of weeks."

She shuts her eyes again.

"Mm." She yawns. "I wouldn't say two. I guess I didn't know it was possible then."

"When did you realize it was possible?"

"After my mum first took me to a doctor," she says. "They sort of mapped out what my life could look like."

"How did that feel?"

"Life stopped feeling black and white," she says. "But I guess knowing what was possible was hard in its own way."

"Why's that?"

"Hope can suck," she says. "Knowing that it could all change made the wait unbearable. I don't know if that makes sense."

"I can understand that."

Can I? The closest I have is the moment I had enough money to book my flights to Thailand. Having the trip in front of me made working at the till more boring, even if it gave me something to day-dream about. I almost say it, even though I know it's ridiculous to compare it to Alex's surgery. It'd make her feel worse. I feel out of my depth. What do I really know about anything?

"Did you speak to the hostel manager this morning?" she asks.

"Yeah," I say. "They said I don't have to move rooms."

It feels odd, staying in the hostel alone without her, waiting for her to recover enough so we can move into a hotel. Even the idea of the hotel feels odd, especially since she's paying for it. She won't let me contribute. She said her mum gave her money, that I could just pay for some food instead, that it'd just be nice that I was there, but that I didn't have to stay if I didn't want to.

She cried last night in our room, after we had sex. She's been off her hormones in preparation for surgery since she got to Thailand. *It's like a deep ache inside, Vincent. It's coming back. It's not how I'm supposed to feel.* I haven't noticed any change in how she looks. It's not like you go off hormones for a little bit and everything reverses, right? She said that doesn't happen, and yet she's filled with panic that it will. I have no idea how to relate to any of this. Sure, I know what it's like to feel out of place, but I've never really thought about hormones, what medication might mean. I tell her she's beautiful, but it's like a plaster over a gash. I'm trying to understand it all, but I guess there's too much distance there. I wonder if there's always going to be too much distance there.

I'M LYING IN BED, AWAKE. I keep twisting in the sheets. One leg in. One leg out. Both legs in. One foot out. Different permutations to get my body temperature right in the cold, air-conditioned room. She's lying right next to me, on her stomach, not snoring but breathing steadily, that kind of deep, deep breath, so natural and undisturbed that her lungs are on autopilot. This is a lot, isn't it? Surgery like this. She's been waiting for it since she was two.

I get out of bed and walk to the bathroom, turn on the light and sit on the closed toilet seat. I look up at the lightbulb in a daze, and I start to feel an ache in my eyes. I don't look away, as if I'm hoping it'll scratch an answer onto my corneas. My head falls back toward my lap. Maybe I can deal with the change. I have to deal with the change. It's not that I can't deal with the change. It doesn't matter to me, but I don't know what recovery means, what it looks like, staying with her while she's bleeding out and stuff. I don't know, it just seems a little intense, and I feel like I'm going to fuck it up. A couple of weeks ago I thought I was traveling with this girl I really liked, and now I'm holding her hand at the most important juncture of her life. I don't know how I got here or what to do, and I can't help but think this isn't what the trip is about. I was supposed to come here with Fred and have fun. I should be with Fred having fun.

I don't pee, but I flush the toilet anyway. When I return to the bedroom, Alex is looking at me—blank stare, blank face.

I crawl back into bed. Neither of us says anything.

The shopping mall's a white modern building with criss-crossing escalators, organized with little architectural rhyme or reason, all modern white-tiled floors, white walls, an enormous skylight through which the daylight penetrates. We get soft, doughy, cinnamon-sugared pretzels and walk in silence to an H&M. I sit down, watching her pale fingers rifle through racks of clothing.

What do I do when she goes in for surgery? What do I do when she comes out? I saved for months and months to go on this trip, and now I'm spending all that money walking around shopping malls, pretending I live somewhere I don't, without a job, just living in the day and having sex in the evening. It feels like I'm missing out on something important. And it all just feels so heavy. *Hey, Vinny, how did you spend your gap year?* I met a girl and took care of her after she got vagina surgery in Thailand. Of course I wouldn't be able to tell people that, which is all part of the fact that the world is a certain way. Maybe the world will change, for better or worse, but can we really wait for any of that?

Alex holds some skimpy bikini bottoms against her hips, ones she'll be able to wear after the surgery. She's lost in her own reflection. I wonder what she's thinking as she puts the swimsuit back on the rack.

At the top of the shopping mall, the white tile turns to black tile and there are sprawling movie posters.

"We could watch *The Hunger Games,*" she says.

We get lucky with the times and go straight to the theater for the two-thirty showing. The seats are near empty.

"Have you read the books?" she whispers to me.

"No," I say. "Have you?"

"Yeah," she says. "They're not very good."

We sit through the adverts. One for McDonald's. Another for Nissan. One for a Thai insurance company. Movie trailers. I mow through my popcorn. At one point Alex holds my wrist, just as I'm about to throw more of the caramelized kernels into my mouth.

"Slow down," she laughs. "The movie hasn't started yet."

I drop the popcorn back into the box and fiddle with my sugared fingers, spreading the stickiness across my palms. The movie starts. Jennifer Lawrence hunts animals. Everyone's wearing gray rags because they're poor. I can't focus on any of it. I feel like I'm sinking into myself, deeper and deeper into the cushion of the seat, further and further away from the post-apocalyptic death match among some children played by children and other children played by people in their late twenties.

Should I really be here? My parents would fucking kill me. I texted my mum last night, lying about pretty much everything, even the fact that I'm in Chonburi. *I'm in Chiang Mai! Fred's great. Having lots of fun with him.* None of this is right.

We get up when the credits roll.

"Do you want to eat here?" I ask.

"Why don't we go somewhere else?" she asks. "Last meal before tomorrow."

"Before the bowel cleansing."

She frowns—she doesn't want to talk about surgery prep. I meant it to sound lighthearted, but none of this is funny. The floor's made of eggshells.

"We could get a couple of drinks as well," I add.

"I should probably have an early night."

My heart is in my stomach. We get a taxi to the waterfront, stopping by a 7-Eleven to get a couple of bottles of lemon iced tea. The sweet liquid settles my nerves a little. Maybe it's an apology, but what is she apologizing for? I want to cry. Could I just tell her that I don't want to stay? But that feels cruel and wrong. It wouldn't put her in a good headspace for surgery. It'd be unfair. If I don't say anything now, we can at least try to enjoy the evening. We sit on a bench.

"Have you thought about what we might do after I recover?" she asks.

She's reading my mind. I feel tense.

"I'm not sure," I say. I think of Fred. "I guess we could go to Chiang Mai or something."

"Yeah," she says. "Chiang Mai sounds nice."

Why did I get myself into this? She would've been fine on her own. That was her plan all along. Hope can suck—she said so herself. Why was I so quick to give it? I could've just left her, then met up with her elsewhere, after, and that would've been fine. But promising felt so easy. Sure. I'll stay! What's a month, anyway?

Alex holds my hand, and I fight the urge to snatch it away.

WE GO BACK TO THE hostel after dinner. In our room, Alex presses her boobs up against me as she leans in to kiss me. It's passionate, but for the first time I don't really want to have sex. We move to the bed. I moan as she goes down on me, shutting my eyes, reaching down to play with her dangling nipple. All of it feels like I'm acting by way of coded instruction, all synthetic, distracting myself from sex to have sex. And when it's time for me to fuck her, I fumble a little with the condom, and it suddenly feels quite tight, and I can't quite get it in, and it's more difficult than normal. The sex is more mechanical. We don't say anything after I cum, and it seems the longer I stay quiet, the more she'll know, and so I probably have to say something.

"I think I'm nervous about your surgery," I say.

She meets this with silence. It's the truth. I am nervous. For her safety, sure. But there's a raft of worries. Maybe this is all I need to say. She takes a deep breath.

"Me too," she says.

"You don't need to be."

"Then why are you?"

"I don't know," I say.

I get up to throw the condom in the bin. I wash my hands and return to bed. She's lying with her back to me. We don't cuddle, but both of us twist and turn for most of the night. Short spells of sleep. An hour. Half an hour. An hour and a half. All incomplete, but replete with dreams of Alex. Mishmashes of the weeks past and the weeks that could come. A dream where I'm having the surgery done, which freaks me out, and when I jolt awake, she's not in bed, but the bathroom light is on. I pretend to fall back asleep before she returns.

In the morning, both of us look tired. She's getting dressed for the clinic, which means she's packing, which means that I'm going to be in the hostel alone.

I sit up in bed, watching her collect her things.

"When are you off?" I ask.

"In ten minutes."

"Right."

I get out of bed to piss. When I get back, she's nearly packed up, and she's standing by her suitcase staring at me, like she's about to say something.

"Are we okay, Vincent?"

I stand stunned, and I know I've stayed silent for just a moment too long.

"I mean, yeah," I say. "Why wouldn't we be?"

And her face falls a little, and mine must be falling a little, too.

"Okay," she says.

We hug, then kiss hard on the lips. No tongue. No passion.

"You're going to be great," I whisper in her ear. "It's going to be fine."

We separate, though not completely.

"Can I call you tonight?" she asks.

"Yeah," I say. "Yeah, of course."

We let go of each other, and she wheels her bag out of the room. I close the door behind her, and then I start to pack. I scour the room for my things. Everything in a bag, then into my backpack, clothes lazily folded, all zipped up, locks on, and then I'm sitting at the edge of the bed ready to go, even though I have another night in the room.

I don't want to think about it too much. In fact, all I really want to do is speak to Fred. Pretend none of this ever happened. I open up my phone to message him, praying to God that he's on the other end. I'm going to leave. I have to leave.

MAX

XV

SIMONE IS DRIVING US FROM MARSEILLE AIRPORT TO BONNIEUX. SHE has shown up to the holiday with an attitude and I can tell Fred and Aisha don't know what to make of her. She hasn't taken her sunglasses off, except for a brief moment to get through immigration. Every time a work email comes in on her phone, she shushes the car so that I can read it out to her from the passenger seat.

I yawn, resting my head against the window. I haven't been sleeping well. There's a recurring dream I keep having, of surgeons leaning over me with a melon-baller, scooping out the excess tissue, except they don't stop there: they keep going until everything is gone. The harder I try to dissociate, the more my panic about surgery infiltrates my subconscious. Simone said she's going to work from my flat for the first week I'm recovering, and Vincent has asked for the whole week off, and might even ask for another. I've tried to feel a little less suffocated, a bit more appreciative.

"Where'd you spend summers growing up, Max?" Fred asks, as if that is a normal question.

"After we moved to Hong Kong we'd sometimes come back to England for a bit to see my granny. On my dad's side."

I hated those summers. The pink-carpeted floors at my granny's, which spread even into the bathroom. No friends. Her insistence that eighteen degrees was not cold, scoffing at the fleece I refused to take off.

"How about you, Aisha?" I ask.

"Mostly around Asia. Lots of time in Thailand," she says. "We'd go skiing in New Zealand quite often, just because of how the ski seasons teed up there." I look toward Simone, and though I can't see her eyes I know that she's rolling them. "Did you go to Hong Kong much?" Aisha asks Vincent.

"No," Vincent says. "Only a couple of times."

I feel the hard jolt of Simone accelerating up a hill. She swerves round a corner.

"Where'd you learn to drive?" Fred asks.

"In London," Simone says. "Last year. My girlfriend let me practice with her car."

"Is your girl—"

"I broke up with her in January."

"Oh, cool," Fred says. "Have you been dating?"

"No," Simone replies, her voice curt.

It worries me that Fred may pity her. He seems like the kind of guy who pities single people. I notice Simone's grip on the wheel tighten, the car accelerating.

"By choice," I say, which I immediately regret.

The land is split over several levels, connected by a winding set of stone steps. The first is adorned with spindly fig trees and a small, bean-shaped pool, the second with a grove of a dozen or so apple trees, and the third with a one-story house.

As we climb up the final few steps, I turn around. The house looks over the hills of Provence, flowing from one to another like cursive letters. Blue-shuttered windows run along its face, with glass folding doors separating the patio from the living room. Aisha leads us in.

"How do you know who owns this house again?" Simone asks.

"A friend from Harvard," Aisha says.

"With a house in France?"

"She's Italian."

Simone makes an mm sound, as if her parents don't also have a holiday home. Aisha turns round to face us.

"So there are two bedrooms here, and then a bedroom which is that one at the back." She points to her right. "Next to the outdoor shower."

She's referring to the roofed and windowed shed next to the house.

"The hut?" Simone asks.

"It's not a hut," Aisha says.

"Who's going there?" Vincent asks.

"Simone, I think?" she replies, turning to Simone. "It's the smallest room."

Aisha hands her the separate key on the counter. Vincent looks to me.

"We could go in there?" he suggests.

I look at Simone. It is nice of him to offer, but I could literally be dead in a couple of weeks.

"Don't worry," she says.

Even through her sunglasses, Simone's face says it all. *I'll go, but I hate your friend.*

"So I guess me and Fred can take the room at the end," Aisha says. "And you and Vincent can take the one next to it?"

We lug our bags through the living room and toward the bedrooms. Ours is much smaller than Fred and Aisha's, windowless bar the skylight. The soles of my feet gather dust as I walk the outdoor path to Simone's.

"Simone?" I call with a knock.

"Come in."

The double bed takes up more than half of the room. She's

crouched down by the far wall, plugging her phone in to charge, wearing nothing but a mesh bra and high-waisted panties. A sexy, squatting goblin.

"How's the hut?" I ask.

"Don't."

We lie on the bed together, our legs dangling off the edge.

"I'm just not into these super-hetty holidays, Max."

"I'm really sorry," I say. "I promise it'll be fun."

"They just make you feel like luggage."

"The people, or the holidays?"

"Both," she says. "Why would Fred ask me if I was dating? Isn't that insane? Like, why is that the only interesting thing about me?"

"I think it was a pretty normal question," I say. "But it's often an annoying one. People should ask it less."

I have some sympathy for Fred, who is, despite all his charms, a little gormless, desperately grasping for what he imagines could be common ground with her. Simone sighs. It's strange for us to not be on the same side, for me not to be in the hut with her. Instead, I'm granted entry into the house, and it's hard to feel good about it. It is, after all, an insecure tenancy, at the mercy of an eviction notice scribbled on the back of a surrogacy pamphlet.

"They might just be intimidated by you. Like, they probably see you and feel a bit bad about their lives." I pause, and I think about Aisha and her neighbor, and of telling Simone about it. I'd be betraying Aisha, but it's Simone. "Their marriage isn't doing that well." I contemplate the words. Maybe Simone needs to hear them. She perks up, like a dog who knows a treat rests in a closed fist. "She wanks in the window with the guy across the street. She wants to take it further."

"What?"

"Yeah," I say. "She told me."

"She just"—she scrunches her eyebrows—"told you?"

"I told her about the brain tumor first. I think it was like some fucked-up quid pro quo or something."

"Does Vincent know?"

"No," I say. "I've kept it secret."

"God, that explains it."

"What?"

"Locking me in the hut," she says. "They're going through their own shit."

Simone's phone buzzes. She checks it and then hands it to me with a grunt. Aisha has sent us all messages with suggested meal plans.

If it's okay I'll handle lunches because they're smaller?

Max and Simone will do dinner tonight? And Fred and Vincent will do dinner tomorrow

Let everyone know if there are any issues for you?

The texts read as strangely inflexible despite the illusion of suggestion. What are the question marks for? Does she think she's being relaxed? I struggle to picture Aisha relaxing, outside of an induced coma. When I imagine Aisha making rugs, it is always feverish.

SIMONE INSISTS ON DRIVING TO the supermarket. She's more engaged in conversation, which means that, to my and Aisha's relief, she is driving slower. Fred and Vincent are having a look at the boulangerie near the house.

"What's your work like?" Aisha asks.

"It's not hard," Simone says. "It's just about having an eye. And then there's lots of admin."

"Do you work a lot with other people?" Aisha asks.

"I have an assistant now who runs the show when I'm away. But besides her, not really." Simone takes a right. "It's kind of nice that nobody knows my business."

"It's tricky, isn't it?" Aisha says. "I feel like I have to make an active effort to keep my life private at work."

Finally, rapport!

"They know I have a partner," Aisha continues. "That's about it."

There is a split second when I think a friendship could unfold between Aisha and Simone.

"It's interesting you refer to Fred as your partner," Simone says.

I am wrong.

"What do you mean?" Aisha asks.

"Well, he's your husband," Simone says. "I feel like partner's reserved for more untraditional arrangements. Long-term partners who you're not married to. Dating someone who uses gender-neutral pronouns. Not necessarily a cis-het couple who've entered into the most traditional form of union."

I keep my eyes on the road in front of me, pursing my lips.

"I'm not sure I agree," Aisha says. "Anyway, it's important to leave room for other things to exist. Maybe saying husband creates a climate of restrictiveness for other people."

"But they can see your wedding ring, right?" Simone asks. "And the engagement ring? Isn't it just lip service? You've kept all the symbols, except the one which presents the least cost to you."

I have indeed seen the engagement ring. It's huge. And the wedding band, which for some reason also has diamonds. I allow myself to look at the rearview mirror, and I can see Aisha looking out of the window. I nudge Simone. She doesn't care about this. Nobody cares about this. I'm pretty sure in another setting Simone would encourage everyone to use the word partner. There are bywords more pressing to eradicate, like Other Half or The Missus. Simone just likes to fight.

At the traffic light, Simone pulls the sun visor down to apply a dollop of Korean sunscreen out of her bag.

"Simone," I say. "The light's green."

The car behind us honks. Simone, unfazed, twists the cap shut, closes the flap, and hits the gas hard.

"My sister said she was going to raise her baby gender-neutral,"

Simone says. "Not like gray tunics or anything, but kind of that vibe until the baby could choose. So, she has the baby, and lo and behold, the baby is dressed up in bows and dresses and everything frilly. And when I asked her why she was doing it, she said it was because people kept thinking her baby was a boy."

"It's quite hard to raise a baby gender-neutral, though, isn't it?" Aisha asks.

I feel like the car is waiting for my contribution, and so I decide not to offer one.

"I agree," Simone says, looking back at Aisha, eyes off the road. "But I think that's why it's important to not lay claim to achievements we haven't earned."

The car goes silent. I wonder if she'd be as vicious if Vincent was here.

At the supermarket, Simone and I attack the list of ingredients while Aisha decides to hunt for a specific kind of Provence rosé.

"It's so light and crisp," she says. "You'll want it for the pool."

I'm unsure why she can't just tell us the name. There are many stands and boxes of produce, ball-pits of blushing tomatoes. Simone and I veer off toward shelves stacked with jars upon jars of pâté.

"Try to be nicer," I say.

"What do you mean?"

Simone's smirking.

"Please," I say.

I find some chickpea flour for the farinata, and then ingredients for the aubergine parmigiana and fresh salad. We reconvene with Aisha at the checkout. She picks up the bill, immediately putting the large sum onto our shared digital tab.

"I wonder what the boys have been up to," Aisha says as we carry out jute totes to the car.

"The boys," Simone laughs.

"What?" Aisha asks.

"It's sort of, like, how we used to talk about men when we were at school. Like, a group of girls pre-drinking asking when the boys are going to arrive. It's just quite funny to hear it."

Aisha offers a passing laugh. I look down at my feet.

"Could I drive back, actually?" Aisha asks, her casualness forced. There's an awkward pause. "I don't get to drive much in London."

Simone throws her the keys and gets in the back.

At home, Vincent and Fred carry the heavier things back up to the house. Two totes hang off Simone's narrow, bony shoulders like weights off balance scales.

"Thank God the boys are here to help," Simone laughs.

"Yup," Aisha says, terse.

The rough weave of the bags' straps cuts into my shoulders, digging in as they swing. Vincent trots down when I'm at the final stretch and relieves me of them. Slicks of sweat have gathered in my armpits.

"What'd you get up to while we were gone?" Simone asks.

"Got fresh bread," Vincent says. "And some pastries. We had some time to see the church at the top of the hill."

"We got this," Fred says, holding up a baggy filled with hash.

He looks proud of himself. Vincent looks a bit sheepish.

"Why?" Aisha asks. "You literally never smoke."

I look at Simone. Her eyes dart between Aisha and Fred. I can't help but feel people shouldn't embarrass those they love.

"We're on holiday," he says. "I bought it from a French teenager. When me and Vincent walked up to the church. I thought we could make a dessert or something. Like, a small cake?"

I think Fred expected us to congratulate him for some reason. I feel bad as I study his expression, quietly anxious, looking for approval.

"I'm not sure people want to do that," Aisha says. "It'd be a waste of a day."

"We could do it at night," I say, wanting to throw Fred a bone. "After dinner or something."

"I'd be down," Simone adds.

He smiles, which makes me feel even worse. There is something so wrong about first impressions. When I first met Fred, I was taken by his confidence, his big arms and his square, Nordic face. Now that I know him better, I see a boy unsure of his gifts. Maybe that's why he's so deep into Aisha's.

EVERYONE'S SITTING BY THE POOL, full from a late lunch of preserve-stuffed baguettes that Aisha made. Vincent is inspecting the fig tree at the corner of the patio. Some of the figs are green, but the skins of those higher up have bruised to a plump purple. He plucks one, then two, then three, then four, reaching deeper, holding the soft orbs in his palm. I feel Simone's eyes on me, and when I turn to her there's a layer of tacit approval in her smile. She returns to her phone, obviously still working. I can't wipe those emails from my brain. What could she be typing? *If you don't grow up and bleach your hair, I'll fucking shave it.*

I look back at Vincent. A branch has scratched him, leaving a crimson streak, a tally mark across his ribs.

"I got five!" he shouts.

I catch one. It is rich. Sweet, but more texture than taste, whispers of caramel. Simone holds out her hands, resting her phone on the taut belly of her one-piece.

"Aisha? Fred? Figs?" Vincent asks.

They decline. Vincent tucks in at the edge of the pool.

"You know there's a dead wasp in every fig," Fred says.

"What?" Vincent asks.

"I think I've heard that," Aisha says.

"Not all of them," I interject. "Just some species." I have everyone's attention. Even Simone's. "Female wasps carry pollen into an opening in a fig. Sorry, male fig. They get trapped once they're in, and then they lay their eggs."

"Why do they get trapped?" Vincent asks, rolling a small fig around his palm.

"I think because they lose their wings on the way in," I say.

"Then what?" Simone asks.

"I think the males hatch first and mate with the unhatched females."

Disgust smears across Simone's face.

"The males then dig holes for the females to get out," I say. "Then the males die, and the females hatch and find their way out, taking some of the pollen with them to go and pollinate other figs. Everything else dies in the fig. The life cycle repeats."

"How do you know that?" Aisha asks.

"My dad once told me there were wasps in figs, so I looked it up."

"Wait, so what happens if the female wasp climbs into a female fig?" Vincent asks.

"She pollinates the fig. That's how we get the fruit," I say. "But the structure of the female fig means she can't lay her eggs in it."

"She dies alone?" Simone asks.

"Yeah," I say. "She dies alone."

We sigh into silence. A few moments later, Vincent squeezes my foot from the edge of the pool.

Simone pours chickpea flour into a bowl. I raise an eyebrow as she places a flat palm inside it, then jump upright as she hits my bum.

"What is wrong with you?" I shriek, looking back, seeing only the faint yellow outline of a couple of fingers. "It didn't even work."

Simone laughs, then brushes the flour off me with a tea towel before rinsing her hand in the sink. She combines the flour with some water, and I drop in the chopped rosemary and salt.

We take a break to look through Emily's social media posts. Many updates on the wedding. I often think of content creators, how at some point their platforms would've been fledging, how they must've shared just as much of their lives then as now, because otherwise their platforms wouldn't have grown. But to see someone do it to such a small audience is a little excruciating. Cringe. It is someone pretending to be what they aspire to be, in the hope that life will imitate art.

Fred appears from his bedroom.

"Can I infuse the butter now?"

"What?" Simone asks.

"The hash," he says.

"Oh! Of course," Simone says, with enough brightness to keep the air in Fred's chest. "Do you want help?"

Fred moves farther into the kitchen, and Simone hands him a pot and a spatula. I sit on a stool and watch as Simone looks over Fred's shoulder.

"Is that too much?" Simone says. "I actually can't remember the last time I did this."

"We might as well just use all of it."

He holds up the spatula and tastes a dot of butter with his finger.

THE DARKENING SKY DOES LITTLE to absorb the day's heat, which continues to emanate from the tips of our noses. We've been drinking for the last hour and a half. Simone and I brought out a tray of martinis, and we're on our third bottle of wine. I've hardly thought about the tumor today. Such is the value of distraction, and of drinking—any dread pales against the warm glugging glow of a bottle. I could die, but everything is fine. In the middle of the table there are crisps in a linen-lined basket, next to a bowl of hummus.

"Isn't this going to ruin dinner?" Aisha asks.

Simone swipes a crisp into the hummus.

"Just save room for cake," Fred says. There's a light slur in his voice. He's been mainlining the rosé. He leans back in his chair and looks at Simone. "Aisha was saying you don't believe in marriage?"

I can't help but think he's trying to stick Aisha in it rather than make Simone uncomfortable. You can tell by the look on his face. He's charmed by Simone. Everyone's charmed by Simone, except when she doesn't want you to be. She gives Aisha a wry smile, willing to play the game.

"Do I not?" she asks.

"Well, no." Aisha looks askance at Fred, then back at Simone. "I didn't put it like that. But you didn't like the word partner, and I just got the vibe you weren't super into tradition, which is a good thing."

Simone holds another crisp over the bowl of hummus, then decides to eat it plain. The table is on tenterhooks for what might come next. I'm trying hard not to laugh.

"Do I think marriage is a little pointless? Yes." She clears her throat and takes another crisp. "Do I think it's just another legal tie to keep people together, despite all the reasons they should probably be apart? Also yes. As does Max." She gestures toward me, though I'm not sure I've ever said that. "It's not like my views are particularly untraditional, or particularly revolutionary or academic. I suppose me and Max just have slightly different vantage points."

Vincent is looking at me. I can feel it. I meet his eyes. It's a placid smile. Not a despondent one. Maybe, if I look hard enough at the corner of his lips, it's even an appreciative one. I don't know. Maybe a smile is just a smile. Aisha looks a little flushed.

"I just feel like you've put me in a box," Aisha says.

"You want to be in the box and not in the box, though," Simone says. "You're Schrödinger's Aisha."

I laugh. Vincent laughs. She looks to Fred for support, but he's sniggering into his glass. I think about the affair. It's all a little sad. The oven timer dings.

"That's dinner," I say.

Simone and I get up at once. In the kitchen, Simone takes the food out as I lean back on the fridge.

"Christ," she says.

"I know."

We return with the dishes. Fred looks even drunker.

"How are you feeling about surgery?" he asks.

Aisha glares at him.

"Fred—"

"I feel okay, actually," I say. "At least right now. It's easy to forget about, until you remember, then there's a bit of panic, but it's okay, really." It's a difficult feeling to describe, and I'm not sure everyone will get it. The thing I can most relate it to is those moments when I've been on the dance floor, happily shifting my weight from foot to foot, but then intrusive thoughts about rising sea levels, or how we might not save the bees, or how my parents will die one day flood in. Is that something that happens to everyone? "It'll be over in a few weeks." I pause. "Thank you for asking." I don't really mean it, but smile at him, and he seems pleased—too pleased, as if all he wanted was to be told he was doing the right thing. I want to close the conversation. I don't want to think about death.

"You guys have had such a shit year," Fred says, almost to himself. "Vincent's dad. The tumor."

Vincent dishes himself some aubergine, his focus on the bright steel of the serving spoon. I reach for the salad tongs.

"Does it help?" Fred asks.

"What do you mean?" I ask.

"To know someone who's going through that kind of stuff."

That kind of stuff. So trite. Oh, you know, I'm just going through some stuff now. *What kind of stuff?* A tumor. Vincent looks exasperated, but I don't want to be annoyed with Fred. He's trying his best and I sense he's in a weird place. He doesn't have a tumor, but still.

"I don't really know him, though," I say, and I wonder if I should say it, but I'm drunk and the words leave my mouth before I can finish the thought. "He doesn't know about me."

I feel the table collectively wince.

"Really?" Fred asks.

Everyone falls silent and I look down at my plate. Simone places a slice of the farinata on there. I run the tines of my fork over it, like hands mapping the surface of a face. Fred looks at Vincent.

"Your dad doesn't know about Max?" Fred asks.

"You know that, Fred," Vincent says, in a short-fused snap. "You know that."

"But I thought you would've since."

"No," Vincent says.

There's heat in my cheeks. Simone's hand on my knee. It's humiliating, a re-humiliation. It's also my own masochistic doing. Vincent's face melts into a pleading look, like he's begging Fred to stop. Fred seems surprised and doesn't look away.

"But you're living together," he says.

"What the fuck, Fred—"

"It's not like we've been together that long," I say, though the words are limp out of my mouth. It's true, but it's simply not enough.

Vincent doesn't look happy with my answer. Simone's glass of wine hasn't left her lips.

"But the tumor," Fred says. "You didn't think—"

"My mum knows, Fred. My dad doesn't. Just stop it."

His mum does know. She even wished me well through Vincent, which was nice, but it's hard to look at someone lowering themselves to wish you well for brain surgery and call it progress. There's a wall between me and Vincent. It'd be easier if we were stoned right now, so that we could at least slump into each other, melt the ice with the heat of our bodies.

After mains, Fred brings out the hash-infused lemon drizzle cake. The cake is tiny, high, and delicate. Three layers cut out of a single sheet of sponge. The now-solid drips of lemon icing were carefully arranged. It was nice watching Fred and Vincent make it, all the way from the sofa, fussing over its construction like two engineers. It was, in some way, like a portal back in time—to a time when I was years from knowing Vincent.

Fred slices the cake.

"Does anyone taste anything?" Aisha asks.

"I think the French teenager took you for a ride," Simone laughs.

"You can definitely taste it," I say.

"Right?" Fred asks.

Surprisingly, the hashy pong complements the lemon.

VINCENT AND AISHA GO TO bed after doing the washing-up with Fred. Simone, Fred, and I sit on the patio with glasses of wine, passing a bar of chocolate between us. He's sobered up a little. Maybe he was never that drunk, and just felt like stirring the pot. Regardless, the facts aren't mutable by intention; Vincent hasn't introduced me to his family, his dad doesn't know about me, for reasons that are sort of sensible. People's parents are different. Cultures are different. He had a heart attack. None of this dispels my resentment that it has to be a thing, that there is something wrong with me. Simone yawns loudly. None of us feel the cake yet.

"I'm going to go to bed," Simone says.

Fred holds out his arms for a hug, into which she leans. It's a deep kind of embrace. I think she's taken to Fred, and that Fred has taken to her, and this makes me wonder if this is just another way for her to stick it to Aisha. I've never understood Simone's vendettas, but part of me will always enjoy them. Fred tops me up from the open bottle.

"I like you, Max," he says. "You're good for Vincent."

I wasn't looking for his approval, but it still feels nice.

"Will his parents think that?"

Fred laughs.

"They will." He pauses. "He just has some thinking to do. And maybe it makes sense in a way. For you. You've got surgery. It'd just be another thing to stress you out."

"Yeah."

He's right. Maybe I should stop indulging. Talking about it feels like I'm making it more of a thing, but at the same time, tonight has reminded me that shame still hangs in the crevices, and perhaps this is an opportunity to lift it, to let words fall out onto the terrace, like wind-snapped leaves or old skin, to be swept away or replaced by the next sad bitch who visits Aisha's friend's house.

"Sometimes I feel like I'm a complication," I say. "Does that make sense?"

"It does." He takes a drag of his cigarette. "Maybe it's a bit rich coming from me, but isn't that always going to be a fact of life?"

"It is a bit rich coming from you." I nudge him with my elbow because I don't want him to think I'm mad. I'm not mad, because he's right. "I know I have to accept the way the world is, but I still have to talk about it, because otherwise where does it go?"

"For sure," he says. "I just don't want you to think it's to do with you." He takes a deep breath. "It was always going to be tough work with Aisha's parents, even though you'd sort of expect it to be the other way around. As in, you'd expect my parents—super white, super Home Counties—to be the ones with an issue."

"Were they?"

"Not at all," he says. "So I just thought her parents would come round. I mean, they mostly have, just not all the way." He pauses. "I'm not sure I ever feel entirely good enough. Or even good. I guess even with life in general. It's hard when your partner's family reminds you of that."

"Partner?"

Fred laughs. We sit close. Elbows and forearms touching.

"Is love ever enough?" I ask, unthinkingly.

"No, probably not."

I feel a deep sadness about Aisha exposing herself to the man across the street, and likely to several unsuspecting families. Even sadder for gossiping about it to Simone. My stomach rumbles, even though I'm full. I really hope that Fred, at least sometimes, knows that he's good, even if he doesn't always feel like it.

"Do you remember when we were at dinner," Fred says. "And Aisha was listing those things that her parents disapproved of?"

"It was kind of excruciating." I pause. "I don't mean that in a judgmental way."

"No," he says. "It was excruciating. But she wasn't being mean. It is just really hard for her. For both of us." He scratches his chin. I yawn, so wide that it feels like my jaw is testing its hinges. He catches it. "It's hard, but I'm glad we're open about it, that she and I can share it. The realities of it. It's us and it's them."

"Mm."

Us and them.

"Do you want children?" I ask.

"Yeah, for sure," he says. "I want to feel that kind of love. I think it'd be really good for me. Do you?"

"I never gave it much thought before this year. I guess with stuff with Vincent's family and my brother—"

"How is your brother?"

"Coping," I say. "I hope he changes a little. If people can change."

"I think they can. They definitely can."

I lean back on my chair, tilting my head toward the stars.

"You would hope a tumor would give me some clarity."

"On what?"

"Kids and stuff, the kind of life I want to live," I say, "but at this point I just want to be alive."

"I think I'd want to spread the seed as soon as possible."

Nobody on God's green earth should be allowed to say that sentence.

"Gross."

Fred laughs.

"I think I've been feeling like a bit of a broken person," I say. "Just not normal at all. It sounds so—"

"No," he says. "It makes sense. I get it. But you're not."

"Neither are you."

"Thank you."

Fred and I exchange a tender stare. What a wonderful man. He'll make someone very happy one day—maybe even Aisha. I hear the sound of a closing door from inside.

"Do you feel normal with Vincent?" Fred asks.

"Family stuff aside?"

"Yeah."

"Yeah, I do."

"I'm glad."

I set my glass of wine by the foot of the chair. My eyes feel extraordinarily heavy.

"I think I'm going to bed," I say.

He holds out his hand. I squeeze it, then let go.

In my and Vincent's room, the blue silk of my dress falls to my feet, grazing my toes and sliding onto the tiles like jelly. Vincent stirs a little as I climb into bed.

"I'm sorry," I say.

He doesn't say anything, but reaches out to hold my hand.

WHEN I WOKE UP A few hours ago, I was the highest I've ever been in my life. This is the worst I have ever felt. I initially thought it was the tumor, that somehow it'd grown the wrong way and I was dying and it was too late, but then Vincent started groaning, and I knew that it was the lemon drizzle. My brain is circling through ridiculous thoughts while my body is sludge. There's no part of me that's remotely capable of anything.

Vincent and Fred are slumped over the couch. They could be dead, but I'm too zoned out to check. Simone and I are cuddled up on the large armchair. Aisha jerks up from the carpet.

"I think we've been poisoned," Aisha says, her voice thrumming with panic. "With Novichok or something."

"Is she fucking serious?" Simone whispers to me.

Is Novichok still a thing? Seems behind the times.

"I think maybe we should call an ambulance or something," Aisha says.

"We just overdid it." Simone sighs. "We weren't thinking of dosages. All of it went into that tiny, tiny cake. And we ate it on a really full stomach so it took a while. Imagine eating five hash brownies in one go."

"I don't fucking eat hash brownies!" Aisha snaps.

"Fucking hell," Simone says.

I'm on Simone's side, but even so I still pick up my phone and search if you can overdose on weed. The results suggest it's unlikely. I've searched this just about every time in my life I've gotten too stoned, and certainly every time that I've eaten an edible. I once made Simone lie in bed with me with her fingers to my neck because I thought my heart would stop.

"You can't overdose on weed," I say. "We'll start feeling normal again in a few hours."

All five of us in the room drift in and out of sleep. During a brief conscious stint, I hear Aisha on the phone to someone. She's outside, near Simone's hut, but the voice travels through the porous stone and open doors.

"I just don't feel okay," she says. "I really need to leave. I'm really not feeling good. I'm freaking out." She fades in and out of audibility until I hear, "Okay, miss you."

My eyes widen. I look at Simone, who's looking at me, and all I do is nod. I look toward Fred and Vincent, who are still comatose, but then Fred begins to shift. My heart begins to pound. Did he hear

Aisha? Does he know? Was that even what I thought it was? And then Fred gets up, silent, and walks to the bathroom just off the kitchen. His primal retching echoes through the house. I can hear the bile splashing in the toilet water, an acidic waterfall. I'm overpowered with nausea. I run to the second bathroom and projectile vomit over the toilet bowl. Streams of it fly out of me. Last night's aubergine parmigiana. Yesterday's baguette. An avalanche of Aisha's fucking meal plan.

BY EVENING PEOPLE ARE FEELING better, which means that we have enough energy to start pointing fingers. Vincent is frustrated. For the last few hours he's been whining about the day being wasted, and consumed with worry about me. *You have surgery in a couple of weeks, Max. You can't be ill like this. This isn't good. This is really bad.* He keeps asking if I'm okay, so much so that I begin to question it, searching if having a brain tumor makes you more likely to overdose on weed, or if weed makes tumors grow faster. No results.

I'm reading the news on my phone, and Fred's sitting next to me. Vincent is at the kitchen counter with his face in his palms, scolding him.

"Why'd you use the whole thing?" Vincent asks Fred.

"I thought it'd be fine."

"It was really fucking stupid."

"Calm down," Fred says. "I didn't know."

"Always doing shit like this," Vincent says. "You need to grow the fuck—"

"Vincent," I say. "It's fine."

"It's not fine," he says. "It's fucked, Max. I don't think you're even supposed to be drinking." He looks panicked, and I feel an unfamiliar braid of discomfort and guilt and care, because while it's never nice to see someone like this, the fuss is warming. Still, he's spiraling. I've never seen Vincent spiral like this, and it's annoying because I'm trying extraordinarily hard not to do the same, to keep the thought of scalpel and coffin at bay. He seems so anxious. From the weed. Or Novichok. He addresses the room.

"She could die," he says.

"Jesus," I say. "It's not going to affect surgery, or the tumor. Can we try to be positive, please?"

"Yeah," Fred says. "Just be positive."

Vincent grunts. He storms off and goes to the bathroom. The one that I threw up in. He marches back out a minute later.

"It still smells like sick in there," he says. I feel like he's mad at me. "It's disgusting."

Fred and I sit still. It's like we're watching a one-man play, starring one angry man.

"I just want this fucking day to be over," he says.

"But you've spent the last couple of hours complaining about wasted time," I say. "We've still got some."

"Today's already ruined," he says. "We're not coming back from that."

"Come on, Vincent," Fred says. "You don't need to talk to Max like that."

"Fuck off, Fred."

I notice that Simone's standing by the entryway to the living room. She's never been one to stray far from a fight.

"You can't talk to your girlfriend like shit just because you're unhappy," Fred says, standing up. I'm choosing silence. This no longer feels like it's about me. "You're the one saying it's a delicate time for—"

"Oh, shut up, Fred," Vincent snaps.

Fred takes a step toward Vincent.

"Don't tell me to shut up."

"Or what?"

Fred reaches out toward Vincent—not to hurt him; it's a reconciliatory reach. Vincent whacks his arm away.

"Vincent!" I say.

"Why are you taking his side?" he asks me.

"I'm not taking anyone's side."

I've raised my voice now.

"This isn't about sides," Fred adds.

"What the fuck do you know?" Vincent shouts. "Fucking swooping in. All that you're-trans-in-a-world-that-isn't stuff. You have no fucking clue what any of this is like, what Max is—"

"You were listening?" I ask.

"You can hear everything in this house," he says, not quite looking at me.

"You're being unreasonable, Vinny," Fred says. "Just calm down. Max was upset about your parents and—"

"Oh, fuck off. Max doesn't know, you know," Vincent says. "You can stop all of this repenting."

"What are you talking about?" Fred says.

"Know about what?" I ask.

"Yeah, know about what?" Simone asks.

"Never mind," Vincent says, waving his hand.

"No, no," I say. "You don't get to say I don't know something in front of another person." I look toward Simone. "Two other people."

Vincent and Fred stare at each other. Male anger. If they could growl, they'd be growling. Two dogs in stasis, daring each other to say another word.

"Tell me what you're talking about," I say.

Silence floods in. I wish someone would look at me.

"Vincent," I say. "Tell me what the fuck you're talking about."

He sighs, as if he thinks I have to know, and I wonder if that's true, if I really have to know.

"Fred—"

"Fred what?" I snap.

"Fred beat up a trans woman when we were traveling," Vincent says, eyes still on Fred. "On our gap year in Thailand."

I look at Simone. Her jaw's on the floor. My stomach's twirling. I could throw up again. I don't know what I feel. What am I supposed to feel?

"I didn't beat her up," Fred says.

"She was black and blue."

"What the fuck?" Simone barks. "Seriously. What the fuck?"

Vincent and Fred are looking at each other. It seems strange that we're here. There are moments in life when you blink and the set has changed around you, invisible hands moving props, swapping the pen in your hand for a knife. A comedy becomes a thriller, a romance a horror. No matter how you reverse engineer, it never quite makes sense. And yet, you cannot force it back, you must play with your surroundings. The past is in the incinerator.

I look at Fred's face. A winded frown. Downturned lips. I understand that this may have been sacred between them. Vincent has snapped a cross in two. Over edibles. Over my brain surgery that will still happen despite those edibles. I'm in shock. A groggy Aisha appears from her bedroom.

"What's going on?" she asks.

"Your husband beat up a trans woman in Thailand," Simone says. "Just so you know."

Aisha's jaw drops, but I can't tell if she's surprised at the information, or surprised that it's out.

"Why did you beat her up?" I ask.

"She didn't tell me . . . She didn't tell me she was—"

"Why would she need to tell you?"

"He hooked up with her," Vincent says, his voice depleted of energy, already soft with regret.

I think about last night, Fred comforting me on the terrace, and now those words feel laced with lead. They're inside of me and I want them out.

"So you beat her up?" I ask.

"I—I only found out after, and I just—"

"But then how did you find out she was trans?"

Nobody answers me. I look at Vincent, who looks shaken. Simone takes the seat next to me. Everyone's staring at Fred now, who cuts through the silence.

"Vincent told me," he says, and it almost looks like there's a smile in the corner of his lips. "He told me afterward because he knew it'd freak me out. Right? That's why you did it?"

"Is that true, Vincent?" I ask.

"What?" Vincent throws his hands up. "Why does that matter?"

"Of course it matters," Simone and I say, in unison.

"It matters a lot," I add.

"He was jealous. He knew she liked me and wanted to get back at her. Or me. But he told me, and I just flipped out." Fred looks at me. "It was really fucked up, what I did. I know that. I don't think I can communicate how awful I feel about it."

"Well, I'm sure you could try," Simone says.

I notice that Fred has addressed none of this to Aisha. She must've known. He would've told her, confessed to this horrible, terrible thing he once did. Cleaning his conscience with Aisha's forgiveness, her acceptance that today's Fred is not gap year's Fred. And I wonder whose right it was to forgive. To rinse Fred of his guilt. Is Vincent a jealous man? Is that what all of today's charade is? His anger for Fred. His care for me?

"Did you ever apologize to her?" I ask Fred.

"Yeah," Simone says. "Did you ever say sorry? Or give her some fucking money or something for beating the shit out of her?"

Fred looks at Simone with a brief flash of annoyance. Vincent's leaning with his butt against the kitchen counter. Fred sighs. His face falls a little.

"No," he says.

"Why?" we ask.

Fred buries his forehead into his palm. He shakes his head a little, keeping his fingers firm and still, the skin of his forehead sliding around. I don't think any of us really know how we got here. Simone turns to Aisha.

"You're awfully quiet," she says.

"What do you want me to say?" Aisha asks.

"I just think it's interesting you're so quiet."

"You're such a cunt, Simone," Aisha says.

Simone doesn't argue. If anything, she probably likes Aisha a little more.

The room falls silent. I'm struggling to process. Fred beat up a trans woman. Vincent disclosed her identity. He told me that he'd never dated a trans person. That was one lie. Does not telling me about this girl, this clusterfuck with Fred, constitute another? I get up and go back to my and Vincent's room.

A few minutes later, Vincent enters and sits next to me on the bed. I'm looking down at my lap. I still feel queasy. He lets out a belch.

"Sorry," he says. "I still don't feel well."

We sit in silence.

"Did you date this woman?" I ask. "This girl."

"Yeah," he says. "I suppose."

"So you lied?"

"It was really complicated."

"Why wouldn't you just tell me?" I ask, and my voice cracks a little. "I feel really stupid. To have found out like this."

"How would you have reacted if I'd told you earlier?" he asks, as if he's pulled a trump card. "You would've walked."

"It would've felt better than this." I take a breath. "This is a horrible way to find out."

"And I'm sorry for that," he says, "but I didn't mean to lie, and I'm not sure if I even—"

"You did."

I hate when an argument dissolves into a game of words. Logic might diagnose wounds, but it doesn't close them.

"And this isn't just about the lie," I add. "You and Fred did something really fucked up. Like, more fucked up than I could ever imagine."

"Max," he pleads, placing a tentative hand on my thigh. I glare at it and he retreats. "It was more than ten years ago. I'm a different person. Fred's a different person. We shouldn't have gone into it." He pauses. "What were you like ten years ago?"

I'm angry at him for saying that. So angry. It's not the same. We are not the same.

"Is this why you and Fred drifted? When you went to uni?"

"I don't know," Vincent says. "I mean, yes, looking back."

"What?" I ask. "Did you just . . . never talk about it?"

Vincent's face is blank.

"What the fuck," I say. "Men are fucking insane."

"Max—"

"Tell me why you stopped seeing her."

Vincent sighs.

"She was in Thailand for the surgery," he says.

"What surgery?"

"The surgery."

"Bottom surgery?"

"Yeah." He sighs. "I went with her to where she was getting it done. She wanted me there."

That's not an answer. I give him a look.

"I freaked out about it," he says.

"What does that mean?" I ask.

"What?"

"That you freaked out."

Vincent pauses. He takes a deep breath, his face still a little ashen.

"I left her," he says. "When she went in."

This blows my jaw open.

"You left her alone after surgery?" I cry. "Vincent."

This is all too perfect. All that subterranean panic bubbles up like lava, oozing from the craters. I picture myself alone in a hospital bed, just like New Year's Day, waking up to the chalk outline of my once boyfriend, and suddenly death feels closer.

"I wasn't sure"—he stumbles—"I didn't know if I was supposed to stay."

"You didn't know?" I raise my voice. "You didn't ask her?"

Vincent starts crying, mushing his face up with his hands. He doesn't deserve to cry. It's pathetic.

"For me," he says. "I didn't know if I was supposed to stay for me."

"For you? Because you were on holiday? Do you know how fucked up that is?" I shout. "When I'm having surgery?"

"But it's not the same, Max. I wasn't sure then."

"You weren't sure?"

"I was nineteen, Max."

He looks so childish. Nineteen. How deep was this buried? I move just a few inches away from him on the bed. I don't want him near me.

"I was nineteen," he repeats.

"You've said that a few times, Vincent."

"Come on, Max."

"You outed a trans woman, then abandoned her when she was about to have surgery. No, sorry, while she was literally having surgery. It's so fucked—"

"It was more than ten years ago."

"You were an adult," I say.

"Would I have dated you ten years ago?"

No. I scrunch up my face.

"That's fucking disgusting," I say. "How dare you?"

My transness is not a moral wrong. I can't help but worry that all of his closeness, his attention, his care, was just born out of an instinct to repent, which I fear renders it meaningless, such that the relationship falls into question, because nobody wants to be a means through which others correct past wrongs. Ten years is a long time, but time is a funny thing. It bends and contracts, splices and recombines, all according to what you plot on the perpendicular axis. Education. Jobs. Transition. Trans girlfriends. Two people more than ten years apart become hand in hand. Is that all I am? A means to correct past wrongs?

"Have you thought about it at all?" I ask. "Knowing what's coming up for me?"

"Why, Max?" he pleads.

"Have you?"

He sighs.

"Yeah," he says, "obviously it triggered things a bit." Vincent shakes his head. "Like, this panic that I didn't expect. I guess the two things feel so close—"

"Things?"

"The surgeries."

"Did you want to abandon me?"

"No, Max, why would I want to do that?" he says. "I didn't want to back then—"

"But you did."

"People change, Max," he says, exasperated. "You should know that more than anyone. How different people can be."

"Stop comparing!" I scream.

He goes quiet. I force some saliva down my coarse throat. I can't look him in the eye.

"What was her name?"

"Alex."

A moment of silence between us. Alex. Her name pains me. No doubt, like me, she cut up her deadname to get her new name.

"Why does it matter?" he pleads. "Alex wasn't my girlfriend. It doesn't matter. I love you."

I imagine her on the hospital bed, blood from her crotch collecting in a pouch, and think of her doing it all alone. Maybe that was her plan all along, but to have the hope of company ripped away, to wake up and to see the blank space that she'd long suspected she deserved. A reminder that, for her, hope would always be an irresponsible feeling. I can't imagine how horrible that would be. I feel the tumor in my head. I really feel it.

"I love you," he repeats.

"I have a brain tumor, Vincent."

"I know."

"The tumor," I say. "You abandon one trans girlfriend—"

"She wasn't my girlfriend—"

"If you felt a certain way about her. If she's hung over you for this long, then it doesn't really matter whether you called her your girlfriend, Vincent. She was important."

Vincent pauses.

"Ten years ago, Max. More."

I'm bored of him. I'm bored of all of them. I clutch my head. It's aching. There's too much noise. Vincent places his hand on my back. I recoil from his touch. His hands are like maggots, legs upon legs upon fingers.

"Max."

"I'm going to sleep in Simone's room tonight," I say. "Then tomorrow morning we'll go to Bordeaux." I pause, churning over what words should follow. "I need some space."

"Space?"

His deflated tone angers me. It's so helpless, like he's timed-out on the naughty step and I've put him there.

"I need space, Vincent."

"What?"

"I don't know if you get it," I say. "Because maybe if you got it, you'd understand without me having to tell you—"

"It was so long ago, Max."

The whimper in his voice grows.

"Exactly," I say. "You've had a really long time to get it."

Vincent lies back on the bed, hands over his face. He starts coughing. It's chesty. There's still part of me that wants to roll him on his side, pat his back, ask if he's okay, but I don't.

"I'm really sorry," he says, crying again through his hands.

I look at him.

"For what?"

"Everything."

"Okay."

I get up to pack my bags. It is a quick operation, on autopilot. I feel his eyes on me the entire time, but I move as if he's not there. My hand touches the doorknob, and cold brass cuts a hole in the safety net. I feel myself falling, my lip wobbling, tears to the floor.

"I love you," he says.

"I love you, too," I mumble, carrying my stuff to Simone's hut.

"I don't want to talk," I say to her.

She nods, then goes to the kitchen to get a platter of cheese, bread, and pâté. There's a whole tomato on another plate.

"Fiber," she says.

We eat, cross-legged on the bed in silence. Afterward, we leave the plates on the floor. Vincent, Fred, and Aisha can deal with the ants. I can't even be bothered to brush my teeth. I lie down facing away from Simone, and she spoons me from behind.

"What did Vincent say?" she asks.

"He said sorry."

"For what he did to her? Or for not telling you?"

"I think he's sorry for both."

Her pillow rustles. I feel flickers of her breath on my neck as she speaks.

"Does sorry cut it?" she asks.

"I don't know," I say. "I mean, no."

Simone hugs me closer, squeezing me tight.

"I'm really scared, Simone."

"Of which part?"

"All of it," I say. "That he's going to leave. That I'm going to die. That I'm going to die alone." I can't hold back my tears. "Like a fucking fig wasp."

"You're not going to die." She presses her arm into my ribs. "And you're not going to be alone."

I know that she's saying she'll be there, that perhaps this is a moment of revelation for the power of female friendship, but I don't feel comforted at all.

"I could really die, Simone. I feel like I'm trying to be chill about it, but I could really fucking die and I just want time to stop."

Simone goes still. There's nothing words can mend, only a tighter squeeze.

XVI

Simone will do the six-hour drive to the wedding venue in four. We left without saying goodbye, as soon as we could sort out a second car. We ride in silence for the first hour, then, as our grogginess fades, we turn on the music and sing to Simone's playlist.

"Bless the Telephone" by Labi Siffre plays. Simone looks away from the wheel periodically to sing sections to me. *Strange how a phone call can change your day, take you away.* That line always makes me well up a little. I think it's one of the most beautiful lines in songwriting history, even without one of the most beautiful women I know singing it to me in the hills of southern France. A simple line captures how much hope a glimmer of someone can instill in a person. It's lovely and painful. There's so much room for disappointment.

There's an ache to forgive Vincent, already ripening only half a day after the fact. It disturbs me. I wonder if accepting moral complexity is a sign of my poor standards; if my desperation for love and belonging and for care—in the general sense, but also in the immediate post-surgical sense—is so expansive that I'm willing to allow someone who outed and abandoned a trans woman, perhaps at the height of her vulnerability, back into my arms. Or maybe it's the inverse, that all the pain I sometimes feel has forced me to become just a little more compassionate. A little kinder. To men who do bad things, who regret those bad things, who claim to have changed, who've hurt people. People like me.

An email comes through on Simone's phone. She makes me read it out to her and she dictates to me a level-headed response. As I click send, Simone asks me to play the song again. This time there are tears in my eyes. The morning rush means last night's heaviness hasn't fully caught up with me: that Vincent and I slept in separate rooms, that he outed a trans woman, that Fred beat her up, that Vincent abandoned her when she got bottom surgery, and that there is a tumor in my head due to be excised in a couple of weeks. Simone looks at me.

"Are you feeling okay?" she asks, turning the music down a little.

"Not really, no."

"Just give yourself time."

"I obviously have to break up with him, right?"

She curves along a winding road, looking at me when the tarmac straightens.

"Do you?" she asks.

"Yes," I say. "I do."

She pulls down the sun visor. I shut my eyes and feel the warmth on my eyelids, the light glazing them orange.

"Would you break up with him?" I ask.

"Absolutely," she says, sitting a little more upright. "But you're not me."

"Is that a bad thing?"

"It doesn't have to be."

I look out of the window, at a field of withered sunflowers.

"I want to get really sanctimonious about it all," I say.

"Which you can." She slows down a little. "Is this our left?"

"The one after."

She speeds back up.

"I think how I choose to handle this will say a lot about me. Like, would forgiving him mean I have a lack of self-respect? Is that just a completely narcissistic way to be assessing this?"

"No," she says. "It's not narcissistic. I think it's totally normal. But I am also a narcissist."

"How are you feeling?" I ask.

"About what?"

"The wedding."

Simone sighs.

"I just think these things are getting a little more real. It's no longer—wow, you're getting married, that's so fucking quirky. It's just normal now." She pauses, but continues before I can say anything. "I know I have a lot, but those environments make me feel like I have nothing."

We arrive at the old distillery-cum-wedding-venue in time for an early dinner in the large rustic dining room. It's the four of us—me, Simone, Emily, and Michelle—and, of course, Emily's mum, Julie, all in matching pajamas.

I feel compressed by the years elapsed. I haven't told any of them about the tumor. I thought it'd be a vibe-kill if I told Emily, but sitting here with them, I decide to. I explain that I have surgery coming up after the wedding, that I should be okay but that I'm also scared of dying. They pile on to me, their pity infectious, causing the ropes holding me together to fray. I cry. I'm not sure if that's because of the tumor, or Vincent. I really love these girls. Women.

Amid the lost years between us, Vincent almost feels like a blip, much like if the history of planet Earth was a day, then humans will only have been here for five minutes. There is a feeling—a knowing—that time will move forward, that eventually a certain pain will fall further and further behind.

* * *

I WAKE UP AT FIVE. For a murky few seconds, there's really no reason to believe that things aren't okay, but then I remember. I want a tourniquet to stop the bleed. When my tears subside and my breath returns to pace, Simone still unstirring, I think of Alex again. Part of me wishes that I could speak to her, but what would I even say or ask? Are you okay?

I fall back asleep, and when it's brighter, I feel grateful for the vapid day ahead. What better than tradition to displace confusion. There's a knock on the door, and a few moments of silence before Julie enters wearing a wedding dress, on her daughter's wedding day.

"Wake up, girls!"

It is low-cut, off-white, barely containing her two waterbed breasts. Why or how she is already dressed is unclear to me. The wedding's not for seven hours. When I first saw her yesterday, I was taken aback by how thin she was, much thinner than she was when we were at school. Julie was on Atkins throughout our entire teenage years. She changed to keto a couple of years ago. I thought they were the same, but apparently the change made all the difference. Her hair is blonder. I still can't believe she went through with that dress.

Simone and I sit up in bed. Julie stands in front of us, hands on her hips, waiting for us to compliment her.

"Wow, Julie," Simone says. "You look amazing."

"Yes," I say. "Amazing."

"Everyone's up and getting ready," she says. "You've got your kimonos?"

We nod. She leaves.

"Fuck," Simone says.

"I still haven't washed my hair," I say. "Or shaved my legs."

"Me neither."

Neither of us moves toward the shower.

* * *

WE FIND EMILY IN THE bridal suite, sitting in a chair with a makeup artist next to her, everyone in their silk kimonos. The sun blasts through three large windows. Someone else is curling Michelle's hair. There are so many people here. We are on a movie set. The girls scream at our arrival, but none of them turn their heads. It's like a horror movie. I go up behind Emily and look at her in the mirror. She radiates synthetic beauty—her skin caked in foundation, her eyelashes unacceptably long. The makeup artist takes a step back, allowing us a moment.

"You look gorgeous," we say.

Emily makes a face at me that suggests she may cry, placing a hand to her sternum, but there are no tears in her eyes.

"Okay," she snaps. "You and Simone need to sit down in those chairs. Did you wash your hair?"

"Yes."

We sit down and a hairstylist descends on my locks, brushing the oil out of them. She looks suspicious.

"Did you wash—"

"Last night."

A makeup artist begins comparing Simone's complexion to a palette of foundation. I take a deep breath, preparing myself. We talk for a bit, more about Bonnieux, though we omit details of the lemon drizzle cake and of Vincent. Simone tells them about Aisha and the window. The girls are scandalized.

Back in our room, Simone and I get into our bridesmaids' dresses.

"I still feel really uncomfortable," Simone says.

"I still hate my shoulders in this."

"No," Simone says. "You look great. I really thought I'd feel fine, but I feel uncomfortable. I don't want to do this. Wear this."

We go back upstairs for a few behind-the-scenes pictures. All of us are holding glasses of champagne. Emily reminds us that we are to take no more than four sips.

"One for each of us!"

After the photos, the bridesmaids and groomsmen are brought downstairs for a quick rehearsal of the ceremony, which is, in fact, a lesson in walking in pairs. Simone goes first, walking with Barney, who I also met at Fraser's birthday party. He told me he was a musician. I told him I was a poet. It was only after the party that I learned that, like me, he is not a successful one, even though he wears a Cartier watch. His girlfriend is twenty-two. Michelle walks with the only Asian groomsman. The pairing feels uncomfortably deliberate.

I meet the man I'm to link arms with. He is tall, broad, bearded, and handsome. He seems like the kind of guy who is just as likely to pay for my dinner as he is to stuff a fiver in my panties, and to him these two acts would be one and the same. I wonder if Emily put me with him because his hypermasculinity masks my transness. When I'm in heels next to these ladies I look like Godzilla. We link arms and begin walking down the aisle.

"I'm Max," I say.

"David."

"Why haven't we met?"

"I've been living in Singapore," he says. "I'm an old friend."

"Me too," I say. "We all are."

We reach the end of the aisle, staying there until we're told to leave.

"I'll catch you again in a little while?" he asks.

EMILY IS WALKING DOWN THE aisle with her father. I glance toward Julie, who is crying, though I wonder if she hoped she'd be asked instead, given the affair. Emily hardly speaks to her dad anymore. *How could he do that to my mum, Max?* For the most part, she's kept to her word. They hardly see each other. But here he is, walking her down the aisle, all in the name of tradition, all in the name of seeing men as who we want them to be and not as who they are.

It's hot. The sun feels relentless. Emily looks beautiful, enduring her white dress, complete with lace train, through the late-summer heat of Bordeaux. All of it, for now, is unmarked, unblemished. Who is she fooling? She lost her virginity when she was fourteen, though maybe in some senses that is, in its own way, extremely traditional. I turn toward the slanting vineyards that stretch far back, ripples in an ocean wave. I will never forget this image, and if I did, the images sprouting from the clicking shutter of the camera, still a little audible over the string quartet, would remind me. I feel a tear run down my cheek. I already miss Vincent, and this is emotional porn.

The strings play "Thème de Camille" from *Le Mépris*. It's a choice that probably makes them seem cultured, or at least beautiful, because when it plays in the movie and Brigitte Bardot looks over her shoulder it is certain that she may be, at that very moment, the most beautiful woman in the world, immortalized in the gelatine and crystals of photographic film. Did Emily think nobody would remember that Brigitte Bardot leaves her husband and dies at the end of the movie? Or that the French authorities have fined her several times for inciting racial hatred?

I turn to Michelle to share a smile, but she's smiling with tears in her eyes at Austen, standing among the crowd, her maybe soon-to-be fiancé. For a moment, I want to look out into the sea of faces and see Vincent's. It's not as if he could've been here, given Emily's one-year rule. Nevertheless, I'm still confronted with his absence. I try to harden. I can't forgive him just because it'd be nice to have him at the next wedding. Better to become inured to people asking me if I have a partner and replying no. I shouldn't sacrifice my principles. But what principles? Built around what commandments? Tell the truth. Don't betray your loved ones. I can't help but think I should be outgrowing axioms. The truth feels more complicated. Betrayal seems reductive. I think of Jamie, still so angry and unforgiving, his attention on a life that should've been, hammering long nails through his own feet.

The landscape behind the altar is so pristine it could be a screensaver. And I wonder what this is all for. To bring people together. To celebrate! What will change about their relationship after today? Not much. If anything, it'll get worse. The wedding cements their transition to bucolic placidity, commuter trains, a tighter circle of friends, a script already written. I think about how she'll look at these pictures, at how beautiful she looks, and reminisce, and it makes me feel a little sad. Nostalgia demands some admission that the present is not so good.

The scene fills me with dread. All the white. Losing weight to be stuffed into a dress that could've just been a bit bigger. And yet it feels like what I'm supposed to do, how I'm supposed to live my life, which is terrifying. Yes, these are things that I've long assumed were never meant for me, but perhaps I haven't spent enough time reflecting on how that's a gift. My life would be terrifying to Emily—it is insecure and often alone—but her life is terrifying to me. I used to worry about how Vincent and I would fit into a life like Emily's, but maybe we don't have to. I think I know that he really is, at the end of the day, down for whatever. Maybe that's remarkable for someone like him, for whom the traditional has always been an opt-out, not an opt-in. With his family, and what they expect of him. He, for whom my vision of life may be an adjustment. And yet he's fine with me, delighted with me. Is that enough? Am I enough? With Vincent I often feel it, even if I don't always believe it.

Emily and Fraser start saying their vows.

When you came into my life, I never thought I'd be so lucky as to one day call myself your wife. She is an endlessly kind heart in the most beautiful packaging. Have you seen him? I am so grateful!

White rapids flush out of Emily's eyeballs, and yet her makeup stays perfect. Tip the makeup artist.

"I do."

I look back at Simone and smile. She looks catatonic, but holds my hand. I exchange tender glances with the groomsmen. David looks back at me in a certain way. I look out at the vineyards and wipe a tear. I think he wants to fuck me. Life is beautiful. Maybe this is just what most people want. Dressed up in different forms of commitment, markers of stability, connection, the same fucking sponge cake in different flavors of icing.

"I do."

They kiss, everyone claps. Emotion pours through the hills. What a time to be alive.

I'm KEEPING MY EYE OPEN for quirks to the wedding. I've learned that there are certain things that very heterosexual couples do to convince themselves that they're defying tradition, queering the institution of marriage; like having a gay man as a bridesmaid or having wheels of cheese instead of a cake. I almost respect that Emily has done none of these.

The dinner begins. The groomsmen and bridesmaids have been split up, except for me and Simone. We have resolved to get fucked up, because we're stuck on a table with Emily's university friend group. Simone and I are separated by Sandra, one of Emily's actual best friends. Over the starter of salmon tartare, she tells me she has a new job in marketing, working for a grocery delivery service that puts grass-fed tenderloin into the nannied mouths of Kensington toddlers.

"Wasn't the ceremony incredible?" Sandra says. "They're going to have such beautiful children."

Is this shit you can say? Simone perks up and mouths what the fuck to me. I laugh. A clink of a glass shuts us up. It's Emily's dad. He's sweating through his shirt, profusely, like a boiled dumpling straight out of water. I can't take my eyes off Julie. She's seething, gritting her teeth. Why isn't Julie speaking? It's absurd.

The speech reads like a spoken-word performance of Emily's CV. Hong Kong. Exeter. A first! A job in the City at Oliver Wyman, where she met Fraser, and now a career in New York. Emily, he asserts, as if it is so hard to believe, is intelligent. He refers to Julie as his wife, which is strange, given the separation. There is a brief mention of grandchildren, with excitement, as if he'll somehow be more present this time round, all the way from across the Atlantic. When he finishes, the room claps. Emily lifts a finger to wipe a tear, although her eyes look bone-dry.

Fraser stands. His jacket is off. From what Emily has told me, he's always been very careful with his figure, and frequently fasts for days on end. If he were a woman, we may have been quicker to venture that he might have an eating disorder. Fraser provides a litany of evidence of Emily's kindness, and as he does this, I think about how he ghosted Emily when they first started seeing each other, after which she wormed her way further into his circle of friends, until he eventually changed his mind. Persistence wins, ladies.

I glance over to the table next to us, with Fraser's friends and a couple of the groomsmen. David and I look at each other. He lifts his glass and takes a sip of wine, not breaking eye contact. It feels nice.

Mains come. We eat beef Wellington. In summer. In France. It is delicious, but it's not right, and I can already feel the meat sweats begin to coalesce. The acid in my sweat stains the satin, leaving a small number of rings like those in a young tree, an invasive species in the forest of my armpit. I make eye contact with David again. Does he think I'm pretty? There will always be other men. Other than Vincent. Other than David. That's a good thing. We continue eating dinner. Then dessert. At no point does Emily speak.

THE DANCE FLOOR IS LITTERED with bodies, two of which are mine and Simone's, unrhythmically gyrating to the wedding band. The slimy frontman sings "Dancing in the Moonlight" in a French lilt, tempting geriatric hips into dislocation. Simone spots Austen at the side of the dance floor and brings him to us. They shimmy together. The girl can work a room. An older man spins me round.

I dance with David for a while. He's solid in his movement, a little awkward. I suppose that when the body is trained to a certain size it starts to lose function, strength over mobility, muscles in the way. We're dancing in front of each other, but the fact that we're at a wedding is complicating the mating ritual. There's little touching, and I start to question if he's actually into me. I peel off and dance with my friends, and then I notice that David is gone. Is it weird that I turned away from him? Examining social conventions quickly becomes like saying the same word over and over, in that if we do it enough, they all begin to unravel. Simone seems a little less tortured in the dress than she was before, although more checked out. One more song, and then I tell her I need to use the loo.

I move outside the marquee. Emily's mum, Julie, stops me on my way into the house.

"Max, I wanted to thank you for putting me in touch with Peter."

"Oh," I say. "Of course."

I gave Emily my dad's email to pass on to Julie after our dinner a few months ago.

"Send my love to him and Melinda."

"I will."

"You look beautiful," she says, giving me a deep hug before allowing me on my way.

When I return from my pee break, I see Simone sitting across from Michelle, holding her hands. They look like they're having a moment. Maybe they're talking about Michelle's mum. I try to find David instead. I haven't been thinking of Vincent much for the past few hours, which forces me to think about Vincent. Thoughts about him do nothing to abate my desire to chase a stranger's attraction to me. I can't help but feel entitled—I'm dying.

David's at the bar. He has no sweat patches, no saline beads on his forehead. It seems impossible. Unfair. Why am I so sweaty? I keep my arms neatly at my sides. I don't want him to see the stained satin.

"What would you like?" he asks.

"I'll stick to white wine."

He orders for us. It's an open bar, but there's a power in the way he hands me the glass that makes it seem like he's paid for it.

"Do you smoke?" he asks.

"Sometimes."

We walk toward the quiet side of the house, a few meters away from a smoking couple. We smile at them. Being a bridesmaid at a wedding almost feels like being a celebrity, when people are aware of your existence and identity, and you have absolutely no clue who they are.

"Are you single?" he asks.

I pause. I feel a little sad, but I'd prefer to feel strong, and it seems like the strong thing to deny Vincent's existence.

"I think so," I say. "Are you?"

"I am."

"There's something about weddings that makes a person feel very single."

He cocks his head.

"Not used to them yet?" he asks.

"Not yet." I turn my body so that my shoulder is on the wall. David follows suit, though the leaning feels too delicate for his frame. "I don't love weddings. I think I'm going to start saying no to them." This makes him laugh. "The ceremony's just a little weird, isn't it? I mean, the tradition."

He smiles, lifting his head toward the sky, at something, or thinking of something; me, the stars.

"I mean, it's nice," he says. "It's just two people saying how much they love each other."

"What are we really adding, though? What's going to really change after today?"

"Nothing, I suppose," he says. "Do you think that Emily and Fraser think things will change?"

"I think so," I say. "Why else would they say things like, this is the start of the rest of our lives?"

"To justify the expense, maybe." He rests his back on the wall, closer to me. "I think it's about bringing people together," he adds. "These things are getting harder. Haven't you noticed how far away people feel?"

"Yeah," I say, because I have noticed. In those years since university, friends have become remote. People are busier. People become things other than themselves: their partner, their job, their tumor. "Maybe I'm too cynical."

"Emily once said she was a mean girl at school."

He nudges me, and we laugh, and we settle somewhere that we're touching.

"What do you do?" he asks.

"I'm a lawyer," I say, and I pause, wondering if I should say it. "I had a book of poems published, too."

David drops his jaw. He holds his hands on either side of his cheeks. In any other circumstance I would think he was taking the piss.

"That's incredible," he says. "To be published. That's really something."

I fight the urge to deny it.

"Thank you," I say. "I've been on a bit of a break, to be honest."

His face falls a little, but with sympathy, not disappointment.

"Why's that?"

I could dive into those feelings of failure, of feeling like a fraction of a person, of not knowing how to be, but I think I'm tired of wallowing.

"I've been trying to write again," I say instead. "I wrote a poem in the car on the way to the wedding."

"Can I hear it?"

"You wouldn't want to—"

"Come on!"

I bite my lower lip.

"Fine." I reach for my phone and find the poem I typed out in the car. I clear my throat and begin. He's smiling too much. "Stop smiling like that. You'll ruin the reading."

He laughs, then settles into a more serious face.

"Very good," I say, taking a deep breath, looking at the words on my phone. I read the lines from the poem, and soon the embarrassment fades. I'm quickly happy just to have a willing ear. I breathe some soft expression into the lines as I reach the end.

He ponders for a moment.

"What's it about?"

"I think I broke up with my boyfriend," I say. "Over something he did a long time ago. I've been processing."

"Shit," he says. "I won't ask what. I broke up with my girlfriend a couple of months ago."

I smile at him and, choosing politeness, afford him a chance to bring the conversation somewhere else.

"It's horrible, isn't it?" he asks. I nod. "You feel so certain of yourself at the time, but then you're alone and suddenly you're not sure anymore."

I keep my face still. I know it feels like precision, telepathy, but really I know it's because we're all just the same, living the same life in different colors.

"Are people ever wrong?" I ask.

"What do you mean?"

"As in, do we ever get it wrong?"

I realize I've done no more to clarify, though a softness registers in his face.

"I'm sure sometimes," he says. "That's part of life, right? You know that. You're a poet."

We smile.

"What do you do in Singapore?" I ask.

"I work in futures trading."

"I've never really understood what that is."

"I don't think anybody does."

We pause, and I return to the thought of his girlfriend. Maybe I don't want to be polite.

"Why did you and your girlfriend break up?"

He sighs, looking forward into the dark.

"I cheated on her. I know that's not good. She went through my phone and sent screenshots to my parents."

My jaw slackens.

"Oh," I say. "That's not good, either, is it?"

"What's not good?"

"All of it," I say. "The cheating. I mean, especially that. Definitely that. But also sending screenshots to your parents, I guess."

He chuckles.

"Yeah. I think we were both fumbling a little, to be honest." He looks at me. "I think the worst part is that she wanted to stay together. Begged. That's when I knew it couldn't work." He searches for a response in my face. I nod. "I'm not proud of it. I'm not proud of it at all. I wonder if anyone looks back at their relationships and feels proud, though. Like, sees it all and thinks, wow! That was the absolute best version of me. I really showered myself in glory."

I think of Vincent, and I wonder if that in fact was the best version of me, or at least a better version of me. Maybe it was. Maybe I am.

"What's the worst thing you've done to a boyfriend?" he asks.

"I kept all these debt collection letters," I say, not missing a beat. "He bought some clothes on one of those pay-later services and forgot. I opened the letters and never passed them on. I wanted to fuck up his credit score."

"That's not that bad."

"No," I say. "It's not."

"So what did he do?" he asks. "Did he cheat?"

"Not even. He said we were going in different directions."

"Were you?"

"Yes."

He laughs. I laugh. I've done worse, things I'm not proud of, including standing here in the dark with David. I know there's a little bit of hypocrisy there, but there are shades of hypocrisy in everything. Our principles stretch like elastic bands. My crimes don't snap mine. Alex does. Our laughter quiets, and David laughs once more, a death rattle. He looks me in the eye.

"I'm probably being a bit forward," he says, "but do you want to maybe have a few drinks at mine?"

"Do you live around here?"

He laughs.

"I meant in my room. In the house."

I think about Vincent for a moment, and I'm drunk enough to not really care, or pretend I don't. I'm Max. I left my weeping boyfriend in Bonnieux. I have a tumor. I'm in a lot of pain today, and I want to remind myself that the world is vast and sweeping. These all feel like reasons why drinking in David's room is acceptable, or at least sensical, even if I'll come to regret it. It is logical, rational, just not totally explainable.

"We could also go to yours?"

"I'm sharing with Simone."

"Ah, I forgot about that." He smiles. "She's welcome to join."

"That'd be a firm no."

I bite my lip. I remember the unforgettable.

"You know that I'm trans, right?" I ask.

"Yes," he says. "I do."

"Is it that obvious?"

"No," he says. "Not at all. It's just that Emily told me. She talks about you a lot."

I feel bad for a second. I wonder if I talk or think about Emily enough.

"I have to stop by my room first," I say.

"I'm the door at the opposite end from the staircase, on the floor below."

Before we part, he leans in and kisses me. It's a short peck, but it feels intimate. I breathe in his citrusy aftershave through my nose and feel it on the palate of my mouth, and I realize I don't want to go back to his room at all. Knowing that I've crossed a line, I take my leave. The crowd's thinned a bit. The pensioners have rubbed their joints raw, dancing for too long to whitewashed renditions of Earth, Wind & Fire. I hold up my dress, stained brown at the hem, as I walk toward my room. When I enter, I can hear crying from the bathroom. I knock twice.

"Simone?"

"Yes?"

She's sitting on the toilet. She looks at me, her eyes red. I stand awkwardly at her side.

"What happened?" I ask. "Did something happen?"

"Simone," I say. "What is it?"

"I think." She's forcing deep breaths. "I think I just feel really overwhelmed."

I kneel in front of her to hug her. She wraps her arms loosely around my shoulders.

"With the wedding?"

"I think with this whole year."

Her voice is childlike. How we regress. Crumple into little things. She sniffs and lets go of me.

"I just feel really wrong right now," she says, picking at some tissue. "I feel angry at myself for crying."

"You—"

"No!" she shouts, flapping her arms around her. "Don't!"

"Don't wh—"

"It's not"—she struggles to steady her voice—"because I want to get married! It's not!"

I reach for her hand but she withdraws. Simone just wants to fight.

"Sorry," she says. "It's just when you're in an environment like this."

"Honestly, Simone, you don't even need to explain."

She separates from me and pulls a few squares of toilet paper from the roll, dabbing the bottom of her eyes.

"And it fucking annoys me that there's people who'd think I'm just upset because I'm single." She stands up and sits at the end of the bath. "I'm happy."

"I totally get it."

"I am."

"I know."

"I have so much," she says, as if I don't believe her. "I have so much. I have been given so much. I have so much of—of . . ."

"Of—"

"Of nature's gifts!" she says. "And I'm crying like I have nothing." She allows her body to slide into the bath with the grace of a fainting Victorian. "So why do things like this make me feel like I have nothing?"

"Because people have to make you feel that way to justify the expense."

"Do you feel like you have anything?"

"Not really," I say. "I have yo—"

"And it's this fucking dress," Simone cries, gesturing wildly at the pink garment, in which she is a vision, just not her own. "It's horrible. I thought that if I wore it for the entire day it'd go away, but it's just climbing up. This isn't me, Max." She takes a deep breath. "I look insane."

"You look beautiful," I say. "But yes, also insane."

"It's just a dress."

"It's not just a dress," I say, holding her hand. "We look like virgin sacrifices, except really old."

Simone laughs as she wipes her eyes. Her mascara has smudged.

"Why didn't she just let me wear a jumpsuit?"

"Because Emily is Emily."

"Why are we even bridesmaids?" She laughs.

"It's deranged," I say. "But it's really nice we're here. All together."

Maybe I really am just a hater. Emily is a nice girl, and it's really quite sweet that she made us bridesmaids.

"Yeah," Simone says. "It is."

Sometimes I doubt whether Simone and I are particularly nice people. Both of us squirm at the idea of being referred to as nice, as if nice is an insult, as if nice means boring and vanilla and tedious. I should try being nicer. I feel nice around Vincent.

"Is this what it's like to be trans?" she asks.

"Probably."

"I just want it off."

I climb into the bath and sit across from her, knees touching.

"I mean," Simone says, "you look beautiful. And you can just do it. Be like those girls."

"You used to be."

"I know. Maybe that's what makes it harder."

I hold her hand, rubbing my finger in a circle along the crinkled skin of one of her knuckles.

"It scares me a bit," I say. "How well I can do it."

"But you're not actually—"

"But I can do it," I say. "It's weird. And I don't know what to think about it."

Quiet passes over us. Vincent passes over me.

"Do you think Vincent wants this from me?" I ask.

"Have you asked him?"

"No," I say. "I haven't."

"You could always ask."

I pause. She's right. I could just ask.

"Yeah. Maybe I could do this. A version of it."

Simone nods. There's probably a version for all of us.

"I think I was about to cheat on him," I say.

"What the fuck?" She sits up a little. "With who?"

"David. The groomsman with the beard. The really masc one."

Simone laughs, and I laugh with her.

"I think he's waiting for me in his room."

"Are you going to do anything?"

"Obviously not."

"I took a bottle of wine from the bar," she says.

She goes to the room and returns with it. She takes a full swig and passes it to me, climbing back in.

"What if I never find someone?" she asks.

I do not think, for a moment, that Simone won't find someone, and perhaps it feels simpler when I deconstruct what finding someone really means. Life is a series of happy endings and sad endings, a handsome lover or career often marking the border between epochs. She'll find someone, or several people, but I don't think anyone can say any of us will find someone for forever.

"You always find someone," I say.

"But what if I don't?"

"You'll always have me," I say, weakly, knowing how little it stemmed the pain when she said this to me two nights ago.

She looks down into her lap. Her shoulders begin to lift and fall, like the hydraulic suspension on a lowrider car. Is having me really that bad? To induce this kind of crying?

"Are you going to die, Maxy?"

"Simone." I lean forward to hug her. I want to apologize. For this really crappy thing happening to me, for how my life knocks onto hers. "I mean, we're all going to die."

She pokes me between my ribs.

"No," I say. "I'm not."

"Promise," she says, not a question.

"I prom—"

"Promise me you're never going to move to the fucking country-side or get a fucking whippet."

"You are literally the only person I'd move to the countryside for."

We go quiet.

"What if I forgive Vincent and then he leaves me?"

I realize again, just like Simone, how desperately scared I am of being alone.

"You'll be okay," she says.

She hands me the bottle. I inhale an acidic mouthful. I think of that movie I watched recently. *After Life,* in which a film crew inter-views spirits of the recently deceased to help them decide which one memory to take into the afterlife. The crew then helps them film re-enactments. Maybe it was a stupid movie to watch while awaiting surgery, but I wanted to take the sting out of death, if that's something a person can do.

"If you could only take one memory to the afterlife, what would it be?" I ask.

"Can we not talk about death, please?"

"I think mine would be us looking at that James Turrell installa-tion at that festival. Remember the skylight?"

Simone looks at me and smiles.

"I think that'd be my memory," I say. "Us sitting next to each other, looking at that blue square."

"I forgot about that."

"What'd be yours?"

"I don't know," she says. "I would've thought something else. But that one sounds good."

XVII

I don't go home after Bordeaux. I tell Robot Job that I have gastroenteritis and book a connecting flight to Edinburgh, feeling so deserving of a splurge that I don't even purchase the carbon offset. Simone went straight to Paris for work. Mum and Dad pick me up from the airport. I've put a strict embargo on talking about the tumor, or about surgery. They were resistant to the idea, but became pliant when I insisted it would make me happy, that if I was going to live then I would have to act like there'd be nothing to stop me from living.

I'm ignoring Vincent's calls. When I imagine him thinking I've gone missing, I feel a little better. With all this quiet, it's challenging to resist looking Alex up. Not that I could. I don't even know her last name. I could ask Vincent, but that would just be punishing him to ultimately punish myself.

Mum sits in the kitchen as I update her on the last week. I'm chopping vegetables, because although we've ordered Indian takeaway, we always make our own salad. It's a relief for my hands to be this busy. Mum offers maternal platitudes. *Oh dear. What does that mean? And so, this Alex, she's no longer in the picture? That is quite awful.* She offers appropriate praise and slander for Emily's wedding. *You and Simone look beautiful. Emily's dress is a bit low-cut. Julie's aged terribly.* We eat dinner, sitting on the floor around a coffee table, mostly in silence. I rip a doughy edge from a disc of ghee-slicked naan.

"How long will you stay?" Mum asks.

"I'm not sure," I say. "He's still in the flat."

"He's not on the lease, is he?" Dad asks.

"No," Mum and I reply.

I spoon some bhindi fry onto my plate, and eat it with the glistening yellow biryani.

"Would you like me to message him?" she asks.

"Why would you message him?" I garble, mouth full of food.

"We're in contact," she says. "Because of the—"

"Tumor," I say. She puts her hand to her mouth. "Have you told him I'm here?"

She gasps, outraged, like I've accused her of murder.

"Of course not," she says. "Me and Vincent talk, but we're not close."

I roll my eyes.

"I just thought I could tell him to move out," she says. "If that would help you."

I think about all the thirty-somethings who have four children and dead parents, and how at the time the Bible was written the average life expectancy was thirty, and then I reflect on my mum's offer and how absurd it is. Even more absurd is my temptation to take it. And suddenly my being home, my running to my parents' house to escape my boyfriend, transforms into symptoms of arrested development. I'm not sure I've ever felt like a grown-up. I guess nobody ever feels like a grown-up, but are you going to tell me that the biblical wench, crusty on her deathbed from a water-borne plague, still pregnant with her tenth child, didn't feel at least, a little bit, like a grown-up?

"I'm thirty-one, Mum."

Nobody argues. It's a fact.

THE NEXT MORNING, I DON'T get out of bed, only stirring when Jamie calls.

"Are you okay?" he asks.

"Not really."

"Can I do anything?"

"Not really," I say. "How are you?"

"I'm okay," he says. "Just been worried."

"I'm sorry."

"Don't apologize."

There's a knock at the door. I lower the phone.

"Who is it?" I ask.

I roll over. Dad peeks around the corner of the door like a meerkat.

"Hi, Dad," I say, lifting the phone to my ear. "I'll speak to you later, Jamie."

"Okay," he says. "Tell Dad I said hi."

"I will."

I hang up.

"Jamie says hi."

"Oh, that's nice." Dad's surprised. "Your mother says we should go for a walk."

"Why?"

He shrugs his shoulders. I groan, pushing my face deeper into the pillow. I take three deep breaths with my eyes shut, and when I open them, Dad hasn't moved. I should get out of bed.

"Give me a few."

Dad waits downstairs while I change into some tailored but long trousers, which I know will likely get muddy, a boob tube and a jacket. I hate the Scottish countryside. We walk down the long driveway, toward the forested area fifteen minutes from the house. The terrain is uneven, the walking path narrow.

"So, how are you feeling?" he asks, as if we are finally alone enough to talk about it. "It's a shame about Vincent."

A shame. It is a shame. Everything Dad asks will have passed through Mum.

"Did Mum tell you what he did?" I ask, walking through a wooden gate that he holds open for me.

"Something about another trans woman, a while ago. A Thai woman?"

"I don't think she was Thai," I say. "Not that it makes it better. Or worse."

"It sounds a bit over my head, if I'm being honest."

I feel a little sympathy, the way I always do for him, for his downtrodden, mopey shit—dim, unsure, unassertive. But I also feel a scrap of irritation. Can grievous bodily harm really be so beyond one's head? If you really want to understand something, especially something human, you can. Too many people hide behind the guise of being useless. Book-smart people hold their hands up at the end of dinner, saying they can't do the math to split the bill. Men will intentionally start a fire cooking scrambled eggs, and say they can't and should never cook again. Give it a fucking go.

"What do you mean that it's over your head?" I ask.

"Well," he says, "I'm not great with these things. I'm going to fudge up my words."

"Try," I say.

"Okay." He pauses, looking up at the trees, and at the sky, as if the right words might appear from behind the clouds. "Well, I suppose it's hard to know whether we judge people for who they are now, or for who they once were."

"Yes," I say, annoyed at the sheer obviousness. "How do you know he's not the same person? And don't compare it to me being trans."

"What? I wasn't going to compare the two, Maxy," he says, walking slowly. "I wouldn't know if it's right to. I don't think it is, I think. I'm just saying people change. I think . . ."

"What?"

"Um, I don't know . . . I think sometimes we need to give others a bit more of a chance."

"But what does that say about me?" I ask. "That I'm weak-willed. And whether he's changed or not, it's the principle. He did this horrible thing, and there was no accountability. No punishment. It's not right."

"You sound a lot like your brother."

"What?" I stop in my tracks, aghast, even though I know what he means. "How is that anything like Jamie?"

"He's stubborn, Maxy."

"I'm not being stubborn, Dad. That's such a reductive way to look at this."

"Sorry," he says. "I'm trying."

We go quiet. I'm not sure why I'm pushing the point. This is the most, the deepest, Dad and I have spoken in a very long time. He is trying, and he's not wrong. I do sound a bit like Jamie—stubborn, righteous, and unforgiving. The thought has crossed my mind, which is likely why I'm being defensive. I'm spitting back, rejecting nuance with the same heft and aggression I've always thought unbecoming in Jamie. But if I don't want to be like Jamie, then I have to forgive, be a little less righteous, which takes me toward Vincent, and that is, whatever I do, at odds with what I feel to be moral. But moral to whom? Good for what?

"Can I even forgive Vincent?"

"What do you mean?"

"It's Alex's—the girl's—forgiveness to give, right?"

Dad stops to look up at the sky again.

"I see what you mean," he says. "But Vincent hid it from you, didn't he? That's something to forgive."

"And everything else?"

"Maybe that's more about acceptance," he says, setting off again.

"What about Fred?" I ask, falling into step with him. "His friend."

"What about him?"

"Even if I did forgive Vincent, I don't think I could forgive—sorry, accept—what Fred did."

"Do you have to?"

"They're best friends, Dad."

"You're allowed to have time."

"How much time?"

"Months. Years. Longer."

We walk on in silence. I feel like a child. A child fumbling with adult problems. We reach another gate, through which there are clusters of sheep, huddled together like clouds across a green sky. Dad takes a pack of cigarettes out of his pocket and offers me one. He must not realize it's highly irresponsible for me to smoke before surgery, so I take only a couple of puffs and let it burn. We look on at the sheep in silence, doing nothing, all of us vacant voyeurs to the others.

"People punish themselves," he says.

I don't respond, though I wonder whom he's referring to. Me. Vincent. Himself. I check the pedometer on my phone. Six thousand steps. We stub out our cigarettes on the thick wood of the gate before Dad leads the way home.

MUM'S PREPARED LUNCH. COLD CUTS. Quiche. Some of the salad from last night. Leftover samosas. For a woman who loves to say she's Chinese, she sure loves picky bits. We eat on the terrace, outside, at the bottom of the upward slope of the garden. Even though the terrace is large and there is ample space, it always feels like at any second the uphill trees and bricks from the back wall could avalanche down, leaving us in a pile of rubble and piecrust. Stubborn. I can't get that word out of my head. I can't silence the part of me that's unwilling to accept it.

"Mum," I ask, "am I being stubborn about Vincent?"

She looks at my dad, and then I imagine them talking about me and Vincent in their bedroom. *She's being very stubborn about Vincent. Do you think? Of course she is. Is that right? Yes!* Whatever I'm about to hear will first pass through a filter of thoughtful diplomacy.

"You can be stubborn," she says. "But it's probably too early to tell. And we probably don't know enough. Or understand enough."

I chomp on a bit of quiche. The crust is crumbly and buttery, and it's made with roasted garlic. I'll be farting for days. Can I be the person who puts her principles aside? Obviously. I'm no saint. But maybe this isn't about principles. Leaving Vincent would stop him from becoming another book of shitty poetry. I'm pulling the emergency brake on the printing press.

"I haven't told Jamie about any of this," I say.

"Oh," Mum says, dabbing her mouth with her napkin.

"Why's that?" Dad asks.

"I feel like he'd judge me."

After lunch, I notice some letters on the carpet by the front door. One is an envelope filled with a hard, irregular object. On the face of the letter is my name in Simone's handwriting. Inside is a set of keys, and a note.

In case you don't feel like going home, mine's available while I'm in Paris (and after).

She could've messaged me to let me know some keys were on the way, but I like the theatrics of receiving keys in the mail, and I imagine she does, too. London starts to feel more possible. Small movements are what I need right now.

The rest of the day is filled with nothing, and I wonder how my parents survive like this. Doing nothing. Cooking food. Going for walks. Sometimes visiting nearby towns as a treat. A domestic life would've made sense a few hundred years ago, kneading dough and milking cows and squatting over a pestle and mortar, but in the absence of all that noise, the huge amount of work it takes to survive, I'm unsure what the retired make of their existence.

There is a sense, whenever I'm home, of the world contracting. I feel it as I'm watching *Strictly*, sandwiched between my parents on the big sofa. A punnet of grapes rests in my lap. I pluck the plump and oversweet orbs from their stems and toss them into my mouth one by one. The tannins squeeze the wet from my palate.

I hate to admit that Vincent made my world feel bigger, not just because I hate to rely on a man for expansion, but because the things he offered were simple. They were banal, sedate pleasures. Much like sitting here with my parents. With Vincent it never felt quite like contraction, but a revelation that I like things I never thought I'd like. Things from which Arthur ran. And so the expanding force wasn't a prize-winning book of poetry, fun parties, or interesting acquaintances, it was all the boring stuff. Those routines that, in some senses, were dull and traditional. I eat the grapes in twos until the punnet is empty, and then I acquiesce to my parents' offer of ice cream, microwaving the chocolate-chip cookie dough until it's soft enough to eat. Normal spoons for my parents, and a teaspoon for me. I move back in between them. I feel a bit less suffocated.

After the episode, Dad turns off the television. I get up to find a bottle of wine and pour myself a glass.

"Would you like some, Mum?"

"I'm fine," she says.

I sit back on the sofa. Mum bought the wine for me, which was kind of her, but sometimes I feel like drinking in front of my father is cruel. It makes me feel like Jamie, who does it brazenly, punishing my dad for his alcoholism even in his sobriety. Hates him if he's drunk, hates him if he's sober, which probably means that Jamie just hates him.

"I'm going to go home tomorrow," I say.

"Are you?" Mum asks. "I thought you would work from here."

"I have to go home eventually, don't I?"

"Do you feel ready to forgive him?" she asks.

"I didn't say that."

"That's why I'm asking."

I sigh.

"Shouldn't you know before you see him?" she asks.

"I'm going to stay at Simone's."

I feel my mum's shoulders stiffen next to me. I take another sip of wine, hunched over my lap. I know they're exchanging looks behind me. Dad is probably just mirroring her face to her. Dad has always been her mirror.

"What's the difference between Simone's and here? Why won't you let us—"

"It's nice that you want me to stay, Mum, but I think I'm ready to go, okay?"

She sighs, putting her fingers to her forehead. She must be holding so much in. Unable to talk about the tumor. The surgery.

"I'll be back," she says, clearing up the empty containers.

"Thanks."

I face my dad, who's looking at the blank screen in front of us. He parts his lips, then shuts them before opening them again.

"No person is fewer than two things," he says.

"What?"

"Isn't that a line from one of your poems?"

"Are you quoting my poetry back to me?"

"I can recite a lot of it," he says. "I can, really. I read them a lot."

I've seen a copy on his bedside table, but always just assumed that it was sort of there because it had to be. I'd probably keep my child's book at my bedside if they wrote one. We sit in silence for a while. In the matte reflection of the television, I see my mum standing in the doorway. I know she is trying to remain unseen, because she thinks there is something special happening between me and Dad. And maybe there is. We've never really spoken about my poems, because soon after the book was published, I stopped wanting to talk about—

"But you never really wanted to talk about them," he says, and for a moment I'm startled, unsure of the last time it felt like we shared a mind. "So I tried to take your feelings as guidance. Maybe I should've, though, because I did really enjoy them, and when I said they were good at the time, I meant it. They actually made me start reading more poetry generally."

"Better poetry."

"Not really," he says, looking at the black square of the TV. "But again, I was worried that you wouldn't want to hear about other people's poetry that I enjoyed. But I thought you wrote a good book, and it made me enjoy other books, which is a great thing."

"I think I would've loved to hear that," I say, my voice cracking. "Phrased like that. I know I'm not that easy." I look at the television again. My mum's still there. "But maybe if you said it enough times, I'd start to believe it."

"I struggle to talk sometimes," Dad says.

I take my legs up onto the sofa. I'm going to ask it. I'm just going to ask it.

"Do you think it's the fire?" I ask.

This rouses him, and he faces me, like I've said something truly surprising, beyond the realm of the ordinary, and I wonder for a moment if I have.

"What do you mean?"

"The reason you can't talk," I say. "At least to me. We used to be much closer."

"Did we?"

"You used to be much more affectionate," I say. "Then the fire happened."

"That's not how I've seen it," he says. "No, not quite how I've seen it."

"What is it, then?"

"I don't know, Maxy," he says, sighing. I no longer know if my mum's still standing there. I don't want to look at the television. "You don't remember a lot when you drink as much as I did. The how of affection. It's always been difficult for me. Maybe alcohol opened that door. It didn't get any easier just because I stopped drinking. And then, of course, Jamie hates me."

I don't say anything, because denying it would feel unfair and untrue.

"I think Jamie sort of needs to hate you," I say. "Probably because he struggles just as much as you do. To talk, I mean. Hating's easier."

"You've never hated me," he says. It's not questioning. His tone is certain. And he's correct. I haven't ever hated him, I've just felt sad, because distance feels sad. "But I guess things, people, have always been a bit more complicated."

"No person is fewer than two things."

"Or one event."

"Yeah," I say. "Exactly."

"I think you're better than me and Jamie," he says. "At this. You're better at talking about things."

It took me over a decade to talk to Dad about the fire, and so I wonder how much better I can be. I want to ask him something, which I'd never really thought to ask but now seems like an important question, the only question there is. I feel pathetic and unsure, and I crumble, unable to take my eyes from the empty wineglass in my lap, unable to look him in the eye.

"Dad?"

"Yes?"

"Do you forgive me?"

"What?"

"Do you forgive me?" I sniff.

"Oh, Maxy," he says, and he grips on to my arm, softly. I look up at him from my cower, and my tears, old tears, salty and weary, fall out of their ducts. "I'm not even sure what I'd be forgiving."

"I just—I just feel . . ." I struggle to catch my breath. "I'm really sorry. For telling."

I start to cry into his shoulder, and he holds me in a way that is foreign and familiar. I hug him tight.

"I'm really, really sorry, Dad."

"You were a child," he says. "I'm sorry . . . I should be—"

"It's okay—"

"It's not okay," he says. "I love you."

He rubs his hand along my back. He's said sorry before. That's what you do when you get sober. You say sorry. You make amends. He's done all that. Maybe it happened at an age when I couldn't appreciate it, and then at an age when I denied that I needed it. But I don't want him to punish himself, not more than he already does, not like how I continue to do. I forgot how often I feel like there's so much bad inside me. How heavy mistakes and inadequacy and guilt sit on my shoulders. I'm sorry. To Dad. To me.

"Think of where I could've been," he says. "If your mother . . . you . . . even Jamie . . . I mean, think of where it could've gone. How much worse . . ."

"I know."

He doesn't need to say any more. My body convulses again, more wet onto Dad's shirt.

"Love you, Maxy," he says.

Learning about Alex forced Vincent into personhood. Not just a fantasy who bakes cake and takes care of me and makes promises of the future, but a person who fucks up or worse. You can fall in love with an outline, you can even make a home with one, but there will come a time when you can't deny the bones their flesh. No person is fewer than two things.

What happened to Alex was despicable—there are no two ways about it—but there's a life in which bad doesn't always multiply, where the tide shifts, where awful things make people better. This is also the world where people, often women, are doomed to spend much of their lives forgiving the errors of others and suffering for the sake of other people's growth. Sometimes there's nothing to do but leave, and sometimes there's nothing to do but forgive.

"Love you," Dad repeats.

IT's NOT UNTIL MY TRAIN arrives at King's Cross St. Pancras that I realize that, even with Simone's keys, I am at a fork, that in certain terms I will be unable to delay things, at least in any way that's significant. At Highbury & Islington, I stand in the ticket hall, unable to choose which platform to descend to, which eastward train to take.

"Max?"

Lo and behold, it is Arthur. Walking alone, vape in one hand, thin book in his other. His hair still artfully disheveled, a few strands hanging over his forehead, carefully separated from the pack. I wonder if I can hide, but he's already seen me. It's not like I can run.

"What are you doing here?" he asks.

He talks as if he owns North London.

"I'm just on the way somewhere," I say, which could apply to anyone using public transport since its inception. "You?"

"Uh, yeah, good," he says. "I'm just walking home. I live in Finsbury Park now. I'm seeing someone who—"

"The girl with the red hair?"

"What?"

"From Caspar's book launch?"

"Who?" he asks. "Oh. No. Not her."

I can't pretend there's no pinch in my chest. It will always suck, to know that someone who didn't choose you has chosen another. But the nip I feel is brief. It is overrun by knowing a person can be so many wonderful things, and if they do not choose me—continue to choose me—then there's little point in wanting them.

"How's it going?"

"With Stella?"

I nod, imagining Stella—lithe, blond, ironed clothes, unblemished brain—and expect another pinch, but it's faint and fleeting. It's okay.

"It's going well, I think," he says. "I'm feeling more ready."

"More ready?" I ask, even though I know what he means, because for much of our time together he was unready, believing himself to be encased in a pressure cooker that simply wasn't there.

"Yeah," he says. "We didn't get to talk much at Caspar's. Like, catch up."

"No," I say. "I guess these things can be awkward."

He smiles.

"Yeah," he says. "Your boyfriend seemed nice, though. Quite corporate?"

"Yeah, he is," I say. "To both."

"Is he Chinese?"

"Yeah."

"Your mum will be happy."

I laugh, loudly. It's easy to forget how enmeshed he was in my life, the things we used to joke about.

"Yeah," I say.

"I don't know if it's weird for me to say, but I've been doing a lot of work on our relationship."

"You mean talking about our breakup in therapy?"

"Yeah."

"Really?"

Bemusement widens my mouth like a speculum. I almost want to laugh, but—

"I guess it feels inevitable," he says. "You put stuff behind you, but then you meet someone new and the old stuff feels new again."

"Yeah," I say, sinking too quickly into my own reality. I can't help but feel sad, and yet there is a way in which I find it all remarkable. It's easy to forget our roles in the theater of other people's minds. "I know what you mean. Being with Vincent brought stuff up, too."

"I'm sorry."

"What for?"

"Dunno," he says, picking at the skin around his nails with his vape-hand. "That it's brought stuff up. And my part in things."

"It's okay," I say. "Really. I'm sorry, too."

"For what?"

I shrug.

"Nobody's perfect."

"Yeah." He looks up at me and allows a brief chuckle to himself. "How are you, anyway?"

There was a time when I would've told him about the tumor, Emily's wedding, about what has possibly been one of the most tumultuous periods of my existence. I would've done it in part because that's what partners do. Tell each other stuff. But I would also have been doing it in the hope that the news would somehow change him, that somehow my tumor would make him more caring, more doting, more sympathetic. Those tactics never work. People are what they are, and sometimes they're just an ongoing series of small disappointments.

"I'm good," I say. "Not great, but good."

"That's good," he says. "That's good."

We stand in silence for a bit longer, looking at each other.

"Okay," I say. "I'm going to head."

"Yeah, sure. It was nice to see you, Maxy."

We give each other a long hug goodbye. As we walk in opposite directions, I wonder if he's looking back over his shoulder. I guess I'll never know.

VINCENT

XVIII

I'VE BEEN WORKING FROM MAX'S FLAT, OUR FLAT, PRETENDING TO BE ILL enough to stay at home but well enough to work. I've said it's gastro-enteritis.

I don't want Max to come back when I'm away. I'm going a bit mad. No messages. No emails. Max's mum isn't responding to my messages either, which is fair. Simone won't tell me anything. She just says to be patient. *Give her space.* I know how everything looks. They must hate me, think I'm awful, and I don't completely blame them. It looks terrible. It is terrible. I left France early, and because Aisha and Fred needed the rental car, I had to take a two-hour taxi to the airport. Somehow I ordered a limousine. It cost a fortune.

I came right back here, to our flat, Max's flat, because I wasn't sure where else to go. I don't want to leave—I love it here. All the books. The nice round dining table. The *Chungking Express* poster that I'm jealous of. We haven't spoken. She posted stuff from the wedding, but I haven't seen anything since. I know she probably isn't missing—it'd be in the news or something if she was—but I still kind of worry that she's missing. I rub my eyes with my palms. I've done a shit job of this

297

share purchase agreement. There are a couple of minor points I should probably check with the client, but I can't be bothered. None of this feels like it matters. I attach the agreement to an email and circulate it to the other side. I lean into the ergonomic groove of Max's swivel chair. What the fuck am I doing here? Should I just move out? I want her to come back. I'm not saying I deserve it, but I want to believe she still sees the good in me.

When I first told Fred about Max being trans, there was a moment, when he'd waited just a bit too long to say something, when I thought we might finally talk about Alex.

"Cool."

That's all he said, and it became clear that we weren't going to talk about it, and abundantly clear that neither of us would ever forget. We're best friends. Isn't that crazy? All those years passed, and we've never really spoken about it. The closest we ever got was when I met Fred in Thailand after leaving Alex. I still remember the tension in the air. I said something like, I couldn't do it, and he gave me a hug, and we left it at that. We saw a couple more places in Thailand, then went to Vietnam, and Cambodia, but bickered for what felt like the whole time. We were too young to handle the guilt. Our faults. Our shame. By the time we got home, we couldn't stand each other, and so we kept our distance until our guilt was far enough behind us to bear each other's company.

I think deep down I knew Max would find out about Alex, that she would eventually have to. On Simone's sofa bed, when Max asked why Fred and I drifted, I thought I could tell her then, but it didn't feel like the right time. I suppose there's never a right time, but the longer you wait, the more wrong it gets.

I don't know why Alex came to mind that evening, what made me draw the link so clearly between what was happening with Max and Fred and what had happened with Alex and Fred, except for jealousy. I acted out of jealousy, just like I did that night when Fred beat Alex up. The same feelings came up again, more than ten years later. I was stressed because the woman I love has a brain tumor. It's been a hard year. It hasn't been easy with my father. It hasn't been easy with my family, nor with work. Seeing Fred swoop in as some kind of arbiter, telling me that Max was good, and I was bad, feeling something between them, fucked me off beyond belief. I just wanted to punch, and punch I did.

There are a million ways in which I'm not the same person that I was ten years ago, and a million ways in which I'm the same. Some parts get stuck and others move on, until we're all random indeterminable constellations on pieces of graph paper. I still get worried. Irrational. Sometimes my mind makes leaps. I say things I don't want to. But I also think I'm kinder, if that's something you can say about yourself. I know how to take care of people, or at least, I want to take care of people. I'm not scared of responsibility. Maybe, deep down, I thought there was something to prove, but it's not like I thought, hey, Vincent, you're not going to run this time, right? Try really hard not to run this time, okay? It was more subtle, just this niggling worry that I hadn't changed, that I was going to blow it all up. I knew I was going to stay. I didn't expect the karmic ombudsman to step in a couple of weeks early, knock down the door before I'd had a chance to repay.

Yet even if I had wanted to settle the balance, I wonder if it would've been so easy. Life offers few chances of redemption. It's hard to force them. There've been times when I've thought about getting in touch with Alex to apologize, but that's not absolution. Alex was kind, but she was also firm. I could imagine what she'd say. *This apology is for you, Vinny, not for me. Please don't ever contact me again.* And she'd be right: I'd be trying to lighten my own load, not making her feel better, not providing—with interest—the care I stole from her.

I once saw Alex at the top of Broadway Market, or at least a woman who looked like her. I was on a date at the time—not with Max—and

I fucked it, because it was like I'd seen a ghost, an apparition of my sins, and I made up an excuse to walk the other way. For the rest of the evening I was in that room in Chonburi, next to packed suitcases, head in my hands.

When Max and I first started following each other on social media, I checked to see if she and Alex followed each other, and breathed an enormous sigh of relief when they didn't. When I got back from France, I looked her up again. She's still beautiful. She's engaged, and she looks happy, though what do any of us really know about each other's relationships? I hate when you tell people you're dating someone and they tell you that they're so happy for you, without asking much about the relationship, which could be terrible and unfulfilling and with lots of bad sex, as if a relationship is an objective good.

I think people assume I'm an end-result kind of guy. Max made those assumptions, too. I don't know what it is—if it's a race thing or what. I don't think that's the case. I don't think that's ever been the case. There are so many ways a life can go, so many ways a life can be. It's overwhelming, like standing in front of a supermarket shelf selling fifty variations of cheesy Wotsits. Unless I'm unhappy, and especially if I'm happy, going with the flow is pleasant. It sounds like an incredibly flippant way to live life, and completely out of step with someone who's a corporate lawyer, but I mean it. *Your free spirit landed in mergers and acquisitions? Are you okay?*

Still, it's the truth. I'm the same in relationships. And I mean it when I say that my mum really is coming round. This is the starting point. We'll give it time. I've chosen Max. I want to keep choosing Max. I finally told my dad about Max.

"If you are happy, then I'm happy for you," he said.

"We can visit when she recovers."

"Yes," he said. "Of course, of course."

Hearing those words repeated—*of course, of course*—made it seem as if her introduction was a given, something so simple it could remain unspoken. I suppose that since his heart attack, large obstacles have become smaller obstacles. He just wants to live.

Is it too little, too late? I'm worried I didn't communicate to Max how happy I am to see where the ride takes us.

I'm good at knowing when I'm happy. That doesn't sound like much, but I don't think a lot of people look inward and ask themselves whether they're enjoying life. When I moved to Hong Kong for work, my ex-girlfriend and I weren't on the best of terms, and I felt lonely without her there. When I came back to London, I was happy to be back with her, and then I wasn't, and then it was time for a change. I should've told Max that I'm happy with her, that I don't see that changing. I guess at a time like this, when I'm out at sea, when she's not even talking to me, every word unsaid feels momentous, each one capable of great change, all obscuring the simple fact that I obscured the truth.

I leave my desk to make some food. I've eaten tuna-and-avocado paninis for lunch every day for the last week. I'm finding it's all I can stomach. Max and I once spoke about the things we'd avoid if we broke up. We haven't broken up yet, but I've been living in the expectation that we will, unable to satisfy my craving for gimbap from the Korean place nearby because it reminds me of her. I leave the sandwich on the counter and go to Max's room. I'm staring at suitcases. I haven't packed everything, but I've packed the essentials, in case she storms in and asks me to leave.

I'm taking a small break from Fred, but then we're going to talk about it, regardless of where Max and I end up, and we're going to see how and if we can make things right. I'm sure Fred and I will be okay, but we need to talk about what happened, why he did what he did to Alex, why I reacted how I did, then and now. I wasn't ready in France— the fallout from Max was too fresh. I couldn't be in the house any longer. But Fred and I did really terrible things, and we're going to talk about them. We're going to talk about how to make life right.

Max's surgery is in a few days. She has to come back to London soon. There's not much I can do other than prepare for her arrival. I go back into the kitchen and look inside the freezer, as if someone might've moved the containers of frozen meals I made for her to have during recovery. I don't know if that's too imposing, but I wasn't sure what else I could do.

The tuna panini isn't bad. I don't think I would've eaten it for seven days straight if it was. Green pesto, Kewpie mayo, capers, half-moons of avocado. I'm sitting on the couch cross-legged, the same couch we came back to on our first date, the first time I kissed Max. I really want her to come home. There are a million ways to live a life, but I really want to try to live one with Max. When she walks through the door, I'm going to say it to her.

When I'm back at my desk, there's an email from the client saying thank you, no mention of those points I didn't clear. I delegate some intercompany loans and minutes to my trainee, and then I go back to our bedroom and lie on the bed. My eyes feel heavy. I could take a nap. God knows, I need one. I've been sleeping terribly, because who sleeps well in a lurch?

When I'm about to drift off, I hear the twist
of a key
in a lock.
My torso
swings up.
Did I hear it?
"Hello?"

EPILOGUE

Tell me about your job
the gloved man
asks me
The masked man
The stethoscoped man. He
who leans above me
No time to explain
that I am a robot. Not a real robot
That I write strings of words
with surgical attention
Sorry! I'd say to the doctor
I get it! Poetry isn't surgery

When I emerge
from intravenous black
I don't know much
about forgiveness
other than forgiveness
is something to give
Much like vomit
into a vomit bowl
glazing Vincent's
lovely fingers
It happens when you're skinny!
The nurse tells me
Not a compliment
I remind myself

I imagine a future
in which I am well
Where I host New Year's Eve
No drugs
No staircases
Where I may still soak
in disappointment
though no more
than promise
I promise
there is a future
this future
where I let another's hands
hold the bowl

ACKNOWLEDGMENTS

Thank you to Monica MacSwan, Lesley Thorne, and everyone at Aitken Alexander, as well as Kent Wolf at Neon Literary.

Thank you to my editors, Bobby Mostyn-Owen and Katy Nishimoto. Thank you also to Milly Reid, Sara Roberts, Whitney Frick, and the teams at Doubleday and Dial Press.

Thank you to all of my readers. I am so grateful to be able to write books for you.

About the Author

Nicola Dinan grew up in Hong Kong and Kuala Lumpur and now lives in London. *Bellies,* her debut, was shortlisted for the Polari First Book Prize, Diverse Book Awards, and Mo Siewcharran Prize, and longlisted for the Gordon Burn Prize and Brooklyn Public Library Book Prize. It was a finalist for a Lambda Literary Award.

ABOUT THE TYPE

This book was set in Sabon, a typeface designed by the well-known German typographer Jan Tschichold (1902–74). Sabon's design is based upon the original letter forms of sixteenth-century French type designer Claude Garamond and was created specifically to be used for three sources: foundry type for hand composition, Linotype, and Monotype. Tschichold named his typeface for the famous Frankfurt typefounder Jacques Sabon (c. 1520–80).